Praise for the Chronicles of Fionn mac Cumhal:

"A WELL-TOLD TALE, WITH A REAL FEEL FOR BOTH THE GRIM AND THE GORGEOUS ASPECTS OF THE CELTIC WORLD"

Chicago Sun-Times

"THE AUTHORS POETICALLY PORTRAY A LOST CULTURE, BREATHING LIFE INTO ANCIENT MYTHS"

Publishers Weekly

A CELTIC FANTASY THAT COMBINES HEROISM AND GRACE, IT HAS THE AUSTERE AND MYSTERIOUS BEAUTY OF A MOSS AGATE AT THE BOTTOM OF A CLEAR POOL."

Susan Shwartz, author of *The Grail of Hearts*

"PAXSON AND MARTINE-BARNES HAVE PUT NEW FLESH ON THE LITERARY BONES OF THE ENDURINGLY POPULAR IRISH OUTLAW/POET."

Orlando Sentinel

"A SUSPENSEFUL TALE FILLED WITH MAGNIFICENT DESCRIPTIONS OF CHARACTERS, ACTION AND SETTINGS."

VOYA

"UNUSUALLY GOOD CELTIC FANTASY . . . THE STORY SINGS"

Kirkus Reviews

Other AvoNova Books by
Diana L. Paxson *and* **Adrienne Martine-Barnes**

MASTER OF EARTH AND WATER
THE SHIELD BETWEEN THE WORLDS

SWORD OF FIRE AND SHADOW

THE THIRD CHRONICLE OF FIONN MAC CUMHAL

DIANA L. PAXSON
& ADRIENNE MARTINE-BARNES

AVON BOOKS • NEW YORK

AVON BOOKS
A division of
The Hearst Corporation
1350 Avenue of the Americas
New York, New York 10019

Cover art by Jean Targete
Published by arrangement with the authors
Library of Congress Catalog Card Number: 94-49015
ISBN: 0-380-75803-2

First AvoNova Printing: July 1996
First Morrow/AvoNova Hardcover Printing: August 1995

Printed in the U.S.A.

RA 10 9 8 7 6 5 4 3 2 1

To Chris Miller,
without whom Fionn's story
would not have been told . . .

ERIU
Ulaidh
Ben Bulben
Rath Grainne
Cave of Seghais
Bri Leith
Connachta
R. Sinnan
Brugh na Boinne
R. Boann
Inber
Colptha
Midhe
Temair
Gabhra
Ath Brea
R. Liffe
Almu
Cruinmhoinn
Fiacrach
Druim Cliadh
Dun Morna
Laigin
Sid BodbDerg
R. Siuir
Mumu
DLP '93

People and Places

CHARACTERS

[Note: The pronunciations given below are an approximate transliteration of the words as pronounced in a way that can be comprehended by the modern reader. Dh = "th" as in *the*; qh = a gutteral "ch" or "gh" sound. A dash indicates a syllable separation, an apostrophe indicates a hesitation. "Mac", meaning "son of", has been left in the modern form (instead of the medieval "magg"). Gaelic is an inflected language, and names may change their spelling in different grammatical positions.]

Our thanks to Alexei Kondratiev, Paul Edwin Zimmer, and all those who have tried to help us thread our way through the complexities of Gaelic language and literature. Any inaccuracies are the result of artistic license or pure ignorance, and are our own.

Characters are listed in alphabetical order. In the course of the story, the personnel of the *fian* goes through many changes. Fian I was that of Cumhal, Fionn's father, a few of whose members have survived. Fian II was that of Crimall, Fionn's uncle, in which he trained in Volume I, and which he inherits. Fian III consists of the men who join during the first years of Fionn's leadership, and Fian IV, taking shape during Fionn's middle years, includes many sons of men from the first two groups. Fian V is that of Oscar and his friends. Characters marked by an asterisk belong to the Otherworld, and those whose names appear in parentheses are dead before this story begins.

Achtlan [AQHT-LAN]—priestess of Brigid
Aechlach [AYQH-LAQH]—son of Urgriu, chieftain of the Luagni of Midhe
Ailbe [AL-BUH]—daughter of King Cormac by a concubine, later the wife of Fionn
Aidin [AY-DEEN]—wife of Oscar
(*Aillén mac Midhna) [AL-YAYN MAK MEEDH-NA]—a fire elemental who attacked Temair every Samhain until he was killed by Fionn
Aodh mac Ronain [AYDH MAK RAWN-IN]—lord of Gabhair, son of one of Cumhal's enemies, *Fian IV*
***Aonghus Og** [AN'HUS AWG]—son of the Dagda and lord of the Brugh na Boinne, protector of Diarmuid
Aonghus Gae-Adúath [AN'HUS GAH-ALDHA]—(of the Terrible Spear), chieftain of the Dési
Ancient Dripping Hazel, the Hazel Shield that Fionn got in the Otherworld
Birga [BYER-GUH]—Fionn's semisentient spear
***Bodb Derg** [BODH-UV DYER-UG]—father of Sadb
(Bodbmall) [BODHVULL]—a druidess who fostered Fionn
(Bran) [BRON]—son of Tuireann, in dog form in our world
Bressal Bélach [BRASSAL BELAQH]—the king of the Laigin
***Brigid** [BREE-ID]—goddess of healing, smithcraft, and poetry
Cairbre Liffechar mac Cormac [KERBRUH MAK KORMAK]—eldest son of the high king, Fionn's enemy

Cairpre [KERPRUH] of Luighne—Ailbe's lover, killer of Lomna, *Fian V*

Camog [KA-MOG]—one of the hag-daughters of Conaran, killed by Goll

Caoinche [KWEEN'HE]—Dithramhach's daughter, second wife of Goll

Cathal [KA-THAL]—the Archdruid

Ceallach mac Cormac [KYEL-LAQH MAK KORMAK]—son of the high king, later killed by the chieftain of the Dési for raping his niece

Cedach Cithach [KYALAQH KEETHAQH]—a warrior of Alba enlisted in the *fian*, *Fian V*

Ciothruadh [KITH-ROOUDH]—chief harper to the *Ard Ri*

Coir-cethar-chuir [KUR-KATHAR-QHUR]—"Four-Angled Music," one of the names of the magic harp of the Dagda

Conain [KONAN] Mael (the Bald)—one of the Sons of Morna, *Fian I*

Conain mac Luachar [KONAN MAK LOOAQHAR]—the Grey Man's son, *Fian IV*

Cormac mac Airt [KORMAK MAK ART]—*Ard Ri* of Eriu

Crimall mac Trenmor [KRIVUL MAK TRENVOR]—Fionn's uncle, leader of *Fian II*

Cuillean [KWULLYAN]—one of the hag-daughters of Conaran, killed by Goll

(Cumhal mac Trenmor) [KOOWEL MAK TRENVOR]—Fionn's father, dead before his birth, *Fian I*

(Cuchulain) [KU-HU-LAYN]—legendary champion of the Ulaidh

Daire Duanach [DERYUH DOONAQH] **mac Morna**—one of Fionn's bards, *Fian V*

Diarmuid mac Duibhne [DYEEARMID MAK DWIVNYE]—a protégé of Fionn, *Fian IV*

Daolghus [DYLGHUS]—a member of the *fian*, *Fian V*

*__Donait__ [DUNATCH]—a woman of the Sidhe, Fionn's protectress

*__Donn__ [DOWN]—son of Fionnlaoch, transformed into the stag of Inis Bo Finne

Donnchadh mac Diarmuid [DOWNAQHUDH MAK DYEEARMID]—Diarmuid and Grainne's first son

Dubhtach [DUV-THAQH]—a member of the *fian*, *Fian IV*

Duibhne [DWIV-NYE]—father of Diarmuid, *Fian II*

Dubh Droma mac Seanchach [DUV DROMA MAK SHE-NUQHAQH]—*Fian IV*

Dubhán [DOO'WAHN]—a friend of Oisin's, *Fian V*

Eachtach [AYQH-TAQH]—daughter of Diarmuid and Grainne

Eargna [ARGNA]—daughter of Aodh, wife of Conain mac Luachar and mistress of Oisin

*__Echbél__ [EQHVAYL]—son of Bodb Derg, brother of Sadb

Echu mac Cairbre [AH'HUH MAK KERBRUH]—second son of Cairbre Liffechar

Eibhir [AYVER]—a Roman captive who bears Oisin his son

Emer Glunglas [AYVER GLOONGHLASS]—son of Aedh mac Garad, Clan Morna, *Fian VI*

(Eochaid Airemh) [YO-KAI ARIV]—"The Ploughman," high king who fought Midir for his wife Etain

Eochaid mac Diarmaid [YO-KAI MAK DYEEARMID]—Diarmuid's second son by Grainne, *Fian VI*

*__Etain__ [AY-DWEEN]—wife of Midir, reborn as a human and married to King Eochaid

Ethne Taebfada [ETHNYE TAYVADA]—a Leinster princess, queen of Eriu

Fearghusa [FERQHUS] and **Faobhar** [FWEEVAR]—twin sons of Muirne by King Gléor Lamraige (Fionn's half-brothers), *Fian IV*

Fál [FAWL]—the Lía Fáil, the Stone on the Hill of Temair that cried out for the rightful king

Faolchú [FWAYLQHOO]—"of the hard-tempered sword," *Fian IV*

Fergus [FERQHUS]—the poet attached to the *fian*, *Fian III*

Feadha [FADHA]—son of Goll by Fionn's niece, *Fian VI*

Fer-li [FAHR-LEE]—son of Fer-tai and grandson of Goll, a fosterling of Fionn, *Fian VI*

Fer-tai [FAHR-TWEE]—son of Uaithne Irgalach of the Luagni of Temair, *Fian IV*

(Fiacail mac Conchinn) [FEEAKIL MAK KON'HINN]—once of Cumhal's *fian*, Bodbmall's husband and one of Fionn's first teachers, *Fian I*

Falchu mac Cairbre [FEL-QHUH MAK KERBRUH]—elder son of Cairbre Liffechar

Fionn mac Cumhal [FYONN MAK COOWEL]—*Rígfénnid* of Eriu

(Fionnéices) [FYON-EY-GUS]—master poet and actual slayer of Cumhal, Fionn's first teacher of poetry, whom he killed

Garad mac Morna [GARUV MAK MORNA]—Goll's youngest brother, *Fiann III*

Goll mac Morna [GOL MAK MORNA]—chief of Clan Morna, second-in-command of the *fian*, formerly Fionn's enemy, *Fian I*

Glas mac Gadal [GHLASS MAK GADUL]—a friend of Oisin, *Fian V*

Glas mac Enchard [GHLASS MAK AYNUHARADH]—son of Mac Lugach, *Fian VI*

Grainne nic Cormac [GRON-YUH NEEK KORMAC]—daughter of the high king

Grey of Macha—one of Cuchulain's supernatural chariot horses

Iornach [YOR-NAQH]—hag-daughter of Conaran, who tries to trap Fionn
Iuchna Ardmor [YUQH-NA ARD-MOR]—daughter of Goll, mother of Fer-li
(The Liath Luachra) [LIATH LOOQHRA]—a warrior-woman, one of Fionn's fosterers
***Lir** [LIR]—father of Manannan the sea-god, a great lord among the Sidhe
Lodhorn [LOD-HARN]—a *fénnid, Fian V*
Loegaire [LOI-GUH-RUH] of the Swift Blows—son of the king of the Men of Fannal
Lomna [LOM-NA]—Fionn's fool, *Fian IV*
***Lugh** [LUQH]—of the Long Arm, many-talented champion of the Sidhe who instituted the feast of Lughnasa
Lugach [LUQH-AQH]—Fionn's daughter by Cruithne
Mac Lugach [MAK LUQH-AQH] (formerly Gaoine "the Joke")—son of Fionn's daughter
***Manannan mac Lir** [MAN-AN-NAWN]—lord of the sea and king of the Land of Youth, one of the greatest of the Sidhe
***Miach** [MEE-AQH]—son of Diancecht, greatest physician of the Sidhe
***Midir** [MI-DHIR]—son of the Dagda, lord of Brí Leith
Mongfind [MON-GEEN]—chatelaine of Almu
***The Morrigan** [MOR-REE-AN]—raven goddess of battle
Muiredach Tírech [MUREA-DHAQH TEER-YAQH]—Cairbre's grandson
Muirne nic Tadg [MURRN'YUH NEEK TADH-UG]—Fionn's mother
***Niamh** [NEE-UV]—daughter of Manannan mac Lir

***Nuadu** [NOO-A-DHU]—king of the Sidhe, father of Tadg

Oisin [O-SHEEN]—Fionn's son by Sadb, *Fian V*

Olann mac Diarmuid [AW-LAN MAK DYEEARMID]—Diarmuid's son by the daughter of the king of the Laigin

Oscar [OS-KAR]—Oisin's son by Eibhir, *Fian V*

Rionnolbh [RINOLUV]—a friend of Oisin's, *Fian V*

***Sadb** [SADH-UV]—daughter of the Bodb Derg, a Sidhe woman transformed into a doe, Fionn's great love and the mother of Oisin

Sceolan [SKYOLUN]—son of Tuireann, in dog form in our world

Sgeimh Solais [SKAN SOLISH]—"Light of Beauty," Cairbre's daughter

Suibhne [SWIVNYE]—Spear-bearer, smiter of hosts, *Fian IV*

(Tadg mac Nuada) [TADH-UG MAK NOO-A-DHAT]—a great druid and Fionn's grandfather, lord of Almu, later called the "Dark Druid"

***Tuireann** [TURYIN]—Fionn's twin sister, mother of Bran and Sceolan

(Urgriu) [OOR-GRIU]—lord of the Luagni, father of Fionn's greatest enemies

PEOPLES

Dési Temro [DAY-SHEE TYA-WRA]—the vassal people of Temair

Galeóin [GALYOWN]—Gauls, the Brythonic vassal tribes of Eriu

The Luagni [LOOIN-YEE]—a subject race of Midhe

Sons of Mil [MILL]—Milesians, Gaelic-speaking rulers of Eriu

Tuatha Dé Danaan [TUA'HA JAY DANAWN]—the Children of Danu, the Sidhe, euhemerized as the race preceding the Milesians
Sons of Urgriu [OOR-GRIU]—a Luagni clan

PLACES

Alba [ALAPA]—Scotland
Almu [AL-VOO]—a *dun* on a hill overlooking the Curragh, won by Fionn from Tadg
Ath Brea [AHTH BRAY]—a ford on the southern branch of the Boyne
Ben Bulben [BYAWN BULUBEN]—a promontory in Connacht, home of the Dark Druid
Ben Gulban [BYAWN GUL-BIN]—a mountain near Rath Grainne
Bregia, Brega [BRYEW-GHA]—the plain to the west of Temair
The Boann [BO-AWN]—the river Boyne
Brí Leith [BREE LAYTH]—Midir's *sid*, near Loch Ri
Brugh na Boinne [BROOQH NUH BOYNYUH]—the mound of Aonghus Og, Newgrange, on the Boyne
Cave of Seghais [SHAGH-ISH]—near Loch Gara
Connachta [KUN'AQHTA]—Connaught
The Curragh [KURRAQH]—plain surrounding Kildare in Wicklow
Druim Cliadh [DRUM KLEEADH]—Shrine of Brigid on the Clay Ridge, County Kildare
Eriu [AYR-YOO]—Ireland
Gabhair [GOW-ER]—Aodh mac Ronain's *dun* on the Liffe
Gabhra [GOW-RA]—battlefield, near Garristown
Inber Colptha [INVER KOLUPTHA]—estuary of the Boyne

Laigin [LAYIN]—Leinster
River Liffe [LEEFUH]—the River Liffey
Lochlan [LOQHLAN]—Scotland
Mumu [MOO-VOO]—Munster
Paps of Anu [ANOO]—twin mounds in southwestern Munster
Rath Grainne [GRON-YUH]—Grainne's home, near Loch Arboch
Sid BodbDerg [SHEE BODHUV DYERUG]—Bodb Derg's mound near the southern end of Loch Dergdeire
Sliab Bladhma [SHLEEUV BLADHMA]—Slieve Bloom Mountains, Kildare
Sliab na mBan [SHLEEUV NA MAN]
The Sinnan [SHINUN]—River Shannon
The Siuir [SHU'UR]—the River Suir in S. Leinster
Temair Brega [TCHEVER BRAYQHA]—the hill of Tara
Tailtiu [TALTCHOO]—Teltown, in the valley of the Boyne
Tir n'an Og [TYEER-NAN-AWG]—the "Land of Youth" in the western isles
Ui Fiacrach [OOEE FEEA-QHRAQH]—district between Sliab Echtge and Galway Bay
Ulaidh [ULADH]—Ulster

TERMS

Ard Ri [ARD REE]—High King
brat [BROT]—a rectangular cape of heavy wool
**brollachan* [BRO-LA-QHAN]—a shapeless Thing, monster of Faerie
**cluricaun* [CLUER-I-QHAN]—leprechaun, one of the lesser folk of faerie
corrbolg [KORBOLUG]—the magic crane bag, source of treasure

derbfine [DYARU-FINYH]—those included with the eight degrees of kinship, mutually responsible economically and socially, with rights of inheritance and in a royal clan, eligible for election to the chieftainship
**fachan* [FAQH-AN]—a one-eyed, one-legged bogle with a single hand extending from its chest
fénnid [FEN-ITCH]—a member of a fian
fian [FEE-AN]—a division of the fianna
fianna [FEE-ANA]—the "national guard" of Eriu
fidchel [FISCHELL]—"tables," or brandubh, a board game in which a central piece, guarded by his own men, is attacked by a surrounding opposition
fili [FILEE]—a poet
**fuath* [FOO-A]—malicious sea spirits
geas, geasa [GYAS]—a taboo, or prohibition laid upon one person by another
grianan [GREE-ANUN]—"sun house," building where the women work or relax
mael [MAYL]—bald
menhir [MEN-HEER]—a Neolithic standing stone
ollamh [O-LAVE]—a senior poet
**phooka* [POO-KUH]—a bogle in horse form
rígfénnid [REEG-FENNITCH]—commander-in-chief of the *fianna*
**urisk* [UR-ISHK]—a water spirit
Imbolc [IMBULK]—Feast of Brigid, beginning of February
Beltane [BAL-TEEN]—May Day
Lughnasa [LOONASAH]—Feast of Lugh, beginning of August
Samhain [SOW-IN]—Hallowe'en

Prologue

DONAIT WAS AT HER WEAVING.

White hands moving swifter than thought shuttled bright threads back and forth through the tapestry. In the sourceless light of the Otherworld their colors glowed as if from within. Donait's golden hair streamed over her shoulders like a river of radiance, but the tapestries were brighter. Whether the light around her dimmed to dusk or brightened to dawning, they remained vibrant and alive.

Food and drink were hers whenever she should command them, but Donait did not eat often, for the folk of the Sidhe took food to pleasure their senses, not from need. She had been a long time at this work—the story her weaving chronicled was that of a hero, and it was not over. But though the task was lengthy, she sought no other. Fionn mac Cumhal dwelt in mortal lands, and Donait was alone.

But from time to time, even in the unchanging world

of the Sidhe, there were distractions. There came a day—it was early summer in Eriu—when a breath of breeze sighed through the branches that made up Donait's ceiling to tell her that a visitor was coming, and one of the walls shaped itself into a door.

The woman who entered was small, her head crowned with masses of moon-pale hair. Her face was meant to be merry, but for a long time now it had been stilled to sadness. Most of the folk of the Otherworld went clad as brightly as imagination could conceive, but the newcomer's gown was the same colorless shade as her hair.

Donait moved to meet her, opening her arms.

"Sabd, it is welcome you are, but I did not expect to see you. Does your father know you are here?"

A flash of spirit animated the calm features as Sadb shook her head.

"He does not, but if he finds out, I do not care. Already he separates me from the ones I love. What more can he do to me?"

Donait felt the slender shoulders shake as she patted them, murmuring, though the other woman's words made the sword turn in her own heart as well.

"Bodb Derg is cruel—cruel!" Sabd whispered brokenly. "The lives of mortals are so brief, soon enough I would have returned to him! Is it not cruel to keep me from my beloved and my child during the short time they will be alive in the world?"

"It is cruel indeed," replied Donait, *and you are not the only one for whom this ban has caused suffering,* but she did not say that aloud. All the Otherworld knew that she was Fionn's protector; her ability to help him might be greater if they did not know that she loved him as well.

"I came because I heard"—Sadb lifted her head, looking around her—"I have heard about your tapestries. . . ."

"They are very wonderful," Donait agreed. "All the stories are here—" she gestured and a wall glowed suddenly with a scene from the Battle of Mag Tured, in which the Tuatha Dé Danaan had won Eriu.

Sadb looked at her with eyes as dark and wounded as those of the doe whose form she had worn so long. "Donait, do not be tormenting me. You know well which tapestries I would see. . . ."

Donait sighed, knowing her response had been unworthy. It was the deeds of Fionn mac Cumhal that Sadb had come for. *But you lived with him and bore his child,* she thought with a bitterness she had not known she carried. *Once and once only has he lain in my arms.*

"They are here—" she said gently, motioning towards the back of the hall. "See, this is the battle where Fionn's father died, stabbed at the last by Fionnéices the poet after he and Goll had fought to exhaustion, and here is his mother Muirne, fleeing to the forest with the druidess Bodbmall and the Liath Luachra the warrior-woman, to escape her father's wrath."

"The Dark Druid—Tadg mac Nuada!" said Sadb, with endless loathing. "He hated Fionn before his birth because he was destined to take Tadg's fortress of Almu, and even worse after Fionn did so. All my sorrow is his doing—it was he who enchanted me so that Fionn would find me, and then, when I had learned to love him, stole me away!"

"But he did not get your child. . . ." said Donait. "Oisin, at least, is free!"

"My little one—" Sadb's brown eyes filled with tears. "And I am missing all the years of his growing! Soon he will be a man!"

"Well, that sorrow is one that you share with Fionn's mother, for like you, to save her child she had to give him away," Donait said briskly. "Look—this next scene shows Fionn growing up in the forest of Fidh Gaible, when he was still called Demne, and going to Tailtiu and beating all the other boys in the Games."

"He told me once that one of them was Cormac, who is now high king," said Donait with a little gurgle of laughter. "Cormac was furious at being bested, but they learned to be friends when they were grown. Fionn rules the wildwood as Cormac rules the lands of men."

I hope so, thought Donait. For a long time now her inclination had matched her duty as chronicler, for the story of Fionn had been the story of Eriu. On the alliance between *Ard Ri* and *Rígfénnid* was founded the peace of the land.

"And here are his adventures when he served as a dog boy and fire-keeper, and forged his spear Birga when he worked for the smith Lochan."

"I did not know that Brigid had a hand in that forging—" Donait peered more closely at the weaving.

Brigid has a hand in everything, thought Donait, *even more than I know. . . .* "Over there is the Ancient Dripping Hazel Tree," she said aloud, "from which came Fionn's wonderful shield. And you can see also the battle in which he defended me from the Fomorii when they would have destroyed these tapestries, and with them, the soul of the world."

"That was just after he avenged his friend Oircbél,

was it not?" asked Sadb. "There are those among the Sidhe who hate him still for killing Aedh, though it was only justice, as they hate him for destroying Aillén when he tried to burn Temair. But Fionn had no choice! It was his duty to protect his king.

"It is true," agreed Donait. "Our time to reign in the mortal world is done. But there are some here who will not accept that. Even the bargain he made with your father—neither to enter the Otherworld nor attempt to see you if Bodb Derg would deliver you from the Dark Druid's captivity—does not content them. All they can see is that it is Fionn who shields Eriu."

"Do I not know it?" Sadb shook her head regretfully. "Half of every year I was living with him he was out in the wilderness with the *fian,* helping King Cormac to put down rebel chieftains and defending the shores of Eriu from the raiders from Lochlan."

"True it is, and indeed the poor man has made more enemies than any mortal needs. But that is his fate in this life—" She looked up as the branches above her shivered to a rush of wind.

Once more her door had opened. Two more women were crossing her floor, one of them tall and bright as sunlight on the sea and the other small and angular, with her skirts kirtled up as if for running, and a cloud of red hair. Sadb was hovering over the tapestry that showed how Fionn had found his son Oisin about to be torn apart by the *fian*'s hunting pack and saved him, and had not noticed the newcomers. Donait smoothed the lines of tension from her brow and moved towards them.

"Donait, my dearest," said the red-haired woman brightly, "how long it has been since I visited—not, I think, since the day I gave my sons into the keeping of Fionn mac Cumhal!" At the name Sadb had turned, and was staring with widening eyes. "But I see that you have a guest already. Do I intrude?"

"And you just happened to be passing this way and thought you would pay a call?" asked Donait. "You have entered already, so I cannot ask you to come in, but I bid you welcome, Tuireann." If it had been possible for one to age in the Otherworld, she would have said that Fionn's sister looked older.

We all have our sorrows—Sadb is separated from her son and her husband, and the price Fionn paid to win Sadb in the first place was the life of Tuireann's son. This is no chance meeting—I am sure she followed Sadb to my hall. She listened, wondering if in another moment Bodb Derg would arrive in search of his daughter.

The fair girl behind Tuireann looked at Donait, frowning. "She asked me to come with her—is there a problem? I could go away—"

"Stay, Niamh," said Donait evenly. "Indeed, I am glad to see you. Your presence brightens my hall!" It had occurred to her that Niamh's willowy strength might prove useful if Tuireann and Sadb came to blows. The other two women were both small, but all the fiercer for their lack of size. "We seem to have become a party," she added with the same calm. "Let me offer you refreshment—"

For a moment her attention moved inward, bringing to mind the image she desired. Like some process in her own body she felt the shift in her surroundings, as a carved wooden table seemed to grow from the polished stones of the floor. And in a sense that was true, for the Otherworld was not real so much as it was the raw material of reality, its appearances given form by the thoughts of the Sidhe as mortals create their dreams. The Fair Folk might choose to appear as bird or beast, as a blaze of light, or, in the case of Tuireann, as a wind. But most often, the chosen shape was that of humankind.

Mortals, thought Donait, did not understand the fascination they held for the folk of the spirit world. *Or why are we still dwelling beneath these hills, instead of gone away oversea like Niamh's kin? The forms of mortality imprison us, but they also give our existence boundaries and meaning. Perhaps that is why we cling to them.*

On the table beside the central hearth, pitchers of sweet milk were appearing, and golden cups, and a flagon of mead. There were rosy apples in a basket, and a platter of fragrant scones. Niamh, who still had the appetites of a maiden, moved eagerly to the table and began to slather one of them with butter and honey from the comb. Donait took an apple and handed it to Sadb, who held it as if she had never seen one before.

Tuireann filled her cup with mead and drank it down. "So many tapestries—" She looked around her. "You *have* been busy!"

"This one shows how your warning saved Fionn when the Sons of Morna were coming for him—" Donait said placatingly.

Tuireann's eyes hardened. "That was a long time ago. Before he killed Bran."

"He did not mean to!" Sadb exclaimed. "He was trying to stop him from killing me!" They all looked at the hanging which showed how Bran, in the canine form he wore in the human world, had attacked Sadb, herself in the form of a doe.

"He was their uncle," said Tuireann dully. "I thought Bran and Sceolan would be safe with him."

"It was the shape," said Sadb. "Bran had been a dog for too long, and the shape mastered him so that he could not give up the attack even when Fionn called. You gave birth to your boys when you were in the shape of a hound-bitch, and licked them all over when they were born. That is why they were condemned to be dogs in the lands of men. I almost did the same when Oisin was born, but I remembered your mistake and stopped myself, and that is why he is human except for a lick of deer-hair on his brow. Cannot you forgive me, and Fionn? Sceolan has done so—it was he who protected Oisin from the other hounds until Fionn arrived!"

"Oisin. . . ." Tuireann repeated, drifting towards the most recent tapestries. She did not appear to have heard. "Such a fine lad—look at him, Niamh, is he not a handsome boy?"

"He is a child," said Niamh indulgently, but her gaze kindled as she looked more closely. Oisin, his hair blazing in the sun like a young flame, had just scored a goal at hurley on the field below Almu. "Still, he promises well. Perhaps I will keep an eye on him. He might be interesting when he is grown. . . ."

Was that what Tuireann had come for? It seemed a modest revenge.

"Fionn is happy—" she murmured. "He is king of the *fian* and lord of Almu. There he is, sitting with his men all around him and his son by his side." She gestured towards the tapestry.

Indeed, no one would doubt Oisin's breeding, though he lacked his father's height still. But the lean muscles moulded to the long bones were the same, the arched brows and high cheekbones above the strong curve of the jaw, and over the broad forehead, the same strong-springing hair, though some of the brightness had been leached from Fionn's hair by the passage of time. It was the color of weathering wheatstraw now.

"And Sceolan is lying at his feet," Tuireann went on, "who should have torn out Fionn's throat for Bran's blood-price! From whom shall I seek satisfaction?" She turned suddenly on Sadb. "From you?"

"I have suffered already," Sadb replied with unexpected dignity. "What do you know of love? You have only your petty jealousy and wounded pride!"

"Do you think so?" Tuireann's green eyes flashed. "Well, that may be enough to bring your precious hero down!"

"By you?" Sadb's finger's curled into claws and Donait stepped between them. "You do not have the power!"

"Maybe not"—Tuireann bared teeth in a smile—"but I am not Fionn's only enemy!"

From the doorway came a raven's harsh cry. Donait whirled, staring, as black feathers extended into a mass of gleaming black locks and a black mantle thrown back to display the white bosom and crimson gown of the Morrigan. In the silence the only sound was Tuireann's tinkling laughter, like brazen bells in the wind.

"And what may I offer you?" Donait said finally. "A beaker of blood?" Tuireann tittered again, and the Morrigan smiled.

"I will drink ale," she said calmly, and moved past Donait to look at the tapestry.

"He has done well, this starveling who set himself against me at Samhain seven years ago."

"He was mad with grief," said Donait quickly. "He did not mean to challenge you!" She found herself shivering as the Morrigan looked back at her.

"Does that matter? Everyone heard. No doubt he has forgotten, but I forget nothing. This tapestry shows me a man at the height of his pride and powers. I think it is time that I took a hand in his affairs. . . ."

"You cannot, you must not!" Sadb fell to her knees before the goddess. All of the Sidhe seemed divine next to mortals, but the Morrigan was one of the great ones, existing in both the Otherworld and in the minds of men. Her power was fed by the blood of every warrior slain.

"No mortal defies *me*—" she said in a low voice. "The Hound of the Ulaidh tried to do so, but my ravens pecked out his eyes in the end. Is Fionn mac Cumhal greater than Cuchulain?"

"He is different. . . ." A new voice responded, soft, as if the fire had spoken the words. "Cuchulain guarded the Ulaidh; Fionn protects all of Eriu. . . ."

The Morrigan whirled as a column of flame blazed up from the hearth. "You! I might have known!"

"Indeed, you ought to have expected me. . . ." Within the light a woman's shape was forming, and in another moment Brigid herself stepped down from the hearth, her crimson cloak trailing sparks across the stone floor.

"You have your purpose, and I have mine, and Fionn mac Cumhal is part of that plan."

"I will destroy him!"

"You will not—powers greater than either of us have called him to serve Eriu." Brigid gazed around her, meeting Tuireann's defiant stare until the red-haired woman dropped her eyes, looking at Sadb with so much love that the girl began to weep again.

"Then I will help him to destroy himself," said the Morrigan. "His will is his own. Even you cannot protect him if he turns to me!"

"Fionn's will is his own," agreed Brigid. "But if he stands fast, you can do nothing against him. The choices must be his own!"

"Then he will be happy!" cried Sadb.

"Did I say that?" Brigid answered her. "In the times that are coming there will be little I can do to protect him. I know only that he will fulfill his destiny. . . ."

Chapter 1

FIONN MAC CUMHAL MOVED THROUGH THE FOREST like the wind in the leaves. Overhead the sun was shining brightly; as the branches shifted, light and shadow dappled the path. Fionn was one shadow among many, his movements timed to the sway of the branches, his footfalls lost in the whispering of the wind. He was aware that there were other men in the wood without needing to think how he knew it; every rustle that was out of time with the pattern told him, every quivering leaf that did not belong to the harmony.

But what he did not know was which of those betraying movements had been made by his son Oisin.

A yellowhammer was singing among the ferns, a single phrase repeated again and again. Fionn paused beside an ash tree, listening, and felt the pounding begin in his temples once more. They had sat late around the fire the night before, drinking to the success of the lads who were about to be tested for the *fian*. He could not remember how many skins had been emptied as the horns of ale went down. Too many, from the feel of his head. He should have called a halt and sent the men off to bed, but it had not occurred to him there would be a problem. He had always been able to drink down the rest of the *fian* before.

From somewhere to his left he heard a sharp yip as one of the runners was sighted, and the thunk of a javelin hitting a tree. His lips twitched as he remembered his own testing. Today, the men who were attacking only meant to spur the boys to greater effort. When Fionn had been the quarry in this race, some of his pursuers had been trying to kill.

He scanned the tangle of young oaks and hazels ahead. It was not Oisin they were chasing over there. His son could become as invisible as a fawn in a thicket; he would never have let himself be seen. But the boy had to move sometime. In this game the pursuers had the advantage of knowing that the runners must eventually break cover in order to snatch the painted wands that would prove they had made the run. The hunters had given the boys a head start, it was true, but the warriors could head straight for the goal and wait there without worrying whether *they* were seen.

Except for Fionn. It had been years since he himself had participated in the testing, but he had always made it a point of honor to race through the forest as swiftly and silently as any of the lads. He liked to manifest behind some wary runner, pull one of the braids whose pristine arrangement bore witness to the boy's skill, and disappear with only an echo of laughter to identify him. It amused him, and it did no harm to remind these young sprigs that he was their master.

So where was Oisin?

Fionn moved forward. The clearing where they had set the row of wands was close now. Had the boy got there before him? It was to be expected that Oisin's friend Caoilte would outrun them all—he was not the most silent, but he was as fast as Ceallach the Swift-footed had been in his youth, before he broke his wind racing to bring Fionn the news that Sadb was gone. . . .

Fionn blinked, and realized that he was standing stock-still in the lee of the beech tree. *Sadb, Sadb . . .* he thought bitterly, *you still have the power to distract me even after fourteen years. Your child is almost grown, beloved. Do they let you have news of him where you are now, or is your father so jealous still he will not even let you look upon your son? You would be proud of him, my darling. Our Oisin is the fairest youth in Eriu.*

And by now, though Caoilte might be faster, Oisin also must surely have reached the goal.

Fionn shook himself and took the shortest route through the trees to the meadow. As he had expected, Caoilte's blue wand and Oisin's yellow were both gone. The purple stick that belonged to Gaoine, Lugach's son, Cairpre Dubh's green stick, and the rest of the colored wands were still waiting there. No doubt the other runners would be along soon and he could catch them, but today they were not his concern. He was going to have to stretch a little to overtake Oisin.

By this time the boy would be relaxing, proud of having successfully completed the first part of his run. Fionn lengthened his stride, reaching out with senses for which he had no names to the earth song that made him part of the land, but found nothing that did not belong to the forest. He leaped over a resting deer before she was aware of his coming. The startled beast exploded from her brake and crashed through the thickets—that was a mistake that would have alerted any pursuer, if he had been the prey. But in moments the sound was far behind him.

He slowed, gazing around him. A few late violets trembled among the mosses at the base of the oak trees, a shrew-mouse stirred the grass; he heard the robin's cheery greeting, and beyond it, the murmur of voices where the rest of the *fian* waited for the runners to come out of the wood. Already the ale was flowing freely, and the scent of roasting meat drifted upon the air. For days people had been preparing this celebration. The folk of Almu had come down to join the *fian* in Fidh Gaible to prepare the feast. It never occurred to anyone that the son of Fionn mac Cumhal could do other than win acceptance into the *fian*.

Nor do I doubt it now, thought Fionn, frowning. Abruptly he realized that it was himself he was testing today. Something flickered ahead of him and he blinked—had that been a patch of sunlight or Oisin's hair? He started to turn, and felt a sudden sharp jerk on one of his braids.

His first thought was that he had caught it on a branch. Instantly he swayed into the pull, reaching behind him. His fingers brushed something softer than tree bark and abruptly the pressure ceased. He whirled, glimpsed a flurry of bright motion among the hazel boughs, and then nothing, only the slowing swing of the branches as they recovered from the disturbance—only that, and a boy's sweet laughter with the hint of a man's depth behind it that rang through the forest until it, too, was gone.

But I sensed nothing that was not part of the forest! Sight dazzled and dimmed, bright and dark, as the blood pounded in his brain.

When he could think again, Fionn realized that he had been standing there long enough for the branches to still completely. Except for his racing heart, nothing was moving at all.

He caught me! That has never happened before!

A thunder of approval erupted from the field beyond the forest. *Oisin has come out,* thought Fionn. *They are welcoming him. They will be wondering where I am now. . . .*

It occurred to him that he had not sensed Oisin because the boy *was* part of the forest, but it was not much comfort. He should have anticipated that and found some way to track him. *Oisin's woodcraft is better, and Caoilte is faster. I am getting old. . . .*

Slowly, he started towards the edge of the forest. Was this what the Liath Luachra had felt when she realized that her fosterling could outrun and outfight her, when she had to let him hunt and bring her food? Fionn stretched out his arms, a little pale from the winter indoors, but hard with muscle still. His biceps had always been as round as a plum about to burst its skin—were they losing that smoothness? His father's friend Fiacail had had muscles like ropes stretched over a framework of withies. But Fiacail had been old!

As Fionn moved, some other part of his mind had been busy figuring how to emerge from the trees without being seen. If he could suddenly appear among the men without anyone realizing where he had come from, it would be less humiliating, so long as Oisin did not start crowing about how clever he had been.

More shouting hailed the appearance of the other

lads—Fionn heard them crying out for Caoilte and mac Lugach, Rionnolbh, Black Cairpre and Glas mac Gadal and Dubhán. He peered through the screen of blackthorn. The men were all clustering around their young hero, as he had expected. It was easy to slip around behind them, to wait until the crowd parted and Oisin could see him leaning against an oak tree as if he had been there all along.

Smile! Fionn told himself. *This is his moment of triumph! Do not be spoiling it with reservations the way your foster mother Bodbmall stole the savor from all your victories!* His own mistrust had soured even those successes the old woman had left him. At least Oisin had the capacity for happiness. He looked at the boy's shining face. *This,* thought Fionn, *is how it should have been for me.*

"Well, men," Fionn cried. "Have they succeeded? Are these lads worthy to join you as full members of the *fianna* of Eriu?"

The men of the *fian* answered with a shout that shook the earth and frightened the robins from the trees. And the name that they shouted louder than any other was that of Oisin.

Fionn opened his arms, drinking in the sight of his son, flushed and laughing. Folk said that Oisin was growing to be the image of his father. But when Fionn looked at the boy he saw only Sadb's eyes, a deep and shifting greeny dark like a forest pool, while his own were blue. And now, in the moment of triumph, there was a sheen of beauty on the boy that made him hard to look on, even for one who was accustomed to the radiance of the Otherworld.

He is like Lugh in the morning of the world, Fionn thought, his sight blurring. *He is the flower of Eriu!*

Then Oisin grabbed him in a hug that nearly drove the breath from his lungs. For a moment he hesitated, then his own arms closed around the strong shoulders of his son.

"I should have known you would catch me out," Oisin said in his ear. "I've been practicing sneaking up on the other lads for weeks—the men all told me how you used to do it to them at their testing, and never a one of them could touch me. I should have known better than to try it on you!"

Fionn pulled back a little. Was the boy mocking him? But no, his eyes were clear, his face open and laughing. He had no idea that with every word he was turning the knife in the wound. Fionn forced an answering grin, swallowing the bitter rejoinder that Oisin should not have been able to touch him at all.

Then the rest were crowding back around them. Lomna the Fool capered in the van, chanting verses. Fionn found himself lifted onto someone's shoulders with Oisin beside him as the *fianna* bore them off to celebrate their victory.

THAT SUMMER IT SEEMED AS IF THE GODS HAD DECREED a particular blessing for Eriu. There was just enough fighting to justify the *fianna's* hard training, first when two of the western clans were disputing a boundary and refused the high king's judgment and later when six keels of raiders from Alba descended on what they thought was a defenseless shore.

Oisin fought with a cheerful abandon, taking chances that made Fionn tremble, confident that his superb reflexes and growing strength would keep him out of trouble. So far, the assumption seemed to be justified, for the boy had come through both battles without a scar.

"He fights as if he were immortal!" said Fionn to Goll, as they leaned against an oak tree one evening after the *fianna* had withdrawn to the forest again.

"No doubt he thinks he is—" the older man replied. "Were you not the same? I can remember some of your exploits that would make a wise man wonder. Come now—did you really believe that you could die when you were young?"

When I was young . . . thought Fionn, wondering at what moment that had ceased to be true, *I knew death only too well. There were times I would have died gladly to have avoided killing. But my body was always ahead of my heart and would never give in.*

"It is you who are immortal, old friend," he said aloud. Marriage with Caoinche had restored Goll's customary gruff cheer. The campfire coppered the silver in the other man's hair and beard, returning the fiery thatch that marked him as one of the Sons of Morna. But his fire was banked now; it could flare forth if stirred, but for the most part, ash covered the coals.

"Do you think so?" Goll laughed. "All I know is that I have no mind to outlive my strength. I will die with a sword in my hand."

Down the hill by the cook fires a woman screeched. Fionn found himself on his feet without thinking, followed, a little more slowly, by Goll. An angry bellowing split the air; there were more screams, and with them, laughter. Fionn slowed, trying to see.

A distorted figure exploded towards him, closely followed by a second, all plunging legs and flailing arms. As he dodged, Fionn realized that the grotesque shapes were two young bulls desperately attempting to dislodge their riders, who were making almost as much noise as the beasts they rode. Fionn ducked a swinging horn and glimpsed a fair face alight with laughter.

Oisin; but Fionn had already known who it must be. He looked around and to his amazement realized that the rider of the second beast was Diarmuid mac Duibhne, who had been a warrior of the *fian* for fifteen years and should have known better, though in that moment he looked no older than Fionn's son.

By now the rest of the men had come running, whooping with glee. They formed a rough circle, waving their arms whenever one of the beasts came too near and cheering the riders. The bulls had already overturned the cauldron and scattered the coals; the scent of boiled meat mingled unappealingly with the smoke from the singed grass. Dogs dashed in and out, trying to snatch the half-cooked pieces from under the hooves of the bulls, barking hysterically.

That's our dinner they're gobbling, thought Fionn. But the *fian* were used to going on short rations. No doubt they would feel the entertainment worth the loss of a meal.

"Ho, Goll— My new silver buckle against your dagger that Diarmuid stays on longest." Duibhne, who had come up with the others, held out his hand.

"Done," said the big man, slapping his palm. "I'll back Fionn's son against yours!"

"And what about you." Duibhne turned to Fionn. "What will you wager on your boy?" He grinned, and for a moment Fionn could see in his face the youth who had been cupbearer to the *fian* when Fionn first came to them, in his uncle Crimall's time.

"What makes you think that I would wager anything on such foolishness?" he said coldly. "This must be stopped before someone gets hurt."

The other two stared at him in amazement. With the possible exception of *fidchel*, there was hardly an amusement, from hunting to hurley, that did not carry some risk. For the men of the *fian*, the danger was half the fun.

"I mean the spectators, not those two idiots—" Fionn added grimly as the beasts careered around again, flanks heaving, eyes wild. The hide of the one Oisin rode was sweat-darkened to earth-brown; Diarmuid's mount was black with white splotches. Froth flew from their jaws.

"Don't worry," said Duibhne. "At this rate they won't last long."

"I wonder where they found the poor beasts?" observed Goll.

"I daresay the nearest farmer could answer that, and no doubt we'll have him storming out here in the morning, wanting an honor-price for the theft of his cows!" Fionn had not meant to be funny, but Goll began to grin.

"I never tried to ride a bullock, but I mind one time my brother Conain harnessed two rams to a cart and tried to drive them chariot-wise. One beast went east and the other west, and there was Conain in the middle, hauling on the head ropes. I nearly split myself laughing."

Dubh Droma, who was standing near them, responded with a story about trying to ride a pig, and Loegaire said his old granny had owned a goat that pulled a wagon as well as a pony.

I once leaped on a stag's back. Fionn remembered

the great muscles sliding beneath his gripping thighs and how the antlers had lashed back at him. *But it was not for sport, but to bring the beast to bay!*

There was a shout from across the ring and they saw Diarmuid bounce half off his mount and come down sprawled across the animal's neck, clutching at the horns.

"Ho Diarmuid, d'ye think to steer him so?" Duibhne was doubled up with laughter.

The sight stung Fionn to fury. He had not authorized this spectacle and he would not have it. Was he not master here? Diarmuid's bull was plunging towards him with Oisin close behind. He stepped forward and, as the black beast swerved to avoid him, Diarmuid lost his grip and started to fall into the brown bull's path. But Fionn was there before him, reaching for the horns and twisting with perfect timing. The bull's head went down, and, as it somersaulted to one side, Oisin went flying, twisting in midair so that he landed on his feet. He was still laughing.

"Oisin's the winner!" came the cry.

"Indeed he is not," others countered, "for Diarmuid's still holding on to his mount, see you, while the lad is ten paces away."

"But if Fionn had not stopped the beast, he would have stayed on—"

As Oisin's bull staggered to its feet, all the fight gone out of it, men turned to look at Fionn. Diarmuid's animal had quieted as well and, when he let go of its neck, stood with head hanging, blowing gustily.

"I declare it a tie," said Fionn. "Diarmuid's feet touched the ground at the same time as Oisin's." There were groans from the men who had been foremost in the betting, and jeers from those who had not wagered.

Goll shook his head. "And isn't that a pity, just when I was beginning to fancy Duibhne's drinking horn! I've an idea—" He turned to the other man. "I'll give you my buckle and you give me the horn and we'll both win."

"Where did you get the bulls?" Fionn turned to his son.

"They were wandering in the wood—" Oisin began, his eyes limpid with innocence. But as Fionn began to frown they sparkled and he shook his head. "That is the truth, Father. I know—they must have strayed from somewhere. I suppose we could have back-tracked them. . . ." he added, but he did not look very contrite.

They turned at an outburst of shouting from the edge of the camp. Someone was attempting to push through the crowd, greeted by mingled jeers and laughter.

"Indeed, I should suppose that the flower of the *fianna* could do so when even the farmer seems to have been able to follow their trail," said Fionn as a short, broad-barreled man with a very red face emerged from among the warriors. For a moment the newcomer stared around him; then his gaze fell upon the two bulls, and his face became, if possible, even more crimson.

"Look at them—my poor lads! The brown bull of Cualigne was nothing to them, or Finnbenach, the great white-horned bull of Aillil! And just see—ye've run ten stone off them surely, there's naught left but skin and bone!" He turned to Fionn. "I'll have compensation for this outrage, so I will!"

"It is true," said Fionn, "you must be paid."

"And what are we to eat tonight," put in Goll's

brother Conain, "with our dinner spilled all over the grass?"

"It will do you no harm to miss a meal—" Duibhne aimed a playful punch at Conain's gut.

"Eat the bulls—" said Oisin. "I like lean meat. I'll pay their price to you," he told the farmer. "It was worth it for the ride!"

Fionn sighed. It was true that Oisin's share of the loot won from the raiders would more than cover the price of the animals, but that was not the point.

"You *rode* them?" It had taken the man a few moments to comprehend the words. "My princes among cattle, my lovely bulls that I raised from little calves?" He sputtered, searching for words.

"Next, he'll be asking an honor-price for the insult!" said Dubh Droma.

"He would be entitled—" Fionn said sternly. "But I have a better idea. You are laughing now"— he looked at Oisin and Diarmuid—"but you would not find it so amusing if you had ever nursed a sick calf through the night, or walked all day to find a strayed cow and then had to pull her out of a bog. The horned cattle of the forest tend themselves, and you have only to hunt them, but there is a deal of labor in raising the cattle kept by men!"

He supposed their ignorance was not surprising. Neither Oisin nor Diarmuid had ever known any life but that of the *fian*.

"An honor-price you shall have," he said to the farmer, "and with it the service of these two young hotheads for the length of a moon. Set them to mucking out the cow byre or whatever you will—" He paused as Diarmuid's face grew fire-red with suppressed indignation. Oisin's eyes blazed, but after a moment he began to laugh once more.

"It is naught to laugh at," said Fionn repressively, "but neither is it a dishonor. I myself have served among the dogs and the cattle, at the forge and the fire, and I think now that I would have served you better if I had set you to this labor before!"

The high color left Diarmuid's face. In his eyes now Fionn saw shame, and appeal. *He understands now that this hurts me—he is the son of my spirit, and I love him as much as any child of my body, even Oisin!*

"That is well, then," said the farmer, looking a little abashed. "I shall give them no dishonorable labor."

It seemed very quiet in the camp when they had gone. Except for Conain, no one dared to complain about their lost dinner, but they were wary of Fionn as well. Only Goll came to join him once more beside his fire.

"You must not be too hard on the lads—" said the older man. "Remember how it was when you were a boy!"

Fionn looked at him, frowning. "Perhaps that's why I was so angry," he said finally. "I was never allowed to be a boy—not that way. Bodbmall and the Liath Luachra never stopped warning me of disaster if I once let down my guard. My mind tells me that what they did was not so bad, but my heart—I suppose that what I am really feeling is envy!"

BY THE TIME DIARMUID AND OISIN RETURNED, THE FIAN had moved west of the Sinnan to Connachta and the sea. It was by now the beginning of autumn, the nights grew brisk, though there was still warmth in the days. The bracken turned bronze on the slopes of the mountains, with a bloom of purple heather, and the glens rang with the belling of the red stags.

It had been a long time since Fionn had been here at this season; seven years had passed since the day he walked out through the mists of the Otherworld and came upon the *fian* at their hunting just in time to save Oisin from the dogs. Seven years, and Oisin had most of his growth now and was a warrior. But Fionn could see that he, too, remembered. He lifted his head at the sight of Ben Bulben stark against the sky, and his nostrils flared like those of a young stag scenting the breeze.

"I had forgotten this might not be easy for you," Fionn said to his son. "I will soon need a messenger to the high king—I could send you to Temair."

Oisin's dark eyes widened. "I am not sad, Father. I am only . . . remembering. It is for me here as it was for you in the forest of Fidh Gaible. I recognize every tree and stone."

"And cave—" said Fionn grimly. "But the Dark Druid is gone. Whether he is dead or fled no one can tell me, but he is not here." Something flickered in Oisin's gaze, but he was silent. He had never said much about the years he had spent with his mother as the Druid's captive, and Fionn, remembering how long they had waited for the boy to speak in human language at all, forbore to press him.

Even without the Druid, these mountains that looked out over the western ocean were strong in magic, haunted by beings that had not gone into the mounds with the Sidhe who remained in Eriu, nor yet had the resolve to fare away beyond the circles of the world with their kin in Tir n'an Og. This land, where the sunlight paled to silver and islands appeared and disappeared like illusions from the mist on the sea, was half-enchanted. Men walked warily, and few beside the *fian* dared to hunt this way, so game was abundant. The *fian* threw themselves into the chase, Oisin most eagerly of all.

Just past the autumn turning, when folk in the settled lands were getting the harvest in, word came that a boar of Balar the stout-smiter's breeding had gone feral and was ravaging the countryside. Folk said that Balar's pigs were half-wild anyway, and his great sow had got herself in farrow from a boar of the wild kindred when she broke from her pen. Balar made no shift to go after him until the boar began to destroy men's fields, and by then it was too late, for the beast was too fierce for either men or hounds.

It was laid upon the *fian* to go after him. Fionn did not like it much—pigs had always been bad luck for him. But the younger men were eager for the chase, boasting how they would bring the beast down.

"Nonetheless, it is Caoilte that will kill it," said Fionn to Diarmuid as the hunt streamed down the hillside.

"Have you set your thumb between your teeth to get that knowledge?" asked the younger man, smiling.

Fionn grimaced. The power of prophecy that had come to him when he tasted the Salmon of Wisdom was only unloosed when he bit on the thumb with which he had touched the fish, and just as well, or he would have been overwhelmed by knowledge. But he did not like to use it, for he had always such a headache afterward.

"No need," he said shortly. "I know Balar's pigs of old, and they would outrun the Grey of Macha. No man but our Caoilte will be able to catch up with the creature, and if he does not try to kill it before the rest of us reach him, he does not belong in the *fian*. Are you disappointed? Better for you not to be hunting pigs anyhow, even when you know their ancestry."

"I know that *geasa* has been laid upon me, but not why—" said Diarmuid, slackening his pace and turning.

He had grown into a lovely man, thought Fionn, straight and strong. He was of the black-haired breed of Eriu, his curls like charcoal with little fiery glints in them, his skin freckled like a bird's egg where the sun touched it and white as a maiden's where it was covered by his clothes. Caoilte might be faster, but Diarmuid was the most skillful in gymnastic feats of all the *fian*.

"Because of your half brother, that your mother had by Roc mac Dicain, the farmer she was married to after she bore you to Duibhne. We guested with them one time at the house they had near the Brugh na Boinne. It was Roc's duty to tend the mound and make the offerings. I think that perhaps your father was a little possessive of the woman still, but the form it took was that he complained because the child she had borne to the farmer and her son by him, a warrior of the *fian*, were being raised the same."

"The time before I came to you and the *fian* is hard for me to remember," said Diarmuid. "Perhaps I don't want to. I can recall my mother's face, a little. And a dogfight—what happened, Fionn?"

"Someone threw a piece of meat amongst the dogs, and before we knew it the room was full of snapping jaws and snarling and people running every which way. When we got them separated we found your half brother dead on the floor. Roc wanted a compensation from me because they were my dogs, but there was no mark of tooth or claw upon the boy. Though he swore it was not intended, it was Duibhne who had fallen on the child and killed him. I offered to pay the fine, but Roc said the only compensation he would accept were if he should be allowed to deal the same by you.

"At that, Duibhne swore he would take Roc's head, and it was as hard to get them apart as it had been with the dogs. Afterward Roc went a little mad and he took up the body of his son and trussed it up like one of the pigs he slaughtered for offerings, and he gave it to the god in the mound. And that night I dreamed that Aonghus Og himself was standing over you, and saying that the farmer's child that had been given to him as a pig should be reborn as one, and that if you, Diarmuid, should chance to kill that boar, in the same hour your own life would end. And that is why you must not hunt boar, for you do not know which one might be your own mother's son. But the way the women fuss over you it would seem that the god has blessed you with his own gifts, so it is not all bad."

The young man turned away, his face red as fire.

Diarmuid mac Duibhne did not run after the women—he did not have to. The men teased that Aonghus Og, who of all the Sidhe was the most notable lover, must have put a love spot upon him that only the girls could see, for wherever they might go, there always seemed to be some woman trying to climb into his bed, even the daughter of the king of the Laigin, who had borne him a son she called Olann.

Fionn laughed and slapped him on the back. Then a clamor of dogs up ahead told them that the hunters had made their kill. They hurried up the path to meet

Caoilte, who was staggering along with an enormous pig slung across his shoulder.

"I did it—I caught him, do you see!" crowed Caoilte. "Here's meat for the whole *fian*!"

That night the men feasted merrily and called Caoilte a hero. Fionn thought that Oisin was perhaps a little less loud in his praises than the rest of them. He was not used to someone else getting all the glory. *It will do the boy good,* he thought, watching him. *No one can be first in everything.*

The talk turned to remarkable beasts and famous huntings. They sang of how Fionn had killed the black boar of Sliab Muicce as his bride-price for the smith's daughter and forged his spear Birga for the deed. In his youth Goll had killed a wild bull that was tearing up the countryside, and there were others.

"There is one great beast of legend still roaming the mountains north of here," said Fergus the Poet at last. "The great stag of Inis Bo Finne that was once Donn son of Fionnlaoch of the Sidhe."

"A tale!" cried Oisin, "Let us hear!"

"Long ago it began," said Fergus, "before the Sons of Mil came into the land. Donn of Sliab Mis carried off a hundred fair maidens from the mound of Aodh, but Aodh's queen was jealous of him, and changed the maidens to deer to roam the cold hills. And Donn's punishment was to be their guardian, and no deer were safer than they. But the queen still wanted his love, and when she sent for him to come for her, he swore by wind and bright sun, by sea and land, that he would never be hers. In her fury, she replied that if he so loved the deer, then he might see how he liked to be one, and by her magic he became the mightiest stag that was in Eriu. And from that day to this no man has dared to hunt him."

"I will hunt him—" cried Oisin.

"For the sake of your mother that bore you do not," said Fionn.

"Is it a *geas*?" asked the boy, his eyes burning like coals. "No one has ever told me not to eat the meat of deer."

"This deer was once a man of the Otherworld, and you are half of that blood—"

"I know it," said the boy more soberly, brushing back the thick lock of hair to show the patch of deer-hide that still grew on his brow. "But if I am a young stag, all the more reason for me to challenge Donn!"

Fionn stared at him. He had never spoken to the boy about his mother. The years had not dimmed his sorrow so much as they had distanced it. When he was at Almu he slept in a different hall than the one where Sadb had had her bower. His folk knew better than to say her name aloud. Unless Fearghusa and Faobhar, who had been with him that day when they chased the white doe through the forest, had spoken to the boy, how could he know how it had been?

"Your mother . . ." he whispered, and his throat closed as once more he scented the dead, wintry smell of the spell that had held her, and heard the dreadful snap of Bran's backbone as he held the hound from pulling her down. As if sensing it, Sceolan whined and set his pale muzzle on Fionn's knee. Even now he could not speak of that day. Fionn shook his head angrily.

"You must not—" he said again. "The stag Donn will think and feel like a man. . . ."

"Why should that matter?" asked Oisin guilelessly.

"I have killed men. If it is a *geas*, I will not eat his flesh, but you cannot hold me from challenging him."

"Hear, hear!" cried some of the men who were nearest. "It sounds like a rare chase, a prey that will make us stretch ourselves. Go to it, Oisin, and we will follow you!"

"I can hold you—" Fionn stood up suddenly. "Am I not your father and lord of the *fian?*"

"Whose cattle will you set me to herd this time?" flared Oisin, his eyes narrowing. Diarmuid had taken his punishment in good heart; they said all the dairymaids had wept when his service was done. But Fionn could see now that the task had hurt Oisin's pride.

He needed the lesson, he told himself. *And I will give him as many such lessons as he has need of until he learns that he cannot have things all his own way just because he now is counted as a man!* The men closest to them had drawn away, afraid to be caught in the quarrel, but not out of earshot. Fionn grimaced. In a moment they would be making wagers on who would win.

"Indeed, you are my father, and you should not object if I am too much like you, for whom did you obey, when you were my age?" Oisin went on, "Do you deny that you deserted every service you entered?"

"It was not by my will that I left them—" Fionn retorted, then a rage rose in him that he should be questioned by this boy. "You shall hunt no beast of the Otherworld, Oisin!"

"Will you not leave me a little glory? You have killed enough uncanny creatures in your time!" said his son, then his mood changed suddenly, and he shook his head, laughing. "I am thirsty—" He sprang to his feet. "Who will race me down to the stream?"

Fionn looked after him, frowning.

"He did not mean it," said Diarmuid, beside him. "You have no need to grudge him his honors—you are still in your prime!"

"Truly? There are times when I feel old. . . ."

"You have spent long enough in grieving for your lady," said Diarmuid. "Let us look about for a suitable wife for you. You will know yourself young again if you bring home a bride!"

Chapter 2

"AFTER HIM, SCEOLAN! YOU KNOW THE SCENT—IT'S a race we are in, lad, to reach Oisin before he runs the stag down!" Fionn straightened as the hound leaped away, nose to the ground and tail waving like a banner behind him. Fionn sprang into motion after him and heard the picked men he had chosen following as Goll, who no longer had the figure for such a race, and the others who were being left behind with him shouted a farewell.

Oisin deceived me! Fionn's first reaction was still disbelief that the boy had gone against his will. Oisin had not precisely sworn he would not go after the stag Donn, but he had certainly allowed his father to believe that he had given in.

I should have explained the danger, Fionn thought as his muscles loosened and he settled into the ground-eating trot of the long-distance runner. *Oisin is still a child. For all his skills, and despite his breed-*

ing, he knows nothing of the Otherworld. If he understood why he, of all men, should avoid this encounter, he would not have gone.

But it should not have mattered if Oisin understood—that was what it came down to. He should have given up the idea of hunting the stag because Fionn told him to. . . .

At least the lad had not seduced anyone else into rebellion. If he listened, Fionn could hear the light tread of Caoilte at his elbow. The boy had volunteered to run ahead, and no doubt he could come up with Oisin before the others, but without the authority, or perhaps the will, to turn his friend from his purpose, all he could achieve would be a warning. Fionn preferred to have Caoilte right where he was, where he could keep an eye on him.

When this is over I'll assign all the young ones to a troop for special training, and put Diarmuid in command. He's still blushing over that escapade with the bulls, and he'll work them till their tongues hang out, he thought grimly. *I can trust Diarmuid.*

Autumn sunlight slanted through the fluttering leaves of the birch trees in a glimmer of gold. It had rained the night before, and the air Fionn sucked into his lungs was rich with the scent of damp bark and molding leaves. Though the sun warmed his back, the crisp air promised cold to come. It was perfect weather for running, but Fionn scarcely noticed. Oisin could follow a leaf on the breeze; once he learned where Donn was ranging, he would have no trouble in tracking him down. But finding him might take a while. At least the pursuers were following a fresh trail.

Fionn had left the Hazel Shield with the baggage, but the spear Birga was in his hand. Each footfall sent a tremor down the shaft, and wind hissed past the blade. *"Drink blood, hot blood, drink blood soon?"* came the whisper, and Fionn shook the spear angrily. The weapon was all too sensitive to his own emotions; anger especially could awaken it, and it gloried in strife.

"Be still," he thought back at it. *"You may help me give the lad a beating, but there will be no killing today!"*

"Thirsty. . . . " said the spear, but more softly. Fionn straightened, breathing deeply to calm himself, and felt the pressure subside. But Birga was not asleep. That sense of avid anticipation remained with him as he pounded along.

The trail led northward, where the mountains plunged steeply into the sea. To Fionn this was new country, a coast where the clouds trailed purple shadows across grey-blue slopes that rose like gigantic waves from the sea; for all its beauty, its stark peaks and shadowed corries held little attraction for either raiders or honest men. But the eagle soared above the ridges, and the wildcat screamed from the crags. In the brightly bannered forest that unfolded below the bronze of the bracken the red stags trumpeted a challenge to any who would steal their does.

As the terrain grew rougher the pursuers lost some of their advantage. Fionn swore and pushed himself to greater speed though he wheezed like a bellows on the upslopes and slid going down. They munched parched grain from their pouches without halting and snatched a mouthful of water when they crossed a stream. Only Caoilte and Diarmuid, with Dubhán and Faobhar, their best runners, could keep up with him and the hounds.

On the third day they knew they were closing. Oisin was moving carefully now, and slowly, his narrow, high-arched footprints crossing the hoof marks of a great stag. Indeed, deer sign was plentiful, but the tracks of the beast that Oisin was stalking were unique.

For the first time Fionn found his heart quickening with excitement. Much of his life had been spent in hunting, but never had he seen deer prints so deeply marked or with such a length of stride. The forehooves were bearing more weight than the rear—the beast must be carrying an immense rack of horns.

The hound Sceolan breasted a low ridge and paused, nose lifted and plumed tail stiffening. Fionn stopped beside him, his keen eyes scanning the tangled oaks. He could hear nothing, but the dog looked from him to the tree-covered slope ahead of them and whined.

"Do you scent the stag, lad?" said Fionn. The other men came up beside him with the rest of the dogs, who caught Sceolan's excitement and began to pull at their leads.

"They're down there—they must be!" said Caoilte.

"Sceolan, my dear, I will trust your senses. Find them, lad, and keep Oisin away from the stag—" said Fionn softly to the dog, and to the man behind him, "Slip the hounds!" Sceolan sprang forward as if Fionn's gesture had released him, with the knot of yammering hounds uncoiling behind him.

They heard them before they could see—a cacophony of furious barking thinned by excitement, and Oisin's voice cracking as he tried to call the dogs away. A deer burst from the blackthorn brake before them, but it was a doe. The wood was full of does, springing away on every side. Ahead, branches cracked as a heavy body passed through them and a dog screamed. They saw the limp brindled body arc through the air, then, as shockingly as if it had manifested from the wind-twisted trunks of the trees, the bulk of the great stag lifted above them, its rack of antlers stark as the boughs of a winter wood against the sky.

Undeterred, the dogs swept after; the earth shook as the forelegs descended and the stag turned to face them, held at bay against a tangle of briars whose scarlet leaves fluttered in the light wind. Fionn slipped through the bushes just as Oisin emerged on the far side of the clearing. Both stopped short, and even the dogs, catching their tension, hesitated. The stag's head lowered a little, his sides working like bellows, the red lining of his nostrils flaring as he breathed.

He was old. Though the great muscles slid smoothly beneath the red-brown hide, that pelt was marred by scars like the bark of some ancient oak whose age only brings more power. But most of all, thought Fionn as the horn-crowned head swung towards him, it was the eyes that revealed that the seasons in which this creature counted its lifetime were centuries.

Once, in his madness, Fionn had wandered the wood in the shape of a stag of seven tines. Even in that shape he wondered if he could have defeated Donn, who bore ten tines on each branching antler. He had never heard of such a thing before. The were-stag's scornful gaze passed over him, and though Fionn had come to stop the hunt, he could not help wondering whether he could conquer this creature even as a man.

"Stand away, I do not need you!" cried Oisin. "He is my prey. I tracked him down and he is mine to kill!"

"If you can . . ." muttered Diarmuid, eyeing the stag doubtfully. Old Donn might be, but his weariness was less of the flesh than of the spirit. *Men have tried me before, and I withstood them,* those eyes seemed to say. *I have lived longer than your bards can remember, but by all means, attack me—perhaps your efforts will amuse me for a little while.*

"It is not your ability I am doubting—" said Fionn, forcing his voice to kindness, "but your wisdom. Some *geasa* are laid upon a man by another, but there are other things which are forbidden by the very nature of the world. If you need to hear the words then I will say them—it is a *geas* upon you, Oisin son of Sabd, not to kill any creature that walks in a shape not its own, but especially not a deer."

"So be it," said Oisin, looking his father in the eye. "But a third binding there is that you have not mentioned, that comes from within a man's soul. And the fate is already on me not to turn aside once I have come face-to-face with my foe. *Geas* or no, I cannot leave this fight now!"

Fionn opened his mouth to reply, then slowly closed it again. The boy was as tall as he was. When had that happened? For a moment he felt as old as the stag.

Shadows moved in the wood beyond them—the does of Donn's harem, returning to see who would win. Donn's head had lifted again, stark against the moving leaves. Fionn flushed a little at the mockery in the beast's dark eye. Oisin should never have started this, but once his feet were on the trail was there indeed any way he could in honor depart from it? He looked back at his son, his expression softening, and Oisin, taking that as agreement, began to move into position to cast his spear.

The wind, strengthening, blew Fionn's hair forward.

As he brushed it back from his face, his thumb touched his lips, and the world changed. Fionn saw the shape of the great stag as a shadow, and within it, dimly shining, another form, with the attenuated, vivid grace of the Otherworld.

"You argue whether or not that child should kill me? Better fear that I will kill him!" The stag snorted.

"You will not kill him—" said Fionn aloud. Oisin flushed, then frowned as he realized his father was not looking at him. The stag's long-lashed eyes seemed to brighten as they fixed on Fionn.

"*You understand me? You are the one I have heard of, then, who has killed so many of my kin! I am surprised that no one has avenged them—it would not be so for me! My folk live free on the isles of the western sea, not skulking beneath your mounds. Be sure that the man who takes my head will feel their wrath.*"

"I did not fear the kin of Aillén the Fireserpent," said Fionn quietly, "nor do I fear yours. But any who touch mine should fear me!"

"*You are afraid for your son!*" bugled the stag joyously. "*Fight me, then! For more years than you have lived I have been prisoned in this shape, pursued by men who thought me a dumb animal! Fight me like a thinking being, Fionn mac Cumhal!*"

"With you I have no quarrel—" Fionn began.

"*Then I will make you one!*" With a sudden spring Donn leaped sideways, towards Oisin.

"Sceolan—" cried Fionn as Oisin set his feet and lifted his spear to throw. The dog flashed between them, leaping for the hindquarters of the stag, the others swarming behind him. Diarmuid and the others circled uncertainly around the edges. The animal pivoted on hind legs to meet this new challenge, and Oisin's lance sped harmlessly past. Now there could be no drawing back. Fionn ran forward, Birga keening in his hands, as Oisin scrambled to pluck his second lance from the ground.

The stag lunged forward, antlers scything the air. A hind hoof caught another dog in the belly and lofted it screaming across the clearing. Oisin swore and threw; the stag's head jerked, there was a sharp crack of horn against wood and the deflected spear rattled into the briars. In another moment, Oisin was rolling after it. Antlers scored the soft earth behind him. Now no one had breath for speech, but from Donn Fionn sensed a delight that grew with the danger, and as he recognized it, Fionn was surprised by his own answering excitement. For both of them, it was boredom, not death, that was the enemy.

Oh my son, thought Fion, *you cannot understand this foe—leave him to me!* And the spear Birga sang out in enthusiastic echo.

Donn swept round again and he leaped back, his own breath coming harder. The stag was so fast! Oisin had retrieved his spear and was coming in on the other side, while Dubhán, Diarmuid, and the others blocked the stag's escape.

Fionn sucked in air and scrambled for footing, thinking it might take both of them to defeat this beast after all. But as Oisin's long body uncoiled behind the spear, a stone rolled beneath his foot. Instead of the vulnerable spot behind the elbow, his blade struck the stag's shoulder and was stopped by bone—a serious injury but by no means fatal, not even disabling while the heat of battle kept Donn from feeling the pain.

The stag bellowed, his head following Oisin's movement as the boy lost his balance and went down. Sceolan sprang for his hindquarters, iron jaws clamping nerve and sinew. For a moment the stag's lunge was checked. Fionn felt Birga leap in his hands, and it was the spear's hunger as much as his own force that struck through hide and flesh into the stag's pulsing heart.

The mighty antlers drove downward, sharp tines sinking into the earth. Oisin lay pinned between them. His eyes widened, then his gaze went inward as he waited for the stag to strike again. The moment lengthened; a rolling shudder swept the stag's body and he reared upward, pulling his antlers free, but slowly—so slowly that Oisin had time to recover from his astonishment and scramble out of range. For a moment Donn poised, straining against the sky with Birga still fixed in his side, then with the ponderous deliberation of an uprooted oak, the great body fell.

Fionn drew a deep breath. The stag was still alive, his flesh racked by shudders as the spirit struggled to win free. There was a pink froth on his muzzle and his flanks heaved. Carefully, Fionn went forward and laid his hand on the shaft of the spear. He felt its ecstatic throbbing as it fed.

"*Not yet—*" in the stag's gasping Fionn heard words. "*You have killed me—you and your demon spear.*"

"I am sorry," Fionn answered, "but I could not let you kill my boy."

"*I would forgive you,*" whispered Donn. "*I have lived too long, and it is no joy to continue in this form. But for me my kinfolk will demand a heavy honor-price—the treasure you hold dearest . . . It is sorry for you that I am, son of Cumhal, to have my kin against you when you have already been marked for destruction by the Morrigan!"*

For a moment Fionn's memory was darkened by black wings. Donait had warned him about the Morrigan's enmity, but all that time was a confusion he tried not to remember.

"When they come for me I will face them. You are my enemy today, and it is time to make an end."

He tightened his grip on the spear shaft, ignoring Birga's protests, and pulled the blade free. Blood poured out behind it, red as the Morrigan's gown. The stag's great body convulsed a final time, then the dark eyes fixed and began to dull as the lifeblood drained into the earth of Eriu.

Fionn plunged the spear into the earth to muffle its triumphant song and stood waiting, looking down at the creature he had killed. Presently, even the blood ceased to flow. A shimmer rippled through the body, as if the light had changed. But it was the form of the stag that was altering, drawing in upon itself until what lay there was a long-limbed man, his fair skin half covered in tangled red-brown hair, with one wound in his shoulder and a deeper gash in his side.

From the forest around them came a cry of grief as if the very trees were mourning. But it was the does—deer shapes that shifted as he watched into white-limbed maidens who tore at their long hair. Then light flared from the still form. Fionn looked back at Donn, blinking at the radiance. For a moment it burned, then faded until all that lay there was a man-shaped dusting of white ash. The fairy women, too, had disappeared, freed by the death of their protector from the spell.

"I am sorry," said Fionn again, looking now at his son. "But I could not let him kill you. . . ."

Oisin let out his breath in a great sigh and stood up, all merriment for once gone from his eyes.

"There will come a day," he said softly, "when you will not be able to stand between me and my doom." For a moment he considered the spot where Donn had lain, then turned, scooping up his spear, and disappeared among the trees.

"Shall we go after him?" asked Diarmuid finally. Fionn shook his head.

"Let him be. He will come back to us when his pride has healed." He knew, only too well, what Oisin must now be feeling. *His nature is too much like mine,* he thought grimly. And that was a hazard from which he could not shield his son at all.

THAT NIGHT THE WEATHER CHANGED. A BITTER WIND came whirling down from the northwest, bearing winter on its wings. The hunters huddled beneath a rude shelter in the cleft of a corrie, listening to the wind crash through the branches above them as if the Powers of the Air were hunting the last of the summer away.

"Time to go into winter quarters," said Caoilte, warming his thin shanks at their little fire.

"You would not feel the cold so if you would put some meat on those bones," observed Faobhar. "It is a crane's form you would wear, I am thinking, if some druid were to lay a shape-spell on you!"

Diarmuid's gaze flickered towards Fionn and back again in warning, but Faobhar only shrugged. He did not trade upon his status as Fionn's half brother for favors, but he was by nature irreverent, and sometimes pushed his humor farther than anyone else would dare.

But it was true, thought Fionn, looking at Caoilte and hiding a smile. The lad was very like a bird, with his long legs and shock of fair hair. Faobhar was something sleeker, perhaps a lynx, while Dubhán darted like a squirrel. And Diarmuid—surely he was the great osprey of the sea cliffs, mantled in black-and-white feathers, with the pride of a king in his eye.

"Tomorrow we move westward," he said as if he had not heard. "I left orders for the *fian* to head home, but we have come so far north we may as well return to Almu by way of Temair." He was cold, too, though he moved no nearer to the fire. It seemed to him that the chill he felt came from inside him. And that was something that could be warmed by no flame.

FIONN AND HIS ESCORT MADE THEIR WAY ACROSS THE plain of Brega in the last dusk of Samhain Eve. It had begun to rain, and darkness was closing in early. Even the dwellings they passed were lightless, their folk huddled within doors, waiting for the rekindling of the fires. To Fionn it seemed as if they were passing through a land of ghosts. Dimly he could sense the paths of the Sidhe beginning to awaken, but it was not yet time for their riding. Perhaps it was himself and his men who were the spirits, he thought as the rainy darkness closed around them, wandering in some nameless land that was neither wholly the Otherworld nor the world of humankind.

Damp was working its way through the tight-woven wool of Fionn's *brat,* and his shoes had soaked through long ago. But he was used to such discomforts; the chill that troubled him was in his heart. He knew that Oisin was safe enough—no *fénnid* had much to fear from the wilderness, even in wintertide, and young bones would suffer far less from the weather than his own. But he missed him. Fionn had not realized how completely his son's bright face had illuminated his life. It was neither the time of day nor the weather that made the world seem so dark. It was because Oisin was not there.

Ah, Sadb, he thought as they trudged onward, *these past years your son has almost consoled me for losing you. But he is becoming a man. Even when he returns it will not be the same. Honor I have from my warriors, and loyalty, but where will I find love?*

A raven called in the distance and Fionn returned to painful awareness of his surroundings, hurrying to catch up with the others. What had he been thinking? He had been alone and happy before he found Sadb, and would be so again. All he really needed to set him right was a good fire and a full drinking horn.

The shifting wind brought them a strong smell of cattle and the mixed reeks of human habitation. The humped shapes of the rude tents and bothies folk had built for the cattle fair appeared in the gloom with the solid bulk of the hill of Temair looming up beyond them. As they passed down the lane a man came out from one of the huts and halted, staring.

"Who's there?" He braced himself, spear at the ready. "Who dares to walk abroad this night? If you are folk of the Sidhe, begone, for the enclosure of the Fair is sacred ground!"

"Mortal we are," replied Diarmuid, "but there is not much we would not dare. Go you up and tell them to prepare us a welcome, for Fionn mac Cumhal has come to feast with the high king."

The man peered at them more closely, then began to grin, "Well, how was I to know, with you coming out of the mist like a pack of bogles? But indeed they will be glad to see you, my lord—it's been long since you were here!"

He turned and hurried up the path. Fionn and the others followed more slowly. As they reached the summit and passed through the wicket gate, they heard a sound like distant thunder. The folk of the king's house were already gathered at the great gateway on the hill's eastern side, leaving the rest of the *dun* empty. Fionn recognized the golden headdress of the queen, waiting with her daughters behind her. The noise grew louder, and light blossomed suddenly between the pillars.

"The fires! The fires!" cried the people. "The Tlachtga fire is kindled! Hail to the high king, who brings light to the world!"

As they watched, the single point became a trail of sparks and a host of chariots came rushing along the road with torch flame streaming out behind them. A pair of white horses were in the lead, froth spraying from their bits as they labored up the last rise. The charioteer bent forward, urging them on, with Cormac balancing easily behind him, holding his torch high. His white silk tunic glowed and his crimson cloak streamed out behind him. In that fitful light his face was all bright planes and shadows, his ash-brown hair threaded not with silver but with living gold. Neither age nor weakness could touch that radiant figure. It was not Cormac mac Airt that he was looking at, thought Fionn, but the *Ard Ri,* who lived anew in each king who reigned in Temair.

Shivering in his sodden cloak, Fionn felt like a beggar at the gates. He could not meet Cormac this way. *I am Rígfénnid of Eriu!* he told himself, but at this moment it was hard to believe it.

Very deliberately, Fionn set his thumb between his teeth and bit down. He staggered as shadow swirled around him. Someone's hand was on his elbow, but he shook it off, staring around him as his sight cleared.

How could he have thought the hill empty? For every living man he saw around him there were a dozen others, for this one night out of all the year returned from the spirit world. When he looked at Cormac he saw hovering at his shoulder Conn of the Hundred Battles, who had been *Ard Ri* when Fionn was a boy, and a dozen more. No wonder the high king seemed more than human as he blazed in the light of the Samhain fires.

The queen moved in her own entourage of shadows, her pale, high-boned face growing goddess-fair as she offered her lord the horn that honored his sovereignty. Upon the Hill of Temair thronged a great crowd of witnesses, drawn by the power of the ritual that king and queen were enacting now. As the royal procession moved from the Mound of the Hostages to the old god's stone, from the millpond to the Stone of Fál, and made their offerings, the dead came forth to greet them. He saw the fair hair and long-boned frames of his own people, and the rounder heads and sturdy bodies of the older tribes, and folk whose race he did not recognize. And mingling with them were others, men that Fionn had feasted and fought with long ago.

When they realized that he could see them they clustered around him. But he could not hear their words. He had not been drawn entirely into the Otherworld then, only to the threshold. *And that,* he thought with dawning wonder, *is what I am—how could I have forgotten? Even here, within the* Ard Ri's *walls, I walk between the worlds.*

"By all the gods, it has grown cold here," said Faobhar. His voice seemed to come from a great ways away.

"We must get into shelter," said Diarmuid. "Go to the woman who rules the queen's household," he told Dubhán. "Tell her that we have come, and will need water to wash in and dry clothes."

"Fionn!" said Caoilte. "Are you all right, my lord? You are looking so strangely. Come now, we must go in—"

Fionn blinked and forced himself to focus on the younger man. The vision was beginning to fade.

"I am well—" he said slowly, and it was true, for he had reclaimed his own sovereignty. Smiling, he let them lead him into the hall.

THE HARPERS OF KING CORMAC SAT IN A ROW BEHIND Ciothruadh their chieftain, blue cloaks like a spot of sky against the partition on the southern side of the royal compartment, their playing a haze of music beneath the uproar in the hall. Note rippled into note as agile fingers plucked bronze strings, damping the long chords and flicking grace notes into the melody like raindrops into a pool. It was a point of honor for the *Ard Ri* to have the best makers of music in his household, even if they could not be heard, just as he claimed the best brewers of ale and mead, whose talents were being appreciated rather more wholeheartedly.

Fionn, who had been listening to the playing with the same unconscious awareness that he gave to the wind in the trees when he was hunting, turned abruptly as he heard his name. The chief of the king's bards had joined the musicians and was declaiming in a thin, pure voice that pierced the din.

> *"The tale of the battle with the*
> *kings of the Ulaidh—*
> *Oh ye who would fain know it—*
> *the reckoning of the valorous heroes,*
> *I myself know it well.*
> *The House of gift-giving Cormac*
> *and the House of warlike Fionn:*
> *they were in that fray,*
> *and the strong Sons of Morna . . ."*

Fionn caught the high king's eye and grinned. Whether or not the royal bards were the finest, they were no fools, and knew well that there was nothing like having a personal interest to make men pay attention to poetry. Already the clamor was lessening as men waited hopefully to hear their own names and deeds.

Fionn's couch had been set in the center of the hall, where the *Ard Ri* and his honored guests lay. Goll was beside him. Around them the royal household and the other guests were grouped in their own sections, each according to his degree and profession. Diarmuid and the other men were in the first rank of the northern quarter, the direction of the warriors. They seemed to be enjoying themselves, clad brightly in fresh tunics of dyed linen from the royal treasury. But Fionn, though he had bathed and let them clean his hunting leathers, had insisted on putting them on once more. Against the embroidered coverlet of his dining couch those weather-stained garments were as incongruous as a wild beast in a woman's bower.

The effect was intentional—in borrowed clothes he would have looked like a poor relation. Instead, his leather trews and jerkin and the tattered earth-colored chequerings of his woolen *brat* stood out against the ornamented silks and linens like the deep chord that supports the harping, the royal panoply of his own brand of sovereignty. Only the golden torque he had taken from his crane bag of treasures, the great brooch at his shoulder and his golden armrings proclaimed that he wore these garments not from poverty, but pride.

"Surely yon was a good fight," said Goll comfortably, setting down the rib upon which he had been gnawing. He was clad only in a saffron kilt and a voluminous mantle of dark red wool, for there had been no tunic in the storerooms large enough to cover him. " 'Tis not soon they will be raising their hands against you."

"Not soon," answered the king, frowning, "and yet I dare not hope that the matter is settled. The men of the North were ever contentious, and the worst of it is that their clans are sib to my own."

Fionn lifted his drinking horn in salute to the high king. "That is why we fight for you. We are beyond blood feud." In the lull, the bard's voice rang out triumphantly.

"King of charioteers was Loeg who drove Cuchulain
of the battles,
and king of horses the Grey of Macha;
high king of Eriu is Cormac son of Airt, resplendent
in glory,
but hard-smiting Fionn is king of the fian."

"And a better judgment I never made than to give you that honor after you killed the fireserpent Aillén," Cormac said softly. "I was young then—I wonder that I had the wit to see it. But I think we have run well in harness together, you and I. . . ."

Fionn nodded. "Better than on the hurley field—" His lips twisted as he remembered how he had resisted Cormac's leadership of the hurley team when they were both boys, not knowing him to be the grandson of the high king. "I was half-mad with grief that day because I had just lost Bodbmall, who raised me, and the only relief I could find was in hitting that ball."

"You did it very well, too," said the *Ard Ri*. "That was what made me so angry. But it won us the game. I try to remember that when some insult makes me angry—more important than my glory is the good of Eriu."

Fionn looked at him with new respect. "You will have glory," he said softly. "I think that in time to come it is the name of Cormac mac Airt that the bards will praise as the pattern and model for a high king."

Cormac flushed like a girl at the praise, but his son Cairbre, beyond him, was scowling. He looked a lot, thought Fionn regretfully, like his father as a boy. It was not so much his appearance—Cairbre would never match his father's height, and his hair like his mother's was a ruddy brown—but that expression of arrogant truculence that was so very much the same. And yet Cairbre was a boy no longer. At his age, Cormac had already become high king and begun to learn wisdom.

He should give the lad more responsibility, a chance to win a name of his own, Fionn thought, watching them. But he did not say so aloud. His own recent performance as a father was not so impressive that he dared to give advice to another man.

There was a little stir at the other end of the hall. Queen Ethne was coming in with her household to pour mead for the last round of formal toasts before the men got down to the serious drinking. Cormac's wife was still a handsome woman, thought Fionn as she came towards them, tall and long-limbed, like a highbred mare. If nose and jaw were a bit too strong for conventional beauty, her eyes were very fine, large and grey and surveying the company with a benign tolerance as she carried her pitcher down the aisle.

As they reached the center, the young woman behind her started to turn right, towards the warriors. She had the same long-limbed grace as Ethne, but her coloring was all golden, and Fionn knew her for Cormac's daughter. The queen said something, and she flushed and began to protest as the girl who had been hidden behind her, small and dark of eye and hair, turned towards the north to serve the warriors, just a hint of smugness in her smile.

For a moment the golden one stood still, her face flaming. Her mother spoke again, sharply, and she moved in the other direction, towards the craftmasters and musicians. From red she had become very pale, but her eyes were blazing. She looked magnificent.

"My daughter Grainne," said Cormac, following the direction of his gaze. His son Cairbre looked from the king to his sister and back again, his eyes as mutinous as hers.

"She has grown into a beauty—" said Fionn, remembering the freckled lass, usually with a skinned knee or elbow, that used to sit upon her father's knee.

The freckles had become a dusting of gold across her cheekbones, and the boyish awkwardness a limber grace.

"That she has, and as headstrong as she is fair, and her suitors not knowing whether to fear the rough side of her tongue more, or the flat of her hand."

"And the other?" asked Fionn.

"Oh, that is Ailbe, that I got by one of my concubines. A clever lass, but not the equal of my Grainne." He broke off as the queen passed the central hearth and mounted the two steps to the dais.

"Drink deep, my lord," said Ethne, as she poured golden mead into the king's drinking horn. "Peace and good seasons to the four fifths of Eriu while you have the rule."

She turned to Fionn. "And to you, all good fortune. May your strong arm be ever shielding us as it has before." She smiled at him and moved to the others, with a word for each as she filled his horn.

The clamor in the hall stilled again as the queen started out, gathering in the king's daughters behind her as she passed, and men looked expectantly towards the dais. It was for the most notable person among them to propose the toast, and Fionn got to his feet.

"Surely it is the flower of Eriu that we see here before us," he said pleasantly, looking around him. "The noblest and most skillful men of every craft. And so I shall propose to you a riddle. Name me the rooftree of every hall, of every herd the bull, the summit of every hill . . ." He paused, grinning, as they began to murmur.

"*Ni ansa*, not hard is that to answer," he said finally. "For is it not the *Ard Ri* who supports every household and guards every beast and watches over the whole lovely land of Eriu?"

But before he had even finished, horns were lifting. "*Ard Ri*!" the men cried, and Fionn shouted with them. "All hail to the *Ard Ri* of Eriu!"

It was only as he sat down again that Fionn saw the smoldering resentment in Cairbre's eyes. For a moment he could not comprehend it. Then it occurred to him that if he had not appeared so unexpectedly for the feasting, the honor of proposing this toast would most likely have gone to the son of the high king. For a moment he considered a word of apology, but it was such a little thing—if this was the worst disappointment that Cairbre ever encountered, he would be a lucky man indeed.

SOME TIME LATER, WHEN THE TORCHES WERE BEGINNING to burn out and half of the warriors were already snoring on the floor, Cormac heaved himself up on one elbow and stared at Fionn.

"Takes me back—" He blinked owlishly and Fionn grinned. "Takes me back a ways t' see you in leathers again. Remember that Samhain Eve when you stood up an' challenged me for your birthright in this very hall?"

"I remember well," answered Fionn, glancing around him. The beams that the Fireserpent Aillén had charred had been replaced long ago. Now, embroidered hangings covered the walls, and the partitions that separated the compartments were faced with thin bronze, worked with scenes of sport and battle by the best smiths in Eriu. Goll had been his enemy then; now he lay snoring by his side. "But it was a long time ago."

"You look no diff'rent—" said Cormac, patting his arm.

"That's what my men say," said Fionn. He was by no means drunk—at least not so drunk as the high king—but the spirals on the houseposts were beginning to uncurl like vines, and the fire was expanding in a golden haze. "They've been saying I should get married again."

Cormac frowned, considering. "Good idea—ev-er'one should be married. Tell you what—you take my girl Grainne. M' favorite, but a handful. Maybe you can bridle her. What d'ye say?"

Grainne . . . For a moment all Fionn could see was a blaze of gold. She was not at all like Sadb, but perhaps that was just as well. And if Oisin did not like it— He thrust that thought away.

"Good-looking girl, good blood," Fionn nodded solemnly. "Good wife for me!" He reached out and clasped the high king's hand.

Chapter 3

THE HEADACHE WITH WHICH FIONN AWAKENED ON Samhain morning was legendary in proportion. Whether it was from the mead he had drunk at the feasting, or the usual aftereffect of opening up his head to vision, pain stabbed his temples with every step he took and every breath he drew. The only consolation was that hardly a man among them, including the high king, was any better off than he, and the only thing that surprised him was that Cormac remembered what he had said in his cups the night before.

In the cold light of day, when the throbbing in his head made all prospects equally painful, Fionn had been inclined to hope he had dreamed that the high king had offered his daughter's hand. But Cormac, for reasons which Fionn did not want to guess at, held to his word.

"But what if she doesn't want me? I've never yet taken a woman unwilling—" Fionn ducked his head into the chill waters of the horse trough and came up gasping.

"I do not think you need fear," said the *Ard Ri,* shaking his own wet head. "I have never yet been able to make that child go against her own will."

"You've already told her?" Fionn's eyes widened, and he closed them quickly against the blaze of the sun.

"I have, and she answered that if you were a fitting son-in-law for me, then surely you must be a fit husband for her. She asks only the time to make ready her bride clothes and gear. Do you go home to Almu now, and return in the moon before Beltane when the druids shall proclaim an auspicious time. We will celebrate the wedding feast then."

Fionn nodded and, shuddering, plunged his head into the horse trough again.

OFTEN, IN THE MOONS THAT FOLLOWED, FIONN FOUND himself recollecting that conversation. He wavered between dread and excitement and exasperation at the teasing he was getting from the *fian.* It was the first time that this had happened to him. No one had dared to make jokes about Sadb; it had not been with her father's blessing that Fionn had taken her, though he had tried. But his marriage to Grainne was something everyone understood. He supposed it was flattering that they should treat him like any other bridegroom.

The weeks passed, and no messenger came to say that Grainne had refused her father's choice for her. In the end, Fionn found himself counting the days simply so that the waiting should be done.

He took more care with his appearance that winter, embarrassed when the men noticed, but pleased when they praised him. Grainne was not the only one who needed time to prepare a wardrobe. Since he had lost Sadb what he wore had not mattered, and even if he had been able to pack for that Samhain feast, he would have been hard put to find clothing worthy of his standing. But Mongfind, who had charge of the women of Almu, was happy to set them to rummaging through the spoils of twenty years of warfare for lengths of rich cloth and embroidery thread of silk and gold.

"You will shine forth in a different garment each day for a moon," she assured him. "And no king of men will be clad so richly. If the princess does not find you magnificent, she must be very hard to please."

Fionn thought about that, and about other things, and as the prospect became more real to him he realized that since Sadb had been stolen from him he had not touched a woman. He lived through a day of terror over it, until the sight of a well-endowed dairymaid driving her cows homeward suggested the obvious answer to his anxieties. A swift dash to head off a beast that was trying to stray brought him to the girl's side. He pulled his hat down to hide his face and walked along beside her, and by the time they reached the byre had bespoken her so sweetly that when he kissed her she did not pull away.

Things progressed rather swiftly after that, though the girl protested for fear someone might come. But he did not mean to take long. Fionn could feel the familiar tension stringing him taut, like the moment before battle, and soon enough he had her down in the straw, her round thighs opening to receive him. The encounter that followed, if not ecstatic, seemed satisfactory on both sides.

"And to whom shall I send if something comes of this?" the girl asked when he was finished, fingering the fine linen of his tunic. "Are you one of the warriors from up in the *dun*?"

"I am that—" Fionn replied, hiding his smile.

"Is it true that the lord of Almu is going to marry the high king's daughter?" she said then.

"That is what they say," he answered guardedly.

"How will she like that, I wonder?" the girl nuzzled closer against him. "I have never seen the *Rígfénnid*, but surely he is an old man—he was already lord of Almu when my mother was a girl."

Fionn stilled, abruptly losing interest despite the fact that the dairymaid was stroking up beneath the tunic, over the strong muscles of his back and down to cup his buttock in her strong hand.

"I do not care how rich he is. I would rather have a man in his prime," she whispered then, "like you—"

Fionn let out a breath he had not known he held. The girl's fingers tightened in his flesh, and suddenly he found that he was ready after all, and once more proceeded to prove to her and to himself that he was indeed still in his prime.

PRINKED AND POLISHED AND BRIGHT AS A SPRING meadow, with bells jingling on every harness and a ribald jest on every tongue, the flower of the *fian* set forth from Almu to bear Fionn mac Cumhal to his bride. Glittering, the procession wound down the hill and struck off across the rolling carpet of the Curragh, the chieftains on horseback for the sake of their honor and the remainder of the escort trotting on foot behind.

A light wind was stroking across the long grasses so that they lay down silver and came up again vivid green, with the first ruddy blush of the seeding sorrel beginning to show between the blades. It was still crisp, but there was a hint of warmth to come, and the plain stretched before them in the sunlight like some great animal stirring from sleep. To Fionn, riding in the lead, it seemed that he had indeed been sleeping all winter, plagued by uneasy dreams. But he was awake now, and when he thought of the bride who awaited him the blood sang so powerfully in his veins it was almost pain.

The road looped around the ridge of the oak trees before turning northward. As they passed it, Oisin pointed, and they saw that the gate to the shrine had opened, and a red-robed figure was coming down the path. Courteously Fionn drew rein to wait for her.

"My Lady Airmedb—" he began, seeing the white hair beneath her veil. Then she looked up at him, and he recognized the strong bones and scornful dark eyes of Achtlan. She had been greying when he first came here. But he remembered that the one called Airmedb had died several winters ago, and Achtlan was first among the priestesses now.

"Achtlan, well met. What word do you have for me to carry to my wedding day?"

"Is it a word you are wanting?" she said tartly. "Why seek me when you can take consultation with your thumb?"

His eyes narrowed. "The wisdom the Salmon gave tells me only what *is,* not what shall be."

"Ah—then what you are asking is a prophecy. . . ."

"Whatever wisdom you are willing to share, oh *bean drui,*" he answered, "I will hear gladly, or whatever word the goddess gives you to say—" He had no choice but to bear the woman's teasing, remembering how Brigid herself had saved him when he battled the host of the Sidhe.

"So you remember what you owe to Her," said the priestess dryly, and Fionn felt himself go red.

"Brigid has no need to be jealous of this bridal," he answered more abruptly than he had intended. "I will not forget my duty."

"Nor has She forgotten it," Achtlan said soberly.

Fionn frowned. "Are the omens good? Will Grainne be happy with me?"

"There was never yet a pair, however well mated, to whom that promise could be made. How you fare with the maiden will depend on your own actions, son of Cumhal. Rule yourself, and you need not fear what fate is foretold for you. This much I can tell you—I have seen the two of you living in content when your hair is silver and there are lines of experience on Grainne's fair brow . . ."

"Well, Fionn—that is an excellent prophecy!" Diarmuid clapped him on the back and laughed. "I would be well content if she could foresee as much for me!"

Achtlan turned her dark gaze upon him, and something in her face made Fionn shiver. "For you," she said softly, "I see not content, but love—the great love that devours like a living flame. The bards will sing of your love when your dust has been scattered on the wind. . . ."

"That is more than I ever asked for," said Diarmuid. "I am a warrior, and I would rather be famed for a hero's death than a woman's love. See another fate for me!"

"You cannot evade your doom," said Achtlan scornfully. "But do not complain—the fate you do not wish may still lead to the one you desire!"

"What do you mean?" he began, but she was shaking her head.

"Do not seek to learn more from me."

"Does Brigid bless us?" Fionn asked, as she turned away.

"Do what is right, son of Cumhal, and do not let yourself be led by what men say. Then you will do well. Brigid blesses all who serve Her, in Her own time, in Her own way . . ."

FIONN PULLED AT THE HEM OF THE EMERALD TUNIC, the gold brocade that trimmed it stiff beneath his fingers. Diarmuid and the others had assured him it looked well, but there had been a sardonic gleam in Goll's eye that he distrusted. The material was silk from the Roman lands, heavy and rich, its green on green in striking contrast to the twining tendrils of gold on the strips that had been sewn to it at shoulders and wrists and hem. But it seemed to him that it was tight across the shoulders, or perhaps it was the intensity of the color that seemed to bind him so.

Grainne will think I am got up like the Beltane tree, he frowned unhappily. *All that is lacking is the crown of flowers!*

They had told him she was waiting in the garden behind the *grianan*, the south-facing hall where the women worked on fair days. He pushed aside the cowhide that covered the doorway and blinked, aware of the tall shapes of looms leaning against the houseposts, of bags and bales and benches, and women, many women, whose chatter hushed as they realized who had come in.

But they were only shadows. There were two doors to the house of women, and the other was open to the bright day. A woman stood framed by that doorway with all the radiance of the spring day blazing from her hair, and in that moment she was the only thing that seemed real.

Grainne . . . He could not have said whether she was beautiful. She was light, she was life, all the vitality of the spring day incarnate in woman form.

Fionn had thought about how being married would change his way of living, worried about his ability to satisfy a wife, agonized over his appearance. He had not really thought much about the woman herself. Not until now.

She turned. Somewhere behind him, a woman laughed. Fionn cleared his throat and made his legs carry him forward.

"The blessing of Brigid to you, maiden," he saluted her.

"The blessing of Lugh of the Long Arm be on you, hero—" Grainne inclined her head with conscious grace. *I am a king's daughter,* that gesture seemed to say, *and I know my worth.*

Fionn lifted one eyebrow, but after all, if the girl thought well of herself, she had good reason. That was why he was marrying her.

"Indeed he has blessed me," he replied. "Do I not stand by the side of the fairest of Eriu's daughters? Grainne, daughter of Cormac, your beauty brightens the day." She had her height from her father. He thought about how it would feel to have the whole lovely length of her stretched out against him and felt his pulse quicken.

"Surely the glory of the *Rígfénnid* outshines mine. Your presence, Fionn mac Cumhal, honors our hall."

His lips twitched. She was returning his compliments like a hurley ball. The pertness he remembered from her childhood had become a woman's wit. Of course, she had been very well taught.

"Are the deeds that a man achieves with such striving of more worth than the beauty that is a woman's very essence? He must do and dare continually. She has only to *be*. . . ."

A warm color rose in Grainne's cheeks. Indeed, she *was* lovely! Why had he not realized it until now?

"Then you think a woman is not capable of heroic deeds?" she asked sweetly.

"I did not say so—"

"Did you not? Well then, if my role in our alliance is to be beautiful, what deeds will you do to be worthy of me?" She tipped her head to one side, smiling ingenuously. Fionn's eyes narrowed.

"I was no older than you when I killed the lord of the Sidhe who burned your father's hall."

"I know." She looked him up and down as if she were pricing his gold trim. "And you have protected Eriu all the years of my life. But what will you do for *me*?"

"Try me, and you will learn—" He forced a smile.

"And perhaps you will learn something about me. . . ."

I am sure of it . . . reflected Fionn ruefully. This bargain he had made with Cormac looked as if it would be more interesting than he had expected. Especially, he thought as he allowed his gaze to dwell on the rich curve of Grainne's breast beneath her linen gown, in bed.

"Tomorrow evening—" he said, reaching out to her. She slid away from beneath his hand, and suddenly he remembered how Donait had teased him. That winter it had seemed no burden to wait for his bride, but now, with the warmth of the woman so close to him, tomorrow night seemed very far away. Abruptly he pulled back. "Grainne . . . my bride. . . ." His voice had grown harsher. "I will count the hours."

As Fionn strode away from the *grianan* he heard women whispering, but he did not turn.

ON THE LONG GREEN BELOW THE RAMPART THE younger men were playing. A target had been set up for the spear toss, and the warriors of the *fian* had challenged the king's houseguard. At the moment, Diarmuid was taking the honors, his lithe body uncoiling in a graceful curve as he cast. Wagering was already heavy, but Fionn felt it more tactful to abstain. He sat beside Cormac, discussing the merits of the contestants with what he hoped was cool detachment, though he tensed at every throw.

Except for the girls who poured out the ale, the women had stayed up in the *dun*. But he was sure they were watching—he could feel their eyes on him, and now and again a trill of laughter floated down on the breeze.

"You should offer the ale to our guest first, Ailbe," said the king.

Fionn looked up, and saw the dark-haired girl turning towards him, smiling. She was small-boned but full-breasted like the women of the south. Standing, she would barely reach his shoulder. Sadb and Cruithne had been small, too. . . . But Grainne faced him nearly eye to eye.

Grainne is different from my other women—but then I am different, too. This would be his first formal marriage, despite Oisin, and mac Lugach, the sturdy grandson that his daughter by Cruithne had sent to be brought up at Almu.

"Willingly—" Ailbe's voice was low. "This hero has no need to strive further. A pity it is that he has already won his prize—"

"And what prize is it that you would rather I should be seeking?" asked Fionn, grinning up at her. Beneath her lashes her dark eyes were glittering.

"Fionn mac Cumhal is the master of wisdom. If he does not know the answer, it is not for me to be telling him!"

"Then I fear it must remain a mystery. The Salmon of the Boann knew all the secrets of the waters and the land through which they flow, but even he had no craft to untangle the secrets of a maiden's heart," said Fionn.

But in truth, he could interpret the color in Ailbe's cheeks and the flicker of her glance well enough. The girl wanted him, and though he knew better than to meddle with his betrothed's sister, he took her interest as a good omen.

FOR THE WEDDING FEAST, THEY HAD RIGGED FIONN OUT in a tunic of saffron silk heavily embroidered around the neck and hem, and a cloak of fine purple wool with fringes of gold. He had reached deeply into the crane bag for adornment—around his neck lay a heavy twisted torque of the pale gold of Eriu, carved deeply with spirals. He wore bracelets and armrings, and plaques on his belt, inset with red enamel and jewels. Once his hair had outshone them, but time had faded it to ashy fair.

It was Grainne who shone sun-gold, her hair a greater glory than the metal-wound thread worked into the curves and trefoils adorning her white gown. Her mantle was the deep blue of a summer sky, edged with golden brocade from the Roman lands and held at the breast by a heavy brooch set with amethyst and pearl, but on her head was a crown of flowers.

"My girl is fair tonight," said Cormac, seeing how Fionn's gaze kept sliding past him and Queen Ethne to Grainne, who sat next to her mother on the high king's left hand.

"She is as beautiful as Etain wife of Midir, by whom the beauty of women is measured . . ." said Fionn.

Her brother Cairbre, sitting in the midst of his own court in the compartment nearest Grainne, grinned sourly. It was clear that he did not like this marriage, but then he had resented Fionn and the *fianna* from the time he was a child.

His brother Ceallach, Cormac's older son, was far different, a boisterous man prone to sudden passions. It was as if Cormac's qualities had been divided between them: to Ceallach all the king's vigor and enthusiasm, and to Cairbre his intelligence and capacity for patient calculation. Both qualities were required in a high king. Fionn wondered if the two would be able to work together when the time came, or whether Cairbre would always resent his brother, as he resented so many other things.

As if he had sensed Fionn's thoughts, Cairbre met his gaze. For a moment he held it, and then, very deliberately, sneered and looked away. For a moment Fionn stared at him, then he laughed and held out his horn to be refilled. It was only a cub, after all, and for all its craft, would never equal Fionn's subtlety.

While Grainne had been preparing her bride clothes, her father's people had been preparing for the wedding. Whenever Fionn looked up, it seemed, someone was offering him another platter of food, and mead flowed like the waters of the Boann. Turn and about, the druids of the high king and those of the *fianna* had entertained them. It was the turn of the *fian* now, and Daire Duanach, perhaps the only man of Clan Morna who had ever completed a bard's training, stood up to sing, a stocky, round-bodied man with the ruddy hair of his kin.

He chanted first of the quest of Art, Cormac's father, for Delbchaem daughter of Morgan in the Otherworld. But as often happened in such matings, their union was not fertile. It was the smith's daughter Achtan on whom Cormac had been begotten, that last night before Art, forewarned by omens, went out to meet his death at the Battle of Moy Muchruinne.

"Lamenting," sang Daire, "lamenting loudly, Delbchaem to the Land of Promise did return. But Achtan bore Cormac to inherit his father's glory, and to father in his turn the brightest of maidens, Grainne the fair. . . ."

He bowed to the girl, who blushed and smiled. *Good,* thought Fionn. *She likes him. I will assign him to entertain her when we return to Almu. . . .*

Most of the feasters had finished their meat, and were filling in the last empty corners with cakes made with dried fruit or honey. He heard a burst of laughter and glanced over at the compartment nearest to him, where Oisin sat with Diarmuid on his left hand and Goll on his right. Their faces were flushed with mead, even Oisin, who had been uncharacteristically moody ever since he had returned from the wilds last fall. Joyous and strong, they balanced Cairbre and his frowning companions in more ways than their placement in the hall. Truly he was blessed to have such men as his companions! Fionn lifted his horn in salute, and Oisin grinned back at him.

As Daire moved past to rejoin them, Fionn reached out to him. "Do you go back to the maiden," he said softly. "She liked your singing. Sit at her feet and tell her tales of the *fian*. . . ."

"With pleasure," said Daire. "She is a lovely lady. I will be glad when she comes to your hall!"

"Then go to her. She is leaving one family—tell her of the heroes who will welcome her." He leaned forward, peering past Cormac and his queen and cursing the etiquette that kept him and his bride from coming together until the wedding feast should be done.

"Grainne—" he called, "since I may not sit by you, I send my bard to be your entertainment. Ask him what you please. . . ."

"Oh, I will, I will," she said softly, raising her eyes to meet his for the first time that evening.

Her gaze was clear, but he could not read it. Grainne was altogether a more noble creature than her brother, but it occurred to Fionn that perhaps they did share that ability to plan while giving nothing away. What was she thinking? For a moment he considered biting his thumb to find out, then dismissed the thought as unworthy.

He could not refuse the mead that the servants of King Cormac were continually pouring. No man without a hard head for liquor could hold leadership in the *fianna*, and many a time Fionn had drunk them all senseless and walked out still under his own power to greet the dawn, but as the evening drew on, he found the gentle buzzing in his ears growing louder. King Cormac was laughing more than usual, and his queen smiled vaguely on the company. But from the other end of the table he could still hear Grainne's voice, measured and slow.

"That is Fionn's son at the center of the table nearest him, not so? He is a fair lad, and I have heard much of his skills. But it will be strange to be wed to a man who has a grown son."

"Soon enough you will have sons of your own," said Daire, "and watch them growing. Short will the time seem then."

"Perhaps . . ." She did not sound as if she believed it. "Tell me, who is the long lad who sits by Oisin's side?"

"Ah—that is his friend Caoilte, and truly, they are rarely parted. A great one for tricks and games is our Caoilte, but a good lad for all that, and the swiftest runner in the *fian*."

"I shall take care he does not chase me. . . ." said Grainne. "And the big man next to him with the grizzled hair, is that Goll? I thought he would be older. . . ."

"Who else? But the men of the *fian* are immortal. Goll is wed now to a woman near to you in years, a niece of Fionn's, and has a young son."

The high king said something then and Fionn lost the next words, but he could still hear their voices as a murmur beneath the rising clamor around him. Cormac laid one arm across his shoulders.

"You will be good to my girl?" Cormac blinked, trying to focus as he stared into Fionn's eyes. "—can be a handful, my Grainne. You tame her, but gently, eh? Thing is, she's always had her own will."

"I've never yet met the mare I could not ride," said Fionn, patting his arm. "Nor has any woman been the worse for me. I will know how to rule my own."

From Oisin's side of the hall came a burst of laughter. He and Diarmuid were arm wrestling, dark head and fair bent together, eyes clashing in a battle of wills as fierce as the one their muscles waged.

"And who is that freckled sweet-worded man, with the curling dusky-black hair and the two red ruddy cheeks, striving now with Oisin the son of Fionn?" asked Grainne.

"That man is Diarmuid the son of Duibhne, with the white smile and the bright countenance; folk call him the foster son of Aonghus Og, and 'tis sure that the women run after him. They say he is the best lover of maidens that is in the whole world," Daire replied.

Slowly, so slowly, Diarmuid forced the boy's arm down, holding his gaze like a lover, until at last Oisin laughed and gave way. Fionn stifled a pang of disappointment. Oisin had not come to his full strength yet; the wonder was that he had held Diarmuid so long.

"Pay up, lad," cried Caoilte. "You are fairly beaten!"

Grinning, Oisin handed Diarmuid his silver-mounted drinking horn, and Diarmuid tipped it upward. The muscles worked in his white throat as he swallowed, again and again, until the contents of the horn were gone.

"Indeed, that is a goodly company," said Grainne softly. "But our hospitality is remiss if our guests are forced to do battle for a drink of mead. Father"—she turned to the high king—"is it not time to bring out the great Cup of Manannan?"

"You go, daughter . . . fetch it. We'll drink deep . . ." Cormac hiccoughed, "to your bridal . . ."

Daire the bard got to his feet as Grainne disappeared and turned to the company. "I have sung the deeds of your fathers, oh King. Let me now sing of the golden Cup of Manannan mac Lir, of which so many stories have been told!"

"But they are not true," muttered the high king anxiously, and Fionn grinned at him.

"Have I not had to endure the same exaggerations, all these years? Let the bard sing, Cormac. There was never a man of Eriu that given a choice between the truth and a good story would not rather hear the tale!"

"On a morning near Beltane Cormac son of Art son of Conn the Hundred-Fighter sat alone on Tea's mound. And he saw coming towards him a grey-haired warrior, finely dressed in a purple cloak with fringes and a tunic all worked in gold. But the wonder was this, that he carried a branch of silver with three golden apples across his shoulder, and when he shook the branch, anyone who heard it, even a man sore wounded or a woman in childbed, would be cast into sleep by its melody.

" 'Whence have you come, O warrior?' asked the high king.

" 'From a land where there is nought save truth,' said the old man, 'and there is neither age nor decay nor gloom nor sadness nor envy nor jealousy nor hatred nor haughtiness.'

"Now Cormac was struck with admiration and amazement by this wonder, and it seemed to him good that they two should strike up an alliance."

"And well it might," whispered Fionn in Cormac's ear. "But what work would there be in such a land for a high king?"

"The old man agreed," the bard continued, "and gave him the silver branch on condition that three boons should be granted him in return. And the boons he asked were first the high king's son, and then his daughter, and then his radiant queen. And the first two times the king shook the branch so that the people should not cry out against him, but when the queen was taken, he went after her to the Otherworld. . . ."

"But this is not what happened," Cormac bent close to his ear, sobering now. "The man was a chieftain of the old race, and we were already guesting in his hall. And there was no branch—I don't know from what tale that got in—only the golden cup."

By this time the bard had told them of the wonders Cormac saw in the Otherworld. "And then the old man gave him a great cup of gold," said Daire. "And it was Manannan mac Lir himself that had taken that form to test and reward him. But the virtue of the cup was that it would shatter if falsehoods were spoken beneath it, but the saying of three truths should heal it all together. And here is the cup itself, and the radiant daughter of Cormac bringing it, to prove the truth of my tale."

True it was that the vessel Grainne was bearing between her two hands was a wonder, a broad bowl on a pedestal of the kind that the Greeks called a *krater*, with two curved handles to hold it by. The sides of the bowl were ornamented with scenes of a sea-god, beaten out from behind in half-relief so they seemed ready to spring forth from the gold.

"Behold the Cup of Manannan," said Grainne in a clear voice, "that will endure no lie."

"And is that so?" asked Fionn.

"I do not know," Cormac answered him. "That was the tradition among the folk that gave it to me. Perhaps all my people have been too overawed by the story to dare a falsehood. I can say only that the cup has remained whole."

"I have found that most men believe in the truth of their words, at least while they are saying them," said Fionn, and the high king laughed.

Grainne was coming towards them. She halted before Fionn. Above the broad rim of the *krater* his eyes met hers, clear and a little defiant.

"Hero, what truth will you give in exchange for the drink I offer you?"

Fionn's thumb tingled, but in that moment it seemed to him that to make use of that advantage when other men must make do with their own wits would be a shameful thing.

He cleared his throat. "Daughter of Cormac, it is proud I will be to call you wife."

For a moment longer she looked at him. Then she sighed, and offered the *krater* so that he could drink from it. The liquor was cider sweetened with honey, heavily spiced and heated over the fire. It burned his throat as it went down and burned in his belly when it got there. He licked his lips, trying to identify the herbs, but the sweetness disguised them. Bodbmall would have known. He sat back, his head spinning, as Grainne offered the *krater* to her father.

"My pride is to be giving you to such a hero," said Cormac, and took a deep draught. This must be a drink they had often at Temair, thought Fionn, for the king seemed to taste nothing strange. Nor did Ethne his queen. Grainne, her face without expression, carried the *krater* to her brother and his friends, but Fionn could not hear their words.

Grainne crossed to offer the drink to Fionn's men, but when she had served Goll, she turned away. "You have drunk it all," she said with a strange smile as she passed. "I must refill the bowl."

Fionn tried to think of some suitable compliment, but his tongue felt leaden. *I am losing my head for liquor,* he thought ruefully. But half the wedding guests had drunk themselves into oblivion already, and Cormac was nodding. When Grainne returned he would ask permission to take her to bed. Surely by now he had satisfied the demands of both honor and courtesy.

From his right he heard a snore. Fionn blinked, and realized that he must have dozed. The queen was fast asleep, her mouth a little open, and Cormac had slumped forward, his head cradled in his arms. Grainne was taking a long time to fetch the drink. He tried to look for her, but only his eyes would move, and it was too great an effort to keep them open. He could still hear, though, and hearing trained to detect the movement of a deer through the forest recognized the rustle as silken skirts brushed the straw.

He could not see Grainne, but he could feel her, like a fragrance in the night. He struggled once more to open his eyes, but the drink was hammering in his head. *She has drugged us,* he thought muzzily. *But why, why?*

"Diarmuid son of Duibhne," her words came clearly. "I bring you the drink of heroes. What truth will you give to me?"

There was a short silence, then he heard Diarmuid, his voice low and shaken. "You are the sun at midnight, you are a swan that swims through dark waters, a goddess looks out at me from your bright eyes."

Grainne laughed softly. "Drink, my hero, and I will give another truth back to you—"

Fionn strove to get his eyes open; through slitted lids he could see Grainne's blurred shape. She turned, and he realized that she had unpinned the brooches that held her gown so that half her white breast was bare. Dazed as he was, he understood from that glimpse that Diarmuid had spoken truth. Grainne blazed with the beauty of a young warrior before battle, or a swift horse ready for the race to begin, every particle of her being focused on the man before her.

"I marvel that Fionn mac Cumhal should seek such a wife as I," she said fiercely. "Were it not more fit that I wed with a man of my own years? Fionn is my father's age!"

The words struck through Fionn's heart like a sword.

"Is that the truth you would give us?" asked Oisin. "If Fionn could hear you, he would not take you now, nor would I!"

But I can *hear!* thought Fionn, shaken between wrath and wonder. What was the woman about, to be saying such things?

"Have I asked you?" she said scornfully, and once more she laughed. "This is my truth, Diarmuid. In the old days every woman was held as holy, and she gave herself in her own time and season. In me you have seen the Goddess, and in Her name I put you under a *geas* of danger and of destruction and mighty magic if you take me not with you out of this household ere Fionn and the high king arise from their sleep."

"Woman, it is an evil thing!" exclaimed Diarmuid, "that with all the sons of kings and princes who are gathered tonight in this mirthful hall you should lay this bond upon the one least worthy of a woman's love!"

"Do you think so?" she answered him. "For many and many a day, though I seemed to mark you not, my eye has been upon you. Do you remember that day when you went to the aid of the son of Lugaid in the hurley game he played against my brother? Three goals you won, and I turned the light of my eyes and of my sight upon you. I never gave that love to any other man from that time to this, and will not forever."

"There is not a man in Eriu fonder of a woman than Fionn, and you agreed to wed with him. And in any case, it is he himself who carries the watchword that wards the gate when he bides in Temair."

"I thought that I could endure it—" she laughed shakily. "But I have drunk truth from this cup as well as you. I cannot marry Fionn. As for the gateway, there is a wicket gate by the House of Women through which we may pass."

"It is against my honor to depart in such a way." There was relief in Diarmuid's tone.

"Then do you perform the hero-feat that I have heard you are most noted for, and use the shaft of your spear to help you spring over the wall. I myself will go out by the wicket gate, and by the *geas* I have spoken I bid you follow me."

Rushes rustled. Fionn's breath caught as he heard her approaching him and pause. *I will open my eyes now,* he thought, *and she will see that I have heard, and then she will tell me that this was only a test to prove the loyalty of my men. . . .* But the drink held him as fast as any druid magic. He could not move.

Grainne . . . Grainne . . . his heart cried. Need for her wrenched suddenly through him. The truth that Diarmuid had spoken was his own as well—how could he not have seen it? And why had he not spoken it when she questioned him?

"Old man, I am sorry," she said softly, and Fionn felt his manhood wither at the words. "But when you come to hear of this I will not ask forgiveness. I am a royal woman, and I thought I could serve my father's will by wedding you. Diarmuid lights a fire in my blood, while when I was with you my heart lay in my breast like a stone. I would have brought you nothing but sorrow—forget me, Fionn mac Cumhal. . . ."

And then she was gone. *You are wrong, Grainne, wrong*—Fionn's soul cried. *This wound you have given me will bleed until you rage as I am raging, and grieve as I grieve!* He sank back into himself, fighting the drug that prisoned him. Sometime later he realized that Diarmuid was talking.

"What shall I do? The woman has bound me!" His tone was anguished.

"That is a hard question," Caoilte put in, "but though I have a fair wife of my own, I tell you that if such a woman as Grainne set her mark upon me, I would leave everything to follow her!"

"But Fionn—Fionn—how can anything go well for me if I betray him?"

"How can you prosper if you fail to keep your *geasa*?" was the reply.

"You are not guilty of the *geas* that is laid upon you," said Oisin quietly. "It is my opinion that you must follow Grainne."

Fionn thought that he had no more room for rage, but a sick anger that he had never known before rose up in him that his own son could counsel this treachery.

"But ward yourself well against the wiles of Fionn,"

Oisin continued, "for he will have no choice but to come after you. . . ."

"That is so," Caoilte sighed. "He will be shamed before the men of Eriu if he does not pursue you with all the might that is in him. Still, I would rather have his anger against me than hers!"

"Is that the counsel of you all to me?" said Diarmuid.

"It is—"

Do they all turn against me? Fionn's soul shuddered. *Be it so then, for they have spoken themselves the* geas *that must bind me now!*

"Then I must go, though my death were in it—" Fionn heard the tears in Diarmuid's voice, but they could not move him.

Oh Grainne, you have doomed yourself, and the one you love! If I am old, I am grown old in craft! You have turned my love to hatred, and my protection to a pursuit that will destroy us all!

And then, finally, he ceased to fight the herbs that held him, and fell down endlessly into the dark.

Chapter 4

GRAINNE BENT OVER HIM, HER LONG FINGERS SMOOTHing his hair, a smile like a summer's day lighting her eyes.

"Is it unhappy I have made you? Indeed, I am sorry, but I could not wed with a man who came to me as if he were buying a heifer at the Samhain Fair! Do you know now that you love me?"

"You are the sun in the heavens," Fionn said hoarsely, his body already stiffening with desire. "You are all the warmth at the heart of the world!" He reached up to draw her into his embrace.

But his fingers closed on air. She was all light, and as lacking in substance, her arms and breast breaking up into rainbows as Fionn clutched at them. But he had felt her touch, breathed in the warm scent of her! He cried out her name.

Groaning, Fionn opened his eyes. Around him, the first faint light of morning showed him piled gear and the humped forms of sleeping men. In his dream all had been brightness, but overnight a mist had come up off the river, and it still lay heavy on the ground. No one seemed to have heard him, and he lay back with a sigh. But his heart was still pounding, and the aching stiffness of his manhood was just beginning to ease. He felt the easy tears spring beneath his eyelids and turned his face against the rough weave of his cloak to hide them. She had been so real!

But then she always was, in these dreams in which she came to him, explaining her treachery each time in a different way. The moon had been new when the pursuit began, and now it was waning, and on most of those nights he had dreamed of Grainne. Were the dreams born of his own hurt pride, or a sending to tell him that she loved him after all? It seemed ironic that the one woman whose hand he had sought in all honor had run from him. Would she have rather he tried to steal her away? How could he have known the way to woo her, he wondered then. His other women had always courted *him*.

As Grainne had courted Diarmuid. . . . For a moment Fionn hovered on the edge of understanding. Then Sceolan shoved his cold nose against Fionn's shoulder, whining, and the moment was gone. He looked up and saw Caoilte, who had been assigned to rise before the dawn and range out ahead of them, coming lightly across the grass.

"They lay last night across the river," said Caoilte. "And ate breakfast. But perhaps Diarmuid sensed me coming, for they seem to have left suddenly. There was a piece of uncooked salmon lying beside the fire."

Fionn grunted. Caoilte moved like a leaf on the breeze, and it was unlikely that even Diarmuid could hear him. Unless he were being intentionally clumsy. That was possible, for it was clear that though the men of the *fianna* understood their duty, there was little enthusiasm in this hunting. But he did not think that Diarmuid had fled because of Caoilte. They had found such tokens before where he and Grainne had been camping —flesh uncooked upon a spit, a bannock left unbroken.

Diarmuid is telling me that he has not lain with her—Fionn frowned. At night he dreamed of Grainne, but by day it was Diarmuid, his beloved, his fosterling, the pride of the *fian*, who was his obsession. It had amazed them all that one man, burdened by a woman who though young and healthy was no warrior, could have eluded them so long. They had always known that Diarmuid was good, but the true magnitude of his expertise had never been so apparent as now, when he was pitted against the men who had trained him.

Diarmuid was using all his skill to get Grainne away, so why hadn't he slept with her? Close as the pursuit had been, surely there must have been time for a quick tumble. In the depths of his soul was the boy somehow hoping that they could all still be reconciled?

For a moment Fionn considered it. Surely there could not have been such a mix of love and hatred in a conflict since his father had faced Goll on Cnucha field. The *fénnidi* did not want to kill Diarmuid, who clearly did not want to betray Fionn. Fionn himself did not know what he wanted. Of them all, perhaps only Grainne was sure, and even she might have doubts, if he could believe his dreams.

Ah Brigid, what can I do to free us all from this coil? He drew breath suddenly—for a moment he seemed to hear a shimmer of silver bells. Then there were only the noises of the camp around him. But his heart had been eased. *If I can catch them, I will offer peace,* he told himself. *If we talk, perhaps we can find a way.*

"There is a wood beyond the river. Doire da Both they call it, and Diarmuid knows it well. It is there that he and the woman will be resting. Swiftly, wake the men and let us surround them. It is time this chase were done!"

Caoilte went off to wake Oisin, with Sceolan trotting after him. The dog was as devoted to the boy as he was to Fionn; sometimes it seemed to Fionn that he loved Oisin more. Grimacing, for his muscles had grown stiff lying on the cold ground, he got to his feet and began to straighten his clothes. From the corner of his eye he saw Oisin bending to pet the hound, his copper-gold hair bright against the dog's fur, the two heads close together as if he were murmuring in Sceolan's ear. Then he straightened, and the hound leaped away into the mist.

At the time he thought nothing of it. It was only later, when Oisin's men were unaccountably noisy even after Fionn had asked for secrecy and silence, that it occurred to him that perhaps it was to warn Diarmuid that the boy had sent Sceolan away. But if Diarmuid had received a warning, he had not heeded it, for the scouts found tracks leading into Doire da Both, but none coming away.

"Someone surely is in there," the trackers told Fionn, "for we saw a man's track that looked like Diarmuid's. But we can say nothing of the woman with him, for we do not know the track of Grainne."

"It is Diarmuid, and he shall not leave that place until he gives me satisfaction!" He signaled to the men to move forward and began to push his way through the trees. The mist lay heavy here, coiling among the branches. Fionn shivered, remembering the Otherworld.

"Are you still so jealous?" Oisin followed him. "Why should he stay here, knowing you are after him?"

"Especially since you have warned him—" Fionn said sourly. "Did you think I would not see? There is no escape from a debt of honor, and Diarmuid knows it."

"But he is not a fool," protested Caoilte. "And he also knows you hate him."

Fionn looked at him. *I do not hate him, but I cannot allow him to defy me or I will have no honor, and what use then will I be to Eriu?*

"He is there—" he said, pointing to the interweaving of boughs ahead of them. At his movement, a raven flapped heavily upward and settled upon a higher bough, watching. "Or who is it that has fortified those hazels in the manner of the *fian*? With which of us is the truth, oh Diarmuid?" he lifted his voice. "With myself or Oisin?"

"There was only once that you ever erred in judgment," came Diarmuid's voice from behind the hazels. "And indeed I and Grainne are here."

He sounded as if he was tired of running, thought Fionn with a pang, with the fatigue of the soul that is worse than the body's pain. *Well,* he reflected, *so am I!* The new leaves fluttered and first Diarmuid's dark head, then Grainne's, appeared. Her golden locks were lank and tangled and full of leaves, but she was still beautiful. Fionn's men began to move in closer, poising their spears.

"Surrender—" said Fionn. "You cannot escape me.

It is time to be talking of compensation now. . . ."

He stared at Diarmuid, pleading with his eyes—*Give in, lad! For your own sake and mine, give in!* But Diarmuid was looking at the men who surrounded him, his weary gaze turning to scorn. Then, very deliberately, he took Grainne's face between his two hands and kissed her on the lips.

At the first kiss, anguish stabbed through Fionn like a sword. At the second kiss the raven called from the treetop, and Fionn's anguish became a red rage.

"Diarmuid mac Duibhne, you will pay for those kisses with your head!"

When Diarmuid kissed Grainne for the third time, Fionn plunged towards the hazels, and the spear Birga howled in his hand.

Mist swirled dizzyingly between him and the trees. Fionn stumbled, trying to see. All around him he could hear men crashing into branches and swearing. Then came the clash of weapons; Diarmuid was trying to break through. He heard an anguished cry.

Fionn struggled forward, touched woven branches, and pulled. For a moment he thought he saw Grainne's bright hair. Then came a gust of cold wind that bore the apple blossom scent of the Otherworld. When it passed, the mist closed in again. Fionn slashed at the hazels with Birga and they sprang to either side. On the grass within the enclosure he could see the print of a woman's feet, but Grainne was gone.

THROUGH THE REST OF THAT SUMMER THE PURSUIT OF Diarmuid and Grainne went on. For a time it appeared that the two had separated. Some said that Grainne had been carried to safety by Aonghus Og. When they found their tracks together once more, there were no more tokens of uncooked game. Nor did Grainne come to Fionn in his dreams. But sometimes he would wake to find he had been weeping, and did not know if it were from grief at losing Diarmuid, or Grainne.

King Cormac had given up on his willful daughter, and offered Fionn the girl Ailbe as compensation, but Fionn could not give it over, even when Eriu was raided by men from Lochlan. Fionn was in Connachta then, following a report that the fugitives had been seen there. It was Diarmuid himself who ended up fighting the foreigners. After that, Fionn had to contend with the resentment of the *fian*, shamed that Diarmuid had been doing their work for them.

As Samhain drew near it became obvious that the men were wearying of what they considered a pointless exercise. Had Diarmuid really become so remarkable a warrior, Fionn wondered, or was it his former companions who held back from using all their skills to bring him in?

If I could face him man to man, then we would learn the truth, thought Fionn. But he could sense in Oisin and the others a determination to prevent any such confrontation. Perhaps they had reason. As the nights grew colder, his bones ached more with every morn. He had not been old when he rode to his wedding at Beltane. But he felt ancient now.

And so, as the autumn wind began to pluck the yellowing leaves from the trees, Fionn called in his trackers and ordered the *fianna* home.

THEY WERE CAMPED ON THE BANKS OF THE LIFFE, A little above the ford of the Black Pool, when Fionn heard a shout from the perimeter. Soon he saw Rionnolbh and red Daolghus coming towards him, holding by the arms a small person swathed in shawls.

"She was trying to get through our lines, lord," said Rionnolbh. "But she won't say her name, or why—"

Fionn's heart leaped, but this woman was too short to be Grainne. Scowling, he gestured to the men to let her go. Her breath caught and he wondered if she were going to cry. Then she drew herself up and pushed back her shawl.

For a moment he did not recognize her. Then a quirk of her eyebrow jogged his memory. "Ailbe," he said harshly. "What are you doing here?"

"Fulfilling my father's word to you!"

Fionn stared.

"He promised you a woman of his own blood. I am willing to live with you, whether you give me the name of wife or no," she continued, meeting his gaze until he had to look away. "What is it?" she cried finally when he did not answer her. "Do you reject me because of my birth, or because I am not tall and beautiful?"

Fionn shook his head. "Go home, Ailbe. I have nothing to offer you."

"But perhaps I have something to give *you*!" she exclaimed. "Listen—hear me, all of you—" She raised her voice and heads began to turn. "This is a challenge I am making! If my beauty is less than Grainne's, my wit is more, and so I challenge you to a contest of riddles, Fionn mac Cumhal. If you cannot answer the three riddles that I shall set for you, you must take me home with you to Almu."

There was a murmur of mingled appreciation and apprehension. It had been a while since anyone had dared to mention Grainne's name where Fionn could hear. The men had certainly all heard Ailbe's challenge. They were gathering round like dogs by the cook fires, waiting to see what he would do.

"Very well—" he made his decision suddenly. He doubted that she would be able to match a man who had studied in the bardic school of Cethern.

They ate first, then settled themselves by the fire, the senior warriors arranging themselves into a kind of jury while the others clustered behind. Fionn supposed he could hardly blame them. This year there had been little enough amusement for the *fian*.

"Are you ready, then, lady?" asked Daire Duanach the Bard.

For a moment Ailbe looked at the ground, then up at Fionn.

> *"Of good and ill I am the giver,*
> *Yet I remain unchanged forever;*
> *Who stays the same will see me never."*

Fionn frowned, for it had been a long time since he had needed to think in this way. Then he remembered a night when the students at Cethern's school had spun tales about their futures, and his friend Oircbél's laughter.

"*Ni ansa.* Not hard to say—" he replied, though his voice cracked as he remembered. "It is 'tomorrow.' "

"That is the answer," said Ailbe. If she was disappointed she did not show it. "But do you understand it?"

"Go on, ask the next one—" said Daire encouragingly. "He must answer all three correctly."

She nodded and smiled. Her voice was calm and clear as she spoke again.

"Both harvest and seed,
Upon my source I feed,
My lack fills its need . . ."

Fionn gazed at her blankly. He could think of a multitude of things that satisfied two of the verses, but no answer that had the stamp of *rightness* that he had learned to look for. He had got out of the habit of thinking in this way, and to seek the answer in his magic would be unsporting. The men were beginning to murmur, and someone laughed.

"A child, nursing at its mother's breast—" Ailbe said at last. "It is a woman's riddle," she added kindly. "No shame if you could not guess. We are one to one now, but I will be generous. Let the third riddle decide."

Fionn did not trust his voice. He nodded, and she closed her eyes, seeking inward for the right words.

"The more I give, the greater I grow,
The more I question, the less I know,
The more I stand fast, the farther I go . . ."

In Fionn's mind, there was nothing, not even a guess that might be wrong. He had never known this riddle—at that moment he felt as if he had never known anything at all. He looked around him desperately, but most of the men were frowning in confusion.

Ailbe knelt before him, and at last he had to meet her eyes.

"It is love, Fionn—" she whispered, "the love that I am offering to you. I am not the one you were wanting, I know it, but I will do the best I can." Her head bent, and he felt a tear hot on his hand.

"You have won, then," he said, trying to sound gracious, as if he had allowed it to save her pride. No man would refuse such an offer. Especially not a man whose love had recently been so completely, and publicly, rejected . . .

That night he took her into his bed. It was a brief and rather brutal coupling. Ailbe was a virgin, which he had not expected. By the time he realized her inexperience it was too late for a considerate courting. As he thrust against her, Fionn was himself possessed by his own need, and by a rage that was in its own way equally unexpected.

As he drove towards his consummation, he found himself muttering, as sometimes in battle he chanted the name of his foe.

"Grainne. . . ."

Afterward, he could feel the woman trembling beside him.

"I am sorry," he said abruptly. "I did not mean to hurt you."

"It does not matter," Ailbe said brightly, but he could hear the strain beneath her words. "I am sure that I will grow accustomed. It will be better when we are at home in Almu."

Fionn rolled onto his back, staring up at the stars. *Almu* . . . He had not thought about that, but he could hardly send the girl back to her father now. As sleep washed over him, one thing was clear. He would not give her the bower in which he and Sadb had shared such joy.

* * *

DUIBHNE, WHO HAD WITHDRAWN TO A LITTLE HOUSE he had over near Sliab Muicce, died that winter. The message said it was an inflammation of the lungs that had killed him, but gossip held that it was heartbreak to see Fionn at odds with his son. Fionn pretended not to hear. It was a sorrow to him that they had parted coldly, and that another man from the old *fianna* was gone. The younger men could not know how it had been when glory waited around every bend in the road, and all the world was new.

He installed Ailbe in one of the lesser houses, ignoring her broad hints that they should sleep in the bower that had been prepared for Grainne, and things grew easier, if not much better, between them. He told her that when the *fian* moved out in the spring she could sleep where she pleased, and did not like her any better when she hid her gladness.

Just before Beltane, when Almu was all astir with preparation for the summer's campaigning, word came that Grainne had borne Diarmuid a daughter, whom they called Eachtach.

"LEAVE THEM BE, FATHER—WHY CANNOT YOU LEAVE them be?" said Oisin as they stood watching the loading of the wagons from the walls of Almu. "You have a woman of royal race for your bed, and surely after this you would not be wanting Grainne."

Fionn sighed. White clouds were piling up in towers to the westward but the sky was clear above Almu, and there was just enough warmth in the air. He had supervised the preparations without his usual enthusiasm, but he had even less stomach for staying in Almu, so he had kept to his work with a dogged persistence. The *fianna* seemed to have caught his mood, for there was little of the usual joking and horseplay. He tried not to remember the joy with which they had ridden out only a year ago.

"It is a question of honor," he said patiently. "Do you think I keep Ailbe here because I love her? To have the high king's daughter as my concubine is useful, but there are still men who will laugh because Diarmuid ran off with my bride."

"No one will think the less—" Oisin stopped as Fionn turned on him.

"Do not be such a fool! You might have spent all your life as a deer for all you know of the world! Next they will be saying it is because I wear the horns that you got your name. It is not strength alone that makes me *Rígfénnid*, but reputation. We will have to fight for our rights all over again if the people begin to laugh at me.

"*That* is why I must pursue Diarmuid, to the death or until he gives Grainne back to me." He felt the wind freshen and glanced westward. The clouds were closer now.

"I see that you believe it, Father, and I will stand by you," Oisin said unhappily. "But I wish—"

Fionn gave a grunt that was not quite laughter. "You used up all your wishes when you counseled Diarmuid to run off with that bitch a year ago." As astonishment and guilt chased each other across Oisin's fair face he laughed again. "Do not try to deny it, lad. I *heard*. Perhaps now you will understand why I am not inclined to make you my counselor!"

It was hurt that showed now in Oisin's eyes. Fionn sighed, but no more than with Ailbe could he find words to ease him. After a moment Oisin turned away, but Fionn did not call him back again. The wind from the west blew strongly, threatening rain.

IT RAINED, OFF AND ON, FOR MOST OF THE SUMMER. But Fionn had pity neither for the fugitives nor for his own men. Pursued and pursuers alike slept wet and scraped the mold off their leathers and the rust off their steel. Grainne's child had been fostered somewhere and she was back with her lover. It would appear he was teaching her his woodcraft, for the little slips that had betrayed them the year before grew fewer. She was learning well. The woman who at the outset had been so weak that Diarmuid must steal the king's chariot horses to carry her was now able to keep pace with him easily.

It was too bad, thought Fionn, that Cairbre and not Grainne was Cormac's son. Though he still felt a sick rage when he thought of her, admiration was growing as well. After Lugach, a few women had passed the tests to join their company—if Grainne had come to the *fian*, she could have won her own glory instead of having to live through her man.

By the time Midsummer had passed, word was coming to Eriu that the weather had been bad everywhere. As the barley began to hang down its head and the stiffening wheat ears opened to the sky, Fionn gave over the chase at last and began to tell off battalions of the *fianna* to the coasts of Eriu to guard against raids from Lochlan.

They spent the feast of Lugh at Tailtiu, then began to move slowly southward. The second night out they slept at the clanhold of Caoilte's young wife, who spent the summers with her family on their lands between Temair and the sea. In the morning they went out after deer, for it was still their season to live off the land.

The morning was overcast. From the ridge above the *dun* they could see the grey waves of the bay at Inber Colptha rolling away into the mist offshore. Turning inland, they looked over pale squares of emmer wheat and barley scattered amongst the tangled green of the woodland. Rain had already spoiled much of the harvest, and as each field began to ripen, the folk worked furiously to cut and stack the grain. From here the figures moved antlike, working back and forth across the fields in rhythmic symmetry.

For most of the morning they ranged the hills without picking up a scent, but as the sun reached its nooning, one of the hounds at last gave tongue and the others, catching the excitement, plunged after him.

Fionn took a deep breath and began to run. Sceolan was already a pale blur among the leaves. He could hear the yammering of the other hounds, and an occasional crash among the underbrush as the enthusiasm of one of the warriors overwhelmed his skill. He ducked to avoid a low-hanging branch, frowning. The men were growing careless. He would have to set them some exercises to improve their woodcraft.

He leaped a rushing stream and started up the slope on the other side. For a moment the cover opened ahead of him and he saw the deer, a young buck of four tines, silhouetted against the sky. Then the beast disappeared. Breath sobbing in his chest, Fionn labored after it. He had thought himself in condition, but clearly he needed the work as much as his men.

Now the chase led downward. The trees were thinning. Ahead, Fionn glimpsed the straw-gold of a field. Someone began to shout. He burst through a thicket and saw an old man, his beard wagging furiously as he tried to hold off the warriors with the wooden rake in his hand.

Dogs frothed about the feet of the hunters, whining anxiously and adding to the confusion. Indeed, the only thing about the scene that was quite clear to him was the trail of the deer, which led straight to the center of the ripening grain.

"Ye cannot, lads—for th' love o' the Dagda—ye must not go in there an' trample the ripe grain!"

"Reap it then, if it is ready," said Aodh.

"All the folk we have are working as fast as they can, lord, in the field down the hill, but they will be here by the day's ending, surely, and when they have finished, then you can cross the field!"

"But by then, our dinner, which is hiding now in the midst of that field, will have fled far away," said Oisin. "Would you have us go to bed fasting?"

" 'Tis more than you will be fasting, my lords, if you spoil that grain. The harvest this season will be poor enough without you warriors rooting around in it like hogs on a hill!"

Fionn heard a shout and turned as Caoilte, rather flushed and breathless, came running up behind him.

"Listen to him, Fionn! Listen to me! That field belongs to my wife, and if we spoil the grain, I will never hear the end of it!"

The men began to laugh, but Fionn was still considering the trail of broken stalks that led towards the center of the field. In his youth he had helped with farm work, among other things. The grain looked ready for reaping, but overhead the clouds looked to be ripening as well, for a good crop of rain that would ruin the wheat as surely as the feet of his men.

"If my lads must sleep hungry, *I* will never hear the end of it," he said to the old man, "but an idea has come to me. We will do a good turn for the lady and for ourselves as well, and reap the field!" He gestured down the hill.

"They keep extra sickles for the harvesters, do they not, to use while the first set is being sharpened? Go you to the next field and bring them, man, and you will see what we can do! It is a challenge, see you—" He grinned at his warriors. "The first reaper to win to the center shall have the honor of killing the deer!"

"I do not know," the man stammered. "The lady will have to agree to it—"

"Then bring her, Caoilte," said Fionn, grinning. "Daire can sing to her while we labor. Think of it as a new competition for the festival of Lugh!"

While they waited, he set the hounds and their handlers to ring the field so the deer could not break free. Trying to demonstrate the proper bend and swing of the sickle with a curved branch was good for more amusement. By the time the peasant came back, his arms full of wicked curved blades, and Caoilte's young wife rattling along in her chariot close behind him, the *fénnidi* were laughing.

The laughter began to fade before the sun had moved a handspan across the sky. To bend on one leg, pulling the grain in with a measured stroke that would sever the stalks at an even height for stubble while the other hand held the cut stalks against the standing grain until the reaper had cut a generous handful soon set the muscles of leg and back to screaming. The reapers crept crabwise across the field, followed closely by the binders, who gathered the handfuls into sheaves and tied them with twists of the lank grass that grew at the edge of the field. If Fionn had not kept them trading tasks, they could not have borne the strain.

Building the sheaves into stooks was another skilled task, as was sharpening the blades with wooden strickles dipped first in grease and then in sand. Once he had demonstrated his own expertise, Fionn was kept busy orchestrating the labor on one side of the field. He set Goll to supervising the other. For a time the only sounds were the hiss of the sickles and the rustle of straw, the grunting of the reapers as they stretched, and, binding them together, the strong, striding rhythm of Daire's song.

Now, perhaps, they will have more respect for the folk who feed them, thought Fionn, as he finished sharpening a sickle and handed it back to Faobhar. His half brother's fair face was flushed dangerously, but the set of his jaw told Fionn it would do no good to suggest that he rest for a while. Two of the men had already succumbed to the sun, whose warmth they could feel even through the clouds.

But they were making progress. The stand of tall grain in the center was growing ever smaller. At times it quivered; the creature who hid there must know his time was being whittled away by the steady advance of the men.

You are Diarmuid, thought Fionn, *and one day you will feel my grip tightening inexorably around you and know that your time is done. . . .*

No doubt by now the deer could be startled into breaking cover by a little shouting, but they had pledged themselves to finish the field. Behind them, the stacked sheaves stood like sentinels above the stubble. Fionn remembered how, when he worked in the fields for a time as a lad, the last sheaf in the field had been bound to the last reaper, manhandled, and doused in water in mock sacrifice. The last sheaf was the old woman—the spirit of the corn that dies so that new life may come. But this time, they would be shedding the blood of the deer in a strange commingling of the hunter's and farmer's mysteries.

It was at that moment, as he straightened, gazing upward to see if they were likely to finish before it began to rain, that he noticed a shadow too dark for cloud, and coming from the wrong direction.

"Dubhán—" he called to the most long-sighted of their warriors. "Run up to the top of the ridge and look seaward. Tell me what you see!"

But by the time the young man gave the long, carrying trill that signaled the approach of a foe, Fionn was already certain. Smoke was rising from the seashore. Raiders from Lochlan had landed and were marching inland, burning the farmsteads as they came.

Fionn reached for his spear and swore. The spear was the only weapon he had, the only real weapon any of them had brought out with them today. Their war gear was all back at the *dun*. One did not need a shield and sword to kill deer.

"You must flee," cried the woman. Her horses plunged as she hauled on the reins and Daire scrambled out of the chariot. "You cannot face them unarmed!"

"Is it so?" murmured Fionn, looking at Goll. "Must we retreat, or can we hold them somehow?"

Goll's mouth had tightened, but his eyes were sparkling. "A man's spirit lives after his body dies, but not after the death of his honor."

Caoilte's wife gave a little sob as she heard him.

"You are mad!" she cried. "You are all going to die!" She whipped up her horses and sent them bucketing down the road.

Goll does not care if he dies, thought Fionn, looking at his old friend. *He is getting old, and he has always intended to go out fighting.* Fionn could see expressions change as that knowledge came to all of them. But no one was suggesting retreat, and though faces grew grim, none showed fear. His heart warmed with pride in them.

"I can run faster than the enemy, and faster than the horses that foolish wife of mine is driving," said Caoilte, blushing. "Let me race back to the *dun* and collect our weapons, and I will bring them to you in time to meet the foe sword in hand."

"Go then, and swiftly—" Fionn made his decision. "And as for the rest of us, I think we may yet find some stratagem that will both save our honor and confuse the enemy!" He looked around him. "Dubhán, Dubh Droma, Loegaire—" He named three or four others. "Take your sickles to the woods and cut branches the length of spears."

"We have spears already—" someone began, but Dubhán was already asking how many.

"As many as there are stocks in that field. . . ." Fionn grinned, and as he told off another crew to gather up the sheaves and set them up again in a line across the road, the rest of the men began to grin as well.

Fionn's warriors scurried furiously to carry out his orders, and a word to the peasant got the reapers from the other fields doing the same. By the time the earth begin to quiver to the regular tread of marching feet and they knew the raiders were coming, a staggered line of humped shapes, spear shafts poised and ready, wound across road and fields. With the sun behind them, details would be hard to see. They waited in patient menace for the enemy to arrive.

"Daire, you are as loud as a dozen men, and even raiders from Lochlan will respect a bard. Will you go out and give the challenge? Delay them as long as you can!" As Daire trotted off, Fionn glanced anxiously behind him. He doubted neither Caoilte's speed nor his loyalty, but wagons would be needed to transport weapons for upwards of a hundred men.

When he heard Daire's shout he crept forward through the trees. From behind, his strawmen looked pitiful, propped up on their stick spears. But from the other side they must be more convincing, for the foe came to a halt.

"Who dares to tread the holy soil of Eriu?" the *fili* cried.

"It is Dolor, son of Trenfhlaith, a chieftain of Alba and high prince of Lochlan who comes. Who dares to oppose us?"

"The very land itself opposes you," answered Daire. "But if you wish to face human weapons, it is the swords of the *fian* of Fionn mac Cumhal that shall take your heads!"

"Dolor is the victor of a hundred battles, ring-giver, mead-giver, feeder of ravens—" The Albans had begun to beat the butts of their spears against their shields. But from the side of Eriu came only silence. When the enemy realized it their rhythmic clacking faltered.

You are right, thought Fionn. *There is something uncanny here. Believe it, fear it, and flee!*

"Fionn mac Cumhal was fighting battles when your

lord was sucking his mother's tit. He killed Laigne mac Mor despite all his magic. He slaughtered Colgain mac Teine, your high king, standing in the fords of the Sinnan!"

A mutter of anger grew among the enemy and Fionn grinned ruefully. It was all true, but saying so had not frightened the Albans, only made them hotter for revenge. Where was Caoilte? If he did not come soon with the weapons, there would be no point in coming at all. He heard a sound behind him and whirled, Birga singing to awareness in his hand.

"He's back—" came a whisper, and Oisin slipped silently from between the trees. He was armed already, and held out the Hazel Shield and Fionn's sword. Fionn felt a tingle run through him as he touched them, and met Oisin's grin with one of his own.

"Bring the men—tell them to creep forward, just behind the line of sheaves. By the time the Albans see how they have been fooled, the illusion will be a reality!"

He settled the shield strap across his shoulder and began to worm his way towards Daire.

"Blood will flow for that deed!" shouted Dolor. "Children now in the womb will rue that day!"

"Children will wail," answered Fionn, rising to his feet behind Daire, who jumped, flushed as he saw who it was, and sidled gratefully behind him. "But they will be your children, not our own. Listen well, for this is the last warning you will receive from me. The grass will reach up to entangle you and the rivers rise to drown you if you try to come this way."

Silent as a breath on the breeze, he could feel the *fénnidi* easing into position behind him.

"The grass will fight us?" barked Dolor. They had come close enough now that they must be able to see the shocks of grain. "Straw is all you do have to fight with, it seems to me!"

He gestured, and the men of Lochlan began to trot forward. Sheaves toppled as they pushed past the line of straw men. Laughing, they flailed about them with their swords, scything down the cut grain. And then, screeching like the *bean-sidhe,* the *fian* of Fionn mac Cumhal rose out of the earth before them, and began to reap their own bloody harvest with sword and spear.

Once they recovered from their confusion the Albans fought valiantly. But the edge of surprise they had lost they never recovered, and soon streams of blood watered the stubbled fields. Where the battle had raged the gleaners came after, gathering up the scattered bundles of wheat and barley and stripping golden torques and armrings from the fallen men. In the end, the fighting had brought them back to the field the *fian* had been harvesting. The grain in the center still stood, but when someone finally thought to push his way through it, they found the deer they had been chasing, dead without a mark upon him in the midst of the golden grain.

"Died of fright, I suppose," said Faobhar, looking down at the stiff limbs.

"Not surprising," his brother Fearghusa answered him. "I nearly died of fright myself when those buggers came over the hill!"

Everyone laughed then, for Fearghusa had fought like a hero—they had all fought like heroes, and they had the victory.

Chapter 5

THE SHIPS THAT THE MEN OF LOCHLAN HAD LEFT beached at Inber Colptha yielded a rich harvest of gold and goods and captives from earlier forays. Fionn shared the booty out among the warriors, with a tithe for the high king and a share for the farm folk who had helped them set up the sheaves. Soon the tale was all over Eriu, and it grew no less in the telling. But that was nothing new.

One of the surviving Albans, a tall, auburn-haired warrior called Cedach Cithach, surprised them by asking to join the *fianna.* He was a king's son, outlawed for an accidental kin-slaying and owing service to no man. It was only a chance blow from a man on his own side that knocked him out so that he could be captured, and he proved to be a good fellow, more than able to pass the tests for the *fian.*

Oisin took as his share of the spoils a slender, upright woman whose skin had a warmth to it like southern ivory, and whose hair shone like antique gold. He called her Eibhir. Her face, too, reminded Fionn of the aquiline images on old coins from the Roman lands. They could only assume that she came from the south, for she spoke no tongue of Eriu, and Oisin spoke no language she knew. But clearly they communicated well in other ways. By Midwinter, Eibhir was with child.

Fionn thought that a woman who could not talk back might be restful. Sadb had been silent the first few moons after he found her. Ailbe, on the other hand, talked constantly.

After a year at Almu, it had become clear to her that Fionn would never install her as lady in the place that had been prepared for Grainne. Old Mongfind still ruled the household, and Ailbe busied herself with whatever she could find, complaining loudly about all she had to do. No one, it would appear, gave her the respect due to her, if not as Fionn's wife, at least as his acknowledged concubine. For a time she thought to find a kindred spirit in Eibhir, but Oisin's woman, silent though she might be, tended his quarters and worked among the women with an unassailable dignity.

"She must be highborn," said Oisin to his father, watching her carry the mead-horn around the hall. "It shows in every movement, even when she goes heavy with child."

I thought every move Sadb made was touched by magic, Fionn recalled wistfully. But it was true that Eibhir, without saying a word, had won more respect from the folk of Almu than Ailbe for all her talking. Yet she did not seem happy. Despite Oisin's devotion and the coming child, she went about her tasks with a weary courtesy and watched the falling rain as if she longed for some sunnier land.

It was on a morning a little after the Feast of Brigid when Fionn found out her secret. He was in the storehouse where he kept the *corrbolg*, whence he had fled a more than usually acrimonious encounter with Ailbe, when Eibhir came in, carrying some linens that would not be used again until next year.

"Let me lift the lid of that chest for you," said Fionn as she hesitated, her arms full of cloth. "It would be awkward for you, I think, even if your arms were free—" She made no sign, but waited patiently until he had gotten the heavy lid up, then carefully laid the linens inside.

"Wait—" he said as she turned to go. "You understood me. I suspect that you understand a good deal of what we say. Do not you think the time has come for you to be saying something in return?"

Her eyes met his and she colored a little, then shrugged helplessly. Sadb's speech had been stolen by magic and restored by a spell; it was reason he must use with Eibhir.

"Are you afraid you would not speak correctly?" he asked. "Well, you can surely nod your head if I say something that is true—" He looked around him. In the years Fionn had lived at Almu, the storehouse had received the produce of many lands, and all that was not used remained. There must be something here that came from her home.

"I will show you things, and you must let me know if there is something you recognize—" He began to paw through the piles, amazed himself at how much had been collected over the years. *I shall have to hold a feast and give some of this stuff away,* he thought, putting down a moth-eaten bearskin mantle from Alba and sneezing violently.

He turned to another chest, partly filled with the parchment rolls on which the men of the south imprisoned their words. He was about to close it again when she reached out, touching one of the rolls with a trembling hand.

"You know how to interpret those things?" he asked her. "Are you from the land of the Greeks, then?"

She shook her head, caressing the roll. "*Italia . . .*" she whispered. *"Puella Romana . . ."*

"From Rome! I suppose you were taken on the way to the country of the Britons," he said thoughtfully. It occurred to him that her family might pay well if they sent her back again. But he would not do that to Oisin. "If the manuscripts will amuse you, take them," he said then. "For certain they are no good to anyone here."

Later, it seemed as if finding her own tongue again had given Eibhir the courage to try another. Though she never spoke in public, she did master enough of the language of Eriu to make herself clear. Oisin was grateful to Fionn for his kindness, though he could not manage the words to say so. But now when his father sat down on one end of a bench he did not immediately get up from the other. Fionn could hope that someday he and his son would be friends once more.

AS EIBHIR'S BELLY BEGAN TO GROW LARGER, THE DAYS lengthened towards summer. The *fian* moved out, and since no war parties from Alba were so obliging as to raid the shores of Eriu, took up the pursuit, or as some said, the persecution, of Grainne and Diarmuid once more. They did not say so where they thought Fionn could hear, but he knew well enough that the *fian* had lost all interest in revenge.

There were times when even Fionn found himself wondering why he was so driven to find the fugitives. These days he could think about them being together without feeling physically sick, but imperceptibly the stakes had changed. Grainne had never been more than a dream. It was Diarmuid whose betrayal made him writhe, Diarmuid, who had been like a son to him, to whom he must prove that he was still the better man.

But throughout that summer's campaigning the runaways eluded him. At the end of harvest, when the king stags were beginning to battle in the glens, the warriors turned homeward, Fionn's *fian* travelling in company with the part of the *fianna* that wintered with Goll. As they passed through the Sliab Seghsa they paused to hunt, for those hills were rich in game.

TOWARDS MIDAFTERNOON, FIONN FOUND HE AND Sceolan had become separated from the *fian*. He paused to drink at a stream, and when he had finished, sat back, taking in the quiet around him as thirstily as he had the water. He realized then that he had not lost the others entirely by chance. Even when the *fian* was in the field he was always surrounded by people, and it would be worse when they returned to Almu. It was good, sometimes, to be alone.

As the water stilled Fionn saw his own face taking shape like some manifestation from the Otherworld, at first distorted, then settling into a more familiar configuration of high cheekbones and long jaw and deep-set eyes beneath straight brows. But the skin was like old wood worn until it shows the grain.

A trick of the light, he thought, or of the hidden currents running underneath the surface of the stream. Sceolan poked his cold nose into Fionn's shoulder and he straightened, shivering. Mist was rising from the damp ground, shadowing the day. Moment by moment it thickened, swirling in grey veils among the trees. The autumn sunlight grew pallid, leaching all color from the world.

Suddenly he hungered for a cup of ale and a fire and the sound of men's laughter. "Come, lad,"—he snapped his fingers to the dog—"it's time we got back to the *fian*." Sceolan darted ahead as Fionn retraced his steps up the hill.

But the path that had seemed so plain in the afternoon sunshine was invisible in this dusk that was so swiftly coming on. He bent to look for his own tracks, difficult with no contrast of light and shadow to define them, but surely no challenge to his woodcraft. The soft earth beneath that oak tree would take prints well—he bent over it, but the only track he saw there was unshod, broadly splayed with strong, gripping toes, and much smaller than his own.

Frowning, he pressed onward, coughing as the damp chill caught in his chest and began to invade his bones. The curdling mist made everything look strange.

Such mists swirled on the borders of the Otherworld.

Fionn slowed, his skin prickling with unease, and Sceolan pressed close to his knee. There had been a time in his life when Faerie had been as near to him as his next breath, but it had been many years since he had spoken with one of the Sidhe—not since the bargain he had made to free Sadb from the Dark Druid had closed the Otherworld against him.

But sometimes the folk of Faerie walked in mortal lands. . . . For certain he was close to something uncanny here. Even if his own neck hairs had not quivered, he would have known it from the way Sceolan was whining. He tightened his grip on his spear.

From somewhere up ahead came a clamor of ravens. He moved forward cautiously. No doubt the birds were calling because one of the hunters had brought down a deer, but ravens were strange, at home in both worlds. Especially the one who was also the Morrigan.

Fionn kept going. Even if it were only some beast dead in the course of nature, he was growing hungry enough to scavenge with the birds. The mists had now closed in completely; trees and stones were no more than shadows in a featureless expanse of grey. It was hard to sense any progress, for this damp chill sapped strength as well as spirit, and each step took more effort than before.

Directly above him, a long "caaark" split the air. Fionn stared up, heart pounding, and saw a dark shape spread jagged wings and flap heavily away. He strained to see where it was going, then began to hurry towards the flicker of light in the dark bulk of a hill.

It must be the Hill of Seghais, a stony hump in the heart of the forest. Fionn had never heard there was a cave there, but the light was coming from within. It was a moment before he realized that Sceolan was not following. He tried coaxing, but the hound hung back whining. Someone laughed, the sound an echo of the raven's cry.

Three women waited beneath the rocky overhang. Stained teeth showed as they grinned. They were gnarled as old tree roots, weathered and grimed with years and toil, peering at him beneath tangles of rusty-red hair. Fionn was reminded uncomfortably of the hags his grandfather had conjured up to threaten him when he conquered Almu, but those apparitions had left the dogs untroubled. Whatever was here was real enough to send Sceolan scuttling into the mist. He supposed he should find that even more disturbing, but he was too weary to care.

"My greetings to this house, and the women of it," said Fionn politely. "Have you a cup of ale for a wayfarer, and a seat by the fire?"

"For the son of Cumhal we can find a welcome," came the answer. He thought it was the middle sister who had spoken, but he could not be sure. "It is Iornach, Camog, and Cuillean who give you good welcome—"

The women might be repulsive, but the aroma of boiling meat that was wafting from within the cave made his mouth water. He nodded and stumbled towards them.

The inside of the cave was like a wild beast's den, hung with badly cured skins to keep off drafts, and littered with bones. Sceolan had been foolish to run away, thought Fionn, as the warmth of the fire gradually began to restore sensation to his limbs. He could have kept busy for a week gnawing what lay on the floor. Fionn reclined on more skins, heaped in a corner, and sipped gratefully from a beaker of bitter beer.

Above the fire an ancient cauldron of riveted bronze was suspended from a bar supported by two forked branches set into the ground. The stew inside it bubbled merrily. Every so often one of the hags would taste the broth, then add a pinch of something or other, whispering into the steam. Fionn could not identify the animal they were cooking, and thought it better not to enquire. He suspected that most of their flesh-meat came from small scurrying things that the *fianna* would have scorned. But he had lived on squirrels and voles and the like when he had to, and knew better than to despise food, whatever its form.

Presently one of the women ladled some of the stuff into a bowl and brought it over. It had been thickened with barley, and the tang of the herbs made other flavors hard to identify, but it was hot and filling. He spooned it down gratefully.

As he tried to finish his third helping Fionn found his eyelids growing heavy. This did not alarm him. Coming into a warm room after the cold and eating heavily always made one sleepy, and he had drunk a fair amount of beer. With an effort he managed to set the bowl down on the cave floor without spilling it. Then he fell back gratefully against the hides and let his eyes close.

For a time Fionn floated contentedly in the warmth, too exhausted even to dream. He did not know how long it was before he began to drift back towards consciousness, but it must have been a while, for he could sense even through closed eyelids that the fire had burned down and it was much darker in the cave.

Someone was speaking. He listened, at first without attempting to make sense out of the whisperings. What brought him closer to awareness was the sound of his own name.

"See how he sleeps, the son of Cumhal . . ." said the first voice. After a moment Fionn connected it with Iornach, the youngest of the sisters.

"But the daughters of Conaran are awake," tittered another, probably Cuillean.

"He is in our power!" The third voice must belong to Camog.

Conaran . . . Fionn recognized the name, but he could not remember in what connection. He turned his head uneasily, and the whispering ceased. He could feel their eyes upon him, and held himself deliberately still.

"He wanders in dream," said Cuillean at last. "He will not resist us." Their laughter creaked like dry bones.

"*By strangled squirrel and netted hare—*"

It was all Fionn could do not to jump, for the voice had been very close to his ear.

"*By barley bent and nettles twined—*" the next chimed in.

"*By stone trapped toad and lime-stuck wren—*" said the third.

His stomach churned uneasily; the ingredients of the stew had been worse than he suspected.

"*By herbs of power this soul we bind!*" the sisters chorused gleefully, and Fionn felt suddenly cold.

But he did not move. At first it was because he was trying to understand their purpose. Then, with growing horror, he realized that he *could not* stir. As in Cormac's hall, the uneasy twitchings of a drugged sleep were all that remained to him. Perhaps he really was dreaming—that recipe would give anyone nightmares. But how could he have known about what was in the stew, if he had not heard?

"Sleep, Son of Cumhal," Camog's voice grew gentle. "The spell twines about your limbs. You cannot move, nor do you wish to. Rest—you are tired, Fionn, worn out with war. Why should you make the effort? It will only bring you more worry, more labors, more pain. . . ."

It was true, he thought dimly. He had never been allowed to rest from his responsibilities, even when he was a child. . . .

"Sleep, lord of Almu," It was Cuillean's voice that lulled him now. "You have grown old. There is no strength in your bones. Your sinews wither and your juices are dried up. You are a withered leaf floating on the stream. Let go and the current will whirl you away. Let go, let it all go . . ."

Cool darkness swirled around him. It would be easy to obey. But Iornach was speaking now.

"Sleep, Fionn, and find peace. What do you want with the world of humankind? Everyone you ever cared for has betrayed you—your mother and Bodbmall, Grainne and Diarmuid and your son Oisin. Even Sadb let herself be lured away. If they loved you, they would not have left you. Sleep, and you will feel no pain. . . ."

Faces whirled in Fionn's memory—his mother, weeping, Bodbmall on her deathbed. Once more he seemed to hear Diarmuid's challenge and Oisin's defiance. And Sadb—but all his memories of her were loving, and as they emerged from that hidden place where he had prisoned them to keep the hurt away he seemed to hear her voice crying, *"Shield of Eriu, remember Conaran!"*

Memories exploded in his skull—the stiffness of hide armor against his skin, the stench of the dragon, and the eager keening of the Hazel Shield as it sent out its deadly vapors against the hordes that attacked Donait's hall. Long afterward, looking at the tapestry the fairy woman had woven to show that battle, he had seen that there were beings of lordlier race among the monsters. She had given some of them names. . . .

"Conaran—" His eyes opened as he whispered the name.

"Conaran's daughters!" Iornach turned at the sound. "The half-breed daughters that Conaran got upon a mortal woman after your damned Shield blasted his beauty. And we will avenge him!"

Fionn tried to shake his head, but his muscles did not want to obey. Iornach saw him struggling, and laughed.

"If you heard that, you heard the rest of it too. You cannot move, Fionn mac Cumhal. You have no more power than an ancient, or a babe!"

"Lie still, you poor man." Cuillean's voice parodied sweetness. "Why exhaust yourself with struggling? Let the dreams take you, and it will all be over very soon. . . ."

I am not old, Fionn told himself. *I am strong, strong!* But the bonds that held him were stronger still. If he had been able to speak, perhaps he could have countered their spell, but it was hard even to think in words. Was this truly what it was to be old, impotent in body and feeble in mind? Was there no choice but to let himself drown in that dark stream?

For a moment an image flickered in his memory—a wrestler giving way in order to let his opponent's own momentum bring him down—then Camog bent over him, a stone knife gleaming dully in her hand.

"We will cut you up and cast you into our cauldron, Fionn mac Cumhal; we will boil your bones . . ." she crooned. "Sticks and stones, shrieks and moans, the holy and eternal bones. . . ."

"And then we will eat you!" tittered Cuillean.

"You will need new flesh to make those bones live again!" snarled Iornach. "Where will you get it, Fionn, do you know?"

"Never!" Fionn managed to get out the word.

"Foolish man! Do not you understand that only by going into the cauldron can you be free?"

Fionn tried once more to escape; his limbs twitched as if he were having a seizure, and spittle dribbled from his slack jaw. Then he felt warm wetness on his thighs and realized he had pissed himself like a babe.

"Cut his head off!" said Camog, brandishing her knife of stone.

"We must hold him over the cauldron, or the blood will be lost—" objected Cuillean. Her sickle was bronze, green with age with a bright edge where it had been newly honed. Fionn groaned as hard fingers dug into his flesh and the hags started to drag him across the floor.

"You hold him, and I will cut—" cackled Iornach. She gripped a farmer's sickle, whose black iron was pitted and worn.

"That you will not!" came a new voice from the doorway.

Goll! thought Fionn in wonder. No one else had a voice like the booming of a midwinter storm. The breath went out of him as he hit the floor. He heard an impact and saw blood spray; there was a screech as if someone had tied a dozen wildcats together by their tails. Above the curve of the cauldron he glimpsed a bewildering tangle of limbs.

There was another thwack; a head arced above his body and plopped into the pot. With a flicker of satisfaction Fionn recognized Camog. *We will see whose bones are boiled now!*

As Goll turned to look, the remaining sister darted under his arm towards the door. As she reached it, she paused, and he saw it was Iornach.

"Fionn mac Cumhal, farewell—" she cried. "You feared us, but in time to come you will think the fate we offered you was kind. But as for Goll, he has chosen the blade, and by its edge he shall die!"

He made a grab for her, but in the same moment she darted into the darkness and disappeared. Goll made a harsh sound of disgust and turned back to Fionn. "Good riddance to her and all her kind! Ah, lad, what have they done to you?"

Fionn could only groan in answer. Goll sighed, gave a quick glance around the cave to see if there were anything worth looting, then upended the cauldron over the coals. As the steam hissed from the embers he gripped Fionn under the arms and dragged him out into the open air. A flurry of barking split the stillness and suddenly Sceolan was there, licking Fionn's face and whining.

"Thank the gods for that hound of yours," said Goll. "He wouldn't leave me alone till I followed him—but he wouldn't go inside that cave!"

Somehow the night had passed, and a pallid light was diffusing through the mists that still hung in the trees. Fionn took a deep breath and coughed as the damp air caught in his lungs, then winced as the prickling in his toes and fingers began to spread up his limbs.

"Drink some of this! I warrant it will wake you—" Goll unhooked a leather flask from his belt and set it to Fionn's lips. It was *uisquebagh*, and it went down

Fionn's throat like fire. He sputtered, but sensation was racing through his body more quickly now. He bit his lip against the pain.

When the convulsion was over, Fionn felt weak as a new lamb, but his limbs were his own. Goll gave him more of the spirit, and now it was a pleasant warmth that spread through his veins.

"I thank you—" he croaked when Goll pulled the flask away again. The other man grinned and took a swig himself.

"Usually," he wiped his lips, "I don't like to kill females. But those weren't women—"

Fionn sighed. He was no longer quite sure what they had been. Not human, certainly, but it was not enough to call them hags of the Sidhe. They had shown him his future—they had turned him into an old man, but at the end there had been some other dimension to their words. Abruptly he wondered what would have happened if Goll had not rescued him. If he had consented to be boiled in that cauldron, in what form would he have come out again?

"And I don't care for their curses, either," Goll went on. "To prophesy death in battle for a warrior hardly takes a druid's powers. And what end would be more fitting, eh? I've no mind to dwindle into a doddering ancient that can do no more than shiver by the fire. If I could choose my ending, it would be to die on my feet like Cuchulain, with a bloody blade in my hand!"

Fionn had always assumed that would be his own ending. Why should he go out in any other wise than as his fathers had gone? But whether they meant to or not, the daughters of Conaran had allowed him to glimpse another future, the one that passed through the cauldron. But that was a magic that he did not yet understand.

Goll stayed with him for the rest of that day and another night. It was not until Fionn woke with the next dawn that he felt strong enough to face the *fianna*.

"A good thing for you that you are fair-headed," said Goll, as they tramped back through the forest. "Red or brown will show the frost, but your hair only grows paler. You are Sceolan's color now!"

And that was how Fionn learned that although he felt almost his old self in body, his hair had gone white in the Hill of Seghais.

For a few days after that he took care to drink and shout with the rest of them. But no one seemed to have been worried much by his absence, and no one had much time for introspection. They were too glad to be going home. At least, thought Fionn as he breathed deeply of the crisp fall air, he had drawn closer to Goll. It was comforting to be with someone who could still call him "lad."

IT WAS NEARLY SAMHAIN WHEN THEY CAME HOME TO Almu; the skies behind them were heavy with rain. The women of the *dun* came out to meet them, drawing their bright mantles over their heads against the damp. Oisin broke ranks and ran ahead, and Fionn, remembering how he had raced home to Sadb, did not call him to order. He could see Eibhir now in the midst of a cluster of women who held a shawl above her and what she held.

Of course! How could he have forgotten? By now she must have borne her child. Oisin had stopped short before them, staring. Fionn hastened to come up with them.

"Fionn—do you see? It is a boy! Eibhir has given me a son!" Oisin turned to him, his eyes glistening with joyful tears.

Fionn swallowed, not trusting himself to reply. That was one joy that had never been granted him. He had never seen Sadb with Oisin in her arms. But it seemed to him that if fate had been so kind, she would have looked happier than Eibhir seemed now. There was pride in the foreign woman's gaze, and affection, but also the sadness that since first they brought her to Almu had never left her eyes.

He peered at the bundle in her arms, and she smiled a little and lifted one corner of the blanket. The child must have been born a month or so ago. He had lost the crumpled look of the newborn, though the features still seemed somewhat large for one so young. He already had a fair amount of flaxen hair. As if sensing all the attention, the baby opened his eyes. With a shock of recognition, Fionn met that thoughtful blue stare. Folk said that all babies looked like their grandfathers, and it must be true, for he was looking at the face he had seen reflected in the stream.

He looked up. Ailbe was watching him from behind Eibhir's shoulder, a mix of envy and exasperation in her gaze. But he had seen how she treated the servants. He was not at all sorry that he had given her no child. For a moment their eyes met, then he deliberately looked away.

"Indeed, there is no doubt of his breeding!" Fergus the Poet, too crippled in his joints to take the field, had come out with the women from the *dun*. "But the lad must have a name. We have only been waiting for his father to return."

"Say then, oh *fili*, what the name of this child

should be—" said Oisin, smiling radiantly.

"You are Oisin, the little deer, and so this babe must be the one the deer loves!" answered Fergus. "Call him Oscar—"

Oisin nodded, and held out his arms for the child. The baby made a little grunting sound at the unfamiliar touch, then stilled, looking around him with vague, wondering eyes.

"Oscar, 'tis a hero's greeting I give you! And before all the *fianna* I proclaim you—Oscar, son of Oisin, son of Fionn, son of Cumhal of the House of Baoisgne and the lineage of Trenmor!"

"And what of the mother's line?" said someone behind him. Oisin turned, his face darkening, but Eibhir's head had gone up proudly.

"It is high as his—in my own country!"

There was a sudden silence. The folk of Almu were grinning, but among the *fianna*, Fionn was perhaps the only one who was not surprised to hear her speak in the tongue of Eriu.

"Lady, we never doubted that," he said smoothly. "Do you tell us now the names of your father and kin."

"I was Æmilia Lucilla. My father was senator in Rome. My mother's clan are the Severii. One was emperor who died in Britannia."

"Septimius Severus!" said Fergus, whose business it was to know such things. "She comes of high kin indeed!"

"My cousin is married now to governor. I came on ship to visit her—" she swallowed and turned her face away, drawing the shawl closer to hide her tears.

"That is well, then," said Fionn across the hum of comment. "But so wellborn a babe must have a proper fostering. Who shall we choose to teach him, Oisin?"

"Let me take the child." Lugach's son shouldered to the fore.

Fionn stared, then nodded. Perhaps it was fitting. Mac Lugach was the first of his grandsons, the child that his daughter Lugach had so unwillingly borne. He was only a year older than Oisin. Sturdy and a little dour in temper, he was a good enough warrior, though not greatly popular with the men. But he had always been unfailingly loyal to his young uncle. Fionn looked at Oisin, and after a moment the younger man—he could hardly think of him as a boy now that he had a son of his own—nodded as well.

Mac Lugach held out his arms, and Fionn carefully, and with a reluctance that surprised him, transferred the warm bundle to the other man.

"My lady, this is a great gift you have given me." Oisin turned back to Eibhir. "And I will make you my lady indeed and marry you in all honor with a contract and bridegifts as if you had come to me from your kin."

For a long moment she looked at him, and all could see that her eyes were wet with tears.

"That is honor," she said carefully. "I know. But I do not want it. I have borne your son. Keep him and let me go. You were kind to me, but I do not belong in this land. Send me back to my kin, Oisin. That is the only gift I want from you!"

As she spoke, Oisin's weather-bronzed face had gone ashy pale. By the time she finished, Fionn was at his side.

"Let us go in—" he made his voice carry above the whispers. "We have much to celebrate, and much to tell. Mongfind—bring out the ale. We have here a horde of thirsty men!"

The *fénnidi* surged past him, but Fionn stayed with Oisin. "Let it be—" he whispered. "It is long since she has seen you. When she lies in your arms she may think differently."

"Do you believe that?" Oisin asked bitterly.

In truth Fionn did not, but as they went through the gate of Almu he gave the boy what comfort he could. Oisin loved this woman from the foreign land as he himself had loved Sadb, and Fionn was only too familiar with the pain the boy would feel if she were to go.

Chapter 6

AT INBER COLPTHA THE WIND BLEW FRESH OFF THE sea, fringing the little green-grey waves with silver foam, and rolling the strands of dulse and mermaid's lace towards the shore. It was as fair a day as Fionn could remember, the clouds puffs of white in an azure sky. The world was filled with sunlight, blessing their backs with warmth and glittering on the leaves and the waves and the polished ornaments and horse harness of the *fian. Surely,* thought Fionn, *when she looks on such a day, Eibhir must change her mind about leaving Eriu.*

They could hear the Greek trading ship before they saw her—a babble of foreign voices like squabbling gulls. *How will she stand it?* he wondered. But perhaps it would not sound like yammering to Eibhir.

Then they rounded the hill and the full force of the wind set horse gear to fluttering and blew the hair back from Fionn's brow. The Greek ship was anchored a little offshore, her faded sail furled along the spar, but two round, hide-covered curraghs went bobbing back and forth between her and the pile of goods on the shore, like bees bringing honey to their hive. They were in time, but there was not much left to be loaded. It was probably just as well—there was no sense in long good-byes.

He glanced back at the horse litter in which Eibhir was being carried. Oisin rode by her side. He motioned to Caoilte, who could outrun a horse, and would rather walk than ride.

"Go on ahead and tell them we are coming. Find out how long we have until they sail—"

Caoilte nodded and started off, his loose stride looking deceptively easy until one realized how quickly his figure was dwindling. The rest of the party continued at the same plodding walk with which they had covered the ground from Almu. No doubt Oisin wished they could go slower still.

"We have until the sun is above the headland," said Caoilte, trotting back towards them. "The master wants to catch the afternoon tide."

Fionn saw that Oisin had heard. He bent in the saddle to speak to Eibhir, and she pulled back the curtains to see. She had told them how to construct the litter in the Roman fashion—even if she had ever learned how to ride she would not have had the strength for it now. For a moment he saw her face, gold-kissed skin drawn tight over the bone of cheek and chin.

Throughout the winter after Oscar's birth they had watched Eibhir grow ever more sallow and thin. By this spring it had been clear even to Oisin that he could keep her with him and watch her die, or send her home. And so they had sent word to the officers of the *Ard Ri* at Inber Colptha to hold the first well-found ship from the southern lands that came in to trade and send word to Almu.

The ponies that followed the litter were laden with treasure and Fionn was sending Eibhir's maid and a strong youth to serve her on the way to Rome. If the Æmilii were reluctant to take her back after a year among the barbarians, no doubt wealth could buy back honor as well in Rome as elsewhere.

Presently they came down the slope and the hooves of the horses crunched on sand. The sailors, bronzed and active, and stripped down to their loincloths, looked up curiously until a barked order set them back to work again. The man who had spoken wore a striped tunic and a gold ring in one ear. Fionn kicked his pony and trotted towards him.

"You are Demetrios of Brindisium?"

The captain hooked his thumbs in his sash and grinned, his black eyes assessing the value of Fionn's gear. "And you are great king of the *fianna*, mightiest of warriors, Fionn mac Cumhal."

Fionn snorted. "Do you understand what we need of you? The lady must be delivered to her family in Rome. I have here the gold for her passage. If you get her there safely, your port tax here will be paid for the next seven years. If you fail, you will never trade in Eriu again."

"I know, I know. But we must go now, while the weather holds, eh? You bring the baggage now and then the lady. The tide turns soon."

Fionn nodded and turned back to tell Oisin, who had dismounted, and was standing next to the litter, holding Eibhir's hand. He could not hear what his son was saying, but he could see his face, rigid with agony.

Oisin was paler than he had been after that fight last year in which his battle-fury had been such that he had lost half his blood before he noticed the sword slash that had opened his thigh.

Oh my son, he thought despairingly, *if only I could have spared you this pain.* The sorrow in seeing one's children grow up was that one could no longer protect them. He had grown accustomed to watching Oisin take risks in battle—or perhaps he had come to share his son's confidence in his own immortality. But when they were fighting he himself was too busy to worry. In a way, sitting helplessly by while Oisin suffered this sorrow of the spirit was harder. Would it have been better if the boy had never loved at all?

Would it have been better if I had never loved Sadb? At this moment Fionn could consider it a mercy that she had been stolen away from him. He did not think he could have given her up voluntarily, as Oisin was giving up Eibhir. For a moment a deeper understanding came to him—*sometimes the greatest love lies in letting go. . . .*

He still dreamed of Sadb, even when he lay at Ailbe's side. In a sense, perhaps, he had done the same as Oisin, pledging that he would not try to find or see her on condition that she should be rescued from her captivity. But he had not seen her. Could he have given her up if he had been required to personally deliver her into her father's hands?

The baggage was loaded, and then the two slaves. Oisin himself lifted Eibhir from the litter and carried her to the curragh. They had arranged furs for her to lie on, but he would let no one else touch her. Fionn watched as the curragh danced across the water to the ship, saw Oisin, tiny with distance, lifting his lady over the side. He followed to see her settled, and Fionn felt his own heart growing hollow as he waited for him to return.

It seemed a long time before he saw Oisin's bright head above the rail. For a moment the boy looked down at the curragh, then he leaped into the sea. He swam as if he were fighting the sea, and the water churned foamy in his wake, but at least he was heading towards shore. Fionn was ready with a cloak to dry him as he came up out of the water. For a moment he held him tight, relearning the hard swell of muscle, the strong drumbeat of the heart. Oisin groaned once, then was silent. It was Fionn whose eyes were pricking with tears.

"There was no other way—" he began, but his son motioned him to silence. They stood without speaking, watching as the strip of sand between them and the ocean grew wider behind the retreating tide and the Greek hauled in his anchor, watched as the faded sail was set and the ship swung over to the wind and slid away. They were still there when it rounded the headland and disappeared.

THAT SUMMER IT WAS MEN OF THE ULAIDH WHO threatened the peace of Cormac's kingdom. Leaving most of the Almu men to watch the southern coasts, Fionn and his household marched north with the half of the *fianna* led by Goll. Goll himself and Garad, his youngest brother, were now the only surviving Sons of Morna, Airt Og of the Hard Strokes having died in battle several years ago, and Conain Mael, apparently of overeating, the winter before.

As he worked his way through the feast that Clan Morna had started preparing when he arrived at the great *dun* on Loch Dergdeire, Fionn wondered if the same fate would be his. He lay back on his dining bench, feeling very much like the boar whose stuffing had been bursting from every orifice, which he had been served, and wondered if the headache he felt coming on was from the smoke or the ale.

The great feasting hall of Morna was as big as the one he had built at Almu, and older, hung with skulls of the great elk of the marshes whose antlers branched as wide as a man was tall, and festooned with tattered trophies from a hundred wars. The chieftain's high seat was spread with the skin of a great red bear, and big enough for Goll to sprawl there with Feadha, his son by Fionn's niece Caoinche, by his side.

Fionn looked around him at those mute but eloquent witnesses to the clan's pride and power, and was glad they were no longer his enemies.

He was washing down the last of his meat with a horn of ale when two boys, or perhaps they were young men, though these days anyone younger than Oisin looked like a child, strode up and took their stand before him.

"I am Aonghus son of Airt, and this is Aedh my cousin!" said the larger of the two, whose flaming hair made introductions almost unnecessary. Fionn raised one eyebrow and looked over at Goll, who sighed.

"Aedh is Garad's son," said Goll, "and they are both too young for the *fian*."

"Not so!" exclaimed Aonghus. "We can run and climb and fight as well as any warrior in the *fian*!"

And argue, too, thought Fionn, wishing the pounding in his temples would go away. "We do not take untried warriors on campaign. Come to me when we return from the north and perhaps you can join the group of lads who are now in training."

"You would send us to play with a bunch of *boys?*" asked Aedh. For a moment he looked exactly like Dael mac Conain, who had been Fionn's tormentor in the House of Youths at Tailtiu, and he felt a flicker of ancient rage.

"We will not accept that," said Aonghus truculently. "Send us on a quest or set us a feat that we may perform for you to prove our worth!"

"A quest I will set you then, since you are so insistent!" said Fionn, anger getting the better of him. "Bring me the head of a warrior or a handful of berries of the Quickentree of Dubros."

At the second phrase, Oisin, who had been drowsing beside him, sat up suddenly.

"Fionn, tell them you were joking!" he exclaimed, then looked at the boys. "The head is that of Diarmuid mac Duibhne, perhaps the best warrior ever to come from the *fian*. I would not like to go up against him myself—" There was a short silence.

"And the berries?" asked Aedh stubbornly.

"Ah, that is a story, and I will not tell you all of it," Oisin grinned, trying to turn it into a game, "only that the tree grew from a berry that was dropped by the folk of Faerie when they came to play hurley with the *fianna*. Their taste, I have heard, is like mead. No disease or sickness seizes anyone that eats three berries, and his youth returns to him."

Perhaps I will hold them to it, thought Fionn, rubbing his temples. *For that is surely what I need now.*

"Why should getting them be such a feat? I should think folk would be lining up to wait for the berries to fall!"

"Ah, well, there's the difficulty," Oisin answered him. "For the tree is guarded, do you see, by a creature called the Searban Lochlannach, that is a thick-boned, large-nosed, crooked-tusked, red-eyed, black-bodied giant. One eye he has, in the middle of his brow, and no weapon can harm him. He has made the district around him a wilderness, and it is there that Diarmuid and Grainne are in hiding now."

He thinks it is a story, thought Fionn. *He never saw the Red-Mouthed Woman, or the creatures who attacked Donait's hall. He is half of the Otherworld himself, but I in my grief was too sore to teach him about the Sidhe and their magic . . .* He felt a momentary pang of apprehension, a sense that he might one day rue that omission, then Aonghus spoke up in reply, and it was gone.

"We will prove ourselves, Fionn of Almu, though all the monsters of Faerie oppose us!" He drew himself up with all the dignity of seventeen, and the two boys stalked away.

"Their mothers spoiled them," said Goll when they were gone. "But they will learn better, if they live so long!" He tossed the bone he had been gnawing to one of the dogs. "Now, lad, I have been thinking, and here is the way I propose we should tackle the northern men."

The conversation turned to routes and supplies and numbers, and the two young mac Mornas were forgotten.

THE MEN OF THE ULAIDH FOUGHT AS THEY USUALLY did, with a somewhat self-defeating ferocity. The campaign against them was notable chiefly because of Oisin, whose own heroism bordered on the lunatic. For the first time since that first year when the boy had become a warrior, Fionn found himself anxious for his son. Nonetheless, Oisin came through the campaign without a scratch. It was Fionn who took a gash in the leg that continued to trouble him as they marched southward. Goll had no wound, but sleeping out on damp ground had given him a cough that did not go away.

Still, the Clan Morna *fian* was in good heart as they came home to their lands around Loch Dergdeire. It was in Fionn's mind to return to the coast and leave Grainne and Diarmuid in peace for another year, but as they were setting up camp at the head of the loch a runner came from the *dun* to tell them that Aedh mac Garad and Aonghus mac Airt had disappeared.

"The young fools!" Goll spat scornfully. "It is not your fault, lad," he said to Oisin. "You did your best to warn them away—"

"Diarmuid will not harm them!" said Oisin swiftly.

"Maybe not, but he will defend himself, and what of that other beastie, the Searban Lochlannach? I suppose we must go after them or their mothers will never let me hear the end of it!" He coughed and spat again.

THE GREAT ROWAN THAT MEN CALLED THE QUICKEN-tree of Dubros had taken root in the country of the Ui Fiacrach that sloped down to the sea. Since then a wilderness had grown up about it. There was only one path through the forest, and that a hard one. Still, from the *dun* of the Mornas on Loch Dergdeire it was little more than a day's journey, easy to understand why the lads had been tempted to try it.

Leaving most of the *fian* encamped by the loch, Fionn, with Oisin, Goll, and the pick of his warriors, headed westward. On the morning of their second day on the trail, they met Aedh and Aonghus coming the other way. Under Aedh's arm was a roughly twined basket.

"You see!" cried the boy. "Here are the berries! We are worthy after all to take our place in the *fian*!"

A murmur of amazement ran through the men. "The Searban Lochlannach is dead?" asked Goll.

Fionn took a deep breath. A hot wind was blowing from the south, and there was a tingle in the air as if a storm were coming on. But when they had risen that day the weather had been fine. His awareness went inward, reaching out for the earth song, and found the same hum of tension that preceded the twice-yearly Ridings of the Sidhe. Suddenly he was very glad that he had brought along the Hazel Shield.

He scooped a handful of berries from the basket, noting how the loose ends of vine had been braided back into the weave in the way they taught in the *fian*. The fruit was ripe and fragrant, glowing in its dark nest as if lit from within. He tasted one and felt flavor expand through all his senses simultaneously. With a pang he remembered the meals he had eaten in Donait's hall.

"This is surely the fruit of Faerie," he said grimly, "but I think it is Diarmuid's hand that plucked these berries and twined this basket. And if so, then it is Diarmuid, not you, who has killed their guardian."

"Is that it?" growled Goll. "You amaze me. How did you persuade the hero to kill the giant instead of you? Well," he went on as Aedh hung his head, "let us go look on this wondertree—"

Aonghus flushed red and met Goll's gaze defiantly as the whole party continued along the trail.

"He told us to get the berries, and we have done so. Does it matter how?"

"It was not we who persuaded him," put in Aedh,

evidently thinking he had been insulted. "It was the lady. She is with child, and when she heard of the fruit she could not rest until she had some."

Fionn blinked. He had not known that Grainne was expecting again; but why should he be surprised? Would he himself not have fought all the hosts of Faerie to bring Sadb a flower she wanted when she was carrying Oisin? In the end he had been able to do nothing for her at all. Diarmuid was more fortunate. Or he had been. The Sidhe would want a blood price for the death of their son.

The quickentree grew in the midst of what had been a pleasant clearing, though now the sod around it was gouged and torn. At the foot of the tree he saw the seared outline of an almost-human form upon the grass.

"It was a great fight," Aedh's eyes kindled. "The Searban Lochlannach had a kind of bed built in the tree, but he came down when Diarmuid challenged him. Like a boar and a bear they battled, but in the end Diarmuid got the monster's iron club away from him and used it to smash his head in. And then—and then, the body glowed white for a moment and disappeared!"

Fionn nodded—that would be the only way the creature could be killed. The wind had faded, but the air was weighted with a strange warmth. He felt the fine hairs rising on his skin.

"And afterward—did they go away?" He looked up, but could see nothing through the thick leaves.

"Fionn, for shame!" exclaimed Oisin. "Are you still so eaten with envy as to think that Diarmuid would stay trapped in a tree, knowing that you are intent on slaying him?"

Not this time, he realized with surprise. He would cheerfully have fought Diarmuid himself, but he would win no honor by leaving his enemy to the wrath of the Sidhe. He shrugged, feeling sweat start on his brow. *Cannot Oisin feel the tension? His beloved Diarmuid is in more danger from Oisin's own blood kin than from me!*

The boy could read the trampled ground as well as he could, and no doubt was hoping Fionn had not seen the trail of footprints that led to the foot of the tree, where a low branch made it so easy to pull oneself upward, and did not lead away. Diarmuid was there, all right. Fionn bit back the appeal that was on his lips. If he called to Diarmuid to come down and flee, not even Oisin would believe it was not some trick to put the fugitives in his power. So long as the *fian* was in the neighborhood, Diarmuid would not stir from the tree. The only way was to let him think that it was *he* who had outsmarted Fionn, and provoke him into breaking free.

"Then it should make no difference if we rest here until the noon heat is over," he said carefully. "Get out the *fidchel* board, Oisin. To pass the time I will challenge you to a game."

Fionn sat down at the base of the tree. If he had not been twitching with apprehension, he would have laughed at the look on Oisin's face, but the boy had no choice but to agree. The *fidchel* pieces were made of beechwood bleached white or stained red, lighter than silver or gold for travelling. They clicked ominously as they were set out upon the board, the white kingpiece in the center guarded by his own men, while the red pieces were ranked in companies on the four sides of the board.

"There sits the chieftain in the center, with enemies all around him," said Fionn. "Will they overcome him, or can he break free?"

"I will play the chieftain," said Oisin, "and defend him from you as well as I can."

Fionn made his first move, seeing at the same time the pattern before him and all those that might grow from it, as once in vision he had seen the colored roads spiraling out from the skirts of Brigid's gown. He had laid his spear upon the ground beside him; as his hand brushed the shaft he felt it thrumming expectantly. *Hurry,* he thought, waiting for Oisin to make his next move, *even Birga knows they are near!*

Move by move the game developed, and Fionn's red-stained warriors moved in. He looked at the board and saw his trap closing around Oisin. The men had grown tense and silent, watching the play.

"There is only one move that will win the game for you, Oisin," he said loudly, "but you will not learn it from me!"

As he spoke, a berry fell from among the leaves above them to strike the one piece that Oisin must move to break free. Fionn saw his son grow first red, then pale, as he made the correct play. The heat had grown more intense, and though beneath the rowan the air was close and still, Fionn heard a whispering like a distant wind.

"A chieftain may find help unlooked for," he said then, "but sometimes his enemies are not all on the board. Take care, Oisin, your friend is in more danger than he knows." Once more he let his mind envision the branching patterns and began to play.

As the new trap unfolded he saw Oisin glance upward in appeal, and as he had expected, at the last moment another crimson berry flicked down to mark the man Oisin should move to take the offensive once more. Fionn resisted the temptation to look up. Oisin was too impulsive to be really good at *fidchel,* but Diarmuid had been the only man in the *fian* who could take Fionn on and win. Even if he had not seen the tracks, he would have known whom he was really playing now.

Diarmuid, Diarmuid, his heart cried, *you know my play as well as I know yours! Cannot you see what I am trying to say?*

He pitched his voice to carry. "Spilled blood screams far more loudly than hurt pride. A wise man does not take refuge in the fortress of his enemy!"

He frowned at the board. His options had narrowed, but that was as he had planned it. Sometimes losing was the only way to win. As the thought came to him for a moment he glimpsed a greater pattern, then Oisin made his next move, and the insight was gone.

A breath of wind lifted his hair; the air was still hot, but now it was moving. Birga was keening softly and he could feel the Hazel Shield beginning to wake as well. Around him men stirred uneasily, wiping the sweat from their brows. They were begining to feel the change, but they did not know what it might mean.

He made his move quickly and looked at Oisin. The white kingpiece had almost won to the edge of the board. Oisin's glance moved quickly from one piece to another, knowing his next move would decide the game. Behind them, a man was trying to change his wager; the *fian* had never seen Fionn so close to losing before.

The rising wind hissed ominously in the treetops. A few leaves fell as if it had dislodged them, and among them a berry that dropped with the same casual accuracy on the man Oisin must move to win.

The men shouted in wonder, but louder still was the sudden wind.

"Your chieftain is free!" cried Fionn, "He should run while he can, for well I know you would not have won that game if Diarmuid himself had not been prompting you!"

"He would never stay—" began Oisin, but his words ended in thunder. The hosts of the Sidhe were speeding between the worlds.

"Am I right, Diarmuid?" he cried. "Are you there?" He leaped to his feet, scattering pieces and board.

"Your judgment is always good," came a voice from above them. The branches shook and Diarmuid's head appeared among the leaves. "Grainne and I are here." Heat lightning flared on the horizon as the hooves of Faerie horses struck mortal air. A look of alarm crossed Diarmuid's face as the tree swayed.

"Then call upon your defenders, for your enemies are here!" Fionn snatched up his shield and spear.

Oisin was staring at his father as if Fionn had conjured up the Faerie hosts to help him. Blue light flared suddenly around the clearing and the men grabbed for their weapons. A flight of ravens appeared in the air above them, screeching a challenge.

"Diarmuid, come down!" yelled Oisin. "I have won your freedom, and I myself shall be your surety. Unless the sky should fall or the earth swallow me, neither Fionn nor the *fianna* of Eriu shall wound you. By my body and my life I pledge no evil shall be done to you today—"

An ill-chosen oath, thought Fionn hysterically, as the world began to go mad around them. The barriers were very thin now; fair faces flickered in and out of vision, distorted by rage.

"Run!" he shouted to his men. "Get out of the way!"

The quickentree shook as Diarmuid began to help Grainne descend. Fionn shoved Oisin towards the trunk to help them and stepped in front of him, raising his shield. His son's expression shifted from astonishment to joy as he understood—at last—what Fionn had meant all along. Then Oisin was reaching up for Grainne. For a moment Fionn saw her face, its radiant youth refined to an enduring beauty like gold in the fire. Then a sudden cold wind swirled around them; the scent of apple blossom suffused the air. When Fionn could see again, Oisin was looking about bewilderedly and Grainne was gone.

Aonghus Og has got her, thought Fionn. *At least one of the Sidhe is on our side.* Then the Faerie host came upon them, and Birga began to sing.

For a time he was too busy fighting to think anything. His mind rang with the terrible harmonies of his Shield and spear. Then came a moment when the tumult contracted to a dreadful humming stillness, as if they stood in the eye of a storm. He realized that Diarmuid and Oisin had taken up position to either side of him with their backs to the tree. Though his arm was weary, he held out the Hazel Shield a little farther to cover them all.

"*Fionn mac Cumhal, why should there be war between us?*" came a great voice from the cloud that whirled around them. "*Give us the slayer of the Searban Lochlannach, and you may go free—*"

Diarmuid made a convulsive movement forward, and Fionn saw he was on the edge of the fighting-madness that counts no odds. "I will give them a slayer," he growled, as Fionn swung his spear to bar the way. "Let me go!"

"There are too many—" whispered Oisin.

"*They* will not accept your surety," answered Diarmuid. "Why should you die for me?"

"The blood of the Otherworld cries out for vengeance!" called their challenger, and ravens echoed him. *"Stand aside!"*

"That I will not," Fionn replied. "My claim for vengeance is older, and if anyone kills him, it will be me!"

"Slay me, and they will let you go!" Diarmuid turned to face him, and Fionn flinched from the passion in those blue eyes. Like the woman, he too had changed; the pursuit had revealed his essence, hammered and drawn out and tried in the fire until all that remained was true steel. And Fionn felt his heart shake in his breast.

"It is the wrath of Bodb Derg that shall fall upon you if you continue to protect him, and the curse of the Morrigan . . ." came the raven's cry.

"The unfriendship of those two was mine already." Fionn forced his voice to steady. "Look to your own defense, ye warriors of the Sidhe!"

"Why?" asked Diarmuid, and his voice shook for the first time that day. "After what I did to you, why protect me?"

"Dear heart, I do not know myself." Fionn coughed to hide his own emotion. "But this I do know, there is no foe in this world or the Other that can defeat us three when we stand together in arms."

"Well then!" cried Oisin, baring his teeth in a grin. "Let us give them a fight!"

Both the younger men were trembling with the onset of battle-madness now. Fionn could feel it radiating from them like heat off a forge. Even as he recognized what was happening, he felt the same fire shock through him. The Hazel Shield writhed on his arm and Birga's keening became a scream as he launched himself forward. Or perhaps it was his own body contorting with fury, his own battle cry.

Fionn's arm swung down and a *brollachan* with bristling hair and a single, red-rimmed eye shrieked and rolled away. He sensed Oisin and Diarmuid moving to either side of him. Like a single, six-armed being, as terrible as any monster of the Sidhe, they waded into the fray.

"DO YOU THINK THAT THE RAVENS CARRY TALES OF battle?" asked Oisin. "The bards have begun to make stories about the killing of the Searban Lochlannach already, and scarcely a hand of days has passed. . . ."

Fionn peered at his son through the steam of the high king's sweathouse, noting where pink skin was beginning to appear at the edge of healing gashes, and the rainbow shadings of the bruises on his fair skin. But none of the damage was permanent, which rather amazed him, considering the odds. He did not know how Diarmuid had fared. When at last the battlestorm had ended, they had all three collapsed where they stood. When Fionn awakened, Diarmuid was gone.

"More likely it was the messenger we sent to the *fianna* to tell them we still lived," he replied. The men who had gone with them had been scattered by the violence of the storm. Last he heard they were still straggling back to the *dun*. But most of their stories were of the events that had gone before the fighting. When confronted by the Otherworld, the human mind tended to protect itself by revising the unearthly into something familiar or blanking out the experience entirely.

Unfortunately for his peace of mind, Fionn himself remembered almost all of it, but at least he had suffered no serious hurt, though every bone in his body felt as if it had been wrenched apart and jammed back into place again. The last time he had fought the hosts of Faerie his hurts had been healed by Donait's magical bath. He wished he were lying in it now.

"I suppose so," said Oisin. "They did not see what really happened. That was a fight to sing about surely. I wish that I had the skill to tell the tale. . . ."

Fionn gasped as the servant poured more water over the glowing stones and steam billowed into the air. If he could not have Donait's magic, the *Ard Ri*'s sweathouse would have to do. A wave of heat rolled over him, obscuring the whitewashed walls, and he stretched out his long legs with a groan.

"Say nothing," he croaked when he got his breath back, "about Diarmuid."

"Nothing?" Oisin glanced at him sidelong. "But you spared him—"

Did I, wondered Fionn. In retrospect, that game of *fidchel* seemed no less fantastic than the battle that had followed it. He relived the moment when he had looked into Diarmuid's eyes in his dreams. He cleared his throat.

"He has sent a messenger to Cormac to make terms. . . ."

Oisin let out his breath in a long sigh. "At last!" Then he smiled. "I'll keep silent, Father, if you'll take them. I can see that you'll have more leverage if the *Ard Ri* thinks he has to persuade you to give in. What is he asking for?"

Fionn shrugged. "A dowry and her father's blessing on his marriage to Grainne, his own father's lands, and forgiveness for his deeds while outlawed. If I will give Ailbe the name of wife, Cormac will turn over her dowry to me."

"It will be good to hunt with Diarmuid once more—" Oisin began, but Fionn shook his head. The men of the *fianna* could not bear to remember the creatures of the Otherworld. But the thing that Fionn dared not remember was the light in Diarmuid mac Duibhne's eyes. The god of love had made Diarmuid to be beloved of women. It was not until that moment beneath the quickentree that Fionn had realized that the magic might apply to himself as well.

"It is a condition that neither I nor the *fianna* shall hunt or pass over Diarmuid's lands, and that he and his woman will stay far away from me. This is peace, Oisin, not friendship. There has been too much between us. It will be best if Diarmuid and I do not meet again."

Chapter 7

THE PRIESTESSES OF BRIGID HAD FINISHED BLESSING the fortress and the folk of Almu and gone back down the hill into the purple dusk that veiled the plain of the Curragh, leaving Fionn and his people to celebrate the festival. The salt beef and mutton, the rounds of cheese and boilings of barley and herbs and the little cakes all studded with dried fruits and smeared with honey had been reduced to crumbs and fragments. The time for serious drinking had come.

Fionn upended his horn and let the golden mead flow down his throat like a river of gold. It was a gift of the goddess, but this year he had avoided speaking to Her. Even mediated through the flesh of Her priestess, Brigid could awaken the kind of emotions he had been trying very hard to deny. He was a long way from being drunk, but the mead was beginning to soothe a pain that he did not even acknowledge except at moments like this, when drink, or sometimes music or a fight or the sky on a spring day, gave him a moment's ease.

Women did not do so. Not even the one he called his wife. It was duty, not desire, that drove him to Ailbe's arms.

> *"A lark in the sty, a pig in a tree,*
> *If I knew how to fly, then I would be free—"*

Lomna the Fool cartwheeled across the floor, gasping out a verse each time he came up again.

> *"If I had no eyes, how well I would see!"*

He finished facing Fionn, who flicked a piece of dried apple into the open mouth. For a moment Lomna gaped; then he got it down, and laughing shrilly, reversed himself and bounced away.

"If I had no heart, I would not miss her. . . ." muttered Oisin, who had gotten a head start on the mead. Fionn needed no translation. Half-drunk, "*she*" was always and only Eibhir. Sober, he never spoke of her, and even now, three years after they had seen her ship sail away, he would reach the edge of consciousness before he could say her name.

"You could not keep her," Fionn said softly, uselessly. They had had this conversation too many times. "Eibhir needed her people. It was killing her to stay here."

"I need her . . . Oscar needs her. . . ."

Fionn glanced across the hall, to where Oscar sat on his foster father's knee. If Oisin never spoke of Eibhir, Oscar never spoke at all. At four years old he was well grown, but the sweet and smiling child who had been the darling of Almu had become silent and surly, lumpish as a changeling, when his mother disappeared.

We've none of us had much luck with women, thought Fionn. *Not Oscar, not Oisin, and certainly not I. . . .*

When he was not drinking, Oisin chased women. Fionn had already had to pay an honor-price to several farmers whose daughters Oisin had seduced and then cast aside when he found they could not fill the emptiness Eibhir had left behind.

"Be patient, lad." He laid an arm across Oisin's shoulders. At least the boy was still talking to him. "The pain will pass."

"Will it?" Oisin blinked up at him. "Then why'd you spend so long chasin' . . . Grainne? Women . . . 'r no damn good." He nodded solemnly. "Always let y' down!"

Fionn winced. Even half-drunk the boy could hit a mark. Grainne and Diarmuid were living now at the *rath* her father had given her, away to the north in Connachta, near the sea. Rumor said that she had given him another child, this time a son. He reached for his own mead-horn once more.

From the other side of the hearth where the women had gathered, he heard a high peal of laughter. Ailbe, got up in purple silk and all the ornaments she owned, was putting away her share of the mead. Defiantly she met his gaze, then looked away. Fionn sighed. She had, at last, the name of wife and the big bower. What sorrows did *she* have to drown?

Then he saw that it was dark, handsome Cairpre who had made her laugh, leaning over the rail of her compartment while she lay back on her bench, face flushed and the brooch that held her gown unfastened, as if she were too warm. As she moved he glimpsed the curve of a white breast and felt a flicker of interest tighten his loins. Tonight, perhaps, he would seek her bed. Perhaps it would be different this time.

Lomna had ceased tumbling about and was standing by the hearth, juggling.

"Look!" Oisin giggled softly. "He's juggling heads!"

Fionn blinked, for a moment seeing as his son did. Distorted features flickered in the firelight as the grisly spheres flew through the air—his own face, Lomna's, Cairpre's, and Ailbe's painted smile. In times past, warriors had played hurley with the heads of slain enemies or made balls from their brains. These days, it was sufficient to set the head of a particularly notable enemy on a stake outside the door. He stared, seeing a terrible significance in those swift orbits, then he blinked, and they were only a set of painted balls.

"Go to bed, lad, and sleep it off!" He clapped Oisin on the shoulder. "You'll be seeing serpents twining up the houseposts if you drink any more!"

"I'm all right—" Oisin smiled sweetly, but his eyelids were drooping. "You don' need t'worry 'bout me. . . ."

"Sleep here then," said Fionn, "and forgive me for leaving you, but I should move around, talk to our guests in the hall." *And clear my own head,* he added silently. That moment of vision had disturbed him more than he wanted his son to know.

Oisin grunted and closed his eyes. Fionn looked down at him, seeing the innocence of the child he had loved hidden in the face of the man. He had tried to strengthen his defenses, but they had not held against the appeal in Diarmuid's eyes, and they could not protect him from loving his son. "Sleep well, my dear, and let fair dreams soothe your sorrow," he said softly, but Oisin did not stir.

Fionn moved around the hall, stopping at each group of benches for a joke or a word. When he came to Fergus the Poet and Daire he sat down and even took up the harp for a time, continuing to talk as his fingers wandered over the strings.

"What is it you are playing?" asked Fergus, cocking his head to listen. Fionn frowned, repeating the phrase.

"I do not know—a tune—they come like this sometimes when I am idling."

"I would like to learn it," said the bard, and Fionn played it again. But with all the noise in the hall it was hard to hear, and no doubt both of them would forget by morning. Words could be written down in ogham if one had the craft, or in the strange crabbed letters the Romans used. It was a pity there was no way to preserve a melody but for one harper to learn it from another. He lifted his fingers from the strings, and as they shimmered to rest, the firelight drew an ogham of music in lines of shadow on the post behind him.

An ogham for harp notes! Why not? Fionn wondered suddenly. The system had been used to catalog battles and fortresses and names of trees. It should be possible to use the patterns of lines scored in wood for music as well. To figure out the way of it would be a nice distraction from his other worries. He was smiling as he continued around the hall.

Further along, he found some of the older members of the *fian* sharing a pitcher of spiced ale.

"Aodh mac Ronain! How goes it with you?" His

horn was empty and he held it out to be refilled. It seemed a long time since Aodh had come storming up to the gates of Almu demanding compensation for a dead deer and stayed to join the *fian*. He was showing his age now, thickening around the middle and going grey.

"Well enough, but when the returning swans begin to herald the spring I find myself missing the wetlands by the Liffe and my *dun* at Gabhair. It is in my mind, Fionn, that my *fénnid* days are over. I will not take the field with you this summer. It is time I went back to watch over my own lands and my lovely girl."

"I have heard that your daughter Eargna has grown very fair," said Fionn politely.

"Enjoy her company while you can," said Faobhar. "Soon enough the lads will be driving cows to your gate for a bride price, seeking her hand!"

"Never with my will!" Aodh rounded on him, face flushing with fury.

"Peace! I meant no wrong!" Faobhar held up a hand, eyes widening.

"Nor will you, nor will any man," growled Aodh. "She is the light of my life, the treasure of my house, and I swear by my head that no man shall go away unscathed who seeks her in marriage from me!" He drank thirstily.

"He is drunk," said Conain mac Luachar softly. "You must not mind him."

"Nor will we," Fionn assured him, "but it is a pity for the sake of the girl. You have marched and fought by Aodh's side for twenty years, and when have you known him ever to break his sworn word?"

"That is so," Faobhar shook his head, "and it makes

no difference to me. But I am sorrier for any young hero who might desire her!"

When Fionn was certain that everyone's temper had cooled, he moved on again. According to the druids' reckoning, the Feast of Brigid ended wintertide, but this was the most dismal time of the year. The holiday released enough tension to get them through the next moon or so, until the weather warmed and fresh food was available once more. Drinking helped too, but though mead could heal a quarrel or seal a friendship, there was always the danger, when it flowed too freely, that a careless word would make blood flow as well.

As he crossed the hall, he found Lomna by his side. "Well, fool, you have fooled well tonight," he said kindly, ruffling the other man's shock of hair. It had always been the same shade, somewhere between sand and grey, as if the man slept in the ashes. And though Fionn knew that the fool must be near his own age, Lomna's face was as smooth as a child's, his skin translucent as if the years had worn his substance away.

It is grief that graves lines in a man's face, he thought sadly, *and responsibility, and memories. For Lomna, there is only today.*

The man had turned up at his gate some years ago, talking nonsense, but helpful around the *dun.* There was talk that Lomna had been meant for a druid and lost his reason, as sometimes happened, when he began to work with the higher levels of power. He knew ogham, and there were often odd bits of wisdom embedded in his riddling that suggested it might be true. With no word said, his status had become accepted, his foolery licensed among the warriors.

It had taken longer for Fionn to realize that Lomna

had come to Almu not for food or shelter or the company of heroes, but because he himself was there. He knew it because he, too, had been mad a time or two in the past, a wanderer in a world he did not understand, and there were times when he understood Lomna's strange pronouncements only too well.

"It takes a fool to know a fool, and a blind man to see—" chanted Lomna cheerfully.

It was possible to get straight speech from the fool, but not often. One did not always know when his rhymes were meant to be entertaining, and when he actually had something to say.

"And enemies make the best lovers, I suppose?" Fionn replied.

"Ah, my dear, you of all men should know that love is a two-edged sword—"

His father's sword blazed suddenly in Fionn's memory and he turned on the other man. For a moment Lomna's face showed naked fear, then he turned a handspring and came up laughing.

He does not know. Fionn drew a long breath, then another, willing his pounding heart to still. *He does not know how often I have destroyed what I loved!*

"What is the difference between the fish and the sea?" Lomna asked brightly. Fionn forced himself to smile in answer. Silly riddles—he had never liked them since Ailbe won her riddle game. But that was not the fool's fault, or if so, it was the wrong fool!

"The fish sees the sea without knowing; the sea knows the fish without seeing?" he offered. Lomna faced him, his eyes open and innocent, and laid his hand on Fionn's arm.

"But a fish out of the sea makes its presence known. Beware of seeing without knowing, my dear!"

Fionn frowned at him, trying to figure out whether this were another riddle for him to untangle or Lomna's train of thought had just become disconnected.

"Either I have not had enough to drink to understand that, or you haven't," he said finally. "Go on, lad, and get yourself some mead."

There were more men to talk to as the evening went on. At one point he glanced over and saw Ailbe being charming to the fool. It struck Fionn as odd, for she had always seemed to dislike the man. But maybe she had drunk enough to grow mellow as well.

That night, when they lay in the great bed that had once been prepared for Grainne, Ailbe came eagerly into Fionn's arms. She had anointed herself liberally with oil of roses; it almost overwhelmed the sour scent of the mead. But he was no better, he thought, stroking back her soft hair. Hoping he had not drunk enough to unman him, Fionn let his fingers play along the smooth neck and down to cup Ailbe's breast.

Her breasts had grown heavier in the past few years, but they were still firm and round. He ran his fingertip around the nubbin of her nipple, hoping he could arouse her quickly. He could feel his own interest growing, but he did not know if he could sustain it for long. He had tried thinking of Sadb when he made love to her, but the contrast between them always made him angry. It was better to let their joinings remain an encounter between two hungry bodies fulfilling a mutual need.

"Love me, Fionn," she whispered breathlessly. "Hold me tight in your arms."

He had not felt her nipple harden, but she must know what she was feeling. He let his hand slip downward to the warmth between her thighs. Once, he had known how to play a woman as he played his harp, plucking and stroking in ascending arpeggios until she sang. Ailbe gasped as he probed her softness, and though it did not seem to him that she was ready, she reached down to fondle him in turn.

"Take me—I love you. Take me now!" she snarled against his ear, and with her hands urgent upon him he could see no reason not to comply. As he rolled atop her soft body, she opened her thighs to receive him, and his own need driving him at last, he thrust in.

Even then he would have tried to be skillful, but Ailbe bucked beneath him, her nails scoring his back as she whimpered his name. And as his completion overwhelmed him, Fionn forgot for a few blessed moments who she was, and who he was, and found peace.

AS THE DAYS GREW LONGER, THE WEATHER FINALLY began to warm. The folk of the *dun*, tired of winter's confinement, spent as much time as possible out of doors. One day a little past the Equinox, when the air resounded with the bleating of new calves, Fionn took the trail to the bathing pool. Except during the hardest storms of winter it was his practice to go down to the stream each morning. Over the years his feet had worn a pathway into the rocky soil of the hill.

Today some of the men had come with him, though most of them usually made do with the horse trough or sought their own favorite spots up and down the stream. The living gold of springtide lay scattered beneath the trees—green-gold of tansy, creamy glow of primrose, and the brighter gleam of the buttercup all shining against the dark soil. Sceolan lolloped ahead, sniffing out all the new scents and pissing on top of them in an ecstasy of canine involvement with the world.

Fionn grinned at him, wishing that he could understand all the messages that were coming to the dog's nose. He could remember, a little, how it had felt to roam the woods in beast-shape. There were times when he was sorry he had returned to human form.

The others followed more slowly, swearing as they stumbled on the unfamiliar ground. It was Conain mac Luachar and Loegaire, Faobhar and Fearghusa who had come with him, all men in their thirties or forties who had been with him for years. Most of the younger *fénnidi* were still sleeping off the effects of trying to match drinks with Oisin.

Early though they were, someone had been this way before them. Fionn noted the occasional track of a man's bare foot on the earth of the path. Fionn frowned, but when they got to the stream there was no one there. It was not until they started back up the hill, tingling pleasantly from the cold water, that they discovered what the stranger had been doing there.

It was Faobhar who noticed the stave fixed in the earth where the path entered the woods and bent to see.

"It's written all over in ogham! What does it say?" He jerked the piece of wood from the ground and handed it to Fionn.

Fionn's fingers twitched as he suppressed the impulse to cast the thing away. A message so secret, or shameful, that it could not be delivered publicly—and so important that it must be left where he would surely see it? Perhaps it would be better not to know.

"It is only lines on a stick—" he began, but the others laughed at him.

"Have I not seen you make sense of the striations on a stone?" asked Loegaire. "Surely you have not lost your skill—"

The stave felt oddly heavy, as if the meaning it carried were weighting it down. Fionn sighed and turned it so that shadow would make the lines clear.

"*Fearn*—an alder . . ." He traced the three lines scratched inward from the edge and continued to the next grouping. "A stake . . . in a palisade of silver."

"And what does that mean?" asked Faobhar.

"A woman in her court . . ." said Fionn, casting back through his training for the symbolism.

"And the next lines?"

"A sprig of hellebore in a bunch of cresses—" Fionn traced along the indentations. "It means, I think, that her intentions are unwholesome." Against his will he continued to read the ogham, his lips moving silently.

"*The willing husband of an unfaithful wife among a select band of tried warriors." Surely*, he thought with a sinking heart, *that is meant to be me.*

"What is the rest of it?" asked Loegaire. Quickly Fionn moved to the end.

"Something about Luighne," he shrugged as if it made no difference. "But that is up near Taltiu. I do not understand . . ." But he did understand; it was the old story all over again, with Ailbe playing her sister's role. The first betrayal still fettered him. He could not go through it again. With a violence that startled the others, he cracked the stave across his knee, flung it into the brambles, and started up the trail.

"I wonder who it could be," came Loegaire's voice

behind him. The others replied with ribald speculation.

"We do not know," said Fionn as they reached the *dun*, "and it will not do to be spreading rumors. I beg you—keep silence about what you have seen!"

BUT OF COURSE THEY DID NOT OBEY. IN THE SPRING OF the year, when the world was beckoning them to action but it was not yet the time to take the field, everyone was restless. There were more gossip and accidents, and more quarrels.

"Dubhán broke Rionnolbh's arm in a fight over one of my maids—" Ailbe came to him complaining. "If they have nothing better to do than persecuting my women, find some work for them."

"Are you sure the girl did not invite their attentions?" Fionn said blandly. *The maid models her behavior on that of her mistress, I have heard.*

He had heard a great deal, moving silently about the *dun*. The story of the ogham stave had grown in the telling. Even so much as the men knew was enough to stir speculation, and since Fionn was the man who most often took that path, they did not need the third line to guess it had been meant for him. No wonder if the men were beginning to eye Ailbe oddly.

"How dare you? Let them whitewash the ramparts or clean out the stables!" she exclaimed. "Perhaps that will cleanse their minds, and yours!"

"So hot in defense! One would think someone had accused you. . . ."

Her face went white at his words and Fionn's heart sank. It was true, then. He had expected to feel rage, but there was only this sick sorrow. He did not even want to know who had been cuckolding him. He must find an excuse to send her away before someone went beyond riddling to words he would have no choice but to hear.

"FIONN—SIR—THERE'S A BODY UP AHEAD OF US, BEneath a fallen tree!" Caoilte, who could outrace them all, came loping back down the trail.

Fionn had ignored the suggestion about the stables, but he did start the men on training runs out from Almu. With a little luck, they would finish too tired to get into trouble. In any case, Beltane was coming, and it was high time they got back in fighting trim.

"Been there long?" He signaled to the nearest three to follow while the other men continued their run.

Caoilte shook his head, but he still looked rather ill.

"What is wrong, then? Do you know who it is?" Fionn felt a worm of unease begin to uncoil in his belly.

"And how could I be knowing that," Caoilte burst out then, "when the poor fellow has not a stitch of clothes on him, nor his head neither? This was a foul deed, Fionn. Did the murderer think the head would open its lips to accuse him, that he must carry it away?"

"Perhaps—" A little out of breath, Fionn came to a halt by the tree. It had been newly felled, presumably to cover the body that lay in the shallow trench below, and more brush dragged around it. But animals had pulled it away. One of the feet had been gnawed on, but the rest of the body was protected by the branches. Fionn motioned the other men to stay back and looked around him for tracks, but the only ones he could see were Caoilte's. Indeed, the ground had a curiously smooth and even look for wild woodland. The murderer had swept his tracks away.

Fionn sighed. "Nothing to be learned here—lift the tree away." It had been cut, he noted, with the efficient strokes they taught in the *fian*. The knotting in his belly was getting worse. Secret murder was bad enough, but it was beyond all bearing that such a thing could have been done by one of their own.

The corpse had lain there no more than a day. Despite the first stages of discoloration it was clear that this man had been no warrior. His skin was too pallid, his frame too slight. His flesh, though sinewy, did not have the muscles built by hefting shield and spear.

"Who is it?" came the whispers. "Where did he come from?" "How did he die?"

Fionn fought revulsion. Words, images, whirled in his awareness. Some part of him knew the answers but would not admit it. *Does even my mind betray me?* he wondered angrily, set his thumb between his teeth and bit down.

"*Lopped by no common farmer's blow—*" As the trance of Illumination by Rhyme came upon him, the verses burst from Fionn's lips unbidden.

> "*Or by Laigin's folk brought low,*
> *Murdered not by boar, I know,*
> *Nor by falling came this woe,*
> *And not in bed, I see also. . . .*"

Suddenly he saw everything—the supple body and the long-fingered, clever hands, the narrow foot that had left its print on the trail to the stream not so long ago. And with the images, the pattern of his verses came clear to him—**L O M N A**. . . .

"Lomna!" he said aloud. The sickness burned in his throat, or perhaps it was rage. "It is Lomna whose body lies here! Oh my poor foolish lad, is this the answer to all your riddles? Why could you not spill out your suspicions in plain words that would force me to action? Your cleverness has killed you—" He stopped himself. It was his own fault, not Lomna's. The fool had warned him. It was his own foolishness that had refused to understand.

From the tree above him, a raven called. As Fionn looked up the bird cocked its head; one black eye glittered back at him.

"Is that you, Great Queen?" he whispered harshly. "Begone—this meat is not for you! But do not go too far, for I will give you blood to drink, and soon!"

As if it had understood, the raven opened inky wings and flapped heavily away. Fionn laughed mirthlessly.

"Make a litter to carry the body back to Almu," he said to the two younger men. "But you, Caoilte, stretch your legs and go before them. Bring the best of the dogs back with you. Tell Oisin to bring Sceolan!"

THE MURDERER HAD WIPED OUT HIS TRACKS, BUT HE could not hide his scent from the clever noses of Fionn's hounds. They were not used to tracking men, and inclined to give tongue whenever they scented a deer, but Sceolan understood Fionn's instructions, and led them to the pile of blood-soaked leaves where the killing had been done. The murderer had set the head in the fork of a tree while he dragged the body away, then came back for it. For a little while thereafter he tried to cover his trail, and the pursuers grew grim as they began to realize that such woodcraft could only belong to a man of the *fian.*

Then, in haste, or thinking he had done enough, the murderer had ceased his attempts at concealment. Now they saw the prints of a man who was running swiftly, carrying a burden that from time to time left a spot of blood upon the leaves.

Why take the head? Fionn wondered. Obviously a body was hard to hide, and he could understand cutting the head off to delay identification, but if that were the purpose, why not hide it separately in a cleft in the rock or sunk in some deep pool? A warrior carried off the head of his enemy when he wished to boast of his victory, or perhaps to prove to someone else that the deed was done.

Darkness fell, but though they moved more slowly, the *fianna* were accustomed to operating at night, and Sceolan needed no light to sniff out the trail. And presently it became clear that the trail was curving back in the direction of Almu.

"Will he lead us back to our own gates?" Oisin swore.

"I do not think so . . ." Fionn said in a low voice, remembering the last ogham on the stave. "I think it is the Hill of Ualainn that he is making for." *And I can guess whom he will be meeting there.*

They all knew the place, a bare, heath-covered hillock above a brook several arrow-shots north of Almu. And when they neared it they no longer needed the dogs to follow the scent, for the smell of woodsmoke came down to them on the breeze.

"Oisin, Caoilte—" Fionn chose three other men skilled in moving silently. "Surround the hill and make your way towards the top. But do not let him hear you. You must be like mice in the tall grass, or moths on the wind. Do not move until I call!"

With a nod they faded into the darkness. Fionn gritted his teeth and began his own stalk, testing each step before he let his weight down, sliding between branches, and then, as the brush grew more stunted, dropping to his belly and slithering through the heather. The summit was somewhat hollowed, and as he reached it he saw that it sheltered a small fire.

"What was that?"

Fionn froze where he lay. It was a woman's voice. Ailbe's.

"Nothing. A night bird—a mouse in the bracken," the man replied. "I told you that no one could follow me, and if they did, from here we would see them. Is that not why we chose to meet on this hill?"

The voice was sardonic, and familiar. Fionn slithered closer. Two shapes moved beside the fire; he glimpsed Ailbe's face, pale and strained, and something else—The fire blazed up and Fionn stilled, biting his lip to stifle an oath. It was Lomna's head they had there, watching from a stake driven into the ground.

Its mouth was a little open, as if in permanent surprise. Shifting shadow lent the features a horrid animation, and firelight reflected balefully in the empty eyes. It made Fionn uneasy, and his only sin was stupidity. How could the murderer bear that unblinking stare? With black laughter in his heart, Fionn began to work his way around to that side of the hill.

As he got closer to the head, he smelled fish and saw that the man had caught a salmon in the brook and was cooking it on a hot stone. Beyond the fire he saw two more faces—Ailbe's manservant and her maid. Several bundles were piled beside them.

Grainne went forth with no companion but Diarmuid and nothing but a cloak for bed, he thought grimly. *Could you not be your sister's equal, Ailbe, even in running away?* He was behind Lomna's head now, peering through the fronds of fern.

"Here's a portion for you," said the man to Ailbe, cutting into the fish and pulling some of the pink flesh on to another flat stone.

He turned as he did so, and Fionn saw his face at last. *Cairpre!* Black-haired Cairpre, who had imagined himself the darling of all the women ever since Diarmuid went away. Fionn had seen the man flirting with Ailbe and never guessed it went any further. His head was beginning to hurt and it was hard to think, but as the wind stirred the heather he seemed to hear Lomna whispering.

"A speckled, white-bellied salmon burst forth from spawn. It ate, and ate, and now it is eaten. But we all come to that one day . . ." Fionn blinked, for the lips that had formed those words were his own.

"What did you say?" Cairpre had gone dead white.

"I said nothing!" Ailbe replied with an edge of malice. "Perhaps it was an owl on the wing!"

Cairpre bit his lip, and with trembling fingers pulled off more of the salmon to give to the servants.

"What kind of division is that?" asked Fionn, this time pitching his voice with intention to imitate the lilting singsong of the fool. "A drunken groom could do it better! But I will have a piece of the stomach, if you please!"

Cairpre leaped to his feet, staring. So did Ailbe. Clearly, this time she too had heard.

"Get rid of that wretched thing!" she hissed. "Did

you think I wanted you to bring it here?"

"You doubted me—" said Cairpre. "You didn't believe that I could silence the fool! When you learned about the message he had written, you wanted to throw yourself on Fionn's mercy."

"But you *haven't* silenced him!" Ailbe's voice rose hysterically. "He is still talking now!"

And indeed he was, or Fionn was—he was no longer sure from whose lips came the laughter.

"A stake you stuck into me, and a rod of flesh into her, but it is a spear that will pierce you. Fionn will cut you into little pieces when he comes!"

"You! Take it away!" Cairpre motioned to the manservant, who was hiding behind the maid.

"He will burn this hill with fire—" Fionn cackled cheerfully, and the servant, whose eyes were already white-rimmed with fear, gave a moan and fainted dead away.

"Then I will bury it myself!" cried Cairpre, reaching out to take the head.

"You are wrong—that honor belongs to me!" cried Fionn in a great voice, and, uncoiling from his hiding place, he plunged his spear into Cairpre's belly and thrust upward with all the strength he had.

Ailbe screamed. As if that had been a signal, the warriors of the *fian* leaped up from their concealment. Where before had been night and stillness was now a circle of armed men. Fionn looked down and saw Cairpre struggling feebly as he lay curled around the spear. The point had not quite pierced the heart, thought Fionn with an odd detachment. Another jab would do it, though. He reached for the shaft.

"I only took . . . what you . . . did not want!" gasped Cairpre.

"Did you think this was because of the woman?" snarled Fionn. "It is Lomna I am avenging!" And with those words he gripped the spear and began to push upward, not ceasing his steady pressure until the untidy twitches stopped and Cairpre lay still.

"And the woman," Oisin said very quietly. "What do you want done with her?"

Fionn jerked the spear free, and wondered distantly what his face must be showing to make men avert their gaze. Ailbe huddled on the ground, curled around her fear as her lover had embraced the spear.

"So . . ." He spoke with weary distaste. "You are no better than your sister after all. You chose me, knowing how little I had to give. What shall I do with you?"

Her head jerked up. "I am a king's daughter. If you are going to kill me, do it quickly—" There was a murmur from the men as they agreed.

"You are a king's daughter indeed, and so I shall send you back to Temair, where all can see your shame. Spread dissension in Cormac's house, Ailbe, not in mine!"

He turned and very gently began to work Lomna's head up off the stake on which it had been impaled.

"What shall we do with *him?*" Caoilte pointed at Cairpre's body, speaking with the same exaggerated care.

"He left Lomna to the birds. Let him feed the Raven now!"

Chapter 8

AFTER SAMHAIN, WINTER BEGAN TO CLOSE IN ON Eriu. But sometimes there would be a day of golden ripeness, when the warmth of the afternoon sun held the underlying chill at bay. Fionn sat on the ramparts of Almu with his back against the stout logs of the palisade. If he stood up he could see out over the expanse of the Curragh, its frost-seared grasses tawny in the sun. Below him were the well-thatched roofs of the halls and houses that clustered within the *dun* and all the busy activity of the folk within. But here on the wall he sat poised between them all.

He shifted the harp forward on his lap, plucked a phrase of melody, frowned, and tried it again, then added another ogham to the line he had scratched in the whitewash on the wall. It had been a challenge, to find a way to write down music, and as he experimented, gradually his old skill with the harp had begun to return. His fingers were no longer so flexible as they had been when he studied in Cethern's poetic school, but he could play well enough for his own pleasure. The music he composed for himself was clean and pure, without associations. He found rest in its regular harmonies.

But he made no verses to go with his melodies. Once, the craft of words had been a key to release the passions within him. These days he was more concerned to keep his feelings locked up than to reveal them. In the five years since he had sent Ailbe back to Temair he had not slept with a woman, and he had spoken neither spell, nor riddle, nor poetry.

Fionn had finished working out the first part of the music and was thinking of going down when he heard shouting from below. In another moment a small shape shot out from the cookhouse with another, heavy-fleshed and draped in shawls and female, close behind him. Fionn recognized Mongfind. The woman moved swiftly for her age and bulk; a large hand closed on the boy's ear and hauled him up short, gasping.

"Oscar, Oscar, you evil imp—" Mongfind swung the child around and boxed his other ear. "That milk was setting for cream! Folk work hard to feed you, and now you have spoiled it! Ungrateful brat, d'ye think you are living with the Sidhe, that can magic food from the thin air?"

She smacked him again, and Fionn's lips twitched. She sounded so much like Bodbmall in a rage. Oscar twisted and turned in her grip, but he had not made a sound. *Neither did I when I was his age,* Fionn thought ruefully. Mongfind made a final sound of disgust and released her captive, who scuttled off with a speed that suggested the hurt had been mostly to his pride.

For a moment Fionn wondered whether he should say something, but he himself had got worse beatings and survived. Oscar might sulk for a while, but no doubt he would forget by dinnertime.

But the evening meal was almost over, and Fionn had almost forgotten the incident, when mac Lugach came to find him, his sandy brows bent in a frown.

"Mongfind's just come to me," he said softly. "Oscar has disappeared."

"What does your son say?" asked Fionn. Mac Lugach's boy, Glas, was two years younger than Oscar, and slept with him in the loft.

Mac Lugach shrugged. "Doesn't know or won't say—I can't tell."

Fionn nodded. Oisin was off somewhere, probably with a woman, but even when he was at home he had little time for the boy, as if he blamed the child for his mother's defection, or perhaps hated the reminder of what he had lost. He would have to deal with it himself, and perhaps, he thought as he remembered the afternoon's altercation, it was time he took a hand.

Mongfind had looked in all the places one might expect the boy to hide. The *fian*, with a certain amount of ribaldry, searched the unlikely ones as well, but Oscar was nowhere in the *dun*. As soon as dawn broke Fionn set out to find him, taking with him mac Lugach, and Conain mac Luachar, who since the death of his wife was living once more at the *dun*, and Sceolan.

The child moved lightly, and he had made a surprisingly good job of hiding his trail. Following it, Fionn thought he knew how the Liath Luachra might have felt when he himself, in disobeying, had yet done credit to her teaching.

"I used to wish my woman had given me a son,"

said Conain, as he jogged along at Fionn's heels. "But now I wonder. I'm a little old for fathering anyway, so I suppose I'll never know."

Fionn glanced back at him, one eyebrow raised. He had been Conain's age when he fathered Oisin. "I've another idea—why don't you marry again? Find some strong girl to give you a family."

Conain laughed ruefully. "The only girl that's taken my fancy is Aodh's daughter Eargna, and you know how far I'm likely to get with him."

"Well, you could always go see her when her father's away and carry her off," said Fionn. "The man is your friend, and if you haven't actually *asked* him for his daughter's hand, then his vow will not bind him to cut off your ears!"

Conain laughed, but as they went on he grew thoughtful. Fionn grinned to himself, then let the matter slip from his mind, for Oscar's traces were growing more obvious now, the small footprints blurring with fatigue.

It was nearly noon when they found him, curled into a pile of fallen leaves and so deeply asleep that it was not until Sceolan licked his face that he knew they were there. Oscar sat up abruptly, fair skin flushing to a deep crimson as he realized he had been discovered after all.

Fionn squatted down, considering him.

"Well, lad, what have you done, or had done to you, that's so terrible you had to run away?" His tone was carefully mild, conversational, and he did not try to touch the boy. There was a long silence as Oscar looked back at him. *Trying to decide if he can trust me,* thought Fionn, with a pang he had not expected to feel.

Oisin had always had an elfin grace, whether as a child fleeing the *fian*'s hounds, as a grown man half-drunk, or caught up in battle's ecstasy. To look at Oscar, he would not have known the boy to be of Oisin's breeding. But he recognized the stiff shoulders and outthrust lower lip, the sullen bending of the brows, and, above all, the hurt in those grey eyes, recognized them from within. It was as if he looked at the ghost of Demne, the confused, hostile child that he himself had been. And yet, for all his pain, Fionn had always been able to delight in the flight of the wild swans or the sheen on a butterfly's wing. What could give this child joy?

"Mongfind *beat* me . . ." Oscar said slowly at last. "And it was not mischief! I didn't drink the milk—it was for the puppies. Their mother's sick, and old Ferdia said if she couldn't feed them, the pups would have to be drowned!"

Mac Lugach had grown very red as well. It was clear how much he loved the boy, and in another moment he would be ranting at him for having frightened them so. It was a natural reaction, but the wrong one. Fionn held up a warning hand.

"Oscar . . ." he said softly. Slowly, the frowning gaze came back to meet his own. "We will save the puppies if we can. And from now on, remember, if there is trouble, you can always come to me. But sometimes I cannot be here. I am going to leave Sceolan with you, Oscar." The hound's head came up abruptly. He looked from Fionn to the boy and back again. "He is as brave as any *fénnid*, and smarter than many." Conain coughed to hide his amusement and Fionn frowned. What he had said was literally true. "Take care of him, and he will take care of you."

A sound suspiciously like a sob came from Oscar's throat, though his face showed no sign. Then, with a convulsive movement, he threw his arms around Sceolan's neck and buried his face in the silky fur. Above his bent head, the hound's eyes met Fionn's, and there was a light in them that he had not seen there since Oisin was a boy. Sceolan had sired puppies, but they were only dogs. In a sense that he himself barely understood, Fionn's children were his own.

THAT WINTER, OSCAR BECAME FIONN'S SHADOW. THE men laughed to see their leader's mannerisms reflected with the clumsy fidelity of a puppy following an older dog. It was a pity, thought Fionn, that the child seemed to have taken on his grim spirit as well. What was fitting for an old warrior was disturbing in an eight year old. Fionn saw and regretted it, but his own heart had grown a rind as hard as horn and he could not change. And so, no matter what attempts folk made to amuse him, Oscar never laughed.

Conain took Fionn's advice and carried off Eargna one day when her father was away. Aodh laughed when he found out what had happened, for in truth he and Conain had been good friends. It seemed that a peaceful life by the Liffe had not been as attractive as he had expected, for he returned to Almu in time for the Feast of Brigid, and settled back into the life of the *fianna* as if he had never been away.

And so the winter passed. The next summer they were kept busy by raids from Alba, and were glad to go home that autumn and lick their wounds. At the beginning of the campaigning season the following year, the *Ard Ri* summoned the *fianna* to accompany him on a tour through the lands of the subject tribes.

Things had been peaceful for some time, and a tactful display of royal power was a good way to keep them that way.

And so it was that as the fields began to ripen after Midsummer Fionn found himself in Midhe, marching into the green and fertile lands of the Dési Temro, the vassal races of Temair. Their chieftain was another Aonghus, called Gae-Adúath—"Terrible Spear"—a big, blunt man who reminded Fionn of Goll.

"THESE HOUNDS, NOW, ARE OF A LINE WE'VE BEEN breeding since my grandsire's time," said Gae-Adúath proudly, as he led them down the path towards the kennels. The dog that was pacing beside him looked up at the words. For a moment Fionn saw in the domed brow and brown eyes, the long brindled hair and loose skin of the muzzle an echo of the man, as if the hounds had been bred from as well as by the chieftain's line.

He suppressed a smile. He, of all men, should not find that strange, remembering Bran and Sceolan. It seemed odd to walk without the great white hound at his side, but he had kept his word and left him, this summer as last, with Oscar.

"Your hounds are famed throughout Midhe," said the *Ard Ri*, who was walking on Gae-Adúath's other side. "I look forward to seeing them."

The country here was a patchwork of cleared fields and patches of woodland, gently rolling, as if they rested on a green sea. The kennels were clustered in the lee of the rise. They could hear the dogs already, singing out with excitement as they scented a friend. Fionn looked at his host and saw that he was carrying a stained leather bag. No doubt the dogs were smelling the tidbits it contained as well.

"Better stand aside—" said Fionn to the high king, as the note in the yapping changed. He took Cormac's arm and pulled him out of the way as hounds hurtled from one of the pens and engulfed the chieftain in a rippling grey and brindle tide. The yammering reached a hysterical pitch, then calmed as Gae-Adúath shouted them down. One by one, the great beasts sat, tongues lolling, waiting for the man to give them a bit of the meat in his bag. When they held still one could see there were only five, including the one who had come down at Gae-Adúath's heels, their coats a bit rough, for these were working dogs, but their eyes bright with health.

"How did you know they were coming?" asked Cormac, lifting an eyebrow as Gae-Adúath squatted down in the middle of his pack and began to examine ears and paws while they licked his face and hands.

"I spent a year as dog boy to the king of Benntraige," said Fionn. "It was a long time ago, but some things you don't forget." Living with the hounds he had eaten better and slept warmer than at any other time during his wanderings. "These are fine animals," he added, watching the ripple of muscle beneath the shaggy hides. "He is right to be proud of them."

Gae-Adúath finished his inspection, and returned to them, the dogs, the first edge of their excitement blunted, frothing about his knees. Clearly they had always been well treated, and they assumed that anyone their master walked with must be a friend. Fionn felt a cold nose poke his palm and instinctively began to stroke the head behind it. Gae-Adúath, seeing the high king rather hesitantly do the same, grinned.

"I hope you like doing that—" he said. "Now that they know you, they'll not leave you alone. Ah, lads, surely you have been sore neglected." He ruffled the nearest shaggy head. "And no one ever petting you or feeding you, or giving you any attention at all!"

Escorted by the hounds, they moved past the breeding pens, where the nursing bitches lifted their heads and slapped the ground with their tails in greeting without disturbing the fat fur balls that suckled them. Ahead was another enclosure, high walled and roofed over. From inside came an enquiring whine.

All the dogs stopped short, ears pricked, tails still. Then the males began to move forward with a curious stiff-legged gait, neck hairs just a little lifted, but tails waving gently.

"Ah, look at them, the silly fools!" said Gae-Adúath indulgently.

"A bitch in season?" asked Cormac, as the tip of a pink cock peeking from its sheath made the nature of the dog's interest clear.

"A princess of a bitch," confirmed the chieftain, "that I bought from a Connachta man at the last Tailtiu Fair. 'Tis time to strengthen the line with a little outbreeding, and she's a beauty for sure—" His hand sketched the flowing line of back and tail.

"And which of these is to be the lucky dog?" asked Fionn, as the chieftain started to haul aside the wicker screen that covered the top part of the door.

"He sounds as if he would breed her himself if he thought it would serve—" whispered Cormac, and Fionn suppressed a smile.

Two broad paws appeared atop the lower half of the door, with a large head, white as Sceolan's, behind them. The bitch whined again, and the males launched themselves forward. The first banged into the door and was thrust back by Gae-Adúath, while the other two collided before they reached it. In the next instant they were at each other's throats, snarling hideously while the others circled, barking.

Gae-Adúath lunged for the third dog and grabbed the scruff of his neck, shouting for the keepers. Fionn, reacting with the speed of long practice, waded in among the hounds. The two combatants rolled over and over, teeth locked. Fionn poised above them, waiting for the moment when they released that death grip like wrestlers searching for a better hold, then dove in. A sharp tooth scored his arm, but his hands closed on rough fur. He gripped, lifted, and flung the dog across the yard. As it hit the dirt he reached for the other one, his arm cutting off its wind while the frantic keepers ran to secure the animal he had thrown.

"Ye cannot blame them—" said Gae-Adúath when the bitch had been shut away once more, and the loose males all securely tied up so that the dog boys could tend their wounds. "It was the scent of the female, see you, that drove them mad."

"Females!" said Cormac in disgust, as he and Fionn walked back up to the *dun*, leaving the chieftain to supervise the doctoring. "It is not dogs only they drive mad. Cairbre is a dull stick who keeps his poor wife pregnant, though as often as not, she loses the child. Two living sons she has borne him, and one daughter, who is growing very fair. But his brother Ceallach makes up for him. You would not believe the sums I've had to pay out in compensation over his love affairs."

Would I not? thought Fionn. Oisin was in the south

with the rest of the *fianna*, and with luck they would keep him too busy to chase any more women for a while. But he supposed that by next winter the boy would be on the prowl once more. *He is looking for another Eibhir,* he thought, *but you cannot replace one lost love with another. I should know!*

"Females that make trouble, and males that make fools of themselves because of them," said Fionn. "There's not much to choose between them, so far as I can see."

By this time they had reached the gates, and more guests were arriving at the *dun*. The yard was full of warriors bearing the badge of some minor chieftain and ponies laden with gear.

Cormac stopped short, consternation crimsoning his cheeks. "Females—" he said again. "I am sorry, Fionn. Ailbe is here."

IN TRUTH, THOUGHT FIONN AS HE SAT DOWN TO THE evening's feasting, he should have expected it. He knew that Cormac, tiring in his turn of Ailbe's complaints, had married her off to one of the Dési chieftains. It should be no surprise that Gae-Adúath would have summoned them with his other vassals to honor the *Ard Ri*. At least Cormac had been able to request that she stay with the women in the *grianan* instead of serving mead in the hall. But perhaps she would not have done so in any case. From the size of the vats lined up against the wall, the night would be a wet one. Tonight the meadhall would be no place for any woman of breeding, even Ailbe.

Later that evening, when most of the food had been cleared away, Fionn went out to relieve himself before they settled down to the serious drinking. Stars twinkled faintly through a veiling of high cloud that had come in since sunset, and there was a damp chill on the western wind. *Rain by morning,* he thought as he started back to the hall, and slowed his steps, breathing deeply of the cool air.

"Getting ready for the fray?" came a voice from the shadows. "Or have you been puking already?"

Fionn's body recognized those bitter tones before his mind did. Muscles that had tensed to whirl cut short the impulse without relaxing. That was unfair! He could gauge to the drop his own capacity! He took a deep breath and forced himself to be still. Ailbe knew that what she had suggested was untrue, but despite the terms on which they had parted, they had lived together for long enough for her to know it would sting.

"Honey-tongued as ever, Ailbe—" he said softly. "Does your new master appreciate your wit?" Carefully, he turned.

Swathed in a shawl, she was a darker shape in the shadow of the milk shed. He could not see whether she looked older, only the tension in her body told him she had grown no more serene.

"Must you be insulting? Have you not done enough to me?"

"It was not I who began this conversation," he retorted. "And if your life is not to your liking, you can hardly blame me!"

"Can I not?" she said bitterly.

Fionn felt a flicker of anger in his belly and knew it was time to go. But as he turned to go she reached out and hard, clawed fingers closed on his arm.

"How dare you! How dare you walk away?"

"As I recall, lady, it was you who ran away from me!" he hissed in reply.

"It was your fault! You forced me to it!" she exclaimed.

For a moment sheer amazement held him still. "You offered yourself to me! I gave you a home, wealth, the name of wife—"

"The name!" Ailbe echoed. "That was all you gave me! I offered you my heart, and what did you give back to me? I needed love, Fionn mac Cumhal—do you even know what that means? You did not pursue Grainne out of love but from pride. I would rather have had your hatred than that cold courtesy."

"I tried to tell you—" He could feel his hold on his temper slipping. Damn the woman! If she did not cease, he would end up by hitting her, and whose fault would that be?

"It was your own fault that I sought love elsewhere," Ailbe rushed on. "And you killed him, killed him for loving me!"

"I killed Cairpre because he murdered Lomna." Fionn's voice shook. "Not for you!"

"No wonder Grainne ran from you! Killing is the only thing you know how to do!"

"Stop it!" Fionn grabbed her. "Be still!"

"You bring death to anyone who tries to come close to you!" Ailbe hiccoughed hysterically.

Fionn shut his eyes, but faces swirled in his vision as if summoned by her words—the Liath Luachra who had taught him, his first friend, Bran mac Conail, Fionnéces the *Fili*, Oircbél, his fellow student at Cethern's school, Dithramhach his half brother, his nephew Bran. Dead, they were all dead, and how many more good men who had served in the *fianna*? He could not count them, but their spirits wailed around him. His hands were still on Ailbe's shoulders; he slammed her against the wall.

"That . . . is . . . not . . . true!" he cried, but voices inside him that had been silent for years were shrieking otherwise.

For a few moments the only sound was the harsh rasp of their breathing. Then Fionn forced his fingers to unclench and swayed back from her, jerking his dagger free. She sagged against the wall, eyes widening at the flash of the blade.

"Take it—" He flipped it so the hilt was towards her hand. "If I am so evil, take the knife and thrust it home!" He shoved it into her palm and she flinched away. "Are you afraid? No one will know it was you!"

"I am not afraid—" Madness edged Ailbe's laughter. "You are! And so I will not kill you, Fionn mac Cumhal. Instead I curse you to outlive your health and strength and honor—I curse you with a life that lasts until you stand alone and helpless before your enemies!"

Still laughing, she flung the dagger at his feet and ran.

Fionn stood without moving for a long time after Ailbe had gone. He stood until his pulse slowed and the sweat grew cold on his skin and then was dried by the wind. A voice within was yammering at him to go inside, that it was foolish to let a woman's curse upset him so. But it was a very small voice, no match at all for the numb silence that had frozen him, as if he already stood alone in a world from which all other life had disappeared.

It was not until another group of feasters came weaving back from their own trip to the latrines that he regained the volition to bend, stiffly, and pick up his blade.

"Ho—Fionn! We thought you had fallen in, man!" Conain cried. For the past week he had seemed preoccupied, as if something were wrong, but he sounded very merry now.

"He musta found somethin' else to do," Aodh mac Ronain giggled. "Got a woman out here, Fionn?" He looked blearily around him.

Fionn turned on him and the man stumbled backwards, waving his hands in vague apology. *They must be well on with the drinking by now,* he thought, not trusting himself to reply.

"Come in, lord—" The third, a man called Fer-tai, who was Goll's son-in-law, touched his arm. "You're cold as ice."

Cold indeed, thought Fionn. *There is a lump of ice where my heart should be. . . .* But he allowed them to lead him back into the hall.

"We chased 'em o'er the meadow
an' we chased 'em o'er the lea;
we drove 'em down the mountain
till they jumped into the sea—"

Fifty voices, not altogether in tune, were belting out the innumerable verses of the old drinking song.

"An' then we emptied all their barrels,
an' then we drank up all their beer,
we traded horn for horn,
  from sunset till the morn,
an' we're gonna do the same thing here!"

They slammed into the chorus, lifting horns and beakers, and the music faltered as they drank them down.

Fionn drank with the rest, though he was not singing. He had been trying very hard to get drunk ever since he came back into the hall. His perceptions were becoming a little detached, as though his body was working on a slightly different time sequence than his brain, but he could still remember everything Ailbe had said to him. No one seemed to have noticed. None of those who knew him well enough to realize something was wrong were here—Oisin, or Goll, or Diarmuid—He blinked, wondering why he was thinking of Diarmuid now. It was probably just as well. Let them all stay far away. Then maybe they could escape the curse. He held out his horn to be filled again.

The *Ard Ri* was surveying the company with a benign tolerance which disguised quite well the fact that by this point in the evening he was aware of very little at all. His elder son, Cairbre Liffechar, seemed to be one of those whom liquor made more silent, if indeed he had been drinking at all. Fionn had tried a few times to be friendly, but it was clear the boy was not about to change. Not that he was a boy any longer, thought Fionn, noting the threading of silver in the auburn hair. In some ways it seemed to him that Cairbre had been born old.

Not so his brother Ceallach, whose face was flushed with good cheer. He was already beginning to thicken around the barrel and through the neck and jowls. His eyes, though, shone with boyish enthusiasm as he joined in the next verse of the song.

> *"We gathered up the slave girls*
> *an' we rounded up the sheep,*

we collected gold an' cattle,
an' decided which to keep—"

"Well, we know which you'd choose—" shouted one of his friends. "How many virgins have you slept with, Ceallach? D'ye even know?"

The prince pretended to count on his fingers, then gave up, laughing.

"Not my fault—they keep comin' after me. Guess I got a love spot like Diarmuid. . . ." He laughed again, met Fionn's chill gaze, and suddenly became very interested in the contents of his drinking horn.

Diarmuid never boasted about women, thought Fionn. *And his affairs never had to be settled with payments . . . until Grainne. . . .* He thrust the thought away. The other men were beginning their boasts now—who had the most cattle, the finest hunting dogs, the most notable sword.

Fionn could probably have topped most of them, as he had when Aodh and Conain came to challenge him so long ago, but he did not care.

"My Bran Dubh is the best war hound Eriu has seen since the time of mac Datho's dog!" cried Gae-Adúath. That, at least, was probably true.

The tenor of the boasting shifted from possessions to deeds, each assertion winning a round of affirmations or objections from the other men.

"I can run faster than any man of the *fianna* save Caoilte—" said Conain mac Luachar, holding up his horn.

" 'Tis true," said Loegaire. "He came in second in the men's races last year at the Tailtiu Fair."

What will I say when the turn comes to me? wondered Fionn. *I kill everything I love?*

"My woman, Iuchna Ardmor, daughter of Goll mac Morna, is the noblest of women and the best of wives," said Fer-tai. There were some objections to this, but no way to test a statement so subjective.

"I have never yet gone back on my sworn vow," said Aodh mac Ronain complacently, looking around him.

"What about when you let Conain marry your daughter?" asked someone. Aodh reddened a little, but shook his head. "I swore to give her to no man who asked me, but Conain carried her off without a by your leave, so I'm clear!" He laughed and lifted his horn to Conain, who was sitting quite still with clenched fists, and made no reply.

Something about that smug smile struck a spark through Fionn's chill. "Indeed you kept your vow," he said in a low but carrying tone, "but is it not a shame on you to have let your daughter go with no bride-price or settlements between you and Conain and against your will?"

"Indeed that's so," said the others. "You should get compensation. Come on Conain, would you insult the girl you chose for wife by denying her value?" A red flush began to creep up Conain's neck, and his companions, seeing only embarrassment, redoubled their teasing.

But Fionn, whose senses were not nearly as deadened as he had hoped, saw something in Conain's stillness that made him frown.

"This is not the time to be talking of money—" he began, but Conain, goaded beyond endurance, had already started to reply.

"Eargna was beyond price for the fairness of her face and the sweetness of her voice, and gladly would I have paid whatever Aodh desired had he asked it of me!" Something in Conain's voice was beginning to alert the others. Fionn could see men straightening, trying to blink away the fumes.

"But as for her honor, that proved to be of no worth at all, and not one hair from a cow's tail will I pay for a woman I no longer have!" He met Aodh's gaze at last and the older man's high color faded until he was deathly pale.

"What are you saying?" His voice was like breaking steel. "What are you saying about my girl?"

"I am saying she's gone, man, she ran away from me!"

"She was my life . . ." murmured the older man. "She was my honor . . . I only let her go because it was to you. . . . Ah, I have lost her, lost the honor of my house forever now!"

Ceallach lurched up from his seat and made his way down to the bench where Aodh was sitting. "Come now, 'tis not so bad. My own sister ran off, and no one's accused us of dishonor—"

Two of your sisters were untrue, thought Fionn, but he did not say so, for Cormac was stirring beside him.

"What is it?" The *Ard Ri* sat up, pulling himself together with an effort that showed, but when his gaze focused on his son his eyes were almost clear.

"What did you do?" cried Aodh, ignoring Ceallach and turning on Conain. "What have you done to my girl to make her run from you, eh? This would not have happened if you had not taken her away!" He grabbed for Conain, who dodged out of reach, then reeled back and pulled out his sword, which was hanging with his shield behind him on the wall.

"Hold!" cried the *Ard Ri,* and Fionn felt a flicker of admiration for the tone of command that stopped men in their tracks as if he had shaken a silver branch out of Faerie in the hall.

"While I am guesting here, the same rules hold as in my own royal *dun*—" Cormac's gaze held them. "You shall not insult Gae-Adúath's hospitality by fighting in his hall!"

"Outside, then!" growled Aodh, clinging to his sword.

Conain said no word, but he went to his own weapons and took them down. As he did so he looked up, and Fionn knew it was an appeal. *He wants me to stop it. If I could speak, I could do it.* But the cold in his heart held him and he could say no word.

"You cannot let them do it," said Fer-tai. "They are both drunk, especially the old man."

Cormac frowned, but Fionn remained silent.

"Then I call him coward and knave," said Aodh. He was trembling, but his speech was clear. "Well, Conain, will you live with that name?"

"You know I will not," said Conain in a low voice. "Or you would not have thought me fit husband for *her*. It is death between us, Aodh." He took a deep breath, straightened, and turned to the high king. "Lord, I appeal to you to order the battle, if we are not to dishonor the Dési's hall!"

Gae-Adúath did not seem upset—he looked excited, rather, as he had been when the dogs were fighting that afternoon. But Cormac's face was stern.

"I hear you, Conain mac Luachar, and I ask if you will not rather pay compensation to Aodh, and regain the price from the man who carried off your bride?"

"I will pay nothing . . ." said Conain grimly.

"And I will accept nothing, if it come not from him!" said Aodh.

"Listen then to my judgment. This feasting is ended." The *Ard Ri* pitched his voice to carry through the hall. "Let all men seek their beds now, and if when morning comes, you are still of the same mind, we will go down to the island that is in the midst of the river, and you may do your battle there."

I was right to offer him my service, thought Fionn. *But he has never seemed more the high king than now.*

And yet Cormac should not have had to do this. It was he himself who was lord and leader to the two men who were fighting, and he should have found some way to stop it. The echoes of Ailbe's curse had hardly faded and already it was being proved. But she might as well have stabbed him with the dagger he had offered her, for he could not find the will within him to do anything at all.

THEY AWAKENED TO A GREY DAWNING THAT LEACHED color from the world and hope from men's hearts. But Conain and Aodh, if less belligerent, were no less determined than they had been the night before. Eargna had betrayed them both, and since both men loved her too well, it would appear, to accuse her, they could only exercise their fury upon one another. Fionn wondered briefly what had happened to the girl, but he did not let it trouble him long. They were bitches, all of them.

A light drizzle began to fall as the procession wound down the path towards the riverside. The Boann flowed wide and shallow here, dividing to embrace the island. The Isle of Birds it was called, and an osprey perched on the rowan tree that grew above the upstream point, where the brown waters ruffled as they spun left or right around the shore, and on the downstream side a blue heron stood sentinel among the reeds.

The middle of the island was strewn with sand and driftwood from the winter floods, but flat enough for fighting, and it was in that place that was neither within Cormac's kingdom nor yet in any other, that Conain mac Luachar and Aodh mac Ronain met sword against sword and shield to shield. The reeds and young trees that clung to the shore veiled some of the action, but it became clear that although there were not so many years between the two combatants, Aodh was out of training.

But there was nothing wrong with his courage. Even after the first few exchanges used up the energy his rage had given him he fought with dogged persistence. Conain was holding back, and after a time Fionn began to wonder if they might come out of this without tragedy. He had known a fight to lead to friendship before.

The end, when it did come, was almost by chance—a misstep that brought Conain off-balance, and a last spurt of energy that gave Aodh the force to cleave through his foe's bronze banded helm to the bone. Conain reeled back with a cry, red blood streaming over his brow.

They could see him gathering all his forces to strike; his blow bit with excruciating precision through Aodh's neck and shoulder so that his head leaped one way and his right arm another. Blood splattered across the sand like a crimson rain.

Neither the dead man nor the living moved, but it seemed to Fionn that a voice keened shrill upon the wind—

"Woe to the men who saw this sight,
Woe to the heroes who let them fight,
Woe that they set them—man to man—
the two battle champions of Eriu's fian . . ."

They buried Aodh upon the island, but after six weeks in bed Conain seemed cured. But the venom in his head wound drove inward; he was never quite right during the year that followed. One day a madness took him. From raving he passed to a sleep from which he could not be wakened, that lasted for three days until he died. During all that time Fionn had men searching for Aodh's daughter Eargna, but it was not until the autumn that he got word of her and rode to tell her that her husband, as well as her father, were gone.

And it was only then that he learned what Conain had been too loyal to say in Gae-Adúath's hall. The man who had seduced Eargna away from her husband, and then abandoned her, was Oisin.

Chapter 9

AT FIRST GLANCE THE FOREST POOL SEEMED ENTIRELY still, a circle of peat-brown water on which a few yellow leaves were floating, mirroring Fionn's face, framed by the twined trunks of willow trees. It was only when he looked past the surface that he saw, through the amber depths, distorted shapes of stones and the wavering strands of waterweed stirred by the secret upwelling of the spring.

Fionn cupped his hands to drink; drops spilled between his fingers, shattering the images. When the water stilled once more, it was his son's face that Fionn saw mirrored in the pool. Beneath the autumn gold of his hair Oisin's eyes were the same changeable pellucid brown as the water, but what lay behind them?

Fionn splashed water over his face and then sat back on his heels with a sigh.

"I have been to see Eargna . . ." He did not look at his son.

There was a short silence. "I did not cast her out. It was she who felt dishonored and would not stay with me."

"But it was you who persuaded her to leave her husband," Fionn said heavily. "Because of you, a woman's life is in ruins and two good men have died. . . ."

"Because of me?" Oisin exclaimed. "If I did wrong, at least I did *something*! You sat there without a word, I have been told, and let the quarrel go on until they drew their swords. You would have stopped a dogfight before it got that far—why didn't you stop your men?"

"Because—" Fionn broke off. *For the same reason you took the woman,* he thought, *because another woman ran away from me.* "If you do not know the best thing to do, best do nothing at all," he muttered instead.

Oisin gave a snort of disbelief. "If you really thought that, you would not be leading the *fianna*!"

Fionn lifted one eyebrow, wondering how he had been put on the defensive in a conversation which had been meant to condemn his son.

"I was wrong to take her!" exclaimed Oisin. "I admit that—why can't you admit that you were wrong as well, and accept the invitation to feast at Rath Grainne?"

Fionn looked up sharply, understanding now why Oisin had followed him. When the message first arrived, Fionn's instinct had been to flee in the opposite direction. Peace and friendship they were offering, an alliance to replace the armed neutrality that had been between them so long. For a moment Fionn saw Diarmuid as he had in the mist by the quickentree, and his throat ached with longing. And what had the bearing of five children done to Grainne? He wanted that friendship, but his heart misgave him. Ailbe's curse was still upon him—or perhaps it was his own twisted nature that made him more dangerous the more deeply he cared. Dare he risk seeing Grainne and Diarmuid again?

"You don't understand—"

"I understand some things!" Oisin said passionately. "I understand that when a creature ceases to move—to fight its fate—it might as well be dead! Doing nothing can be dangerous too! Please, Father—we all need this reconciliation. . . ." His voice softened.

It was true, thought Fionn, that the men who had known Diarmuid in the *fianna* had never liked being his enemies. Perhaps they could all make a new beginning with the turning of the year.

"Very well. I will try," he answered. A breath of wind parted the leaves and sunlight flashed from the water; or perhaps it was the radiance of Oisin's sudden smile.

And so, as the moon waned towards Samhain, Fionn and his household did not head home to Almu. Instead, they turned their steps westward towards Rath Grainne, hidden in the forests below Ben Gulban where the headlands sloped down to the sea.

"THE INVITATION WAS GRAINNE'S IDEA," SAID OISIN. Fionn, who had been watching the field where Diarmuid's children were competing at tossing the javelin with the lads of the *fian*, turned, one eyebrow lifting in enquiry.

"What does she want?" The meadows around Rath Grainne were full of fat cattle, her storehouses well stocked with provisions, and rich hangings kept out the drafts in her feasting hall. Diarmuid had earned enough renown for any one lifetime. What could they possibly need?

"Nothing for herself or for him," said Oisin. "It's her daughter, Eachtach—" He nodded towards the field, where Diarmuid's eldest child, her black braids tossing, had just sent a slender lance winging towards the goal. "She's grown husband-high, but she scares off most suitors. Grainne seems to think that only in the *fianna* is she likely to find a man who can handle her . . ."

"I can see the problem," said Fionn, as the girl's second lance plunked into the target close beside the first. "To be truthful, I would rather test her for admission to the *fian*!"

Oisin laughed, his eyes on the girl. "She's good, isn't she?"

"Better than her brothers, though they are young yet and may grow to greater skill. But be careful how you look at her—" his tone grew hard and Oisin flushed. "I do not think it is the House of Baoisgne with which they seek alliance, only the *fian*!"

Oisin did well to blush, thought Fionn, as Eachtach strode forward to take her lances from the target and handed them to her younger brother. If he himself had not the gift to make any woman happy, his son, apparently, had no talent for fidelity. But there must be some lad among the younger men who would be of good enough birth, valor, and character to make Grainne a fitting son-in-law.

It was Donnchadh's turn to throw. Olann, the son Diarmuid had got by Bressal Bélach's daughter, looked on indulgently. When they settled at Rath Grainne, she had taken the boy into her household and treated him like one of her own. The third brother, Eochaid, bounced with eagerness behind him while the two little ones watched enviously. Fionn sighed, wishing that Oscar could do as well. Sometimes he wondered if his grandson's clumsiness was a deliberate attempt to attract his famous father's attention by failure since he seemed unable to win Oisin's affection by trying to do well. It was hard to believe that any child of his blood could be so consistently and comprehensively unsuccessful at any kind of warlike exercise. Perhaps this winter he himself could take a hand and teach Oscar as he had been taught by the Liath Luachra and Bodbmall.

When I was a child they seemed ancient, he thought, remembering how the warrior-woman had switched his legs to make him run, *but how old were they really? Was it age that bent the Liath Luachra's limbs, or all those years in the wilds?* It occurred to him that when he first knew him, even old Fiacail could hardly have been much more than the age he himself was now.

The thought made him shiver. Or perhaps it was just that the air chilled quickly at this time of year. The sun was sinking behind the tableland of Ben Gulban, and with the light behind it, the mountain seemed larger, its blunt bulk looming ominously above the glen and the cluster of buildings around the feasting hall. It was a fancy, surely—he had grown too accustomed to the windswept height of Almu. But he found himself shivering once more. He drew the folds of his *brat* up over his shoulders, suddenly looking forward to food and a warm fire.

THAT EVENING, AS THEY FEASTED ON FAT BEEF AND mutton from Diarmuid's herds, the talk turned to hunting. Fionn was content to let the conversation eddy around him, allowing his eyelids to droop as if he had grown sleepy from the heat of the hearth. But his hooded gaze returned ever and again to the faces of Grainne and Diarmuid, as if they were a puzzle he must solve.

That was as good a way to think of it as any, it occurred to him, as young Eachtach refilled his horn with ale. These were the two people whom he had loved and hated as much as anyone in the world, and if they were to be friends in the future, he needed to understand them.

Fionn had been afraid that he would be overwhelmed once more by Grainne's physical splendor. But five children and her wanderings in the wilds had taken the edge from her beauty. Now, however, Fionn was beginning to wonder if he had claimed immunity too swiftly. True, the sun-bright hair had darkened—now it was the tawny gold of the turning leaves. Childbearing had thickened her waist, but her added bulk only made her look stronger. And her skin, that had been so fair, had not been browned so much as ripened by the wind and sun.

But it was none of these things that was making it so hard for him to look at her, but her eyes. They had blazed with defiance in Temair and he had been dazzled. Now they held depths he could drown in. *She has grown . . .* Fionn decided, and turned his gaze away. It was easier to stare into the fire.

"I remember, Oisin, when you hunted the stag of Inis Bo Finne," said Caoilte. "That was a hard trail, and a harder fight at the end of it, eh?"

"It was Fionn who actually killed him," said Oisin quietly, as if the subject were still sore.

"That was after you had brought down the feral boar of Balar, was it not?" asked Dubhtach. For this visit Fionn had brought as many of the men who had been Diarmuid's companions as were still with the *fianna*. It was like turning back the years to see them all laughing around the fire. But he found that even now he was not quite ready to look closely at Diarmuid.

"Now *that* was a pig!" exclaimed Caoilte expansively. "Fierce, and fat —I could scarcely carry him, and he fed the whole *fian*. I've never heard of one like him since that day!"

"*I* have!" young Donnchadh turned to him eagerly. "There's a boar called Gulban who roams our mountain. He's a big, black beast almost as old as my father—at least he's been there since before I was born. He tears up the farmer's fields sometimes, but so far he has evaded or killed everyone who tried to hunt him."

The boy's voice had gone low and thrilling, and he was glancing around him to see if he had impressed anyone with his tale. It was only to be expected, thought Fionn. Every district had its black beast, whose exploits grew greater with every telling. There was no reason why hearing about this one should make him shiver as if the boar he had killed on Sliab Muicce when he was scarcely older than this lad were glaring at him once more.

But some boars were more than pigs. And even allowing for a boy's exaggeration, this one had lived beyond the span of his kind.

"Has he now?" said Oisin, his own eyes kindling. "Well, perhaps he has been waiting to meet the hunters of the *fian*!" Diarmuid sat up like a hound at the packmaster's call.

"If that pig needed killing, my father would have done it!" said Eochaid. His brothers, little Connla and Selbsercach, grinned up at him.

"You know our father never hunts boar—" began Eachtach, but Oisin interrupted her.

"What do you say, Fionn? Shall we go out tomorrow and show this beast who rules the forests of Eriu?"

The glow began to fade from Diarmuid's eyes. *Good,* thought Fionn, *he is remembering the* geas *that is upon him.*

"Not if you are wise," he said aloud, trying to hit the right balance between repression and amusement. He had to discourage them without stirring too much curiosity. "The time is drawn too close to Samhain Eve to hunt a boar who may be a creature of the Sidhe."

"And when did we ever fear *them*?" asked Caoilte.

"Never," said Fionn evenly, "when there was a reason for fighting. But even a *fénnid* does not stir up a hornets' nest just to see if they can sting."

Everyone laughed, and the conversation turned to other things, but Diarmuid was looking into the coals on the hearth as if he saw visions there, and though with so many people inside it the feasting hall was almost too warm, Fionn's skin prickled with chill.

FIONN AND THE SENIOR MEMBERS OF THE FIANNA HAD been given beds inside the feasting hall while Oisin and Caoilte and the rest made camp in the meadow below the rath. The sleeping furs were comfortable, but he found himself drifting in and out of consciousness, listening to the snorts and sighs of the sleeping men. Grainne and Diarmuid lay in a roundhouse of their own, as did her children, and Fionn was glad.

He would have found sleep even harder if he had lain in the same house in which Grainne slept with Diarmuid in her arms.

A little before dawn the demands of nature gave him an excuse to rise from his bed and go outside. As he was returning, a call, like the howling of a hound but purer and sweeter than any dog Fionn had ever heard, drifted down from the mountainside. He stopped short, listening.

"What's that?" came a voice from within the roundhouse he was passing—the voice of Diarmuid.

"A dog, my darling. Perhaps the *fianna* have decided to get an early start on their hunting." Grainne's voice wavered drowsily.

"That is no dog from Fionn's pack—" he persisted. "I know the voices of his hounds."

"Then it is some hound of the Sidhe, howling to tease you. Lay your head against my breast and I will shield you from the sound."

Diarmuid laughed softly, and Fionn found himself shivering, but he did not stir. When Diarmuid and Grainne had first run off together he had tormented himself, wondering what they said when they lay in each other's arms.

"Sleep, my love," she said softly, her voice deepening as if she chanted a spell, "as Dedidach of the high poets slept in the south when he took the daughter of Morann from Conall of the Red Branch. Sleep, my darling, as Finnchadh of Assaroe slept in the north when he took stately Sláine. Sleep, heart of mine, as Aine daughter of Gailian slept in the west when she fared by torchlight with Dubhthach. Sleep, you sweet man, as gallant Degba slept in the east when he bore away Coinchenn daughter of Binn."

In the distance, the hound howled once more. She stopped speaking; it seemed to Fionn that he stopped breathing, as they waited for it to call again. One of the *fian*'s dogs barked and was hushed. An owl called from the hill. Then there was silence. Fionn heard Grainne sigh. Then she began to sing.

> *"Sleep awhile, a little here,*
> *dear lad to whom my love I give,*
> *For sure there is no need to fear,*
> *Sleep in my arms, and thou wilt live."*

That might even be the truth, thought Fionn bitterly, for certainly some magic had preserved Diarmuid throughout the years when he was hunting him.

> *"The hornless doe does not know sleep;*
> *she watches o'er her spotted fawn.*
> *The lovely linnet, chicks doth keep,*
> *and so shall I, until the dawn.*
>
> *The duck her little ones among,*
> *dares neither slumber nor take rest;*
> *tonight the grouse with sheltered young*
> *is wakeful on her storm-tossed nest."*

Fionn closed his eyes. Donait had sung to him when he stayed with her, and his mother, one time only, so very long ago. But no other woman, even Sadb. Grainne's voice was warm and low. Perhaps he could carry the sound of it with him and sleep himself when he got back to the hall.

> *"West from Greece, no match for thee*
> *in valor lives; and so I wake.*

If thy sweet face I did not see,
my loving heart would surely break."

Fionn's eyes opened. The spell continued, but it was not for him. A fragment of memory teased him—Brigid's priestess, promising Diarmuid "the great love, that devours like a living flame." There had been more, but he could not remember it, for Grainne's song claimed him once more.

"If children from their home were torn,
such were the parting of us twain,
or body from the soul were lorn,
oh hero mine, so I remain."

Grainne's voice trailed into silence, and Fionn gathered his forces to move away. Then he heard the sound of a kiss.

"What, have I not sung you into slumber?" Grainne's voice trembled, but not with laughter.

"Come here, witch. It is not sleep to which your spell has sung me," said Diarmuid in a voice Fionn had never heard from him. "Come, my beloved, and I will show you—" There was more movement, then he heard her gasp.

"Never parted—" she whispered.

"Body and soul—" Diarmuid replied.

There were other sounds, and Fionn shook where he stood, his own body feeling what they were feeling as a leaf reflects the movements of the wind, until at last he heard Grainne cry out and her lover's long groan. He fled back to the hall and burrowed into his sleeping furs, where he lay, alternately sweating and shivering, until uneasy slumber claimed him.

FIONN HAD HOPED TO REST AT LEAST UNTIL THE OTHERS were stirring, but he found himself awake, the sweat still clammy on his brow, just when the first light was edging the hide that covered the door. For a moment he could not imagine what had awakened him. Then he heard the belling of a hound, not the unearthly howling of the nighttime, but a very mortal singing that was echoed by a discordant yammering.

Cursing softly, Fionn fought free of the sleeping furs. He needed no magic to understand what had happened. Oisin and Caoilte were going after the boar of Ben Gulban. As he pulled on his leggings he wondered why he was so anxious. The boar was not forbidden to the *fianna,* only to Diarmuid. But he could not deny the urgency that drove him to stuff some scraps left from last night's feast into his pouch, and to take up his tight-woven *brat* and his spear.

"So you've decided to join in the hunting after all—" said Loegaire, as Fionn pushed past the hide and daylight rushed into the hall. But Fionn did not answer him.

The early morning air was chill, and before long Fionn's brogues were soaked with dew. But he was used to that. He lengthened his stride, following the *fianna* up the mountain, and soon the exercise loosened stiff limbs and he began to think his anxiety had been born of foolish night fears. Yet still he was drawn upward, as to a meeting long-appointed, and the warmth of the sun on his back did not reach the chill within.

The lower slopes of Ben Gulban were thickly

wooded, young oaks growing strongly out from the hillside, as the land rose, varied by an occasional scattering of pine. Where the little burns came splashing down the undergrowth was still rank and green, and as the air warmed, the damp soil beneath the trees released a rich vegetable perfume.

The dogs should have little trouble picking up a scent today. If they could find the slot where the boar went down to drink in the dawning, they could trail him back to his lair. Fionn took a deep breath—he could almost track by scent himself on such a day, though the hunters were leaving a clear trail. He remembered how the world had been a tapestry of odors when he had been out of his head and roamed for a time as a young boar.

He heard ravens calling and hastened his steps, but he smelled the blood before he found them. Beneath a tangle of birches he saw churned earth and the bodies of two dogs. The birds flapped away to the nearest branches, eyeing Fionn balefully as he noted the typical ripping stroke that had spilled the dogs' entrails on the ground. They had found the boar, or perhaps he had found the hunters, thought Fionn, as he read the trail. But they were long gone, and the chase led upward.

Partway up the slope, Fionn found another body, this time that of a man. The trail grew confused, and he wondered if he would be able to see better from the summit.

Breathing harder than he had expected, Fionn finished the last scramble and came out onto the rolling top of the tableland. After the close woods it was like emerging on top of the world. Light blazed down from the bright bowl of the heavens, blinding him. For what seemed a long time he could only stand leaning on his spear, absorbing that radiance.

When his vision cleared, there was someone else there with him on the summit, his figure sharp-edged by the brightness of the day. Fionn blinked, but the image remained, and he felt his heartbeat booming in his own ears like the beating of spear on shield when a warrior faces his foe.

"Is it you who are holding a hunting on my mountain?" Diarmuid spoke very quietly, but Fionn knew that voice, and hearing it, was able, finally, to focus on the man.

Diarmuid had his favorite dog with him on a chain, a strongly built, brindle-coated hound. He was dressed, like Fionn, in hunting leathers, and held a boarspear, not the Gae Derg, the spear he took to war. An old sword hung by his side. Fionn himself was carrying Birga, but these days that weapon rarely left his side—there had been too many times when an afternoon's hunting turned to war.

How is it with you? he wanted to ask. *How has it been for you through all those years when we were parted? Was Grainne enough for you, or did you miss my companionship at all?* But he could not find the words.

"Oisin and some of the other young fools got up before dawn. After drinking all night, most likely," he said instead. Neither he nor Diarmuid had spoken the other's name. But as he met that hesitant smile, it seemed to Fionn that there were things that Diarmuid, too, did not know how to say.

Fionn had not been able to look at him the night before; he did so now, as a girl looks at the lad she loves, or a father at his son. But Diarmuid was not a boy. He must be—Fionn thought backward—nearly the age he himself had been when he fathered Oisin. When they met at the quickentree Diarmuid had been gaunt with hard living, but the past years of peace had put some flesh on his bones. He looked, not stout, but solid, and there was a threading of silver in the raven hair.

"You are alone. That's unusual. Where are your attendants and companions?"

Fionn stared at him. *Is he implying that he could kill me here and no one would know?*

"I came up after them. I suppose I thought that if I caught up in time, I could stop them, but I was too late. They have found the boar, and he has already begun his killing—" He paused, as the wind carried the sound of dogs and a man's scream from below. "Soon, I think, they will come this way. It might be better if we left them this hill."

"Since when was it the custom of the *Rígfénnid* of Eriu to flee from before an enemy?" Diarmuid chided gently.

"It is not for my sake that I would retreat, but for yours," snapped Fionn. "Or have you forgotten the *geas* that was laid upon you?"

"I remember—" The other man's eyes came up to his, and Fionn could not look away. Grainne's gaze had become like a deep well, but Diarmuid's was clear as the waters of a flowing stream. "I think you guessed why I have never hunted this boar. Do you really believe that Gulban is my brother reborn?"

"I think it very likely," Fionn said hoarsely. A fist of fear had gripped his guts and was beginning to tighten there.

Diarmuid let out his breath in a long sigh, looking

around him as if he had only now noticed the beauty of the day. And indeed, from this height the view was a wonder; to the east, where the land fell away in fold after fold of field and forest until it dimmed into purple distance, or westward, where beyond the blunt prow of the mountain danced the silver shimmer of the sea. A long moment passed when neither of them spoke. Fionn wondered if Diarmuid was also thinking of other times when they had stood so together, delighting in the loveliness of the world. Then he turned abruptly to Fionn.

"Do you remember that other *geas* that Oisin spoke of when we hunted the stag? A man cannot flee forever, whether from fate or from fancies. No more than he can run away from an enemy. Have you made this hunting to trap me, Fionn mac Cumhal?"

Diarmuid had spoken softly, but in Fionn's heart a spark of anger flared.

"Before the gods, it was against my advice that the *fian* began it. If you seek for a cause, why not name Grainne, whose invitation brought us here. Call Grainne the cause of all our troubles, for was it not she who enticed you to that abduction and so destroyed the good companionship that you had with the *fianna* of Eriu and with me?"

"Never Grainne!" Diarmuid exclaimed. "Though I should see her with a bloody sword above the body of my dearest friend, though I should hear her speak treason, I would not believe it. Grainne is the justification for the world."

And that, thought Fionn, as he remembered the singing he had heard in the darkness, might very well be true. For Diarmuid, at least, she must be the justification for the past sixteen years.

Another shout brought his head up. The chase was drawing closer as the *fian* sought to bring the boar to bay.

"You can run when reason requires it," he said flatly. "You fled from me."

"It was not out of fear that I fled you," retorted Diarmuid. "I did not wish to have your blood on my hands!"

"Do you think you could have defeated me?" Fionn felt the old rage rise up within him. On the hillside below he heard a scrabbling and the deep grunt of the boar.

"It was you yourself who taught me—even now I could strike you down—" Diarmuid began, but Fionn scarcely heard.

It was not love, then, that kept him from coming to blows with me? Was it because he pitied me? He was shaking so hard he could hardly hold the spear. Blindly he turned away. *If I stay here, I will kill him and be forsworn!*

"Fionn mac Cumhal, is it my spear or your own anger you are fleeing from now?" Diarmuid's mocking call brought him around.

"Follow me and find out," he said bitterly, "or stay and meet your doom on the tusk of a boar. It is all one to me!" Using the shaft of his spear as a staff, he stumbled back over the lip of the hill.

Diarmuid's voice floated after him. "I have run long enough. If it be here I am fated to die, I have no power to shun it."

FIONN SLIPPED AND SLID DOWNWARD, HEEDLESS OF THE branches that clawed him, until he came to rest against the rotten stump of an old tree. Moss cushioned the impact, and for a time he crouched there, waiting for his heartbeat to slow; waiting for his tears to end. It was the boar's cough of challenge that brought him upright, tense and listening, once more.

He heard the pig squeal its rage, and it seemed to him that the earth trembled as it gouged the stony soil; there was a scuffling in the dry grass at the top of the hill, but no sound at all from the man. He heard a yip and the sound of the hound running off down the mountain. For the time it takes an eagle to fly across the top of the mountain he continued to listen. There came a cry, more of surprise than pain, from Diarmuid, and then nothing at all.

Suddenly frantic, Fionn grabbed Birga and clambered back up the bank. The hillock was empty except for Diarmuid's abandoned spear. But flat though the ridge might seem from a distance, it was scored and folded by ravines. The boar's prints, deeply sunk in the damp ground, led down one of them, but Diarmuid had left no footprints at all.

Fionn looked around him in confusion. Had Aonghus Og sent down a wind to bear his darling away? But the air held no scent of magic. Frowning, he looked once more at the tracks of the boar. Then he began to grin. He thought he knew what had happened, but he wanted to see it. He scrambled down the slope, following the trail.

A few minutes later he caught a glimpse of them, Diarmuid with his long legs clasped tight around the boar's barrel, holding on for dear life to its tail. The outraged pig bounced and bellowed as it tried to dislodge him. Fionn caught his breath on a bark of laughter. For certain, the boar of Ben Gulban was a monster, as big as a pony, and as black as a dead coal. Then the strange pair plunged around an outcropping of rock and disappeared.

Down the corrie and up again Fionn tracked the boar. Through the stream whose waters, picking up color from the red rocks they flowed over, gave their name to the waterfall, and onward he ran. As the trail passed through a patch of woodland, he heard a raven call again. But this time there was only a single bird, though grown beyond mortal size. Her two eyes glittered with flame.

"Ho, son of Cumhal," croaked the raven, "what trail do you follow so eagerly?"

Fionn stared up at her, breathing hard. "What is it to you, bird of ill omen?" he answered, seeing around her the shimmer of the Otherworld.

"I wish to know on whose flesh I will be feasting this Samhain Eve."

Fionn remembered then that it was the last day of the year, and his flesh grew cold. This was no good day on which to meet the Morrigan, and she his sworn enemy.

"It is the boar of Ben Gulban that I follow," he said carefully, "and you shall have your portion as an offering."

"And what of the man who rides him," she asked.

"He is no meat of yours!" Fionn exclaimed, and made to go past her.

"What, are you so greedy?" she said then. "Will you drink his blood yourself for your revenge?"

"I have made peace with Diarmuid!"

"Peace!" As the raven said it, the word was a curse. "What peace can you have, and the groans of his enjoyment of your woman still ringing in your ears? What peace can you have, and your hide still stinging with the lashes of his pity and his scorn?"

The foot that Fionn had lifted to go forward came down again as he swayed. It was true, and he had left Diarmuid to his fate. Why was he following him?

"It is fated that the boar of Ben Gulban shall kill his brother," rasped the raven. "Diarmuid's life has been forfeit since he was seven years old. Go your way, Fionn mac Cumhal, and no man will give you the blame!"

Fionn looked up at her. "Why are you trying to delay me? Is it that I could save him?"

The raven's caw became wild laughter. "Go then, but you will only find sorrow! I care nothing for the fate of Diarmuid mac Duibhne—my business is with you!"

"I deny you!" cried Fionn.

"Do you think denial will serve you? You will serve me, son of Cumhal. With your will or without it, you will serve *Me*!" Black wings snapped open suddenly, and before he could think of an answer, she was winging away.

Gut twisting with apprehension, Fionn looked for the tracks once more. Now they led upward. He pushed himself up the slope, hearing behind him the sound of dogs and men.

The trail ended in a grassy hollow in the hillside that faced towards the sea.

Fionn's foot struck a fragment of Diarmuid's sword. The other half flashed in the sunlight a short way away. And there was the hilt, still buried in the head of the fallen boar. And Diarmuid, lying in a pool of crimson, curled tightly as if that could keep his entrails from spilling out through the great gash the tusk of the boar had torn from his lower belly up towards his heart.

But he was still alive, though with every shallow breath a little more blood expanded the pool. Walking carefully, as if something, perhaps he himself, would shatter if he trod too heavily, Fionn moved towards him.

"Diarmuid . . ." Fionn knelt, whispering his name. The other man's eyes, dilated with pain, fixed on his own. His lips moved.

"You cannot . . . flee. . . ."

"Don't talk—" Fionn started to say, but what did it matter? No man recovered from wounds like these. The only choice was whether one died quickly or slow.

"Heal me . . ." Diarmuid said then.

Fionn stared at him. Were the man's wits already wandering?

"Bring me water in your two hands . . . and I will be easier . . ." As Fionn shook his head, Diarmuid continued, "When you ate . . . the Salmon of Wisdom . . . you gained that power. Sing a spell over the water . . . for me."

"I have no power for healing. Only for destruction," Fionn said bitterly.

"You do not know . . ." breathed the dying man. "Even now . . . you do not know what you can do!"

"By Miach's mighty herbs of healing, Fionn," came a voice from behind them, "get him something to drink if he thinks it will give him ease!" Oisin had come up with the rest of his hunters, who stood round staring in shocked recognition. Their faces seemed shadowed. Fionn glanced up, and saw that clouds were moving in swiftly from the west, veiling the sun.

"I could not kill you, and you could not kill me . . ." Diarmuid muttered. "It is not enough . . . I see . . . now. . . ." His voice trailed off, and Fionn bent closer. "There must be . . . love."

Fionn sat back, his face working uncontrollably. "There is no water here," he said harshly. "How can I give you what I do not have?"

"But there is!" exclaimed Caoilte. "Just down the hill rises a pure cold spring."

"Get the water!" said Oisin dangerously, "or I will strike you as dead as the boar!"

"Do not—" gasped Diarmuid. "It must be . . . freely given!"

The gaze of twenty pairs of eyes pierced Fionn's hide, and all the light was going out of the world. Painfully, he got to his feet, and Caoilte ran ahead to show him the way.

As Fionn cupped the water in his hands, its chill shocked him back to awareness. This was ridiculous! Diarmuid was dying, and his wits were wandering, that was all. He started back up the hill, but as he neared the fallen man he stumbled, and the water ran out from between his hands.

"I can do nothing to help you," he said, flinching from Diarmuid's drowned gaze.

"I did not say so . . . " whispered the dying man, "when Miogach held you prisoner at the ford of the quickentrees. . . ."

"Go again, Fionn," said Oisin, and the *fian* growled its agreement.

Fionn shook his head, but he went once more to the spring. This time he carried the water more carefully, but as he neared Diarmuid, the raven called from the tree. Hearing that cry, Fionn remembered how

Grainne had cried out in Diarmuid's arms, and he started, and his palms opened, and the water slipped away.

"When you carried Grainne off from Temair and shamed me before all the men of Eriu you needed no help from me!"

"The guilt of that . . . was not mine," gasped Diarmuid. "Grainne put a *geas* upon me to carry her away." His gaze sought the pig. "If I . . . had honored this prohibition as I did that one . . . I should not be lying here . . . now." He had always been white of skin, but now his face had no color to it at all. Shock and loss of blood were finishing him fast.

"That is true," said Oisin, his tone less hostile now. "And it is my shame that I counseled him to do as she asked."

"And you, Diarmuid," asked Fionn, "are you sorry that you obeyed Grainne's call, and departed from me?"

Their eyes met, across the sixteen paces that separated them, across the sixteen years. "I loved . . . you," whispered Diarmuid. "But *she* was . . . the Lady. . . ." His gaze lost focus and he began to smile at something only he could see.

Without a word, Fionn turned and went back to the spring. He hurried this time, clamping his hands tightly together, and when he came back up the hill he neither stumbled nor let go. Until he reached Diarmuid's side he held the precious water, held it until he bent over him, calling his name, and looked into eyes that would never see anything anymore.

Even then he held on to the water, rocking back and forth while the men of the *fian* made three great shouts of grief against the sky. It was only when the first drops of rain splashed down that Fionn opened his hands, and the water of the spring and of the sky and of Fionn mac Cumhal's own weeping fell upon the slack face and began to wash the mud and the blood away.

Oisin pulled off his cloak and laid it across the shattered body. "We should make a litter to take him home."

Fionn looked up at the heavens. Even this close to the sea he had never known a storm to come up so fast. The wind was as cold as winter, but there was yet in it a hint of apple blossom that made him weep all the more.

"Leave him—I think it is Aonghus Og himself that is coming now . . ." He looked one last time at Diarmuid's body, then turned to the *fian*. "We must get down the hill, and quickly." The men looked at him doubtfully, and he forced his voice to the old tone of command.

"I swear by all the gods that it was not I who made this hunting, nor I who set Diarmuid on to follow you. Think what you will, but if he finds us here, Aonghus will see only that his foster son is slain, and destroy us all."

Thunder cracked in the distance, and suddenly they believed him, at least regarding the god. No doubt the men of Eriu would hold him accountable when Diarmuid's death was known, and it was yet another reason for the Sidhe to count him an enemy. But as he followed the men along the twisted path down the mountainside, Fionn was not sorrowing for that, or even for the grief that he would be bringing to Grainne soon.

It was Diarmuid's face that Fionn saw ever before

him, and Diarmuid's voice that he heard, and the grief that wracked him was that not until the moment when Diarmuid lay dying had he understood that he had fought the other man so long and painfully not because he hated him, but from love.

Chapter 10

"BELTANE, OH BELTANE, BLOSSOMING BEAUTY—"

Once, Fionn had sung with joy at the coming of summer. But not this year. He could remember the words to his Beltane song, but not the music. The keening of the Guillbinnach, the little curlew whose wailing call haunted the twilight, seemed a more appropriate song. In Fionn, there had been no music since Diarmuid died.

Throughout that winter, sorrow clung like a black beast to his shoulders. Spring arrived wet and cold with an unsettled feel to the weather, as if summer were undecided about coming this year. Nonetheless, Fionn had led the *fian* out just after Beltane. By now they had been in the field long enough for the moon to wane and wax to full once more, but though the weather was finally clearing, nothing had changed in Fionn's soul.

He lay back on the soft grass, but the sweetness of

the wild thyme beneath him and the sharp fresh scent of mint from the moist ground by the stream, gave him no pleasure. Through the interlace of branches he could see the first stars pricking through the purple dusk, but their brilliance did not delight him. The savor of stewing meat was beginning to drift enticingly from the campfires, but he felt no hunger.

On the other side of the trees some of the warriors were talking of Diarmuid, very quietly, as they always did now.

"And did Fionn really kill him?" It sounded like one of the younger men.

"The boar killed him," Daolghus said flatly.

"That's not what they say in the north. I heard that Grainne has sent her children to be trained as warriors so that they can avenge their father when they are grown."

Fionn had not heard that one, but it did not surprise him. Nor did he really care. It would have saved everyone a great deal of trouble if he himself had been the one to die.

"What are we doing this summer, have you heard?"

"Hunting." Daolghus laughed. "If there is anything else planned, there's been no talk of it; I don't think Fionn himself knows what he will do."

"I could go hunting at home—" said the young man dubiously, his voice fading as they moved away.

Someone summoned them to eat and Fionn sat up. He had no stomach for food, but the men would be calling him, and just now he could not face the questions in their eyes. He was a little stiff from lying on the damp ground, but he could still move silently enough to make his way past the sentries without being seen.

When he lost Sadb, he had ranged the woods in beast-shape until he wandered at last into the Otherworld. Fionn would have been equally happy to go from his wits or to go away from Eriu just now. In the years since he had found Oisin he had never regretted so bitterly his promise not to seek Faerie. Lately, visions of Donait's hall had haunted his dreams.

The rising moon silvered the tree trunks and laid a dappled pathway across the forest floor. Unthinking, Fionn followed it. Sometime later he found himself beside a spring that trickled into a small pool. Someone had piled up rocks to hold the water, and from the branches of the willow that grew above it fluttered scraps of cloth tied there in offering. Suddenly thirsty, Fionn murmured a prayer to the spirit of the spring and bent to drink.

The bright surface shattered as he scooped up the sweet water. Even to his dulled ears there was music in the sound the drops made falling back into the pool. When he had his fill, he stayed where he was, watching the shards of light melt back into a silver mirror. But as the surface cleared, the features he saw within it were not his own.

Fionn's heart began to pound heavily in his breast as the moon's pale round became a woman's face, rayed with shining hair. Was it Sadb? He held his breath, but already he could tell that this woman's features were stronger, her hair a shadowed gold.

"Donait," he breathed, not daring to reach out to her lest he shatter the spell. "Donait, I have needed you. . . ."

"I know. Oh my dear one, I know—"

Was the death of Diarmuid already recorded in her

weavings? In her eyes he read a grief that matched his own.

"Donait, my youth is gone," he whispered. "The men of the *fianna* hate me because of Diarmuid, and there is no joy left to me in this world. I do not know if I can go on."

"It is true, the years run so swiftly in the mortal lands," Donait said sorrowfully. "Too soon, yours will be done. But not yet, my beloved. It is not yet time for you to come to me."

"Come to me, then," he cried. "If for only a moment. Your kisses will heal my soul."

After a moment, she replied. "My dear, only one who is greater than I can give you peace, but perhaps—" Abruptly she seemed to make up her mind. "Look behind you where the path of power—brighter than the moonlight—leads from the sacred spring. If you will follow it into the forest, you will find a circle of stones, and in that place which is neither wholly in your world nor in the Other, I will be with you."

As Fionn's breath touched the pool the image of the fairy woman became a hundred shining fragments, each one reflecting its original, shattering and dividing in dizzying repetition until they were too small to see. He got to his feet, staring around him.

Before him a pathway led straight away from the spring. Through bush and briar ran the radiance, deepening to a pallid iridescence like the rainbow around the moon. He stepped onto the Faerie Road and the earth song surged suddenly around him, bearing all his grief away. And then he was running, moving to the music, speeding along the shining path as lightly as a boy.

One did not count time when travelling the Faerie Roads, but by the time Fionn found his momentum lessening, the moon was almost overhead. Before him the forest opened into a clearing. As the world turned towards midnight, the earthpower was begining to define a circle within it. One by one the standing stones awakened with a shiver of light that settled to a deepening glow. The power that ran between them was already strong enough to be felt as a barrier, but Fionn knew the word of power that would let him pass.

Every hair on his body erect with energy, Fionn stood in the center of the circle, watching the moon draw towards its zenith, waiting for the doors to open between the worlds.

He felt it first as an intensification of the light. The radiance extended from one *menhir* to the next until he was surrounded by a shimmering wall. The moon stood round and full above him and its light filled the circle, so strong that he could see the color of the grass. Then he realized that the colors were becoming even brighter and he could see the moon no longer. Instead, between one breath and another, its light had become the silvery illumination of the Otherworld.

Here, the weathered stones of the ancient circle were mighty pillars, their smooth faces carved with spirals and meanders like the curbstones at the Brugh na Boinne. Whatever lay beyond them was obscured by the shimmer of light, but the grass within the circle was smooth and intensely green, and upon it stood a woman wrapped in a blue mantle embroidered with spirals and veiled by golden hair.

He took a step towards her, whispering her name.

Donait's eyes widened. She herself was unchanged, but Fionn could see in her eyes his own reflection, gaunt and wild-eyed beneath a shock of shaggy silver hair.

"The years run swiftly in the mortal lands," he repeated bitterly. He let his hands fall.

"Ah, my dear one, did you think it was for your fine long body and your bright hair alone that I loved you?" Smiling, she came to him and kissed him full upon the mouth.

She tasted like apples. Suddenly Fionn found that he was weeping. He slid to his knees, still leaning against her, and stayed there, resting his head against the sweet joining of her thighs. She held him, crooning wordlessly, until the shuddering stopped at last.

But it was Fionn who pulled away, trying to hide a wince as he forced stiff muscles to bring him upright again.

"What has happened?" He saw the flicker in her gaze and knew he had guessed right. "Is my ending upon me, that you should break the *geas* that kept me from you, or is it your own need that calls?" He hardly cared which it might prove to be.

"The Dagda is leaving Eriu." Donait's fair brows bent in a frown. "He means to abandon his lordship here and pass over the grey plains of the sea to Tir n'an Og. The Otherworld has not seen such an upheaval since the Tuatha Dé Danaan surrendered the land to the Sons of Mil. But since your folk have ruled Eriu, many of the high kindred have set sail for the Undying Lands—the surviving lords of the Fir Bolg first, and then the Fomorians, and their conquerors after."

Nuada, who since the Second Battle of Mag Tured had only been partly in the world, was now departed entirely, and with him his wife Macha and his household. Ogma the Champion was gone, and Diancecht, Gobniu, and Credne. Manannan mac Lir had his dominion in the seas, and rarely concerned himself with the affairs of men. Since then, it was the Dagda whose good hand had ensured healthy cattle and bountiful harvests in Eriu and kept peace among the Sidhe.

"Are you going with him?" Fionn exclaimed. He thought he could face his own doom, but it had never occurred to him that change could come to her.

"Not I—" There was an indefinable sadness in her smile. "Your world still holds too much that I love. Nor will all of the Sidhe be departing. Brigid remains, for she has loved this world too dearly to abandon it. I think sometimes that she will outlast us all. But for the most part it is the younger ones, like me, who cling to each wood and hill, the younger ones who rejoice that the time for them to rule has come at last."

"Who?" asked Fionn, beginning to understand at last. "On whom has the Father of All determined to bestow his sovereignty?"

"At the Beltane Riding he announced it," answered Donait unhappily. "It is to be Bodb Derg. . . ."

Fionn's breath caught. Indeed this was something he needed to know. It explained the unseasonable weather, and even, perhaps, some of his own unease. And it filled him with foreboding. How could he keep peace between the world of men and of Faerie when its ruler was his enemy?

"I thank you for telling me—" he began, but she shook her head.

"That is not the only reason I called you. The decision was not made without disputation. There is another son of the Dagdas who would like to inherit his honors. . . . Midir."

It was a prickling at the back of his neck rather than any sound that warned Fionn they were no longer alone. Slowly he turned. Long knowledge had inured him to Donait's strangeness, but a single glance was enough to tell him that the newcomer was a man of the Sidhe.

"Midir—" Fionn thought of the old tales, and how the Sidhe-lord came ever unheralded, with his golden hair floating to his shoulders and his eyes like jewels. They had said, in the stories, that Midir was fair, but none had told how the eye continually skipped away for doubt it had seen such beauty and was as often drawn back again. With an effort he kept himself from gaping.

"Well met, Shield of Eriu," the Sidhe-lord's voice was music. The golden fringes of his mantle stirred in an invisible wind. "Do not be blaming Donait for not warning you—it is I that could wait no longer. My enemy is your enemy, Fionn mac Cumhal. He keeps you from your desire, but if I were to defeat him, I could set your lady free. Fionn, will you make alliance with me?"

"This war is of the Otherworld. What can I do?"

"You have fought in our world before," said Midir, "when you got the Hazel Shield. But I will not ask you to go against your oaths and obligations. This war of mine with Bodb Derg is a fight for lordship of the fairy mounds of Eriu, which have their being in both worlds, and I above all others know what damage and devastation mortal men can do.

"The Sidhe have been divided by this war. In Faerie, my enemy's strength and mine are well-nigh even. But if you and the *fianna* were to go against the hill that covers Sid BodbDerg as Eochaid Airemh assaulted Bri

Leith, my own fair hall, then I would have the advantage. And so I say to you again, Fionn mac Cumhal, will you fight for me?"

Fionn looked at Donait in question. "I do not know if it be good counsel for you to join with him," she said gravely, "but it was needful that you at least hear his appeal."

The luminous gaze of the Sidhe-lord was still fixed on Fionn, but it was the lovely face of Sadb that he was seeing. Slowly he began to smile.

THE *FIANNA* MOVED THROUGH THE FOREST AT A QUICK trot, their dull-colored cloaks and leather garments blending into the dappled browns and greens of the trees. They were moving well, thought Fionn, turning to look at them as he ran, with an energy that had not been there the day before. It could not be their destination that had made the difference—he had not yet told them what it was. But it had made a difference to him, and they were reflecting it. It seemed to him strange and a little humbling that even now, when they doubted him, they still responded to his moods like good hounds.

What, he wondered, had they seen in his face when he returned to them in the dawning? The light of the Otherworld, perhaps, or of hope; it had been a long time since light of any kind had kindled in his eyes. But after the first moment of surprise, no one had a chance to ask where he had been. They were too busy getting ready to move out once more.

It had been a long time since Fionn had come this way, not since that ill-fated journey he had made with Sadb to seek her father's blessing on their marriage. But he found as they travelled that he remembered it only too well. At times it seemed to him that if he turned, Sadb would be beside him, and only the hope that soon he might see her kept him from weeping.

They had covered half the distance to Loch Dergdeire by the time night fell. They ate dried meat and meal from their pouches and lay down by the fires, too tired for horseplay but not yet ready to sleep.

"Give us a story, Fionn," said Caoilte, drawing up his long legs and wrapping his arms about them.

Fionn raised one eyebrow—it had been a long time since that had been asked of him. It was a good sign, and he thought suddenly how he could use it to prepare the men for what they had to do.

"Very well—" He pitched his voice to carry and the murmur of conversation faltered as men turned to hear. "I will tell you the tale of the Wooing of Etain." Oisin, who had been very quiet ever since they began this journey, gave him a strange look, but the others were settling themselves like good dogs at a feast, waiting for a tidbit to come their way. The silence of the forest closed around them as Fionn marshaled his thoughts and began.

"In the time of our grandfathers' grandsires, long ago by the reckoning of mortal men, there was an *Ard Ri* in Temair called Eochaid, who married a woman so fair that the beauty of Etain became the standard by which since then all beauty has been tested. He did not know that she was a woman of the Sidhe who, through a rival's jealousy, had been reborn in human form. Still, she loved him, and they lived together happily—"

"But not for long, eh?" asked Faobhar. "Or what were the point to the tale?"

Fionn grunted. As a bard, he knew well that what his half brother had said was true. But there must be some way to bring forth a happy ending for his own tale. . . . With a sigh he took up the story once more.

"One day the *Ard Ri* stood within the ramparts of Temair, and suddenly, though the gates were still barred, a young warrior of marvelous beauty was with him there." He paused for a moment, still stirred to wonder that the bards' descriptions had been in this case so very true. "It was Midir of Bri Leith who had come to him, the Dagda's son, and he challenged the high king to match him at *fidchel*."

Swiftly he told the story of that gaming. Though the Sidhe-lord played well, somehow Eochaid always seemed to win, and the forfeits he demanded from Midir were to clear land and build causeways. And forever after Eochaid had the name of "Airemh"—the Ploughman—because he made these things to be. But in the end, Midir said they should play for whatever stake the winner of the match would demand.

"And this game he won, and the forfeit he demanded was that he should be allowed to hold Etain in his arms. And when he kissed her, she was recalled to her true nature, and they rose up through the smoke-hole of the hall and disappeared."

And when I kiss you, Sadb, he thought then, *no matter how your father has hidden or enchanted you, we will once more be one. . . .*

"That is a good story," said Loegaire, "but did the *Ard Ri* sit by tamely when the Sidhe-lord took his queen?"

"He did not," Fionn grinned at him. "He went up against Bri Leith with all his men, and they dug into the Faerie Hill, and rather than let his dwelling be destroyed, Midir had to let Etain go back to Eochaid and live out her mortal years."

"How could mortal men attack a faerie *dun* without themselves passing into the Otherworld?" asked Faobhar.

"The mounds where the Sidhe dwell are no ordinary hills," said Fionn. "They were built in ancient times by mortal men and given to the gods, and so they are a link between the worlds. Once the Children of Danu lived entirely in our world, but they were defeated by the Sons of Mil.

"Afterward, some fled away entirely," he added, remembering Donait's words, "but many of them still loved Eriu, and so they remained, *of* this world though not *in* it. From us they draw the forms they give to their mounts and their homes and even their own bodies, and the link between us is the mound."

"And that is why they fight for possession of the faerie hills?" asked Dubhán.

"That is what I was told. From time to time the Sidhe must return to their hills as a tree spirit to her tree, or they will become no more than voices on the wind."

"They say that the women of the Sidhe are fair, but their love is not always a blessing," said Caoilte reflectively, and Faobhar and Fearghusa, who had known Sadb, tried to hush him.

"Not so," objected Loegaire. "Etain tried to be faithful. It is the Faerie lords who are treacherous."

Fionn frowned at that, but why should Midir seek to cheat him when their goals were the same?

The fire had burned down to coals. Someone yawned, and, laughing, Fionn ordered them all to get some rest. He rolled himself in his cloak as well, but for a long time he lay wakeful, looking for Sadb's face in the waning moon.

* * *

IT HAD BEEN AUTUMN WHEN FIONN CAME TO THE LAKE before. A mist had clung to the dark waters, and the earth had been bright with fallen leaves. Now it was the trees that glowed with brightness, new leaves shining in the pale spring sun. But the red-rimmed lake still seemed shadowed, its waters stained as if all the blood ever shed in battle had collected there.

"This is Loch Derg," said Oisin as the *fianna* came to a halt on the shore. "Are we going north to join up with the mac Mornas? I see no reason to have made such a secret of it, if there lies our way."

"We are going south," Fionn replied, "to Sid BodbDerg."

"But why?" said Oisin in amazement.

"We are going to attack your grandfather," Fionn said flatly. "We are going to destroy the Faerie Hill. There is a war among the Sidhe, and we are called to be part of it. If we succeed, it will be Midir and not Bodb Derg that rules the Sidhe, and we may get your mother back again!"

A murmur spread among the men. For a long moment Oisin stared at him, disbelief, apprehension, and excitement alternating in his face. "The Sidhe. . . . You went between the worlds, then, that night you disappeared. And I suppose that is why you told us the story of Etain. I understand," he smiled sadly. "If I could wrest Eibhir from her kindred by doing so, I would break down the very walls of Rome."

"Will we see the Fair Folk?" asked Fearghusa as they moved along the path beside the shore. He had fallen sick and been left behind when they came here before.

"Last time, Sadb's brother Echbél gave us sprigs of hawthorn to wear," said Faobhar, "and then we could see not only him and his men but the Brugh. Could you sing a spell over something to help us now?"

For a time Echbél had served with the *fianna*, but when Sadb was stolen by the Dark Druid he, too, had disappeared. Would he be fighting for his father, or was he one of those who had already retreated oversea to Tir n'an Og?

"That hawthorn came from the Otherworld, where it is always in bloom," said Fionn. "There will be danger enough in this as it is. It will be better if you cannot see."

Perhaps his meeting with Donait had made him more sensitive, but it seemed to him that he could hear a murmur like a distant wind though the air around them was still. He felt the quiver that changed his spear, Birga, from dead wood to something alive and hungry, and the Hazel Shield grew lighter on his arm. *They feel it too. The hosts of the Sidhe are fighting already,* he thought grimly. *If we are lucky, Bodb Derg will be too busy to notice the threat to his* dun.

Presently the woods fell away to a rather marshy meadow from whose center rose a smooth, grass-covered hill. A flock of sparrows were working over the ground, pecking for worms, but none ventured near the hill. Though there was no difference visible in the turf, the behavior of the birds showed him clearly where the border must be. All seemed serene in the sunlight, but Fionn could still feel the thrumming in the air.

He closed his eyes for a moment, seeking an image of the *dun* as he had seen it when he brought Sadb here. The yard in front of the *dun* had been a swirl of dogs and brightly clad people. But he remembered the point of the thatched roof sharp against the sunset sky.

The doorway would be there, then, on the east. In memory he could see it clearly, and when he opened his eyes once more the image remained for a moment in his awareness, superimposed upon the green slope of the hill.

"And how are we to tackle it then," asked Loegaire practically, "with neither spade nor shovel?"

"Use your axes," Fionn answered him. "I'll assign the cooks to carry the turves away in their pots and cauldrons." With sudden decision, he set about dividing the men into teams to attack the sides of the *dun*.

The day was warm enough that soon the men were sweating. The air was humid and heavy, as if a storm were brewing, but Fionn knew it was no storm of the world. Rather awkwardly at first, but with increasing vigor, they dug into the soil. Fairly soon it became clear that this was no ordinary hill. Perhaps an arm's length under the turf they came to a covering of fine white stones with a filling of loose rock beneath it. No more work for axes here, but spears came in handy to lever up the stones.

Fionn moved from one side to another, encouraging and advising. A pressure was building inside his skull to match the weight in the air, and he found himself blinking away bright spots that swam before his eyes. He had not expected the faerie *dun* to be deserted, and though Bodb Derg and his warriors might be far away, the faerie folk who had remained here were clearly aware of the invasion. And they were growing angry.

Three men were already wounded—apparently by accidents, though Fionn suspected otherwise. Spear shafts snapped and jagged edges gashed bare limbs. Rocks gave way suddenly, smashing fingers or sending a man tumbling backward down the hill. And more and more frequently, a warrior would pause in his labors to massage his temples as if he were beginning to feel pain there.

Oisin was the worst affected. It stood to reason that he would be, with his mother's blood awakening. When he fell for the third time, Fionn had him carried to the grove where the other wounded were lying, a goodly distance away from the hill.

The men continued to work as the shadows grew longer, and by the time the sun began to dip behind the trees the hill resembled a round of cheese at which a number of particularly industrious mice had been gnawing away. Indeed, on one side they had excavated down to the great capstone of the inner chamber. Another day's work would expose the rest to the cleansing light of day.

But there was still danger, especially now, at the threshold between night and day, when even at ordinary times the barriers opened a little between the worlds. Fionn's head was throbbing, and the tumult that rang in his ears was now so loud it was hard to believe the other men did not hear.

As he opened his mouth to call them down from the hill a wave of shadow seemed to pass over the ground, and suddenly they all *could* hear—battle cries and horncalls, hoofbeats that rumbled like oncoming thunder, and a deep voice that called out a single Word of Power that ruptured all barriers. Light and dark clapped together and parted with a rush of chill air. Fionn blinked and saw the *dun* of Bodb Derg before him, with a turmoil of men and horses around it.

He tipped back his head and split the air with his own war cry. Still dazed and blinking, the warriors of the *fianna* rolled to their feet with the speed of long training, scrambling for their spears. Then a faerie horse reared above him; the spear Birga jerked in his hand and Fionn stabbed upward, leaping aside as the horse's scream became a wail of despair. The beast fell one way and its rider another, but it was a beast no longer. Fionn saw the fair face convulsed with agony, but he had no time to wonder, for a spear was darting towards him. Instinct brought the Hazel Shield up to take the blow.

This is better than when I fought the Fomorii before Donait's hall, he thought when next he had a moment to breathe. *This time I am not alone.* After the first surprise, the *fianna* were rallying, clumping together in groups of two or three and standing against the Sidhe. Oisin had flung himself into the action and was laying about him with his sword, his face alight with a terrible beauty, so fair that had it not been for his rough gear, he might have been taken for one of the foe.

A screech behind him brought Fionn about, spear ready. It was a female warrior who was attacking him, angular and ugly, with a tangle of reddish hair. He planted his feet and took her furious blows on the Shield, waiting for an opening. Her screeching had become a mutter of curses, in which he caught his own name.

"Where is the giant that protected you, eh?" She thrust her face close and he recoiled from a breath as foul as her words. "Rather kill him to pay for my sisters, but you will do! Better if you had died when we had you! More grief for you now, eh?" Her words trailed off into a high peal of laughter as she stabbed low with her spear.

"Iornach!" He leaped backward, remembering the

cave and the cauldron. As the spear Birga caught his emotion, its eager hum became a shrill cry. The hag came in again, spear flickering like a serpent's tongue. Fionn felt a lick of fire sear his thigh, and his own anger flared. Roaring, he strode forward, beating her back with mighty blows. Swift as a serpent she might be, but she was not so powerful; her spear shaft blocked one blow, and another, but the third cracked the stressed wood and pierced her shoulder. Wailing, she dropped the spear and sprang away.

Fionn did not try to follow her. There were enemies enough for everyone, from the contorted shapes the lesser fay-folk took for fighting, to the noble forms and glittering mail the great ones wore. A *fachan*, single arm groping from the midst of its chest, whirled on one leg; the shapeless bulk of a *brollachan* rolled across the bloody ground; *fuaths*, slimed with water-weed, attacked with shrill screams. He glimpsed Oisin, his shield gone, the spears he held in each hand spinning a shield of light around him as he whirled.

Caoilte had made his stand nearby. Laughing, he fended off the mighty blows of the high lord who had attacked him, holding him with the greater length of his spear. His opponent was one of the older Sidhe, his beard almost as long as his flowing hair, armed in a shirt of overlapping scales like fishes' mail. Fionn had thought all the great ones had gone oversea or were holding aloof from this conflict, like Aonghus Og, or Manannan. . . . And at the thought, he realized who Caoilte's opponent was—not the god who ruled the waves, but his father, ancient Lir.

Fionn started towards them, not so much because he thought Caoilte needed help as to share the blood-debt if he should succeed in killing Lir. The young warrior grinned as he saw him, then his eyes widened. Fionn jerked around and saw Bodb Derg.

"It is not enough to have half burnt my hall; now you try to tear it down?"

Sadb's father was as big and ruddy as Fionn remembered, and even more magnificent, armed in golden mail. The cloak of russet fur, from a bear such as had not been seen for a thousand years in Eriu, made him look even larger. He looked like a king, and for the first time since he had spoken with Midir, Fionn wondered if he were on the right side.

"Gladly would I have served my lady's father and her kin!" he answered grimly. "It was your own will that put me on the other side. . . ."

Bodb Derg's face darkened. "You took what I would not give—"

"And will again," answered Fionn. "I do not fear you—I have killed great ones among your folk before." He settled into a fighting crouch, shield up and spear poised.

"Indeed, we owe you a heavy reckoning," growled his foe. "But do not boast, mortal, until you have fought *me*!" His own spear swung forward.

Blustering and boastful as the Sidhe-lord might be, he could fight. The Hazel Shield groaned as Bodb Derg struck, and Fionn found himself giving ground. As he parried, it occurred to Fionn for the first time that he might lose. Then a fierce joy rose up in him. Since Diarmuid died his own life had not been so sweet that he would regret its ending. What better way to finish than on his feet, fighting a worthy foe? Sadb might grieve when she heard, but she would know that he had tried to win her back again.

Breathless, Fionn went down on one knee, Birga

screaming in his hand. He glimpsed his foe's muscled thigh and thrust with all his strength. There was a shock as the spear struck, and Bodb Derg roared with pain. It was all Fionn could do to hold on as the Sidhe-lord lurched backward, but the movement pulled him to his feet again as the spear came free. He was off-balance, though, his shield arm swinging out in an instinctive attempt to right himself, leaving him open to his foe.

His enemy's lips drew back in a feral grin as he saw Fionn's breast at last unprotected. "Farewell . . . *Son-in-law*!" He lifted his spear.

Fionn wrenched his body sideways, trying to curl under the shield. He glimpsed his foe's muscles bunching and knew that this time he was not going to make it. He turned then, unwilling to meet death trying to run away—

—and flinched back again as a Sound split the air, his hearing, the world. All the world's despair was in that cry, and all its rage; it was a scream to turn men's bones to water, to congeal the blood in the veins, to shrivel the soul. For a moment Fionn struggled against it; then terror rolled over him in a black wave and he knew no more.

IT WAS DARK, AND HE WAS LYING ON SOMETHING AS rough and cold as stone. Fionn blinked and tried to sit up. It *was* stone; as his eyes adjusted he could see rocks scattered all around him and beyond them the tattered slopes of the Faerie Hill. It was the Scream of the Morrigan, it must have been, that had expelled them from the Otherworld. He wondered if it had destroyed his hearing as well.

Then, from somewhere nearby, he heard a groan.

Biting his lip against his own pain, Fionn crawled towards the sound. Around him, some of the shapes he had taken for stones were stirring. They were not all dead, then, though some might wish it. He reached out and his fingers closed on warm flesh. Beneath his fingers the pulse bounded erratically. Carefully he felt down the body for wounds.

"Fionn . . ." came the whisper. It was Caoilte's voice, but he had already recognized the long limbs.

"Be easy—I am here."

"I killed him, Fionn . . . I saw him go down and the light left his eyes . . ."

Fionn had found the great gash in Caoilte's thigh by then, and was pressing against it, willing the bleeding to slow. "Then you have saved us all," he said softly. "For the lord you killed was Lir himself, and I am thinking it was the keen that the Morrigan raised for him that drove us back into our own world."

"I have done well, then," Caoilte said on a sigh.

"And will do so again—" Fionn answered bracingly. "You have a bad slice here, but nothing that cannot heal. Lie still now, and let us tend to you." Someone had gotten a torch lit, and men were beginning to search the field. He called for water, and in a few moments was relieved to see Oisin with a waterskin.

"Water from Fionn's hands . . . will heal me . . ." whispered Caoilte.

"And will you give it?" Oisin asked bitterly.

"Do you think I have learned nothing?" Fionn looked up, not caring what his face showed. "It is easy to take life; hard to give it back again. Do you think there has been a day since Samhain that regret has not tormented me? But the demon that was in me died with Diarmuid. I will not make that mistake again."

Chapter 11

IN THE GREEN GLOOM BENEATH THE FALLEN ALDER something was moving. Fionn tensed, but saw only the flutter of leaves. He frowned, for this had happened to him several times since the battle at Sid BodbDerg. Was he ill? Or perhaps— Still frowning, he bit down on his thumb and when his vision cleared, looked again. Once more he saw something stir; he stepped closer, and made out the attenuated limbs and pointed ears of a *cluricaun*, like a badly drawn sketch of a child.

"Small one, you are far from home—" he said pleasantly. The *cluricaun* hissed and stared at him from huge, slightly slanted green eyes.

" 'Tis no thanks to you if I am! I know you, Poison-Spear. With all the battling and uproar there is still in the Otherworld, where is there but the mortal lands for a poor creature to go?"

That was it, then. Fionn sighed. "You are welcome

to follow the *fian,* but none of your tricks, mind. I will have them leave out food for you."

He supposed the grimace that followed was meant for a smile. But at that moment a loud crack like a breaking branch rang out nearby, and the *cluricaun* dove into a pile of leaves and disappeared.

Fionn heard the sound of wood striking wood again. It seemed to be coming from the clearing beyond the cook fires, shocking in the damp air. It was followed by a meaty thunk, and after a moment, a strangled cough. From long experience Fionn could interpret the sounds; he wondered which of the boys who had come out from Almu for field training during the break in the weather had just had the wind knocked out of him.

"Fool!" Oisin's voice was as sharp as the blow. "How many times must I tell you—the cut you have just parried does not matter, it is the next blow you must watch for, and the one that comes after. Is it lazy you are, or only clumsy?"

Fionn frowned. Oisin was not usually so harsh with the young ones. He tossed the deer rib he had been nibbling to Sceolan and eased through the fringe of willows that edged the training ground. His son was standing with his back to the trees, the wooden sword still in his hand. Oscar, still clutching his belly, was kneeling in the mud a few paces away.

"Have you nothing to say for yourself?" Oisin flung down his weapon. "I do not even know why I try!" He turned away, his face dark with anger. As he pushed through the trees Fionn saw the pain in his eyes.

I don't suppose he can understand, thought Fionn. *For him it was always easy.* Indeed, Oisin had been a joy to teach, grasping each new skill almost as soon as it was explained. But Fionn remembered only too well how it felt to be matched against an unachievable perfection. Was Oscar really so poorly gifted, or was it only in Oisin's presence that he became clumsy? He was well grown for fourteen, hard-muscled over sturdy bones; he might not be as quick, but Fionn suspected that in the end he would prove stronger than Oisin.

Oscar stayed crouched, listening as his father left him. When it was quiet once more he straightened, his face twisted with such anguish that Fionn felt his own heart wrenched. *I must do something to show him he is not alone . . .*

He was still searching for the right words when Caoilte emerged from among the trees on the other side of the clearing. Intent upon the boy, Fionn had not even seen him there.

"Hey lad, it is not so bad! We've all taken our knocks when we were learning! Would you like to try a turn with me?"

A wave of red suffused Oscar's cheeks, then receded, taking with it all evidence of emotion. "If my father cannot teach me, what do you think you could do?" Scowling, he got to his feet.

His own training sword had fallen near the willows. As he stamped off he picked it up and in the same motion swung it against the nearest tree. As it hit, the stick shattered, and the two pieces went wheeling away. Without a backward look, Oscar followed them. Caoilte was still staring after him when Fionn joined him.

"No sense of humor, that's Oscar's problem," said Caoilte. "It gets in his way when he tries to use his skill."

Fionn snorted. There had never been a time when Caoilte had not been as full of tricks as a *cluricaun*, and ready for a laugh, but he remembered how serious he himself had been about everything at the age of fourteen.

"Do you suppose we could send Oisin off somewhere when it comes time for Oscar to be tested for the *fianna*? Otherwise . . ." Caoilte did not need to finish.

It was hard to say who would be more devastated if Oscar failed his testing, he himself or Oisin. Fionn knew well how difficult it could be to have a famous father, but at least Cumhal had been safely dead when Fionn was growing up, and folk had only their memories for comparison.

"I'll have to think of something—" he began, then broke off as someone shouted his name.

"Fionn!" The big Alban warrior, Cedach, shouldered through the willows. "There's a messenger come from the *Ard Ri*. You are summoned to Temair!"

FIONN FLINCHED AS THUNDER BOOMED ABOVE THEM, making the timbers of the great hall tremble and rattling the shields that hung on the wall. A moment later rain began to roar on the thatching as if someone had upended a tub of water above the *Ard Ri*'s feasting hall.

"Do you hear that, do you hear?" shouted the high king's chief druid, Cathal, in Fionn's ear. "Is that seasonable weather for Midsummer? The young corn will be flattened in the fields. A poor harvest this year for the farmers of Eriu, and it is all your doing, Fionn mac Cumhal!"

"My doing?" said Fionn when he could be heard

once more. "You flatter me. But it is Midir and Bodb Derg you should be blaming. I did not start the war that they are fighting now."

He started to gesture and was brought up short by the fetters on his wrists. He supposed that they and the ones weighting his legs were a compliment as well, and perhaps more justified. Even the walls of Temair would not have kept him in if his limbs had been free. And yet he was a fool not to have expected trouble. This was the first time in years he had come to Temair so poorly attended; there had seemed no point in bringing the men north when they might immediately be ordered to march south or west again. And so he had left the *fianna* under Oisin's command and started out with no more than Caoilte and two serving men, and Caoilte had turned aside to visit his wife before they came to Temair.

"To be sure, it was not good, but we did not face disaster," said the Archdruid. "The weather of the world is always a reflection of conditions in the Other, and a war among the Sidhe was bound to create some disturbance. But it was not until you opened the door between them that we were in any danger! The fault is yours, and you will face the judgment of the druids of Eriu as soon as they can be convened!"

Is the fault indeed mine? Midir desired lordship and I wanted love. Were those such evil desires? What have I done wrong, that I should be denied the consolations of other men?

Fionn stretched as well as he could, setting groups of muscles against each other until his backbone popped and released some of the strain, then sighed. The druids had accused him, but it was Cormac who had ordered him bound. Perhaps tonight, when the

Ard Ri had eaten, Fionn could persuade him to let him go.

But it was late before Cormac finally returned to his hall. Almost since Fionn's capture Temair had been plagued by problems requiring his attention. Not dangers, for the most part, but annoyances like unlatched gates and doused fires. One day the weanling calves had gotten loose from their pen and gone back to their mothers, so there was nothing left for the evening milking. Another time a fire had somehow started at the high king's mill. The Archdruid blamed these troubles, too, upon the Sidhe, but remembering his encounter with the *cluricaun*, Fionn suspected that just now even the minor bogles had better things to do than tormenting the folk of Temair.

Tonight the problem was horses. The high king's prized broodmares had been set free to roam the plain of Brega, and it took him and his houseguard most of the day to retrieve them. By the time Cormac came in, wet hair plastered against his skull and spattered with mud to mid-thigh, it was well after sunset.

Smiling sweetly, Fionn watched him gulp down a horn of hot spiced ale. Then he stretched out his own feet to the fire and wiggled them luxuriously.

"Wet work, was it?" he asked pleasantly.

Cormac winced as he extended his own legs. "I'm getting too old for this sort of thing." Watching him, Fionn was reminded unpleasantly of how his grandfather, Conn, had looked in his old age.

"You would have finished more quickly, had I been free," Fionn observed. He had spent half his life in the open, and would no doubt have found the labor easier than did the high king. And yet they were of an age;

like Cormac, Fionn found his bones aching when the weather changed.

"Wretch! I wish you *had* been. I swear those horses ran as if they were pursued by bogles."

Not bogles, thought Fionn, but it seemed to him that he could put a name to the trickster. No warrior of the *fian* would defy the *Ard Ri* directly, but the realization that at least one of his men had not abandoned him helped Fionn to endure his bonds.

"It is your own fault if I am not at your side. How long do you mean to continue this comedy?"

"Do you consider it a joke?" Cormac asked bitterly. "You are the Shield of Eriu, and you have put Eriu in danger. Until the counsel of my druids or some sign from the gods shows me how to judge this, I cannot let you go."

"It is not like you to look to others for your judgment. It is as if you gave up an eye or a hand. . . ." said Fionn very softly, but the king did not reply.

By the end of the evening, however, Cormac and Fionn were singing songs together, and both had consumed their full share of mead. It was very late when the king called for his torchbearer to light him to the privies before he went to bed.

"Hey—you're not my usual lad—" He peered at the man, who held the flame above his head so that all one could see was a long-shanked figure with a shock of mouse-fair hair and bright eyes. "Look familiar, though—got eyes like that man of yours, Fionn—the runner—Caoilte's his name."

"Bless you, say not so!" exclaimed Fionn. "Is it not shame enough that I should be fettered in your house without accusing one of my *fénnidi* of doing the work of a serving lad?" He let his head sink down on his crossed arms lest his grin give the game away.

Shortly thereafter Fionn heard a roar of rage from outside, but it was not until past midnight that he roused to Caoilte's whisper in his ear.

"What did you do to make Cormac yell so?" he asked.

"Put nettles in the moss set out by the privy trench for wiping and sent him to bed with a burning bum! He is asleep now, though, and I have the key to unfetter you."

"Good lad." As the manacles came off Fionn stretched gratefully.

"I've given the guard at the lower gate enough mead to make him sleep. If we go now, we can be far away by dawn."

"If I run away now, I am still Cormac's prisoner," said Fionn, gripping the other man's arm. "Better to stay willingly and play one more trick to show him where he is wrong."

THE NEXT MORNING, WHEN CORMAC, LIMPING FROM the previous day's exertions, came into his feasting hall, he found Fionn there, unfettered, taking his ease before the fire with Caoilte by his side. Fionn watched him narrowly, prepared to duck if anger won out over amazement. It was a close-run thing, but eventually Cormac tipped back his head and began to laugh.

"Is it that you are trying to drive me crazy?" he asked. One of the women brought him a beaker with a fragrant minty tea, and rather carefully, he sat down.

"We are trying to show you that things are not always as they seem." said Fionn. "I could have disappeared last night with no one a whit the wiser, and the Archdruid would be swearing I'd been taken by the Sidhe. But it is Caoilte here who has been your bogle. If you will look in your scabbard, you will see his sword sheathed there instead of your own."

"But why?" asked the *Ard Ri*, looking from one to the other.

"Your druids do not know everything," said Fionn. "Sitting here in your fetters I have thought hard, and some responsibility I must bear for our current troubles, but not all. Not every bolt of lightning is an omen, and not every storm a punishment for wrong. Caoilte could have played tricks that were deadly," he went on. "Do not you think the Sidhe could do the same?"

"Indeed, I have not truly harmed you!" said Caoilte. "Will you tell me now what would ransom my master?"

"Have you not?" growled the *Ard Ri*. "My buttocks are still smarting! But there is some truth in what you say. Let us put it to the test—" He straightened. "Bring me a pair of every kind of beast that is hunted. If the Sidhe will allow you to do so, I will take that as an omen, and let Fionn go."

THOUGH THE DRUIDS CONTINUED TO MUTTER DARKLY, everyone else seemed relieved to see the estrangement between the *Ard Ri* and his *rígfénnid* ended. Even the weather improved, and Cormac determined to celebrate by inviting the leaders of the *fianna* to feast upon the fruits of Caoilte's hunting. Once the agreement had been made, Fionn remained unfettered, free to roam within the walls of the *dun*. It eased him, though he spent much of his time upon the ramparts, gazing out over the plain of Brega and drawing in great breaths of the clean wind. He was grateful when Cormac agreed that if the weather permitted, the feasting should take place on the grass of the fairgrounds below the *dun*, in the open air.

The night before the feast was to take place, Fionn dreamed—if indeed it was a dream and not some night-wandering of the spirit—that he was in the Otherworld. He walked through a perpetual twilight, seeking Donait's hall. After a time it struck him that the land was curiously empty and those beings he did see fled swiftly away; there were places, too, where the forms were becoming misty. It came to him then that what Donait had told him was true, and that Faerie, for all its magic, took its shape from the human world.

By the time he found Donait's hall, he was ready to weep, and when he saw it he groaned, for it was smaller than he remembered, no longer a palace, but a cottage such as a wisewoman might have in the hills. But when he knocked on the door it opened to him, and Donait was there.

"What has happened here? Were the druids right to give me the blame?" he cried.

"In part—" She drew him through the door, and he saw that the inside of her dwelling was much larger than the outside had seemed, and that her weavings still hung on the walls. "But the beginning was with Bodb Derg and Midir. It is true, though, that when you damaged Sid BodbDerg you weakened the links between the worlds. Some of my people were destroyed in the war, and many more have gone oversea to the Blessed Isles. Those of us who remain here must bind ourselves ever more closely to the human world."

"And who won? Who now rules the fairy hills of Eriu?"

"In such a conflict no one can win," Donait said

sadly, "and I fault my own wisdom not to have seen it before the war began. North of Bri Leith Midir holds the greatest power, while in the west and south Bodb Derg is supreme. But neither one of them can truly claim the sovereignty. Do not expect that all will be as it has been. Change comes, Fionn mac Cumhal, even to the Tuatha Dé Danaan."

"Cormac was right to punish me," Fionn said grimly. "I was led astray by my own selfish desire."

"And by Midir, who can be most persuasive, and by me. We must all share the blame." Donait poured springwater into a silver cup and offered it to him.

"Tell me, Donait, what must I do?"

"Do you still trust my counsel?" she laughed bitterly. "My beloved, in this I cannot guide you. But I see now that Brigid did not save you from the Morrigan to become embroiled in Faerie wars."

"Why, then?" he asked. "What is it I must do?"

"Ah, my dear, you must seek that answer in the leaping flames, or perhaps in the waters of the sacred spring. . . ."

When Fionn left Donait's house the light had darkened. As he moved through the deepening dusk, seeking the glow that represented Temair, Fionn let his tears flow. He was still weeping when he awoke in the dawn.

"Ho, Caoilte, here's a fine bird—what skies did he fly, eh?" Goll waved the leg of swan on which he was gnawing, grinning widely.

"That is one of the swans of Loch Darravagh that swam with the Children of Lir—" Caoilte's voice faltered, for who would mourn for those lost children now that Lir was gone? Fionn reached past Oisin and patted his arm. Caoilte responded with a flicker of smile, and in another moment he was laughing once more.

The cooks of King Cormac, inspired by the story of Caoilte's hunting, had outdone themselves in preparing the game he sent back to Temair. The ducks and geese and swans constituted the first course of the feast, garnished with summer greens. The waterfowl had been roasted to golden perfection, or covered in clay and buried in the coals so that when the mud coat was knocked off the feathers would come. The bakers had been busy as well, producing piles of flat loaves to serve as platters. They had spread lengths of linen upon the grass for tables, one for the *Ard Ri* and his kindred, and one for the *fianna*. Cormac sat in the center of the first with his sons beside him, and across from him, Fionn, flanked by Goll and Oisin.

The evening was so fair that even the druids had to conclude that the powers of nature had been mollified by Caoilte's feat. Remembering his dream, if that was what it had been, Fionn thought it more likely that the Sidhe were too exhausted by their own conflicts to concern themselves with the rivalries of men. The feasters—sixteen men of the *fianna* and another sixteen of Cormac's kin—were enjoying themselves with self-conscious vigor, their shared appetites demonstrating the renewed accord between the royal Gaels and the *fian*.

After the fowl the boys who were acting as servers brought in the small game, the swift-coursing hare, the dormouse, and even a pair of prickly hedgehogs, included as a challenge to the cooks, since only in emergencies was it usually eaten.

"A fine ransom is this," sneered Cairbre, plucking

one of the dormice by the tail from the sauce in which it had been simmered and tossing it to the dogs. "And where are the snails and earthworms and other such noble game?"

Caoilte's eyes widened for a moment at the gibe, then he struck his forehead dramatically. "Lord King, forgive me! Had I known it was worms your fine son was wanting, I would have made shift to brave the danger. Shall I go after some now?"

Cormac shook his head. "I think you have made work enough for my cooks without that!" he said, laughing, and the others, seeing that he had chosen to take it as a joke, laughed too.

Between the courses, women servants made their way up and down the rows of feasters, pouring ale and mead. King Cormac's harpers sat beneath an oak tree making sweet music. No effort had been spared to make this event memorable, and yet Fionn felt oddly uneasy, as if they were all trying too hard.

The pigs were brought in—a boar and a sow from Sliab Muicce, both of them fine and fat. The scent of the roast pork made Fionn's mouth water, but he did not eat the meat. He had not eaten pig flesh since Diarmuid died.

As the guests were finishing, the royal women came down the hill to pour mead before the final course. Ethne the queen walked more slowly these days, and the hair beneath her embroidered headdress was almost entirely grey, but she still moved with royal grace. Fionn was uncomfortably reminded of how she had once led Grainne and Ailbe through the feasting hall.

But this time it was her granddaughters who followed her, gowned in their best, with wreaths of flowers on their hair. The first girl, with the bloom of approaching womanhood still upon her, was so lovely that conversation stilled when she appeared, her hair a deep auburn, her eyes the deep green-brown of a forest pool. Young Oscar, standing behind his father with the other boys, was staring as if someone had hit him. She was fairer even than Grainne in her prime, thought Fionn, but he would not seek her in marriage for himself or for any man of his kin.

"She is a beauty indeed," he said in a low voice when Oscar bent to offer him more bread. "Enjoy looking at her if you will, but think no further. She is Cairbre's daughter, and I suppose he would rather give her to the wild man of Dun Da Bheann than to one of the *fian*."

Oscar went red as fire, but if he had had any notion of trying to speak to the girl, he gave up on it. It was a pity to discourage the boy from any kind of social interaction, but Cairbre was already glowering.

The harpers struck a sweet chord, and four of the younger warriors brought in the noble stags, that had been roasted whole on spits above the fire, with the great heads, one of seven tines and the other of six, borne by two lads before them. By this time the guests were beginning to reach a welcome state of repletion, but the scent of the venison made Fionn's mouth water nonetheless.

"Here are our red cattle of the forest," said Caoilte, as the carcasses were laid down on planks in the space between the feasters. "Let each man carve off his portion according to his rank and honor, saving only the marrowbones, which are the traditional portion of Goll and Clan Morna."

"Then you should make your choice first, Caoilte,"

said Cormac good-humoredly, "for at this feast you are surely the champion."

"But it is you to whom the ransom is being paid, and Fionn who is being ransomed," answered Caoilte, drawing his dirk and bending over the first deer. "So I will carve for you both if you will tell me what parts you desire!" It was an eminently tactful reply, and Fionn's lips curved in appreciation.

"If they are to be honored," said Cairbre, "then surely it is they who should receive the marrowbones. Why should Goll be so privileged, when he is only the servant of Fionn?"

Cormac glared at his younger son, and the older, Ceallach, who had drunk more than he had eaten, began to laugh.

"When Cumhal ruled the *fianna* the marrowbones were his," said Goll's brother Garad angrily. "But since we brought him down at the Battle of Cnucha they have belonged to the mac Mornas!"

Fionn cast a quick look at Goll, and saw on his face the same amazement that must be in his own. When he first became *rígfénnid* he might have expected such a challenge, but not after all these years! But of course it was not really the Sons of Morna who had challenged him, but the son of Cormac.

"And is it you who would challenge us for them, Cairbre?" growled Goll, directing everyone's attention back where it belonged.

"Not at all," Cairbre's smile did not change the lines of discontent graven on his face. "It is only that I wished the guests of honor here to have their due."

"That will be enough!" snapped the *Ard Ri*. "They may have my share of the bones and be welcome!"

Silently, Caoilte sawed off the leg bones and presented them to Goll, who surveyed them quizzically.

"There was a time," he said softly to Fionn, "when I would have cracked these bones with my jaws. But I don't have the teeth for it any longer. If it were not for the honor of the thing, I would give them to Cairbre after all." He began to dig into the end of the bone with the point of his dirk to extract the sweet marrow inside. Slowly, the conversations around them picked up again.

"If you are willing," Goll added presently, speaking loudly enough so that heads turned, "I have a lad or two I'd like to send down to you for fostering. Young Fer-li, who is my grandson by my daughter Iuchna Ardmor and that Luagni chieftain I married her to, and a grandson of Garad's, called Emer Glunglas."

"If they are kin of yours, I will welcome them," said Fionn. He held out his hand to Goll. They held the clasp for a little longer than necessary, making sure that everyone had seen.

"Grandsons. . . ." Goll shook his head and took another swallow of ale. "I've got too many. I find myself calling them by their fathers' names. Even Feadha, that boy that your niece Caoinche bore me, is getting married this year. I'm growing old, Fionn, and I don't like it." He drank again.

Fionn nodded. The only grandchildren of his that he knew of were Oscar and mac Lugach, but he understood what Goll was saying. The lads that came to them for training got younger every year.

The stags were the last of Caoilte's offerings. By the time the venison had been eaten the light had faded from the sky. Upon the grass a great bonfire had been kindled, and the men took their drinking horns and gathered around it to hear the harpers, while they themselves made further inroads into the *Ard Ri*'s store of mead.

Ciothruadh, who at this time had the name of chieftain of the royal harpers, had come down from the *dun* to join them. He stood with folded arms as the great harp was lifted down from the back of the donkey that had carried it, directing the slaves to set up his harping stool where the fire would warm him without being so hot as to put the harp out of tune. As the servants fed the flames their light gilded the edges of the harp and struck sparks from his brown hair and the golden embroidery on his gown. He was a tall man, long-armed and long-fingered; when he played he seemed to have ten on each hand. During the time of Fionn's captivity they had become friendly, but Ciothruadh, who could repeat any song on a single hearing and never forgot anything he heard, only laughed at the idea of using ogham to note down the tunes.

He was in good form that night, and gave them most of the lays of Cuchulain as the warriors emptied one barrel after another of mead and ale.

"True it is, Cormac son of Airt, that you come of a great people," said Fionn.

"A great nation indeed," echoed Cairbre. "The conquerors of Eriu."

"Well, we others are not so lacking," Fionn responded with careful good humor; surely he should be used to rudeness from that quarter by now. "Is it not a hero-feat that Caoilte has performed here to ransom me?"

"A fenian trick it was," Cormac growled, only half in jest, "I gave my word in a weak moment, or I would have had a more worthy ransom before I let you go free."

"If you had asked me, I would have counseled against it!" exclaimed Cairbre. "The subject tribes grow proud and rebellious. We should make these bold men of Laigin go under the fork of the cauldron in token of submission, as their fathers did when our fathers overcame them."

"You would be less than wise," said Fionn very quietly, "if you should try to compel us. In all we have done heretofore, the winning of every game has been mine. If we should be forced to choose sides again, it is you who would rue it." He had not spoken loudly, but his men, recognizing that tone even through the haze of mead, turned to listen.

Cormac drew himself up, still leaning a little—he had drunk a great deal. "Your race did not do so well when Cumhal your father rose against my grandsire Conn the *Ard Ri!*" This sally was echoed by a shout of approbation from King Cormac's men.

"Considering that the odds at Cnucha field were three to one, I think the wonder is rather that the king's men were unable to wound Cumhal at all," Fionn shot back at him. He was becoming angry now. "Had it not been for the men of Connachta and the other subject races that fought on Conn's side that day, your whole kindred could not have made him yield the length of a spear!"

Even as he spoke Fionn recognized that these were only boasts of the kind that men make when they drink before battle. He and Cormac had done it a thousand times before. But now they were boasting against each other, and that was potentially deadly.

"Come now, Fionn," said Garad mac Morna in a clumsy attempt at conciliation. "That is too great a taunt to give the race of Conn."

"They have been just as insulting to us!" exclaimed Oisin. "Tell us, Garad, since you were there on that day—how did Cumhal die?"

Fionn could feel the others moving closer, and knew the guard hairs were rising on their necks as they were on his own. His nostrils flared as if he could smell the change in them, even young Oscar, who crouched beside him with the same look on his face with which Fionn himself, at that age, had confronted his foes. Instinctively he noted where everyone's weapons were.

"Well, he died well," answered Garad reflectively. "For every wound he took he gave two or more, and in the end it was the men he himself had trained who brought him down."

"I do not think that the level of training in the *fianna* has decreased since Cumhal's day. . . ." Fionn said silkily.

There was a murmur of agreement from his men, and suddenly a younger voice that startled them all.

"You would have no trouble getting single combat from the House of Trenmor, even if Fionn were over the sea!" It was Oscar, blushing like fire as every eye turned towards him, but standing his ground.

"And you would get combat from Cormac's sons, puppy, though the *Ard Ri* himself were far away!" Cairbre replied.

"The young dog has young teeth!" cried Oscar, launching himself towards Cairbre. Before he could actually strike a blow, Oisin uncoiled from his place and grabbed him. But all around them on both sides men were reaching for their blades. In another moment the feasting ground would be reddened with the blood of men.

Cormac swayed, blinking, as he tried to sober up enough to understand what was happening, but Cairbre already had his sword. *He wanted this!* thought Fionn, recognizing the look in his eyes. *From the beginning of this feast he has been looking for his opportunity, and I played right into his hands.*

Behind the Gaels, the harpers were trying to pull their instruments to safety. All but Ciothruadh, who still stood behind his harp, watching intently. Considering the number of fights he had sung about, he might well find a real one of interest. But much as the Gaels might need a lesson, it would be a disaster for Caoilte's feast to end in blood.

"Ciothruadh!" Fionn leaped to his feet. "Now is the time to show your skill! Know you the strains that the Dagda played on his harp that he called *Coir-cetharchuir*? Play us a smile-strain or a sleep-strain, harper, lest we shame the *Ard Ri*'s hospitality!"

He saw the hero-light leap in the harper's eyes. Ciothruadh's supple hands fell upon the strings of his harp as a hawk strikes its prey, but the music that exploded from the strings was no battle lay, but a tune so lively that it would have set the folk of the Sidhe to dancing. With chord and run and bright shimmer of melody, the harper plucked out the music, tossing notes from his flying fingers to wing through the air.

Fionn clapped out the rhythm as lustily as he was able. It was a dance they knew well in the *fian*, testing nimbleness and endurance, displaying both a man's coordination and his powers of invention. Caoilte, for all his crane's length of leg, was a lively dancer. He caught on first and whirled away, leaping high. Goll let out one of his deep laughs as one by one the younger men of the *fian* followed.

"Ho, Cairbre!" he bellowed. "On top of a full meal and all, d'ye think ye can match them?"

A number of emotions chased across the face of Cormac's son in quick succession, but his brother Ceallach was already attempting to imitate the swift steps of the dancing, and the other men in the royal party, seeing that no blood was flowing, sheathed their swords.

Now Fionn began to dance as well, wincing as he realized how badly his wind had been affected by the days spent in Cormac's bonds. But for a few moments at least he was able to make a good showing, and that was enough to get most of the others moving.

Ciothruadh played as the harpers of the Sidhe played for their gatherings, when a single night of dancing could take a hundred human years. His music leaped and lilted, the bright notes chasing each other up and down the strings, with grace note and ornament to match the dance steps in complexity, until they became a mingling of partnership and a competition in which each one inspired the other to further feats of skill.

They danced until the fumes of the mead were burned off and they remembered why they had gathered for the feasting; they danced until all the king's men fell down in exhaustion. They danced until most of the *fénnidi* gave up as well, and only Oisin and Caoilte remained upright, moving in graceful figures against the light of the dying fire while Oscar watched them with burning eyes.

When at last the harper's swift fingers began to falter, Fionn slid off one of his golden armrings and went to him.

"Prince of Harpers, take this for your fee," he said

softly, "for you have saved your master's honor tonight, as well as my own." One by one the other men of the *fianna* came forward, each with some token. This night's work would make Ciothruadh a rich man.

Then, as the first awakening birds began to fill the silence left by the ending of the human music, Fionn and the *fianna* slipped away and disappeared into the mists of dawn.

Chapter 12

"WELL IT WAS FOR THE GAELS THAT THE FEASTING did not end in bloodshed," said Oisin grimly, "but Cairbre's insults still burn in my belly." He sat with the other senior men of the *fianna* around the remains of the breakfast fire. A blue thread of smoke twined from the ashes to lose itself among the leaves.

"He was nasty-minded as a child, and has grown no better as a man," said Fionn reflectively, "but Cormac can still rule him."

He leaned back against the oak tree, savoring the mixed scents of woodsmoke and leather and the sweat of healthy men, the essence of the *fian*. It was good to be back in the forest after his captivity indoors.

"That is true," observed Caoilte, "but no man is immortal. Cairbre may well be chosen *Ard Ri* when Cormac is gone. Before that day comes it might be a good idea to show him what the fian can do!"

"Ye cannot attack him, man—" exclaimed Goll,

hunkering down beside Fionn, a half-gnawed deer rib in his hand. "Not the *Ard Ri*'s son."

"To attack *him* was not precisely what I had in mind," answered Caoilte. Fionn looked up quickly and saw the beginnings of his slow smile.

"You are right. Something more subtle is wanted," said Fionn gravely. "Something that will display our skill and style." The two weeks he had spent listening to complaints about Caoilte's tricks while he was captive in Temair had been quite educational. "But it has to be heroic as well . . . at a guess, I would say that Caoilte's chosen target is the *Ard Ri*'s cows."

Caoilte looked disconcerted, then he had the grace to grin.

"I should have known you would guess it!" He turned to the other men. "The thing is, when I was skulking around Temair trying to rescue Fionn, I got to know their arrangements pretty well. Very soon they will be bringing the royal cattle down from the hills, to have them settled before the Lughnasadh Fair. We could seize them easily when they're being driven home."

"I like that," exclaimed Faobhar. "The cattle raid of Cualigne will be nothing to the cattle raid of Temair!"

Fionn grinned with the others, but considering the results of Queen Medb's reiving, he could not help but hope for a better ending to their own enterprise.

FIONN HAD PURSUED HIS SHARE OF RAIDERS IN THE course of defending Eriu; he had never properly appreciated the problem from the other point of view. A cattle raid was not like a pursuit, when one's goal was to make contact with the foe. In this case their purpose must be to redirect several hundred head of healthy, half-wild cattle from the familiar road to their home pastures to some safe location in the hills. They had then to hold them there until they knew if a successful reiving would salvage the *fian's* pride.

Most of the *fénnidi* were more familiar with the antlered herds of the forest than the horned beasts raised by men. For the raid, Fionn had to find men who were not only good fighters and riders, but who, before they joined the *fianna*, had had some experience with cows

Goll laughed hugely when Fionn tried to explain his difficulties. Hey, lad, I wish I were going with you. But it wouldn't do, you know. This particular quarrel is between your clan and that of the high king."

His laugh turned into a cough, and Fionn thumped his back. Everybody coughed in the cold season, but Goll's winter catarrh had been unusually persistent. One grew so accustomed to people's looks, it was not until now that he saw how much bulk Goll had lost in the past year. He was still a big man, but not so solid as he had been, as if his flesh were loosening its hold on the heavy bones. His hair had gone silver, with only an occasional strand of red like a live coal among the ashes to bear witness to its former flame.

But Goll was still a fighter, still strong and canny, the only man he knew who could still call Fionn "lad." Who would have thought they could become such friends, given the enmity with which they had begun? It would have been a fine thing, on this hare-brained adventure, to have had Goll by his side.

They were almost ready to depart when his grandson Oscar came to Fionn, pleading to be allowed to come along.

"Do you think we are going out on a pleasure party? This will be hot, hard, dangerous work with little glory. We are out to make a point, Oscar, not a song."

"You are going to restore the honor of the House of Baoisgne," said Oscar sullenly. "And son to son, I am the last of that kin. It is my right to come with you."

Fionn shook his head and sighed. "True it is that you are kin, lad, but also that you are the youngest—"

"I have turned fifteen!" Oscar exclaimed.

Fionn stared at him. Had it really been fifteen years since Goll had saved him from Conaran's hag-daughters and they had come home to find Eibhir waiting with her young son in her arms?

"But you are not yet a warrior of the *fianna*," Fionn explained.

He supposed that was a problem they would have to face when this was done. Oscar was taller than his father, with heavier bones, his hands and feet still large in proportion, like a half-grown hound. Everything about him was a little bigger, blunter, darker, than Oisin. His sun-streaked hair darkened to an ashy brown, his eyes were the grey of a stormy sky, his nose an eagle's beak inherited, no doubt, from his Roman kin. Oscar had the build to make a fighter, but it was all unfinished. He needed to grow into his bones.

He cleared his throat. "Work hard while we are gone so that you will be ready for your testing when we return."

"It is a game," muttered Oscar. "The practice, even the testing. I cannot do my best because I know it is not real. Give me an enemy to fight. In practice, I am afraid to hurt my friends!"

Fionn stared at him, seeing in memory the face of his first friend, Bran mac Conail, staring sightlessly at the sky. *Brigid be merciful—the boy is entirely too much like me!*

"Practice is what will give you the control you need," he made himself say. "There is no place for a man without discipline on a raid." He got to his feet and stalked away, but he could feel Oscar's gaze burning his back all the way.

IN THE DAYS WHEN FIONN HAD WANDERED THE WORLD with a cropped head to hide from his father's enemies, he had supported himself by serving minor kings. He had been a dog boy and a fire-keeper, a scullion and forge boy, and more than once, he had herded cows. But never, from those days to this, had he seen anything like the herds of the *Ard Ri* of Eriu. As the cattle poured over the rim of the hill, his own emotion was answered by a hiss of drawn breath from the men crouched beside him, an appreciation bred into them by generations of ancestors whose lives had been dedicated to raising, trading, and raiding cows.

Herd by herd they came, as they had been pastured, the bulls guarding the rear and the matriarchs leading, the clappers tied around their necks jangling musically, wreathed with summer flowers. Each bull tended to stamp his get with his own characteristics, so that one herd might be mostly dun and rangy, while another was of stout cream-colored animals, or red and shaggy, or dusty black. But all of them were fine beasts—King Cormac had been taking the best bulls in tribute from the subject peoples for years.

The drovers walked ahead, keeping the beasts to a slow and steady pace, two or three to each herd. They were armed only with knives and light spears to keep off marauding animals; it was not the drovers the *fianna* would be fighting, but the warriors Cormac would send after them when he learned that the cattle were gone. But first they had to deal with the cows.

At Fionn's signal, the men eased back down from the rim of the hill and moved back to the horses that were waiting in the patch of fir wood below.

"There are four herds in the drive," said Fionn. "Close enough together so that they can hear each other. We will divide up, therefore, and fall upon them when I blow my horn. Try not to harm the drovers, but get the cattle going. There are rain clouds moving in already. If you obscure the tracks at the point where each herd is taken off the trail to the refuge we have prepared for it, Cormac's trackers may as well tell him that the Sidhe have taken them, for all the good their skills will do."

Grinning broadly, the men mounted their ponies. Fionn cuffed his dun mare to make her stand still, then leaped, hung for a moment across her withers, and swung his leg over her side. He felt the wind in his hair and the mare's strong muscles working beneath him, and suddenly his anxiety gave way to a wild excitement. They were committed now, and need care about nothing but making this cattle raid worthy of song.

Whooping, the first four riders pelted down the slope, with Oisin, who could ride anything with four legs, in the lead. The drover's curiosity turned to alarm as they neared. He began to shout something about disturbing the beasts, but that, of course, was their intention, and the warriors grinned. The bell-cow threw up her head, snorting like old Bodbmall in a fury, and Fionn nearly fell off his pony laughing. But her outrage at the change in procedure could not stand against the mounting hysteria of the rest of the herd.

The wild-eyed heifers were the first to break ranks, with the older animals following. The bull went after his wayward ladies, bellowing noisily, and in another moment they were all plunging through the gap in the trees. For Fionn, the world narrowed to a confusion of rolling eyes and heaving dun backs. Grimly he clung to the pony's back as they dodged tossing horns and limbs of trees.

The stampede seemed to last for hours, but the sun had only moved a palm's breadth across the sky when their mad career at last began to slow. The frantic scramble became a rocking gallop, which eased to a jog and finally an exhausted walk. Even the mare, her excitement run off at last, seemed content to amble in the wake of the herd, while Fionn's racing heartbeat slowed.

They had come a good way around the eastern edge of the forest, and the advancing clouds were swiftly stealing the brightness from the day. But that was what Fionn had counted on. The ground ahead was broken heath; if they could get the herd across it before the storm hit, the rain would wash out most of the tracks, and by splitting the herd again and again, he judged they could confuse any pursuers. The first few hours were crucial. If they could get clean away in that time, there were a hundred folds and hollows in the hills where a few beasts could be hidden away.

Some of the men were on foot now, encouraging the cows in the right direction with the butts of their spears. Others were following with shovels and brooms. He had forgotten just how frustrating working cattle could be. It was not that they were stupid, exactly, but what brain they had was directed towards such limited goals. However, what they lacked in intelligence they more than made up for in willfulness. Fionn kicked his pony after the bull once more. A damp breath of wind cooled his brow and he felt on his face the first drops of rain.

With the rain, the cattle ceased their resistance and consented to be driven across the heath and up through the oak wood. Then the group was split again and each man herded his beasts on the long circle that would eventually bring them back together once more.

Four days later, saddle sore but exultant, the reivers and their booty were reunited in the home pastures that belonged to Almu. One horse had broken a leg in the chase and several of the men had gashes from tree branches or horns, but the cattle, though gaunt from the lack of grazing time, had come through in good condition.

Fionn's own herds had not yet been brought down from the hills. They would do well enough in the high pastures for the next moon or two, but they would have to do something with Cormac's beasts before Samhain. He did not think that would be a problem. He had already heard about the *Ard Ri*'s fury when his cattle did not show up in time for the Tailtiu Fair.

Cormac's first reaction had been to accuse the other chieftains of the Gaels, especially those who had been his family's principal rivals for the lordship of Eriu. It would take a while for his officers to search their lands. The folk of Laigin were loyal; Fionn did not think that anyone would tell the *Ard Ri* how amazingly the *fianna*'s herds had reproduced this year. And yet the point of the exercise had not been to keep the cattle, but to get away with stealing them, and that point would be lost if Cormac did not eventually find out who had diddled him. Just past the Autumn Equinox, Fionn thought, was when he ought to send his messenger.

AS THE SEASON TURNED TOWARDS SAMHAIN THE weather grew crisp and chill. The belling of the red stags rang in the glens as the Hunter's Moon rolled across the sky. The deer were growing fat and thick-coated—it looked as if the coming winter would be a hard one—and the *fianna* ranged the hills, culling the stags that had lost their mating fights and the old barren does. The cattle raid had been an interesting diversion, thought Fionn, as he trotted down the forest trails, but this was a more proper labor for a man of the *fian*.

It was towards the end of the day, when the new moon was just rising, that the hunters became the hunted, and King Cormac came in search of his missing cows. His arrival was not completely unexpected, but Fionn had not thought he could get here so quickly. As he heard the first shouts he began to curse his own complacence, for the *fianna*'s orders were to head home the next morning, and the hunting bands were still scattered through the hills.

Fionn melted back into the forest, becoming one with the foliage, as four of the *Ard Ri*'s warriors came down the trail. Birga twitched in his hand and he gripped the spear tightly. He could have killed them easily, but that was not his intention. He wanted to talk to Cormac, not fight him, and he would need an equal force at his back if he was going to persuade the king to consider terms.

The forest became musical with birdcalls as the *fénnidi* signaled. The *Ard Ri* might guess that all this avian activity had some significance, but until Fionn was ready for him, the royal war band would not see a single foe. Cormac was intelligent enough to realize that, but he also knew that by leading his men into the forests around Almu he had issued a challenge that Fionn could not ignore.

By evening, Fionn knew that the high king had brought fifty of his finest warriors, veterans of a hundred forays against the coasts of Britannia, and experienced in fighting their fellow Gaels. The best young warriors of the ruling tribes entered Cormac's service; it was one sure road to influence and power, and the *Ard Ri* was a generous master. But although many of these warriors had fought alongside the *fianna*, they had never before had to face the particular skills in which Fionn trained his men.

Cormac's warriors, growing noisier as darkness fell and the shadows made them apprehensive, made a workmanlike camp, thickly posted with sentries. In the center was a roaring fire. Fionn grinned when he saw it, knowing that every time the men on guard turned to talk to their fellows, the brightness would destroy their night vision. It was a mistake no first-year trainee for the *fianna* would have made. Fionn wondered if Cormac had assumed, all those times when they were campaigning together, that the *fianna* kept their fires small and low out of humility.

Fionn's men ate cold meat that night and lay without a fire. By dawn, he had gathered a little over half as many fighters as the high king, but he reckoned that if he used them correctly, Cormac would assume he had more. In the chill hour before the dawning a touch awakened them, and as the mists began to drift down the hillsides, they moved into position around the campsite of the high king.

Their fire had burned down to ashes. Humped shapes lay still around it, and the sentries leaned sleepily on their spears. From across the circle a wren twittered, and Fionn answered it. At the signal, his men rose like the mists, twitching spears from the lax hands of the sentries with one deft motion and with the next getting a lock on the throat and bringing their quarry down.

No one had cried out, but some of the men thrashed about a good bit as their captors overpowered them, and, within their circle, some of the sleepers began to stir. Killing them would have been quieter. Grinning, Fionn set his hunting horn to his lips and bugled a merry tune.

At the first notes, warriors exploded from their rolled cloaks like a covey of flushed quail, grabbing for spears.

"Ho, Cormac," cried Fionn, "it is time to wake up if you would be ahunting. We have netted a fine quarry already!"

The high king knew his voice, even if nothing else made sense at this hour. He turned, lowering his spear a little, though he did not put it down.

"Fionn, you cattle-thieving madman, what does this mean?"

"It means I want to talk to you—"

"We don't talk to traitors!" cried Cairbre, standing at his father's elbow. "Release our men!"

"I was speaking to the high king," snapped Fionn.

"As for your men, if I had meant to betray you, we would have killed them. We could have killed you just as easily as you lay sleeping."

"Put down your weapons, Fionn, and come out to face me," growled Cormac. "And I may listen, but by all the gods you will have to surpass yourself to talk your way out of this one—"

Fionn began to wonder if he had outsmarted himself indeed. Surprise was fine, but he had forgotten how out of temper the high king could get when he had not slept well. Still armed, he moved silently forward, and was pleased to see Cairbre jump as he appeared suddenly between two of the fallen sentries, who struggled anew as he passed them, but no more successfully than before.

Cormac, however, continued to scowl. "Cairbre was right. I have indulged you people too long. It is time you remembered who is master in Eriu."

"Do you think so?" asked Fionn. "It seems to me the spear is in the other hand. I have served you so long and faithfully that you began to take me for granted. It was not well-done, *Ard Ri*, to keep me in fetters in your hall. It was because we were loyal that Caoilte did no more than trick you. It is because I am loyal that I determined to remind you of the *fianna*'s skills by carrying off your cattle instead of burning down your hall."

"You have shamed me before my people, Fionn mac Cumhal," Cormac said heavily. "To avenge that will require a heavy reckoning."

"Oh, I always meant to return your cattle," Fionn said cheerfully. "After all, I have plenty of my own."

"The cattle are nothing!" exclaimed Cairbre. "We too have more. But all over the land the subject peoples are laughing! And that insult to our honor will only be wiped out when their laughter turns to tears!"

"What honor is there in oppressing your people when your quarrel is with me?" asked Fionn.

"The people will weep when they hear of your fate, Fionn," Cormac said grimly. "That is what he means. To avenge this dishonor, blood must flow."

Fionn eyed him unhappily, wondering if he could keep him talking long enough for his mood to brighten along with the day. Oisin had moved into position on the other side of the circle, his face taking on already that intent look it got when he was expecting battle. Indeed, this stratagem did seem to have gone awry; perhaps blood was the only thing the Gaels could understand.

"If you and I fight, no one will win—" he began, but he had forgotten that he was not the only one listening to the high king. One of the captive sentries, more awake than the others or perhaps more affected by his lord's words, chose that moment to try to break free.

He was a big man, and strong, but Fearghusa, who held him, was tough and fast. They rolled over and over, fighting for the *fénnid*'s knife. Steel flickered in the morning light, then there was a scream, and when the knife came up again it was red.

"Do you think so?" Cormac cried in sudden fury, and launched himself at Fionn, putting his full weight behind the spear.

For one nearly fatal moment, Fionn could not move. He had known this course was dangerous, but in his heart he had never believed that Cormac would turn on him. Then he got his spear up, gripping the shaft in both hands as if it were a staff and, twisting, deflected the blow. The high king cursed and came at him again; Fionn settled into a defensive crouch, spear poised. Cormac would be lucky indeed to get a hit in past his guard.

The rest of his men were under no such inhibitions about killing. Outnumbered though they were, the *fénnidi* were fighting furiously, and when the first fury of the king's onslaught slowed, Fionn saw one of the royal houseguard already groaning on the ground. But the others were doing well, and Cairbre, especially, fought with a stubborn ferocity that Fionn had not expected; he had given Dubhán a slash across the arm that put him out of the battle, and now he was keeping Oisin at bay. Fionn did not allow himself to doubt that they would win this one, but he knew it was going to be a close-run thing.

By the time the sun had cleared the trees he was less sure they would even win. Cormac's blows were coming more slowly, but so were his own, and the superior numbers of the Gaels were beginning to make a difference. Fearghusa was down, though still living, and three more of his men lay sprawled in a boneless stillness that gave no hope they would rise again. But even now he did not try to kill the *Ard Ri,* though he rather hoped, since it had come to open conflict, that someone would manage to bring Cairbre down.

A little while longer, and enough of the house guard had won their battles to come to their master's aid. Suddenly Fionn found himself fighting two of them at once while Cormac himself retired to lean panting against a tree.

"This is an ill trick, Cormac, to send your hounds to wear me down while you look on," he gasped, and the king managed a croak of laughter. "On the other hand—" he paused, batting one spear aside and driving Birga in under the ribs of the second man, "these foes I can kill!"

He saw a deeper flush redden Cormac's face, then two more warriors came in to replace the one he had speared, and he had neither breath nor attention to spare for the king.

Fionn was beginning to wish rather strongly that he could take a moment to go catch his breath along with Cormac when a hunting lance sped suddenly past him and lodged in the eye of his most active foe. The man shrieked and dropped his sword, grabbing at the shaft, but command of his limbs was already leaving him, and he collapsed in an untidy sprawl.

Fionn whirled, guarding, glanced behind him to see where the lance had come from, and almost missed his parry as he saw Oscar, now quite unarmed, standing there. But not for long. In the next moment the boy snatched up a heavy branch that had been too big for last night's bonfire and began to lay about him, yelling like a *bean-sidhe*.

With all Oscar's explosive adolescent strength behind it, the log swept through the fighters like a lethal broom, knocking down friend and foe. But since it was the foe he was aiming at, the *fianna* were more likely to be bowled over by falling enemies than by the branch, and quicker to rise again. Presently the branch broke in the middle from the force of his blows and became a club, which Oscar used with equal effectiveness.

When Oisin fought, his eyes sparkled with interest, but Oscar's eyes were glazed with battle-fury, and Fionn knew with sick certainty that this was how he himself had looked when he went mad and killed Bran mac Conail and the other boys on the hurley field. But it was undeniably effective, as if a minor whirlwind had been set down in the midst of the fray.

After the first shock, the surviving *fénnid* warriors renewed their onslaught, laughing as one of Oscar's blows lofted a man like a hurley ball and flung him against a tree. For a time thereafter things were very busy. It was only when he heard one of the Gaels shouting to the others to get the *Ard Ri* away that he realized they had won.

Fionn sounded his horn to hold his men, for he had seen that Cairbre was one of those left on the ground. He had been knocked out, but his wounds were still oozing, and it had occurred to Fionn that Cormac's son would be a great deal more valuable for bargaining than his cows.

Quick orders set the men to work binding those enemies who still looked ambulatory, and binding up the wounds of the others. When at last they counted over the slain, among those who had been taken out by Oscar's club were two chieftains from the *Ard Ri*'s houseguard, and among the *fianna*, young Linné, who had been Oscar's friend.

Oscar himself was still standing where he had fought, beginning to tremble as awareness came back into his eyes. Fionn, who had been watching for this, went to him.

"Be still now, be easy," he said softly. "It is over, over now. Oscar, look at me—you are Oscar, and it is Fionn who is calling you."

"Linné . . ." he whispered, and Fionn sighed, realizing that Oscar's hearing had returned first of all.

"It is not your fault, lad; he moved into your blow. It happens sometimes in war."

"I wanted . . ." Oscar swallowed and tried again. "I wanted to help you."

"Oscar—" Fionn moved closer and set a hand on the boy's shoulder, feeling the fine tremors that ran through the hard muscle beneath the skin. He gave the shoulder a squeeze, and the grey gaze came up to meet his, dark with pain. A difficult childhood had taught Oscar to conceal his feelings, but though he might like to think his heart was made from horn and sheathed in steel, he was flesh and blood after all.

"Oscar, you did help us. If you had not come when you did, they might have won." At least one good thing had come out of the disaster—this shining revelation of Oscar's might.

Oisin had been watching. At the words, he came up to them, hesitant, as if he feared to be sent away. In his face Fionn saw a delight in his son that had not been there since the moment when Eibhir first laid the infant in his arms.

"Oscar, lad," he said with a friendly malice, "your grandfather is understating the matter to cover his own miscalculations. You were a hero, and you saved our hides!"

"It is true," agreed the others. "I never saw anything like it. Gods, did you see how he bowled them down?"

"Has any man of the *fian* performed such a hero-feat before, and with only a piece of wood to aid?" asked Fionn, seizing the moment. "I cannot think of a greater testing. Would any man disagree, do you think, that Oscar mac Oisin is worthy to be one of the *fianna* now?"

"Oscar! Oscar!" The men surged around him, shouting his name, while Cairbre glared sourly above his bonds. Fionn wondered if anyone had ever been so happy about anything Cairbre had done as the *fianna* was about Oscar now. And as the *fénnidi* acclaimed their newest member, at long last Fionn saw Oscar smile.

THE NEXT MORNING FIONN SENT MEN TO BEGIN GATHering the *Ard Ri*'s cattle and herding them home. They had missed the Fair at Tailtiu, and now Cormac could figure out how to feed them all through the winter season. To send them back, unasked, was also in the nature of a challenge, especially when they came with the message that Fionn was willing to discuss terms for ransoming Cairbre at Cormac's convenience, but that he considered the prince worth more than any number of cows.

Cormac would be wondering what he did want, thought Fionn, as he turned homeward towards Almu. Worrying about that would do him good; almost as much good as watching Cairbre try to walk in his fetters was doing Fionn.

The high king's messenger returned to them the next day, confirming Fionn's suspicion that Cormac was still hanging about in Laigin. However, he had agreed to meet Fionn, neither at Almu nor yet in his own fortress, but under the eye of the priestesses of Brigid on the plain of the Curragh below her shrine.

FIONN WAITED IN THE SHADE OF THE OAK TREES, watching the *Ard Ri*'s party approach across the plain. Cormac was followed by at least a hundred warriors, but he himself was not armed or harnessed for battle. That was a good sign, especially as Fionn was clad only in tunic and mantle of forest green. He glanced back at the hundred who had come with him from

Almu, hunkered down to watch two of their number play at *fidchel*, or leaning on their spears with an ease that was deceptive. A single whistle would bring them upright and ready for battle.

It was one of the last golden days of autumn, when the world seems to hold its breath for wonder at the beauty which is so soon to pass. The sky was a thin pale blue, against which the oak leaves glowed every shade of bronze and gold; even the fading grass had a tawny richness. Men's clothing glowed brightly against this background, as if it, too, had absorbed some of the gold. Lest they be remiss in hospitality, a fire pit had been dug and a great cauldron suspended from forks above it, though the pot would not be filled nor the fire started until it became apparent whether their unwilling guests were going to stay.

In this scene of general holiday Cairbre was the only exception. His hurts had been tended and his clothing mended, but his fetters were as like the ones he had persuaded his father to put on Fionn as could be arranged. But where Fionn had tried not to show how he was galled by his captivity, Cairbre had met all offers of conversation with sullen silence. He was not an amusing guest, and Fionn would be glad to get rid of him. Indeed, he thought that if he had to look at that sour face much longer, he might pay Cormac to take his son away.

The sound of the high king's horns echoed with mournful clarity across the plain. Fionn came out from beneath the shade to stand waiting, like any attentive host. A flicker of red from the gateway to the shrine told him that at least one of the priestesses was waiting too. He had an uneasy feeling that this summer's accomplishments were not quite what the goddess had wanted from him, but there was nothing he could do about that now.

He watched while Cormac strode towards him, dressed in purple with golden fringes and most of his jewelry. Clearly he wanted no one to doubt his wealth or his power, but the shining gold only seemed to emphasize how much silver glinted in the *Ard Ri*'s hair. Fionn grinned sourly. As if to emphasize his disdain for such trappings he had kept his own dress simple, with only the golden torque of a chieftain to proclaim his standing.

"Will you sit?" he asked kindly, and when the *Ard Ri* shook his head, glowering, snapped his fingers to one of the lads to bring up a great, silver-mounted horn brimming with ale. "Drink then," he said softly. "Drink to a happy conclusion to our meeting." He set the horn to his own lips, tipped it up, and took a long swallow, then handed it to the king.

"Have you left any for me, or was that to prove it is not poisoned?" muttered Cormac. "There was no need—I would not suspect that of you. On the other hand, I never expected you to steal my cows!" He lifted the horn and did not cease from drinking until it was drained.

There was more than a little relief in Fionn's sigh. If Cormac could face the situation with even this much humor, there was hope for them still.

"Did the cattle reach home safe and sound?" he asked blandly.

"It will take another summer's grazing to replace the meat you ran off them, but they arrived. . . ." His gaze flicked over to his son, then back to Fionn.

"Then it is time to discuss the ransom for your other

possession." A dull red crept up Cairbre's neck, and Fionn showed his teeth in a smile.

"What do you want?" growled Cormac.

"*Ni ansa*— it is not difficult to say, lord King, though it may be harder for you to do. There has been too much talk of the submission of the subject races in this conflict, and the glory of the Gaels," Fionn went on. "All these years, Cormac, it has not been as a slave that I served you, but as a partner in the defense of Eriu. If there are any who think otherwise, then the time has come to show them they are wrong." He turned, as if by chance, so that he faced the cauldron.

"Go under the forks of the cauldron, High King," Fionn said softly. "And take back your son."

"You cannot!" cried Cairbre, struggling futilely against his bonds.

But Cormac was silent. Fionn waited in patience, knowing it was no easy decision. When the royal Gaels had returned from their British exile to reconquer Eriu, they had symbolized their triumph by requiring each conquered chieftain to pass beneath the forks of the cauldron in token of submission and servitude. A murmur had gone through the men of both sides at his words, but presently they, too, fell silent, waiting to see what Cormac would do.

It seemed a very long time before he moved. But the silence became, if possible, more profound as he stalked over to the waiting cauldron, bent with a stiffness that was not entirely physical, and crept beneath the great bar from which it hung. His face was dark with emotion as he emerged, and Fionn felt tension rising among his men like oncoming thunder.

But he himself was already moving, and before anyone else could react, he followed Cormac and himself passed beneath the fork of the cauldron to come up beside the *Ard Ri* on the other side. He held out his hand.

"In this, as always, lord King, when it is for the good of Eriu, I follow you."

For a moment Cormac simply stared at him. Then the fury in his eyes gave way to a reluctant appreciation. With the beginnings of an answering smile, he took Fionn's hand.

Chapter 13

THE WILD WINDS OF SPRINGTIDE BLUSTERED AROUND the walls of Almu, drying the mud in the courtyards and plucking at the thatching, moaning like a lost child. Fionn huddled near the fire in the feasting hall with a blanket around his shoulders, trying not to cough. This year the rheum that swept through the *dun* every winter had been unusually severe. In some, like old Mongfind, it had turned to a raging fever which carried the sufferer off within a few days. But for most the symptoms were shakes and chills and a cough that settled in the lungs.

Even now, Fionn could feel the fluid building again. Though he fought it, the pressure was too great for him; he coughed convulsively, bringing up phlegm in great rasping heaves.

When at last the fit was over, he took a long pull from the horn of mead by his side, and the raw places in his throat were soothed by its golden fire. Mongfind would have been forcing one of her herbal concoctions, almost as foul as the ones Bodbmall used to brew when he was a boy, down his throat by now. Without her strong hand on the reins the management of Almu had been suffering. He needed to find someone to rule his household, he knew, but he had grown used to the old woman ordering them all about. To give another her place seemed disrespectful. The obvious candidate would have been that girl Aidin that they had married to Oscar in hopes of settling him down. But all she seemed good for was to moon after her young husband when he was present and weep when he was gone.

It would be easier, Fionn thought as he stretched out his hands to the fire, if only he could get warm.

A draft made the flames flare as the hide that covered the doorway was thrust aside and Oscar and his companions came in from hunting. Their smells, their noise, and their vibrant good health seemed to fill the space to bursting. Fionn grimaced and pulled the mead horn out of the way of temptation.

But the young men sounded as if they were already well started on their drinking. If he had been healthy, thought Fionn, he might have stopped it, but in the five years since Oscar had been accepted into the *fianna* it had become clear that he could neither be led nor driven. It was not that he intentionally rebelled, thought Fionn, as he watched his grandson sprawl across a bench on the other side of the fire. But Oscar walked his own way always.

The best you could do was to open a path in the direction you wanted him to go and be ready to clear up afterward if the results were not entirely as expected. The year before, Oscar's lads had found an old broom in an abandoned cottage and taken it for their battle standard. They called themselves the "Terrible Broom," because once they began their charge, everything in their path was swept clean away.

Fionn looked at them and sighed. Goll's red-haired son Feadha stood with his head back, laughing at a joke Fear Logha was telling him. Young Fer-li was arm wrestling with mac Lugach's son Glas while Emer Glunglas, the other Clan Morna boy, shouted encouragement. They were the new broom of the *fianna*, this younger generation, eager to sweep all the old men and the old ways aside. When Fionn looked at them they seemed absurdly young—their leader was his grandson, and their newest recruit his great-grandson, mac Lugach's boy. And yet they were no younger than he had been when he won admission to Crimall's *fian*.

He winced as a shout of laughter shook the roof-beams. Oscar's war band reminded him of young race-horses penned in too small a pasture, bursting out of their skins with health and energy.

Oscar himself lay watching, with his long limbs extended in illusory relaxation. At twenty, he had grown into his bones. He towered above most of the other men in the *fian*, and it was all muscle. He looked half-asleep, but the eyes beneath the heavy lids missed little. For a lark or a quarrel he would be awake in a second—especially for a fight. Fionn sighed again, thinking of the compensation he had just had to pay for a farmer's cart destroyed when the lads commandeered it to win a wager. Glad though he was to have them, Oscar and his band could be expensive allies.

Suddenly Oscar swung his feet off the bench and in a single fluid motion stood up, watching the door. Fionn stilled, listening, and in another moment heard the watchman's halloo. A messenger was coming, one of his own men, from the sound of the greetings. Fionn shrugged off the blanket. Even if he was one, he had no mind to greet the fellow looking like an old man good for no more than to huddle by the fire.

There was a time when Fionn would have depended on the *Ard Ri* to give him news. But though their relationship was officially as strong as ever, it had been strained by the episode of the cattle raid and the forks of the cauldron five years before. It had seemed a wise move to establish observers in the various districts and clanholds, and, of course, in Temair. They had a set schedule for reporting, but no one was due just now. He wondered what had gone wrong.

Splashed with mud and worn with fast travelling, the man who entered the hall was hard to recognize as the young *fili* whom Fionn had recommended for a post with Gae-Adúath of the Dési.

"What is the matter? Is the chieftain dead?" asked Fionn, when the man had gulped half of the beaker of beer that Oscar handed him.

"Gods, I wish that were so! He's not dead—he is angry. That fool Ceallach has bedded the little niece Gae-Adúath is so fond of, and he's galloped off to Temair with blood in his eye."

A fool indeed, Fionn reflected, thinking swiftly. Ceallach had always had an eye for the women, willing or unwilling, he did not seem to care. At least Oscar had not caused trouble that way, and since the episode with Eargna even Oisin had taken care. The Dési were a proud people, apt to read unforgivable insult into a matter that would be handled among the Gaels by paying compensation all round.

"When did he go?" he asked.

"Yesterday morning. I left soon after, but by now he'll be at Temair."

Fionn nodded. If he knew Cormac, the *Ard Ri* would keep the Dési chieftain waiting as long as possible, hoping his ire would cool. Gae-Adúath's temper was as terrible as his spear, but he might listen to Fionn, who spoke for the Galeóin peoples of Eriu, where he would not hear the king. Cormac might not know it, but he needed his *Rígfénnid*. If Fionn took his swiftest pony, he might be in time.

"Faobhar, go out to the stables and tell them to saddle up the Grey Swan. Moragh," he said to the serving girl, "pack up my crimson tunic and my warm mantle, and tell young Donall to ready my arms."

"Are you well enough to travel?" asked Oscar. He had never learned tact, either, thought his grandfather, managing a smile.

"I will have to be."

"You should not go unescorted," said Oscar. "I will come with you."

Fionn started to protest that he did not expect to need protection, but he had not expected to be imprisoned when he went to Temair before.

"REMEMBER, WE ARE GOING TO STOP TROUBLE, NOT TO start it," he said repressively.

"We will not have to start the trouble. Cairbre will be there. . . ." Oscar said grimly, and Fionn sighed, wondering what would happen if Cairbre became high king, which after Ceallach's latest escapade, was looking increasingly likely. Neither Oisin nor Oscar had any use for Cormac's second son, who himself had never forgotten that it was Oscar's blow that allowed the *fianna* to capture him.

Where Cairbre was concerned, Oisin and Caoilte were just as much a liability as Oscar, and in any case they would not be back from their own hunting expedition for several days. Goll would have been better; Cairbre seemed more tolerant of the mac Mornas, if only because he thought it would annoy Fionn. But there was no way to summon him in time. It would have to be Oscar or no one. He nodded.

"With you and Sceolan at my side, he will not dare to trouble me!"

FIONN COULD READ THE SIGNS OF IMPENDING CONFLICT even before he got through the gates of Temair. An encampment of Dési warriors had sprouted outside the gates. They rose to their feet as Fionn and his men trotted past, uncertain whether to glower or cheer, but their dogs barked hysterically when they scented Sceolan. Armed warriors paced the ramparts, and there were more men guarding the great gate than he had ever seen before. Gae-Adúath was a brave man, or perhaps foolhardy, to challenge the *Ard Ri* in his own *dun.*

"Lord Fionn," exclaimed the gate-captain, "we did not expect you—"

"If I only turned up where I was expected, I would not be much good to Eriu," answered Fionn, swinging his leg over the horse's neck and sliding down. After three days' swift riding, he ached in every bone.

He held on to the pony for a moment, waiting for his head to clear. A man came to take the horse away, but by then Oscar was at his elbow. Fionn suppressed the impulse to shake him loose, damning him silently for having guessed correctly that his grandfather needed the support of his arm.

"Gae-Adúath has just gone into the meadhall," said the gate guard. "But I've heard no shouting yet, so I do not think they can have begun!"

"ARD RI, FOR FORTY YEARS YOU HAVE HELD POWER AS king over all Eriu—"

Fionn paused just inside the entry to let his sight adjust. The voice was not that of the Dési chieftain, but he thought he should know it.

"Not over the Gael only, but the Galeóin—the Lu-agni and the Fir Domnan and the rest of the tribes that pay tribute to you. It is as lord of Eriu, therefore, that we appeal to you for justice. . . ."

Fionn moved forward. Now he could see the *Ard Ri*, seated on his platform in the center of the hall above the hearth, glittering with gold. To one side stood Gae-Adúath, feet apart and beard jutting defiantly, with two white hounds beside him, while Ceallach, washed and combed and looking altogether harmless, stood with his brother Cairbre behind him on the other. It was the Dési chieftain's chief druid who was speaking, his white robe luminous in the firelight.

"In the judgment of the king is the health of the king-dom," answered Cormac soberly.

His own druids formed a wall of white behind him, setting off the multicolored embroideries of his robes. Fionn suppressed a smile. The *Ard Ri* was decked with all his symbols of authority, from the massive golden torque around his neck to the white wand of kingship in his hand. His hair had been oiled and combed smooth so that it looked more dark than grey; the shadows around his eyes and the lines that care had graven into his brow made him all the more kingly.

I was right, thought Fionn, *to serve this man.*

As Fionn and the *fénnidi* came forward a little stir ran through the warriors of the royal houseguard, who stood ranked along the sides of the hall. The *Ard Ri*'s eyelids flickered, but the only indication he gave of having seen them was the faintest lessening of tension in the set of his shoulders.

Cairbre saw it, and turned, and his own reaction was marked enough for Gae-Adúath to note their arrival as well. For a moment he frowned uncertainly, trying to decide whether Fionn was a threat or an ally, then turned back to the high king.

"Hear us then," cried the druid. "And though the blame fall upon your own kin, justice we require."

"Who is it that brings forward the accusation, and who is accused of the crime?" asked Cormac grimly.

He was skipping no step in the ritual. Despite all the trouble that Ceallach had been, his ebullience made him easier to love than Cairbre's calculating obedience. Fionn, who had had to deal with the consequences of Oisin's escapades, knew that whatever Ceallach had done, his father would do a great deal to save him.

"It is I, Aonghus of the Dési, called Gae-Adúath, who accuse!" The chieftain, unable to contain himself any longer, stepped in front of his druid. "Rape—the rape of my own niece—is the crime, and the man I accuse of the deed is Ceallach your son!"

Cormac's features twitched, but his voice was steady.

"Ceallach, what say you?"

"I did not rape the girl," muttered Ceallach.

"Will ye deny that we found ye pumping away as

ye held her down upon the floor?" sputtered Gae-Adúath.

"I'll not deny that I had her," flared Ceallach, "but it was no rape. She was more eager than I was."

"Why, ye lyin' bastard! D'ye accuse my own sister's daughter of dishonor?"

Fionn closed his eyes, stifling a cough. If Ceallach had admitted his fault, they might have scraped through this, but he was trying to get off with the oldest excuse in the world. Sometimes it was even true. But Ceallach's reputation was bound to count against him as much as his truculent air.

"She wanted me! She led me on! What was I to do?"

You might have tried resisting — The thought was driven from Fionn's mind as Cairbre pushed forward beside his brother.

"It is you who have called your own kin whore!"

Gae-Adúath's roar stunned them all. The rest of them were still blinking with the shock of Cairbre's taunt when the Dési chieftain whirled, wrenched the spear from the hands of a startled guard, and lunged.

The scene shattered into fragments: the two hounds, barking furiously; Ceallach's slack mouth opening in surprise as the spear drove towards him; Cormac, throwing off his royal mantle and leaping down from the dais, drawing his sword; Cairbre shouting, and a confusion of other faces as Fionn himself ran forward.

Afterward, when Fionn tried to understand exactly what had happened, more images came to mind. He could remember blood spraying as Gae-Adúath's spear pierced Ceallach's chest, and Cairbre and Cormac turning on the Dési chieftain; he could see once more the butt of Gae-Adúath's spear drawn back as he tried to meet them. But no matter how many times he worked it through, he was never certain whether Cairbre had been trying to deflect the spear or direct it as the blunt end of the weapon smashed into Cormac's face. The high king rocked, his features contorting in agony, but the smooth arc of his sword stroke continued, gathering light, as it sliced through Gae-Adúath's neck and sent his head flying through the air.

By that time the rest of the Dési escort had plunged into the action, and so had Fionn's men. Fionn tried to cry "Hold!" but he could not suck in enough air. He laid about him with his spear shaft, trying to drive the struggling warriors away from the fallen men, and heard someone gasp as his point struck. He fought his way towards Cormac, who was up on one elbow, blood oozing from his eye.

Something rushed through the air behind him. Over his shoulder Fionn saw Oscar heft one of the long benches and whip it around, clearing the floor. Warriors went flying in every direction. Above the thud of falling bodies, his young voice rang out, and gradually the clamor stilled.

"Cormac—" Fionn went down on one knee beside the *Ard Ri*. "How is it with you?"

"There's . . . still a fight or two . . . left in me." He grimaced and put his hand to his eye.

"You took off Gae-Adúath's head, anyhow. That was a fine blow," said Fionn.

"He killed my son." The pain that throbbed in Cormac's voice had nothing to do with his eye.

The druids were huddling near the walls; some with crimson splashed across their white gowns. Fionn beckoned to those who seemed to have retained the greatest self-possession, and turned, looking for more wounded.

He saw his own warriors gathered around a still figure, and felt his belly clench. Not Oscar—no, he had seen him fighting. Someone moved, giving him a clear view of the body, and he saw a strong throat with a gaping wound where a spear had slashed it and red hair spread across the straw. *Feadha* . . . the only living son of his own half brother's daughter, and Goll mac Morna's last-born child. Oscar looked up and saw him watching, and some bitter sympathy in the younger man's gaze told Fionn that the spear that had made that deadly wound had been Fionn's own.

AS THE SEASON DREW ON TOWARDS BELTANE THE LAND lay quiet, but it was a deceptive peace, full of tension, as the Gaels waited to see if Cormac would recover from his wound and the Dési readied themselves for war. Fionn and his men returned to Almu, but though Fionn was still troubled by his cough, he could not settle. Hoping to build up his wind, he took to ranging the countryside accompanied only by Sceolan. He had offered Goll compensation for Feadha's death, but so far there had been no reply.

On a misty day in the moon before Beltane, Fionn started off for the outcropping of rock that the *fianna* referred to as his high seat. The weather had improved enough so that sitting out was a pleasure, and by the time he got there he was usually ready to rest awhile.

Tired as he was, he might have missed the small change in the sounds of the wood that meant danger. But when Sceolan stopped, ears pricking, Fionn started to turn, and the lance that would have pierced his heart put a hole through the folds of his cloak and spun him around instead. He staggered from the impact, shock sending a rush of power through his veins.

Sceolan had already launched himself in the direction the lance had come from; Fionn heard a crashing in the bushes and a cry.

"Hold him, lad, hold him!" he called, running towards the sound. Sceolan's warning growl came from somewhere ahead. He pulled aside the branches, his own spear poised, and saw the dog standing over someone with hot eyes and black hair.

For one heart-stopping moment Fionn saw Diarmuid lying there. Then his mind began to work again and he focused on a beardless face and gangling limbs, and on the boy's fair face an expression compounded equally of terror and shame. He let out his breath with a croak of laughter.

"Which one of them are you? Let me see—Donnchadh had fair hair like Grainne, and the littler boys would be too young still. You must be—Eochaid—" memory supplied the name. "Did your mother send you to murder me?"

"She didn't—" Eochaid shut off the words, glaring. "Do what you must. I am not afraid!"

"She didn't know? You needn't glower at me, lad. I am not going to kill you—" Fionn paused, considering. He had heard that after Diarmuid's death Grainne had gone to live on her dower lands in Laigin, no more than a day or two away. "I have a better idea," he said slowly. "I think I will take you home."

Sceolan was still growling softly, but his tail was wagging gently as well. Anyone who knew him would realize that his intentions were basically friendly, but from where Eochaid was lying, those white teeth must have looked very sharp indeed. There was no need to bind the boy while the hound was there.

Hiding his own smile, Fionn found a piece of wood,

trimmed it, and after a moment's thought scratched an ogham message on the flat surface. He stuck the boy's lance into the earth and tied the stave to its shaft. Oisin would want some proof his father had not gone mad.

"All right," he said pleasantly. "Let us move on." He motioned the dog back and Eochaid sat up, eyeing him dubiously.

"You mean to go away with me, just as you are?"

Your mother ran off in just such a fashion, thought Fionn. "You think I cannot do it?" he said aloud. "In the *fianna,* we live off the land. On the way to Grainne's *dun* I will show you how."

IT TOOK THEM THREE DAYS, DURING WHICH EOCHAID alternately sulked and raged and twice tried to run away. Fionn himself had found the bare earth harder to sleep on than he remembered, and when he breathed deeply there was a pain in his chest that was growing hard to ignore, but on the whole, he thought he had done well. By the time they arrived at the *rath* where Grainne was living, he hoped that the boy looked more exhausted than he did.

Sceolan's growl silenced the farmstead's assortment of dogs, but the noise brought Grainne to the door. For a moment she stood staring, fear and fury warring in her gaze.

"He is not hurt," said Fionn, grinning up at her, "and neither am I, though 'tis not from any lack of effort on the part of your son. Your children seem to have me confused with the *brollachan.*"

"Why?" she managed finally. "*Why?*"

Eochaid stared at the ground as if he would like to sink into it. By this time word had gone through the household and men were gathering from every side, glaring. Fionn felt his laughter draining away.

"While you were swearing revenge over Diarmuid's body I swore an oath as well, Grainne. I will kill no more of Diarmuid's kin. I have recently seen where the lust for vengeance can lead, and I am tired of it." He moved a few steps forward, spinning his spear suddenly so that the shaft touched her hand. "Kill me yourself Grainne, or let me go in peace, but send no more children after me. To this feud, at least, let us make an end."

Once he had made the same offer to Ailbe. She had been unable to kill him. Could her sister?

Grainne's hand closed on the spear. She was trembling; he felt the fine tremors transmitted along the shaft. Grief had worn away the luxuriance of her flesh, revealing the good bones. Her deep-set eyes were still luminous, her hair still thick, though its sunshine was shadowed now. Though her splendor was muted, she was still beautiful.

Fionn held his ground as she angled the spear point towards his breast, though staying upright was becoming rather an effort as the stress of the past three days caught up with him. He felt the sharp point prick through his tunic, but his gaze still held hers. From the spear he sensed a confused humming. He wondered what would happen if Birga tasted the blood of its maker. Perhaps he should have told her to use a different spear.

Grainne's gaze hardened and the spear pressed more sharply. Fionn could keep himself from flinching, but he could not stop the cough he felt gathering in his lungs. With a gesture of apology he turned a little away, covering his mouth with his sleeve.

The paroxysm was a bad one. When Fionn was able

to straighten, the iron taste of blood was in his mouth and there were red stains on his sleeve. The pain in his chest had been bad enough to make him forget the spear point, but it was no longer threatening him. Grainne had plunged the spear into the earth and was leaning on it, looking at him with a mixture of pity and exasperation.

"Ach, man, why should I give myself the trouble of killing you? You are falling apart where you stand! Come in and I will brew you up some hot comfrey tea."

He would have resented that patronage, thought Fionn as he followed her, if what she was saying had not been so patently true. He had an impression of a well-kept, whitewashed hall, but he was growing very dizzy, and glad enough to drop down upon a padded bench by the fire.

For a time after that it was very bad. When Fionn came to himself once more he was lying in bed. Grainne had her arm beneath his head and was trying to get him to swallow something that tasted foul enough to wake the dead. He would have suspected poison, but if she had wanted his death, Grainne could have speared him, or left him to die like a dog at her gates. He accepted another bitter mouthful, pleasantly aware of the warm breast against which he was leaning.

He wanted to thank her, but she hushed him. "Do not be trying to talk now. You men of the *fianna*—" She shook her head in exasperation. "You drive yourselves until you drop and then a step after and wonder why you fall ill. Do you think I don't know the way of it? Diarmuid was just the same."

Fionn's eyes filled with easy tears and he turned his

head away. Weak as he was, he could hide nothing. It might have been better to die than to be thus helpless in the hands of his enemy. But was Grainne his enemy? Her hands were gentle, and he thought he recognized the taste of some of the herbs with which Bodbmall had dosed him when he was young.

By the next morning he was a little better, though it still pained him to talk. Grainne talked instead—at first of small, inconsequential things—to keep him from fretting. But every topic seemed to lead to Diarmuid. At first Fionn wondered if she were doing it on purpose to torment him, but after a time he realized that she could not help it, and that he himself was perhaps the only person to whom she could speak so about the man she had loved, because at some deep level she recognized that Fionn had loved him too.

"He missed the *fianna*, you know," she said as she handed Fionn a bowl of gruel. He was able by now to sit up and feed himself, though still fevered in the evenings. "He would take out his weapons and oil and sharpen them, though there was no war. And sometimes he went out on the hills, saying he was off hunting. But he did not always come back with game. I think he was running, racing his memories of Oisin and Caoilte and the others, pretending he was still with the *fian*."

"It was years before I ceased to listen for his step behind me, or to remember things I wanted to tell him," said Fionn. "I love Oisin as my life, but between a man and his son there is always the strain of expectation and duty. From Diarmuid I expected nothing, and received everything. He was dearer than son or a brother, that was why—" he broke off, realizing that he, too, had been betrayed into revelations.

"That was why it hurt you so much when he ran off with me. . . ." Grainne said quietly.

Fionn sucked in his breath as if she had speared him after all. Now would be a good time for another coughing fit, but his body remained quiescent. He could not evade her gaze.

"Fionn mac Cumhal, why do you think I have hated you so long, if not because I knew that Diarmuid loved you, perhaps as much as he loved me?"

Grainne looked away, but even in profile he could see the tears on her cheeks. He gazed after her as she left him, feeling as if his soul had become an open wound through which all his defenses were bleeding away.

I must get well and get away from here, he told himself as sleep overtook him. *Or I will die of this pain.*

The next morning he was awake and on his feet before she came to him, a little light-headed and tottery to be sure, but walking. They found it hard to meet each other's eyes, as if they had inadvertently seen each other unclothed. But it was their souls they had been baring. Too much had been revealed if they were to be enemies, but what else they might be to each other he did not know.

Grainne was brisk and practical as she helped him to walk to a seat beside the fire; Fionn, uncomplaining even when he feared he would fall. But from that day he grew steadily better.

"I have spoken to my children," said Grainne a few days later, when Fionn was beginning to think of beginning the journey home. "Donnchadh is easygoing, and can be persuaded to make peace. I think that Eochaid, who was the most bitter, has learned to admire you, though he will not yet admit it, and the two younger ones were following their brothers' lead. But Eachtach, my daughter—" She shook her head. "She was still at the age when a girl idolizes her father when Diarmuid died. She will never forgive you, Fionn, and she is as good a fighter as the boys. Of Eachtach you must still beware."

Fionn smiled at her. "What you have done already, Grainne, is a great deal. I feel, if not like a new man, at least more like the old one. I must not impose upon your hospitality any more."

"You cannot leave today," said Grainne decidedly. "You are still coughing a little, and it is likely to rain. Tomorrow we will see."

"Will you keep me captive here?" He grinned at her and she laughed.

That afternoon a messenger arrived from Temair. Fionn stayed within the hall, but he could hear what was said as Grainne went out to him.

"Is it my father? His wound—"

"Your father is well, lady, and his wound is healing, but the physicians have examined him, and they say that he will never regain the sight of that eye."

"Oh," she said doubtfully. "Well, that is a pity, but Goll has been a great warrior with only one eye for fifty years."

"No doubt Cormac will fight again," the messenger said in the same neutral tone, "but the loss of an eye is a blemish according to the law. The druids of Eriu have deliberated upon the question, and this is the message I am charged to bring. Because he is a whole man no longer, Cormac mac Airt is disqualified from the kingship. You are summoned to Temair at Beltane for the inauguration of your brother Cairbre as *Ard Ri* of Eriu."

Fionn was still holding onto the pillar of the hall when Grainne came in once more. He saw in her face the same blank incomprehension that must fill his own. Cormac had become king when he was barely eighteen; even Fionn, who could remember when Conn of the Hundred Battles had ruled, found it hard to imagine anyone else as high king. And though he had thought himself prepared for the prospect that Cairbre would succeed his father one day, he had always assumed that it would happen after he himself was gone.

"I will not go there to see it happen!" exclaimed Grainne passionately. "Cairbre and I never got along."

"That is something else you and I have in common," Fionn answered grimly. He had been thinking he might retire from the leadership of the *fianna* in favor of Oisin, but his son had never made any secret of his own hostility to Cormac's heir, and Oscar frankly hated him.

"I dare not go," Grainne continued reflectively. "If I know Cairbre, he has already promised me in marriage to some foul-mouthed chieftain who will take me in hopes of getting a son within the royal kindred. If I was going to take a husband for political reasons, I would have married you!"

Fionn blinked. "You will have to take someone," he said slowly. "If your brother wants to marry you off, you can no longer live here alone. The only other choice"—he looked at her apologetically—"would be to come back with me to Almu."

"As your wife?" she asked steadily, holding his gaze.

"As my honored guest, if you will," he said formally. "Though Diarmuid's death was not my doing, it was partly through me that you were deprived of his protection. I owe you that, Grainne, and even if Cairbre were to come against us in arms, I think I could keep you safe at Almu."

"My position would be stronger if I married you," she said. Her gaze was shadowed. He still could not interpret her tone.

"If you will," he repeated carefully, but his heart was pounding. "Almu needs a mistress, and you would honor me. But I make no demands upon you, Grainne. You thought me a bad bargain when this match was first proposed, and I am a worse one now. Come with me on whatever terms you will."

Grainne looked around her, as if silently saying farewell to the hall where she had been mistress of her own fate, the grieving widow of Diarmuid mac Duibhne. Then she turned to Fionn.

"It is as your wife I will go with you to Almu, Fionn mac Cumhal, or not at all."

GRAINNE LOST NO TIME IN SUMMONING THE FEW NEIGHBORS who lived nearby to a feast, and setting her servants to preparing it, lavish with food and drink since she would not need to supply her household through the rest of the year after all. But it was not until the guests had already started their drinking that she announced that the occasion was her marriage to Fionn mac Cumhal. By that time most of them were already growing mellow with mead. If they were shocked to learn the identity of her guest, and even more surprised by her announcement, the mead was good, and she had been a good neighbor. One could hardly say she was marrying without the consent of her kin, since Fionn was the man her father had first chosen for her.

They were willing enough to wish her well.

But the ribaldry usual on such occasions was muted as they escorted Fionn to the bed where Grainne awaited him. A wedding was not legal until the feast had been made and the couple publicly bedded, but Fionn could see that they were wondering if he would be able to do his duty by the bride. He might have been worried himself if he had thought that was what Grainne expected of him. But he had made it clear that he did not intend to trouble her. This was for her protection, that was all.

Fionn had certainly had enough mead to make him sleep well, but after the guests had departed he lay wakeful, acutely aware of the warmth of the woman beside him. One night, he thought, and after that they could sleep separately, and he would not have to lie there remembering how he had dreamed about sleeping with Grainne when they were betrothed so long ago.

After what seemed half a lifetime, she sighed. The straw of the mattress creaked as she shifted position, then, so lightly that at first he thought he had imagined it, her hand settled upon his chest. He jumped as it slid across the skin to touch his nipple, and heard her laugh.

"I have nursed you like a baby for half a moon. What are you afraid of?"

"Grainne—" His voice had gone harsh, and not from the cough. "You are not touching me like a baby now. Is this your revenge on me?"

"Only with your cooperation—" Her voice faltered. "It is customary for a couple to lie together at least once, to seal the bond."

"There is no need—no one will question us," said

Fionn. "Do not feel you must . . . out of pity for me."

"Ah Fionn, Fionn, it is not out of pity I am coming to you! Cannot you believe that I need someone to hold me, after all these years alone." She pulled herself closer and he trembled at the silken touch of her hair. "By Brigid's holy flame," Grainne laughed suddenly, "do I have to seduce all my husbands to get them to make love to me?"

He dared to reach out to her then, his fingers tangling in her hair. She came to him sweetly and he gathered her against him. A moment before, Fionn had still been wondering if he could serve her if indeed she desired it. As Grainne's hands moved across his body, he realized that would not be a problem, the question was how long he could wait. He kissed her urgently, taking swift possession of the splendid body that was being so generously offered to him, seeking the way home.

His climax was like falling into the sun. At the end, carried beyond awareness of himself or the woman by the intensity of his release, for a moment it was Someone Else to whom he gave up his spirit, someone whose hair was living gold.

When at last Fionn lay back, feeling his heartbeat gradually slow, he sensed the tension in the body of the woman beside him and knew that for her it had been too soon. He kissed her gently, then felt her surprise as he began to caress her once more. Long ago, Donait had taught him well.

"I don't suppose that Diarmuid ever needed to do this," he whispered ruefully. "Be still, my dear, and dream that it is he who is touching you."

Chapter 14

At Beltane, the world seemed to pause for a moment of perfect harmony, a moment of blue skies and flowers bright in the rich grass. In the blue sky-fields the swifts soared and darted in intricate maneuvers; from the meadows the corncrake called. When Fionn brought Grainne home to Almu it had seemed as if the land were decked for their bridal. Now, as he rode northward towards Temair, the same splendor was arrayed for Cairbre's kingmaking, and he found it disturbing. The skies ought to have been weeping to see Cormac deposed as high king.

And yet, as they journeyed he found himself smiling at the memory of Grainne's arrival at Almu. To say the *fianna* was stunned was putting it mildly. They had been almost as shocked as they were to hear of Cormac's fall. They could not seem to decide whether to jeer at Grainne for being faithless to Diarmuid's memory, or cheer Fionn for having won her at last. But it quickly became clear that Grainne, at least, had expected their ambivalence and was prepared for it. That should not have surprised him either—he had realized long ago whose mind had guided Diarmuid when they were fleeing him. After all, Grainne was the daughter of Eriu's greatest high king.

Fionn wished he could have been riding to Temair with Grainne beside him. It was still Cormac's legal right to approve their marriage, but who could tell what Cairbre might try once he was in power? The wisest course was the one they had chosen, and so he had left Grainne at Almu, making herself mistress of the place with a somewhat terrifying efficiency, along with enough warriors to defend her.

But her sons, Donnchadh and Eochaid, rode with the *fianna*. As Cormac's grandchildren, they were within the royal *derbfine*. Some would say that their status as sister's-sons to Cairbre gave them an even closer relationship to the new *Ard Ri*. It was their right to witness his elevation, and it might be useful to show that they were under the protection of Fionn. Grainne's sons were still a bit uncomfortable in Fionn's company, but they had taken to Oscar, and marched now in the rear guard with his men.

"Is the *Ard Ri*—I mean Cormac—still in Temair?" asked Oisin, who was riding beside Fionn.

Fionn shook his head. "It is unlucky for a king with a blemish to reside at Temair. After he was wounded they moved him to Achall."

"Unlucky! Unlucky is what this land will be when Cairbre is in power!" exclaimed Oisin.

"I will not contradict you," said Fionn glumly. "But we must find a way to live with him."

"You may be able to do so. Even I might, though it

will be like swallowing sour apples," said Oisin. "But what about Oscar?" They both turned to look back down the line. Oscar's men strode along with springy step and heads high, but their leader's features were set in a sullen scowl that meant trouble for somebody soon.

"Let us all keep our tempers for the next few days; then we can start worrying about the next few years," said Fionn, and Oisin chose to consider that a joke and laughed.

THE ROYAL *RATH* AT ACHALL WAS A RESIDENCE, NOT a fortress, a pleasant dwelling on a hill, shaded by beech trees and surrounded by meadows, where the *Ard Ri* had sometimes retreated when he wanted to rest. But it was not Temair. Fionn set his men to making camp and rode up to the rath with only a few companions. The kingmaking was not until tomorrow, and there would be less chance for trouble if the *fianna* did not arrive too soon.

"Himself is inside the house," said the lad who came out to take the horses. "He has not stirred outdoors today. Go in to him, lord Fionn, perhaps you will cheer him."

There were fewer servants here than formerly, though Cormac was still well attended. No doubt those who had come with him were folk who served him from personal devotion. The glory hounds and toadies would be still at Temair, fawning on the new king.

It was dark inside after the brightness of the day. Cormac had let the fire burn down. He sat alone, a deeper shadow in the darkness of the hall.

"It is a fair day, man! Why are you sitting here in all

this gloom?" He strode forward and stood over the man who had been his king.

"Fionn, is it you?" The other man looked up at him. "I thought you would be with the others at Temair."

"Not until I have to," answered Fionn. "Do you think I am looking forward to seeing that puppy in your shoes? Until I myself am satisfied there is no way around it, I will not hail him as high king!"

"There is none," Cormac said heavily. "If he had been a usurper, I would have fought him, but Cairbre is my son. And the druids have spoken. Unless Miach should return to give me a new eye as he gave a new hand to Nuada I cannot rule."

"Cormac—" said Fionn, hunkering down beside him, "I cannot accept that. You have in your reign preserved the Truths of a king that keep the kingdom in peace. Today I rode through a land blooming with promise—it has not fallen off since your disfigurement. If the druids blamed bad weather on my troubles with the Sidhe, then surely they should ascribe the continuation of this good season to you!"

Cormac reached out and gripped his shoulder. "Old friend, you have argued your way out of so many troubles, and fought your way through the rest, but neither talk nor fighting can stop what is happening now. It would have been much simpler if Gae-Adúath's spear had killed me, for now I am as a ghost among the living. All that remains for me is to exact a retribution upon the Dési for my maiming and the death of my son. I do not think it will take long."

"Not long at all, if I fight beside you," said Fionn, setting his hand over Cormac's. "And when they are chastised, come back with me to the *fianna*. I always thought there were the makings of a *fénnid* in you, my dear. We will range the forests together, and I will give you the freedom of the kingdom I rule."

"Now there is a prospect to trouble Cairbre's sleep!" Cormac observed. "You and me together in the *fian*! We would always be a threat to him. In his place I should not allow it, and I think I have trained him well enough to see the danger. It is a fine notion, old friend, but I will not destroy what chances you have to live in peace with my son."

"Well—" said Fionn, searching for some news that might prove cheering, "you should know that Grainne is my wife now, and safe at Almu."

Cormac gave a bark of laughter. "Have you tamed her at last, then? Or did she tame you?" He shook his head. "Do you think Cairbre will welcome you as a brother-in-law?"

"She was afraid he would marry her off to one of his cronies," Fionn began, but at the thought of Grainne warm in his arms, his voice changed. "But it is more than the best of a bad bargain. There is respect between us. I will give her content, I think, and she—she has given me joy."

A silence fell between them. After a time Cormac sighed.

"Then perhaps the time of magic is not ended. Ah Fionn, Fionn! I remember how I hated you when we were boys. And how I feared you when you marched through the gates of Temair like Lugh in his splendor to claim lordship of the *fianna* of Eriu. I could not believe you did not mean to be my rival. But so many years have passed, and it has been more than the 'best of a bad bargain' between us as well. If I have suceeded as *Ard Ri*, it has been because you were my ally." Cormac paused, cleared his throat, and then went on.

"After . . . tomorrow, I will ride into the Dési lands. Go up to Temair, Fionn, and see what fate the gods and Cairbre will deal you. And then, if you wish, we shall fight side by side once more."

Fionn tried to speak and found he could not. He tried to blink away the blurring in his vision, and Cormac reached up and brushed the tears from his eyes.

"You are weeping . . ." the king whom Fionn had served for fifty years said softly. "Well, we are two old men together; we are entitled to our sorrow. Weeping is something I can still do, even with only one eye."

"HE COMES! HE COMES!" THE SHOUT SEEMED TO RISE from the earth of the royal hill as a flicker of motion appeared on the road beyond the open gates of the *dun*. Even Fionn, hating the occasion that had brought him here, could not help but be stirred. He had been studying poetry with Cethern when Cormac had been made *Ard Ri*, and like most of those here, had never seen the rite of kingmaking before. If the land had not rebelled against Cormac's disfigurement, neither was it resenting Cairbre's accession. The sun was bright enough to make him squint, the sky an uncompromising blue.

As the movement on the road resolved itself into a chariot drawn by two white horses, the cheering became deafening. Unless Cairbre's skills as a charioteer had improved, Fionn doubted that the horses were, as tradition specified, unbroken. But he was handling the reins in reasonable form, and the royal mantle that flared from his shoulders swirled dramatically.

The crowd recoiled to either side as the chariot swept through the gates of Temair. Frowning with concentration, Cairbre set the horses at the narrow course that had been cut through the swell of the hill, and the people surged after him. Fionn slipped around behind them in time to see the chariot make the difficult pass between the two stones called Blocc and Bluigne, and scarcely slackening, head towards the Mound of the Hostages.

The Stone of Fál, sometimes called the phallus of the Great Horse, thrust upward from the base of the mound. The track led past it, but Cairbre was aiming dangerously close to the pillar, as he must in order to complete the ritual. Even Fionn, who would have liked to see him fail, held his breath as the chariot rocked and the axle of the right wheel screeched against the stone.

"The Stone speaks!" "Fál has accepted him!" came the cry.

Fionn slid into place among the *fianna* as the princely charioteer completed his circuit of the mound and pulled the frothing horses to a halt. With a kind of bravado, Fionn had chosen to wear the same tunic and mantle of deep green that he had been wearing when he made Cormac go under the forks of the cauldron at Brigid's shrine. He wondered if Cairbre would remember it.

The senior druids were waiting on top of the mound, their faces set in lines of carven solemnity by the gravity of the occasion, though perspiration glittered on bald heads from the heat of the sun.

"For whom speaks the Lía Fáil?" cried the Chief Druid Cathal.

"It speaks for Cairbre Liffechar, son of Cormac mac Airt!" Daire Duanach replied. "By election of the chieftains he has been chosen *Ard Ri* of Eriu!"

The Gaelic chieftains sat with the sub-kings of the

four-fifths of Eriu, faces reddening beneath the heat of the sun. Fionn knew most of them, had fought against some of them and beside some of the others. He could see Conall of the Ulaidh, looking truculent, and fat Eógan from Mumu; Brión of Connachta sat next to Bressal Bélach of Laigin. There was a boy behind him that made him stare until he realized he must be Diarmuid's other son.

Fionn raised one eyebrow as Daire stepped back into place again. It was proper for a *fili* to take this role, but Daire was *fili* not to the royal clan, but to the mac Mornas. Had none of Cormac's *ollamhs* been willing to perform this service, or was there some other reason for Daire to be playing this role today?

Benches had been placed for the family in the first rank of the circle surrounding the mound. Cairbre's pallid queen sat with her lovely daughter on one side and her younger son, Echu, on the other. The older, Falchu, stood behind her, with his small son, Muiredach, in his arms. Ailbe was sitting there as well, smiling smugly. Fionn thought she looked older than Grainne now that her slim grace had turned to gauntness. Ceallach's son stood next, with Grainne's two boys beside him. Behind them, brushed and polished and glittering with all their ornaments, stood the men of the mac Morna *fian*.

"What is Goll doing over there?" Fionn whispered to Oisin.

"You tell me—" his son replied. "They were here when we arrived, licking their lips like a pack of foxes who know that the door to the chickenhouse has been left ajar."

Fionn frowned, but the druid was speaking once more, inviting the candidate to ascend the mound.

Cairbre, having demonstrated his coordination and nerve, showed a commendable briskness in getting up the hill.

"People of Eriu, Cairbre Liffechar stands before you. Let it be seen that he is fit and without blemish—" said Cathal.

It seemed to Fionn that Cairbre was smirking as they unpinned the royal mantle and took it from his shoulders and assisted him to pull off the crimson tunic he had on. He was wearing nothing under it. As he turned, the heaviness of his arms and the thickening in his middle were quite apparent, but it was clear, also, that beneath the excess flesh were the muscles of a warrior. His skin bore the usual tracery of battle scars, but every member of his body was complete and whole.

"We have seen that he is fit and whole and without blemish indeed," called Daire from below.

"He is whole in body and approved by the people, but what say the gods?" Cathal continued the ritual.

Cairbre had clearly made certain that no step would be omitted that might help establish his sovereignty. The ranks of the druids parted and another man came forward, clutching around him a raw cowhide. He was thin, staring at the crowd from deep-set eyes. Fionn remembered seeing him pointed out as the best seer among the king's druids, but could not remember his name.

"I have drunk the blood of the slain bull; I have slept in his skin; a vision of truth has been given to me. It is Cairbre who has the blessing of the gods!"

A little shiver of awe went through the people and Fionn sighed. Unwelcome though this vision might be, he did not disbelieve it. He knew from his own poetic training that when one fasted for a vision, the mind was likely to move along those paths prepared for it by previous meditation. Even before Ceallach died, everyone had been expecting Cairbre to be the next *Ard Ri.* It would have been wonderful indeed if the druid had seen any face but his.

"Be it so!" cried Cathal. "Let him receive the regalia of a king!"

One of the druids brought out a long robe of white linen, very much like their own, to cover his nakedness. The many-colored royal mantle was laid across Cairbre's shoulders. He looked, thought Fionn, a great deal more kingly when his clothes were on.

"Let the *Ard Ri* be proclaimed before the people! Let his name be exalted! It is Cairbre who has been chosen to hold the kingship. Let the white wand of sovereignty be set in his hand!"

Fionn seemed to remember that this privilege traditionally belonged to the new king's fosterer, or some great man of the kingdom. But in the next moment he understood why the mac Mornas had looked so self-satisfied, for the warrior who was coming forward with the hazel wand clasped carefully in his big hands was Goll.

"By all the gods," whispered Oisin, "what is *he* doing in this ritual?"

Fionn did not answer, but his generalized anxiety began to focus as the prominence accorded the mac Mornas today assumed a new significance. He had the unpleasant suspicion that before this day was done, they would all know why Goll had been chosen to convey the symbol of sovereignty .

Less swiftly than Cairbre, but with a heavy dignity all his own, Goll mounted the mound.

"Here in my hands is the wood of wisdom—the slender offshoot of the sacred hazel tree. To you, oh King, it is given, and in the giving, the peoples of Eriu acknowledge you their master." He bent proudly and laid the hazel wand across Cairbre's outstretched palms.

Fionn gritted his teeth as for a moment he saw on the face of the prince a triumphant smile. Now, surely, if the gods were against this, they would give some sign of their disapproval. But the heavens remained clear.

"Listen, Cairbre, to the ancient wisdom," the druid, Cathal, said then.

"By the truth of the king, great peoples are ruled.
By the truth of the king, death is warded from men,
By the truth of the king, war is carried to the foe,
By the truth of the king, all have their rights;
every vessel is full in his reign.
By the truth of the king, fair weather shall come in every season.
Magnify truth, oh King, and it will magnify you;
Strengthen truth, and by it you will be strengthened.
Preserve truth, and it will preserve you,
Exalt it and it will exalt you;
For so long as you preserve the truth,
Good will not be lacking to you, and your reign will never fail. . . ."

Cairbre listened, holding the white wand in his hands, on his face a complacent smile.

While the druid was speaking, a woman approached from the direction of the spring at the foot of the hill, bearing in her hands the Cup of Manannan. She was small of frame and bone, with a broad white brow and a fall of dark hair, and dressed in the colors of Laigin. It was Medb—the young one, for since before the Gaels assumed the kingship that name had been given, mother to daughter, among that people's royal kin.

There was a little murmur of appreciation from among the men, and Fionn saw a sadness in the face of Cairbre's queen, for they all knew that when night came the girl would be giving the new *Ard Ri* more than water from the sacred spring.

"A bride-cup I bring to you, oh King, drawn from the womb-waters of Eriu. The water of life is yours if you will take oath to me."

Fionn blinked as if the sunlight had brightened, or perhaps for an instant something more than mortal shone through the girl's fair skin.

"To each you shall give justice according to his state and function; you shall oppress no one wrongfully through your might; you shall serve your kingdom as a husband, protecting her against all who would despoil her or do her wrong," said the maiden, and her words echoed in Fionn's soul. Though he had never stood upon the royal mound of Temair, this was his oath also, and as Cairbre answered, his own soul echoed the words.

". . . and may the earth swallow me, the sea cover me, the sky fall upon me, if I fail to abide by these words—" The new *Ard-Ri* took the golden *krater* between his two hands and drank deeply.

With a sigh Fionn let his awareness sink into the sacred soil on which he stood, and felt the earth song pulse triumphantly. *He is king* . . . the force of Cairbre's binding was as powerful as Fionn's own. *He is king, and his oath has been accepted, and there is nothing that I can do. . . .*

He swayed, and felt Oisin and Oscar supporting him. Vaguely he knew that the ceremony was continuing, knew it when Cairbre ate the flesh of the sacrificed mare and kindled the sacred fire. But it was not until the ancient golden trumpets blared forth their triumph that Fionn came fully to himself once more.

"To the four-fifths of the island let it be proclaimed—" cried Daire. "To every tribe and people let the word be carried. It is Cairbre Liffechar who is *Ard Ri* over kings and princes; in Cairbre now rests the sovereignty of Eriu!"

WITH THE PROCLAIMING OF THE NEW KING THE FORMAL part of the ceremonies was ended. Cairbre was carried off somewhere to rest and recover, while the royal servants became furiously busy setting up the couches and benches and tables for the great feast which would follow.

Oisin dragged Fionn down to the little grove above the statue of the ancient god and stuck a horn of ale in his fist while the others gathered round.

"What happened to you?" he asked angrily. "Are you sick? You were white as that treacherous ninny's robe!"

"He is *Ard Ri*. . . ." whispered Fionn. "I felt it happen. Dear gods—Cormac must have felt it too—as I did when Sadb was taken from me, as if a part of myself had gone!" He lifted the horn to his lips and took a long swallow, but the link was not quite broken; he could hear an echo of the land's living waters in the ale.

"He can't be," exclaimed Oscar. "He is not worthy!"

"Worthy or not," answered Fionn, recovering a little, "the power has passed to him, and until he abuses it, there it will remain."

"What a thing to hope for!" said Caoilte gloomily. "But I daresay it will not take long!" The men who stood closest responded with uneasy laughter.

"That is all very well," said Oisin, his fair brows creasing, "but what are we going to do now?"

"We are going to the feast," answered Fionn, sitting up and handing him the horn. "If this is the last time we ever enjoy the *Ard Ri*'s hospitality, let us make the most of it!" He looked around him and saw on some of the faces a lessening of tension. "Eat your fill, lads, but go easy on the ale. And keep your tempers," he added, and saw Oscar flush. "If Cairbre Liffechar is going to destroy his kingship, he can do it without any help from the *fian*."

Oisin grimaced, tipped up the horn, and drank the rest of it down.

THINGS WERE CHANGING—THAT WAS CERTAIN. FIONN could hear it in the way people spoke to him, or kept silent. He could see it in the interest, avid or pitying, that flickered in men's eyes. But when the *fianna*, by the simple expedient of entering the feasting hall early, made sure of their traditional seats on the northern side of the hall, no one dared to displace them. That might come later, thought Fionn, remembering with uncomfortable clarity how vulnerable he had felt the first time he marched into this hall. He wondered if it was worse not to understand what was happening, or to recognize it, even after fifty years, only too well.

As he took his seat, Eochaid came up to him. The boy was still a little shamefaced in his company, but this time he met Fionn's eyes without flinching.

"Cairbre wants Donnchadh for a hostage," he said baldly. "He is calling it fosterage, but his meaning is clear."

Fionn took a quick breath. A king did not usually require hostages from his own sisters, but since Grainne had not come to the kingmaking, it made sense for him to try and control her through her eldest son. He should have anticipated that when he decided to bring the boys along.

"What about you?" he asked.

"I am to go home and carry his good wishes to my mother—" his lips quirked, and for a moment he looked like Diarmuid.

Fionn cleared his throat. "Does he know where your mother is living?"

The quirk became a frown. "He didn't ask. In all this confusion, I don't think he knows we came with you. But Donnchadh was never able to keep a secret. He will talk as soon as my uncle has time to question him."

"Well, if the high king wants you to take a message to your mother, I think you should obey him," said Fionn thoughtfully. "Now—before something changes his mind for him and he decides to keep you here as well. The gates have not yet been closed; no one will question you. I would tell you to wait for us, but I cannot say what road we will be taking, or when. You have the woodcraft to make your way to Almu alone. Bear my love to your mother, and go now, quickly."

He was relieved to see Eochaid's answering smile.

Goll came in shortly thereafter, followed by the portion of the *fianna* that wintered on his lands. Laughing and joking, they settled onto their share of the benches, the red pelts of the mac Mornas like sparks among the fair and brown heads of the other men. They were good fighters, if a little rough in their manners. Fionn knew those men almost as well as he knew his own. How many times, he wondered, had they feasted together this way? The arrangements appeared to be the same, but Fionn could sense a difference, the beginnings of separation, like fat rising to the top of a pot as the broth begins to cool.

Garad mac Morna sat in the front rank with his son Aedh beside him. Flame-haired Aonghus followed him. Fionn recognized Fer-tai of the Luagni, whose son was now Fionn's fosterling. Daire Duanach the bard came in, accompanied by a little ripple of congratulation, and sat down.

Goll himself had chosen a place down by the end of the compartment rather than plumping himself down at Fionn's side. Without comment, Fionn motioned Oscar forward to take the empty place, and Oisin, on his other side, greeted his son with a wry smile.

The hall stilled as the royal women entered, bearing silver-mounted drinking horns. The new queen carried the mead to the chieftains, and Ailbe to the masters of art and craft, though she cast a superior smile in Fionn's direction as she went by. He suspected she would have a different look when she found out that he had married Grainne after all. It was the high king's daughter, Sgeimh Solais, who bore the horn to the *fianna*, so innocently radiant in her young beauty that Fionn could almost forget who her father was. She was almost as old as Oscar, ripe for marriage. But Cairbre had kept her by him, whether from affection or to dangle her temptingly as an inducement for an alliance he did not know. She passed along the front row of benches, offering the horn first to the mac Mornas, who sat nearest the high king, then, after the serving man who followed her had refilled it, moving along the row to Fionn and his men.

No one has told her we are out of favor, Fionn thought, watching how gravely she held out the horn to Oisin, who had been famed as a hero since she was a babe. To Fionn she offered the horn shyly, and he took it with a smile. But when she came to Oscar the color flamed in her cheeks, and Oscar met her gaze with an intentness that reminded Fionn uncomfortably of Diarmuid and Grainne. But this girl did not have her aunt's strength of character or resolution. She smiled a little tremulously as he returned the horn to her, and passed on.

At this feast the new king received the best cuts, so the Champion's portion was not an issue. It was not until appetites had been satisfied and the ale vats were carried in that Fionn sensed a little ripple of tension run through the mac Mornas and knew that the fun was about to begin.

It was the practice of a new ruler to bind men to him by the giving of gifts, and Cairbre had dug deep into Cormac's treasure houses. There were gold chains for the druids, a new cloak for the *fili*, Daire. Underkings received torques and chieftains, armrings, as they pledged their service, and men of art and learning gifts of cows. Through all of this the mac Mornas waited quietly, and so did Fionn.

The drinking horns were refilled again and again. *At*

least he is not stingy, thought Fionn, keeping a sharp eye on his men. But the tension appeared to be keeping them sober. The mac Mornas were not quite so disciplined. Their voices grew louder, and there was more challenge in the way they looked at Fionn.

Now the *Ard Ri* was confirming his officers in their posts. There were some changes here, but for the most part the gifts went to the men Fionn had known.

"Let Goll mac Morna and Fionn mac Cumhal come before the king—"

As he stood up, Fionn felt the knot in his gut ease. At least the waiting was done.

"Since before I was born you have led the *fianna* of Eriu," said Cairbre smoothly, looking at both of them. Fionn smiled, aware of an unwilling admiration for the man's subtlety. "The relationship between an *Ard Ri* and his *rigfénnid* is unique. There must be trust and understanding between them, respect and friendship and community of interest—" he paused, and Fionn smiled tightly.

You have learned a great deal from your father, he thought, *but not all. It was not liking that bound Cormac and me together, but love for this land of Eriu.*

"It is grateful I am to you, Fionn mac Cumhal, for the blood and toil with which you have served Eriu over the years, but I am a different man from my father, and I need a different man to lead my *fianna*—" Cairbre looked down as if in apology, but Fionn knew it was nothing of the kind.

Do they expect me to ask why? he wondered wildly. *My grandson knocked this man silly, and then we fettered him. The surprise would be if he wanted me to stay.*

"Therefore, I have asked Goll of Clan Morna to be

my *Rígfénnid*, and he has accepted that honor from me." Cairbre fell silent, his lips turning up in a little cat-smile.

He is waiting for us to run about and make sport for him, thought Fionn, but Cairbre no longer mattered. It was Goll, whom he had feared when he was a child, hated as a youth, and learned to love as a man, who concerned him now. He looked at the other man, and realized with a pang that sometime in the past years Goll had become old. There was still fire in his eye, but none in his hair, and he moved as if his joints were hurting him. *I cannot blame him—this was not his idea, I am sure.*

"Well, Goll—" As the silence deepened, Fionn took pity on the older man's distress, "what do you say? Must the *fians* of Almu and Morna be parted after we have been brothers-in-arms for so many years?"

"Ah, lad, you must see how it is. I can no longer follow you. There sit your son and your grandson hale and hearty," said Goll, meeting his gaze at last. "But my last-born son is dead by your hand. It is no good to say you did not intend it, man—I know it. But his blood still lies between us."

And your kinfolk are dreaming of ancient glories, thought Fionn, looking at the mac Morna men. With a momentary shock he saw that Fer-li and Emer Glunglas were now among them, the former standing with his father and the latter by his grandfather Garad. But he should have expected that as well. He understood all of them far too well for his own comfort. Their eyes were hot with the same hunger he had seen in the men of his uncle Crimall's *fian* when he was a boy. No doubt the mac Morna clansmen had worked upon the old man until he had seen no choice but this.

The mac Mornas were not the only ones who expected a fight. Fionn could feel anticipation mounting in the room. He looked around the hall and sighed. They were so young, all of them! To these men the enmity between the mac Mornas and the House of Baoisgne was as much a legend as the wars of Medb of Connachta and Ulaldh's Conchobar. To have it start up again would be like having an old tale come alive.

But he did not mean to entertain them.

"Indeed, old friend, I do see how it is," Fionn said softly. "And I agree that for a time it will be better if we follow separate trails. You must stay and serve your king, but it seems to me there is a score still to settle with the Dési, and that is the way I mean to ride. Does that seem good to you, Goll?"

"You are claiming all the best sport, as usual, Fionn mac Cumhal!" said Goll, but his face was flushed with relief, and there was real warmth in his eyes. "It is a good plan, though, and I wish you well."

There was a stifled sound from Oisin's direction and Fionn sent him a quick glance of warning. They were almost clear, if his own people did not spoil it now. In Cairbre's face he saw a bemused exasperation that almost made him laugh. Had he realized that Fionn had not asked his permission for the Dési campaign? He could hardly forbid it, though, when the idea had been publicly endorsed by Goll. Clearly this was not how the new high king had expected things to turn out at all.

"My duty to you, lord King, and my farewell—" said Fionn, and in his voice there was regret, but no mockery. "There is not room for all of us at Temair, and my men and I have a long distance to go. As I heard the oaths you swore this afternoon, so did the land of Eriu.

Yours is a true kingship, Cairbre. I tell you this as one who knows. Keep your vows, and your reign will be prosperous. I wish you well."

It had not been the speech of a suppliant, and everyone in the hall was aware of it. But it was not the speech of an enemy either, and clearly Cairbre did not know what to do. While he was deciding, Fionn saluted him and turned back to the *fian*, whistling, very softly, the call they used to signal a silent retreat from hostile territory.

By the time he had reached the benches, his men were on their feet, the weapons that had hung upon the wall behind them in their hands. Fionn favored the feasters with a final smile and, without even pausing, led the *fian* out of the hall, all of them walking with the same silent and slightly unnerving grace, as if they were moving soft-footed along some forest trail.

A greater silence fell behind them, and as they emerged into the darkness Fionn had a sudden sense that to the men in the hall they had become as ghostly as the spirits he had seen here one long-ago Samhain Eve. And perhaps that was not so fanciful, for he felt a prophetic conviction that never again would the *fian* of Fionn mac Cumhal feast in the halls of Temair.

"Oisin," he said softly when the door had closed behind them, "get you to the gate guard and tell him that we are being sent out on a mission and must ride." When he touched his son's arm he felt him shaking with some suppressed emotion, probably laughter.

"The rest of you gather up your gear and get down there after him. Even Cairbre will be able to figure out something authoritative to do about us, given the time, and we must be well away from here before he makes up his mind!"

The servants who assisted them to collect and saddle their horses were a little surprised by such an abrupt departure, but for so many years Fionn had held the warding of their walls when he was in Temair, it did not occur to them to question his orders. It was not until they paused to rest the horses, many miles from the trap Cairbre had planned for them, that anyone dared to question him at all.

"To see Cairbre's face as you blessed him was almost worth all that has happened," said Oisin. "But what do you intend to do?"

"Just what I told him," answered Fionn. "Cormac means to punish the Dési, and I will aid him. Cairbre gave me no gifts to compel my submission, and took no oath from me. It is his father to whom my faith was given, and whom I will follow."

Chapter 15

"THE KING IS DEAD—THE OLD BULL IS GONE—"

"Cormac who was *Ard Ri* is dead at Cleittech on the Boann. . . ."

"A druid's curse killed him . . . his host Spellán killed him . . . he choked on a salmon bone . . ."

"They have taken him to the Brugh na Boinne to rest with his fathers . . . not so, the river was in flood after the rains, so they have buried him at Ros na Righ. . . ."

In the days just after the Feast of Lugh rumor sparked like summer lightning from Tailtiu to the heights of Brega, from Inber Colptha to Usnech, and from Midhe to the four-fifths of Eriu. The *fianna* of Almu, on the trail of a band of Dési who had sought refuge with their cousins in Mumu, were encamped on the headwaters of the Suir when the news came to them.

Fionn knew that something was wrong even before he saw the messenger. If his strength was not quite what it had been, other abilities, less important when he had been in his prime, seemed to be increasing. He sensed the changed atmosphere in the camp as soon as he came up from bathing in the river. But even before that, the waters themselves had whispered to him of grief, and the earth song turned to mourning. In the western sky, the setting sun kindled the gathering clouds into a funeral pyre.

The exhausted man who sat drinking a horn of ale by the fire was one of the warriors who had been helping Cormac to harry the northern remnant of the Dési. At last hearing, the former king had been so successful that several bands of fugitives had taken ship to try their fortune in Britannia across the sea. But there was no triumph in the way the fellow's shoulders sagged now.

"What has happened?"

At the words the man looked up and his face twisted. "It is bad news I bring you, Fionn mac Cumhal. Cormac mac Airt, who was your friend and ally, is no more."

Fionn nodded and sat down himself, fighting the first wrenching wave of sorrow. *This is how it is when one grows old,* he told himself, *so why does it surprise me? I must learn how to bear the death of friends.* Oisin and the others gathered round, and seeing that he had an audience, the messenger continued his tale.

"It happened on the Eve of Lughnasa, when he was staying at Spellán's hostel on the Boann. We had just defeated the last of the Dési we were chasing, and the men were ready to celebrate. But the king—Cormac, that is—seemed unhappy."

"He would be wondering what was left for him, if his enemy was gone," said Fionn softly.

"He stayed inside when we started the feasting—they killed a bull for the festival, and, of course, there were fish from the Boann. Late in the evening they sent me inside to see if I could persuade him to join us." The man paused, swallowing. "He was lying on his dining couch with his salmon half-eaten before him; his head on his arm as if he had fallen asleep. But he did not move when I touched him—" He shuddered and hid his face in his hands.

Fionn closed his eyes, knowing that they were all watching him, waiting to see how he would respond. But his grief for Cormac was not something that could be shared. Their relationship had been too ancient, and too complex, for explanations. He could not believe that it had come to an end.

The king had been a fury in those first encounters that sent the Dési flying in all directions. He had fought with no care for his own safety. Clearly he had hoped to be killed in battle, but as often happens in such cases, his life seemed charmed.

"Men wondered if Cormac had choked on a fish bone, but the way he was lying was too peaceful. He just . . . stopped." His story done, the messenger's own grief burst forth in great wracking sobs.

"His heart broke," said Oscar, who had always loved the high king. "Cairbre broke it, casting him aside like a worn-out shoe."

"As surely as the Black Bull is offered to release the harvest, he was the Lughnasa sacrifice," said Faobhar.

Fionn shook his head. "It is Cairbre who is the bull—the bull-prince of whom the traditions warn—" Grimly he repeated the words he had learned long ago, when he studied near these same waters at the poetic school of Cethern.

"*The bull-prince is not a well-liked man. He strikes and is struck, he injures and is injured, he tosses and is tossed. Against him horns are constantly shaken. Rough and difficult the beginning of his lordship, hateful and unprincely its middle, unstable and fleeting its end.*"

"May it be so!" growled Oscar, "and may it be soon!"

"You may well think so," the messenger lifted his head. "I heard another rumor on my way down here. They say that as soon as Cairbre learned of his father's death, he ordered Goll to assume authority over all the *fianna* and occupy Almu."

The shout that rang against the heavens as that word swept through the camp must have frightened the remaining Dési all the way to the southern shore of Mumu. The *fian's* rage was all the greater because they still thought of Goll as one of their own. Only Fionn could remember a time when the mac Mornas had been enemies.

"Does he think he can get away with it?" sputtered Oisin. "He'll soon learn differently. How fast can we get the men moving?" He looked at Fionn, who still had not spoken. "You do mean to attack him, don't you? You will have to fight Clan Morna now!"

"I will," Fionn said heavily. "But I do not have to feel happy about the necessity, nor, I'll warrant, does Goll. It is Cairbre who has forced him to move against me. Goll won't be in any hurry to attack the fortress, you know. He'll remember how hard it was to take it before."

"Last time," said Oisin bitterly, "it was defended by the Dark Druid's magic!"

"This time it is defended by Grainne," Oscar grinned fiercely. "And I would back the *Ard Ri*'s daughter to give as good as she gets, any day!"

"So would I," Fionn spoke grimly. "But it need not be for long. I do not intend to let the mac Mornas have Almu!"

THE FIANNA OF ERIU HAD ALWAYS BEEN FAMED FOR their ability to cover ground quickly. Since Fionn had led them, there had been many famous marches to defend other men's homes against a foreign enemy. But the marching the *fian* of Fionn made to raise the siege of Almu was of all their journeys the most worthy to be famed in song, run at a pace that was nearly as fast as a horse could canter, and maintained for longer. A night and a day and a night was the length of that running, and the first light of the second dawn showed them the white ramparts of Almu.

There were scars on those walls to show where the enemy had already tried to scale them, and the massive gates were blackened by fire. But they were still shut.

"Bless the dear woman, she has held them!" breathed Oisin.

"Did you think she could not?" murmured Fionn, assessing the enemy's dispositions. He was no longer foremost in the fighting, but there was little he did not know about how to manage a battle after fifty years of war. "Keep the men quiet—these are our own people we are fighting, not cocksure Gaels or barbarians out of Lochlan. Goll will have sentries out, and they may be hard to see."

"Not so hard as we will be, for we are expecting them, whereas they can have no idea we are already here . . ." Grinning, Oisin melted into the morning mists.

Fionn had considered attacking while the enemy was just waking. But hardy though they were, his men needed rest before fighting a battle, and it seemed to him he might do better to wait until all Goll's attention was on his enemies inside the *dun*, and then attack him from the rear.

The sun rose and the shape of the battle began to appear, like one of Donait's tapestries. Fionn waited as the mac Mornas arrayed themselves before the walls of Almu, shouting their challenges. Men appeared on the ramparts, jeering down at them, and arrows flew. But that was only for form's sake. Now the enemy were dragging up piles of branches. The walls of the *dun* were built of rammed earth braced with timbers, and such ramparts could be breached if the timbers burned.

Let them build their fires, thought Fionn. They would not live to light them. And as lads trotted forth from the camp with torches, he lifted his horn to his lips and blew. From his vantage point on the knoll the earth appeared to sprout armed men. While Goll's forces busied themselves with the attack, Fionn's warriors had crept into their very shadows. Now they rose, shrieking their battle cries.

He saw Oscar's battle-broom flourished suddenly before the gates, where the enemy was thickest, and then Oscar himself, laying about him with the long Roman sword he called "Swoop of Battle." On the right Oisin was leading his companions, and on the left Caoilte surged against the foe. This was the first time he had ever seen a fight take shape before him. In the midst of a battle one saw little more than an enemy's snarling face at the end of a spear.

Thread by thread, the tapestry of battle was woven. The mac Mornas were red strands, twining their bloody path through the fray. The men who rained missiles down from the ramparts were white as their walls. But it was the green band that he watched for, the woodland green of the *fianna* that wove in and out across the battlefield like grass covering a grave.

There was a terrible fascination in watching it happen. But Fionn knew that he could do no more good standing here. The Hazel Shield was quivering on his arm already, and Birga hummed eagerly. Grinning, Fionn trotted down the hill to weave his own thread into the deadly tapestry.

THE GREAT GATES OF ALMU, THAT HAD REMAINED tight-closed through three days of battle, swung open at a word from Fionn mac Cumhal. Limping from a sword slash on the thigh, he led his men into the *dun*, where they were immediately surrounded by their fellows, not quite so battered but almost as weary, who had been defending the *dun*. Grainne, her hair combed but with a smudge of ash still on her cheek, came forward to greet him, the great silver-mounted drinking horn in her hands.

"Here is golden mead for great heroes," she said, offering it to Fionn. "More glad to our eyes this morning was the sight of you than that of the rising sun."

Fionn managed a smile and took the horn. The taste of the mead was sweet and cool. Already he could feel the touch of his own earth reviving him.

"Hey lads—" said Oscar to the men who were

thronging around him, "is there more where that came from? We've been working our tails off down there while you sat about on the walls and cheered!"

"Indeed," said Loegaire, "we did cheer, when you popped out of the heather like the hosts of the Sidhe. We sent off a runner when first we saw them coming, but we did not think you could get here for two days!"

"Neither did the enemy!" Caoilte grinned. "A man sometimes looks surprised when he gets his death-wound, but the mac Mornas were all surprised today!"

Not quite all, Fionn reflected, remembering how the broken ranks of the enemy had fled the field. They had not found valiant Garad among the dead, nor Goll himself, but Garad's son Aedh was dead, and Airt's son Aonghus, and surely there had been many another—men whom Fionn had known and led to battle in happier days. Caoilte had wanted to give chase, but none of the others had any speed left. Better to let Goll go and lick his wounds, thought Fionn. Perhaps he would realize that the enemies of Eriu were the only winners when the men of the *fianna* fought each other.

And if not—if the mac Mornas, having been snared once more by the compulsion to blood feud and vengeance, insisted on continuing the war . . . Fionn's mind shied away from facing what that would mean. He was tired. He swayed as the strain of the past few days began to catch up with him, and Grainne took his elbow.

"Come into the hall, my husband. A feast has been prepared for you. And afterward you can rest."

GRAINNE WAS INDEED A WOMAN IN A THOUSAND, thought Fionn, as he washed down the last of his beef with more ale. Even after a week of siege, Almu looked better than it had when he had left it. Walls had been whitewashed, hangings repaired, the tangle of things stacked haphazardly in corners cleared away. She had even found the time to set dinner to cooking, anticipating their victory. But he should not be surprised if she had the skills to manage a great household, for she had been brought up to help her mother run Temair.

He was beginning to relax now, a warm glow of content spreading through him from the meat and the ale. For his men it must be the same, for voices were growing louder as they clapped each other on the back and began to trade tales of the day. He listened to them, smiling at the minor exaggerations, and only realized that he was falling asleep when Grainne took his arm.

"Come to bed, Fionn. It has been a long day for both of us. The men can take care of themselves."

That was certainly true. Caoilte had leaped upon a bench to describe in glowing terms how he had saved Oisin with a fortunate cast of his spear, and how Oisin had saved his life in turn. The men were still cheering them as Fionn followed his wife out the door.

Grainne had installed the great bed that Fionn had once intended for her in one of the smaller buildings on the southern side of the *dun*, where it would receive the early sun. But before she would allow him to collapse upon it, she insisted on stripping him and with the warmed water her serving woman had ready, washing him and treating his wounds.

There were only a few slashes from today's battle, for by the time Fionn had got onto the field, the surprise attack had taken the heart out of the enemy and the worst of the fighting was over. But he had a cut on his sword arm—from one of the encounters with the Dési—which was still sore. He needed another of Donait's curative baths; he didn't heal as quickly as he used to. But failing that, Grainne's efficient ministrations were very welcome.

And it was very good indeed to lie with her in the great bed, her long body warming his. Fionn had thought he would sleep immediately, but though his body was relaxed, his mind insisted on going over and over the events of the past few days.

"Grainne," he said softly, "there is a thing you need to know—"

"About my father?" she said bitterly. "Goll's *fili* shouted that he was dead when I refused to open the gates to them. I thought it might be some trick to break my will."

"If they thought that would work, they do not know you," said Fionn. "But they were speaking the truth, my dear. We had the story from one of Cormac's men." As he repeated the messenger's account, a grief he had not known he carried rose up in him. He groaned and, as Grainne turned to him, felt her tears wet on his arm.

"Why am I weeping?" she whispered. "He is well out of it. When I heard that Cairbre meant to take his kingship from him I knew he could not last long."

"He was the greatest of Eriu's high kings," answered Fionn, "furious in a fight and reasoned in judgment when the time for peace had come. He should have died on the battlefield, or in his bed at Temair, praised by his warriors. It was not right for him to pass unheralded and alone!"

"Death does not always come when it would be most welcome. If it did, I would have died with Diarmuid. I wanted to—" Grainne's voice shook, "and there are some who blame me for outliving him. But I had children who still needed me. My father had nothing. . . ."

Fionn gathered her against him. "Every man's story has the same conclusion," he spoke to himself as much as to her. "There is no evading it. The only choice we have is whether our deaths will have meaning. I feel as if Cormac's meaning was denied him. I suppose that is why I am mourning, and because a little more of my past disappears with the death of each person who knew me when I was young."

"Sleep, my dear—" Grainne's hand was gentle on his hair. "And may we both find comfort. In sleep is healing for the body and the soul."

Perhaps it was because he lay soft in a woman's arms that Fionn dreamed that night that he was in Donait's hall. But he found it hard to understand her words; perhaps he was only partly in her world after all. Only one phrase remained with him when he woke the next morning: *"Follow your own heart, Fionn, and beware the Raven's song. . . ."*

FIONN ALLOWED THE FIAN A FEW DAYS TO RECOVER their energy and refurbish their war gear. Then he led them out again, leaving the garrison of Almu under Grainne's capable command. Little though he liked it, he knew he must resolve the situation with the mac Mornas before Cairbre himself decided to take a hand. So long as the conflict remained a dispute among the *fianna*, they might still be able to preserve the peace of Eriu.

In the battle for Almu they had given the mac Morna *fian* a good savaging, and the enemy was retreating, as Fionn expected, westward towards his own lands. But the stronghold at the northern end of Loch Dergdeire, though as large as Almu, was not nearly so defensible. And so it was that when they came to the Sinnan, they found the fords held against them.

Fionn remembered only too well the ford below the hostel of the quickentrees, where a few men had held off all the hosts of the king of Lochlan. There were rowans here, too, their autumn bounty of crimson berries blazing above the ruddy banks of the river. It was almost evening already. He pulled his men back to make camp and ready themselves for battle on the morn.

That night he slept badly, and when he woke in the grey hour before the dawning he knew he would not get back to sleep again. Quietly he rose and threw his grey wool mantle over his shoulders, then belted on his sword. The sentry materialized from the shadow of a holly tree as Fionn approached the perimeter. It was young Fear Logha; when he saw who it was he grinned.

"Nothing is stirring, sir, but there is someone on their side who snores like a war drum. I've been in no danger of falling asleep with that din."

Fionn nodded, moved on into the little wood beyond their campsite, and paused to piss against a tree.

The boy had been right, he thought, as he rearranged his clothing. The enemy's snoring was clearly audible, and as Fionn listened, it seemed to him that he had heard that hollow rumble before. Though joints still stiff from sleeping on the chill ground protested at each movement, scarcely a leaf stirred as he passed through the undergrowth to the riverside.

The gurgle of flowing water seemed loud in the predawn stillness, but above it he could hear the snoring. The sound seemed to be coming from within a stand of willows on the other side of the ford. Fionn stuck one bare foot into the water, grimacing at its icy chill, then carefully made his way across. At its deepest the river came to his thighs, and by the time he reached the far shore he was shaking with cold.

But neither the disturbance in the water as he crossed the ford nor the crunch of gravel and stone as he came up the other side had awakened the sleeper. Fionn stepped over a deadfall left by the last flood and parted the branches.

As sometimes happened, a small area of clear sand had been left in the midst of the willows, making a private space screened by leaves. Upon the sand a warrior was sleeping with his spear stuck into the ground beside him. No doubt his patrol lay close by, on the higher ground.

The sleeper lay on his back, grey beard jutting towards the paling sky. One arm had been flung out from beneath the cloak that covered him, the curled fingers looked oddly defenseless, resting on the sand. A few strands of red still glinted in the beard, and Fionn recognized an old jagged scar upon the arm. But he did not need such tokens; he had listened to those snores too many times, on too many campaigns, not to recognize Goll.

Still moving with care, Fionn maneuvered through the tangle until he stood over the sleeping man. If the past few weeks had been as hard on him as they had on Goll, he thought ruefully, they could stand in for a pair of masquers dressed up as bogles at Samhain. Goll had grown gaunt with hard travelling, and beneath the new bronzing his color was not good. He had always seemed larger than life, but he seemed shrunken, lying there.

Listening to Goll's stertorous snorting compete with the early birdcalls, Fionn found his heart wrenched with pity and laughter. Surely this was no fit ending for such a man, a man who had made the enemies of Eriu tremble—who had made Fionn himself tremble, when he was young. They had fought and drunk and laughed together for so long. Most piteous of all was the fate that had put them at odds. There must be some way they could resolve this. Smiling with anticipation, Fionn set his hand to the hilt of his sword.

The tiny splashes Fionn had made fording the river had not wakened the sleeper, nor the rustle of pushing through the willows. But the hard rasp as Fionn drew his father's sword from its sheath brought Goll upright, blinking and grabbing for his spear.

"There is no need—" Light glanced from the polished steel as Fionn lowered his blade. "If I had wished to kill you, I could have done it long since and hung your head from the willow tree."

Goll hacked and spat and shook his head as if to clear it, then he shivered and pulled his cloak around his shoulders. From his good eye he squinted up at Fionn.

"What are you doing here?"

"Man—they could hear you snoring all the way to Temair! I had to come see if it were you or some new monster of the Sidhe!" A little creakily, he hunkered down on his haunches beside his enemy.

"Not so easy as it used to be, is it?" Goll began to laugh, coughed, and laughed again. "Ach—we're too old for all this marching around in the wilderness."

"That we are," Fionn agreed. "But surely between the two of us we should be able to find some way out of it. That is why I have come to you."

"Ah lad, lad—" Goll shook his head. "Too much blood has been spilled already. Garad and the rest of my kin would still keep fighting even if I were to make peace with you, and that being so, I would rather keep faith with them and with my king."

"But if we keep on with this war, neither of us can truly win!"

"We can win honor—" Goll said harshly. "We can go down with glory. What value is long life if those are gone?"

Fionn shook his head, knowing all too well the stubborn jut of his old ally's jaw, and levered himself to his feet once more.

"Then we must play this match out to the end. It is time for me to leave you, old friend. We will meet again on the battlefield." He held out his hand.

Goll took it, and with Fionn's help stood up. His laugh was like the cawing of a crow. "Look again, lad. I do not think your going forth from here will be as easy as your coming."

Fionn turned, and saw that Goll was not the only one who had a problem hearing. While they were talking, mac Morna men had surrounded the willows. There was a double line of warriors between him and the river, Emer Glunglas and Fer-li among them, all of them armed and ready for a fight.

"I myself am ready to go down fighting. What about you?" Goll fixed him with his single eye.

Fionn straightened, hoping his face did not betray how crazily his heart was pounding. He had faced odds like this before and been the victor, but not usually before breakfast, not when his feet were so cold. And yet, he thought, what man, seeing his death approaching wolf-eyed as the mac Mornas were watching him now, ever thought it was the right time? By now the sun had risen fully, glowing in the turning leaves and sparkling on the Sinnan's brown waters. It was going to be a beautiful day.

"If that is the way you wish it," he answered, steadily. "But I promise you that a great many of your kinsmen will die. Or the two of us could fight it out here."

"You had my life in your hand, son of Cumhal, and spared it. Can I be less generous?" Taking his spear in one hand, Goll grasped Fionn's arm with his other and led him between the willow trees to the shore. His warriors surged forward ominously, but a gesture from Goll thrust them away.

"Back, my brave boys, and let him go. The glory of our House would be forever stained if we killed Fionn here, and him so outnumbered. Save your strength to send a fitting guard of honor with him, on the battlefield!" Goll gave Fionn a little shove forward.

His back twitching from the pressure of all the hostile eyes upon it, Fionn strode into the Sinnan's swift-flowing waters. There was a shout from his own side as someone saw him; he held up his hand in warning, not wanting to end up in the middle of an exchange of spears.

Fionn managed to make it across the ford without falling, and climbed up to join the *fian*, who were too dumbfounded even to cheer.

"It was Goll who was snoring over there," he said to Fear Logha, as he headed towards their campsite. "I thought it might be." An exasperated growl from Oisin brought him around to face his son. "I hope you have left me some breakfast," Fionn said briskly. "We must eat and arm swiftly—as you can see, our friends over there are ready for battle, and it would not do to keep them waiting too long!"

If he had failed to halt the war, at least his escapade had given Fionn a chance to count the enemy, and he knew his own *fian* outnumbered them. He could afford to split his forces, to send a band of his men across each ford of the Sinnan, and still retain superiority. The fighting at the fords was bloody, but once they were across the river, the *fian* of Almu re-formed and began to push the mac Mornas westward.

All that day the chase continued, up from the river across the flanks of Cronnmhóin and the bogland beyond it. From ridge to ridge the fighting flared, fierce and unpredictable as wildfire, and Goll mac Morna proved that his own flames were not quenched, despite his great age. Indeed, though the Morna clansmen could run like foxes, when they turned at bay they bit like wolves, and gave Fionn's men a good savaging before giving ground once more.

They left behind them a deadly trail of wounded and dying, but the men of Almu would not give up, and those of Clan Morna would not surrender. It was in that day's fighting that young Fear Logha died. Not until nightfall did the mac Mornas give up the fight, one remnant fleeing with Garad to the south, while the other went with Goll westward. Fionn sent Oscar and his band after Garad, whose strong arm had accounted for so many of their men. But he himself, with Oisin and Caoilte beside him, followed Goll mac Morna towards the sea.

FOR ALMOST A MOON THEIR QUARRY MANAGED TO elude them. Goll's men were killed off one by one, but they sold their lives dearly, and each death bought their leader a few more days. West and north led the trail, into the wild coastlands above Ben Bulben, until at last, with the desperate fury of a cornered animal, Goll went to ground on a rocky promontory.

The crags that headed it rose sheer above the crashing waves; a stony bastion blasted by chill winds off the sea. Wind and water had carved the stone into a maze of spires and overhangs and archways, linked to the rest of the promontory by a narrow neck of land. Unhospitable the place might be, but it was eminently defensible, as Goll demonstrated as soon as Fionn tried to attack him there.

He pulled his men back, hoping that the old man would see the futility of his resistance and surrender, for if they could not come at him, neither could he come out. He was beseiged more straitly on the point than ever Almu had been by his men. In a last attempt at mercy, Fionn sent a messenger to bring Caoinche, his own niece and Goll's wife, who had recently borne him another child.

She had left the baby with a wet nurse, for it was sickly. When she was brought to Fionn, her face was puffy with weeping, but she faced him with eyes like stones.

"Caoinche, by my brother's head I swear to you that I do not want to kill your husband. He has speared everyone who got close enough to talk. But he will let you come to him—tell him that I give him his life if he will come out from there and lay down his arms."

Her appraising gaze saw how the pursuit had worn on Fionn, and a little of the bitterness left her eyes. "Stubborn," she said harshly, crossing her arms beneath her full breasts, "that he always was. But I believe you, Fionn, and I will do what I may."

"Do you think she will persuade him?" asked Caoilte, when Caoinche had gone.

"If she cannot do it there is no one who can," Fionn answered grimly, gazing out at the sea. It looked peaceful now, grey waves glinting coppery in the light of the setting sun, but on this coast, such calm was deceptive.

"But you cannot leave him there to starve!" Oisin said accusingly.

"Can I afford to let him go?" Fionn asked in return, and his son fell silent. A knob of rock was digging into Fionn's back; he shifted position, his eyes never leaving the path up which Caoinche had gone.

"I wish I could go away from here—from all this—" Oisin indicated their rude camp with a wave of his hand. "I am tired of fighting, Father. I am sick of killing friends."

Fionn nodded. In this relentless pursuit of an old man there had been no glory. The only one of them who still found meaning in it was Goll. "But where would you go?" he asked softly. "Where in this world could you find a place without war?"

Oisin stared out across the sea. "See how the sun is laying a path of red-gold across the sea. It looks solid enough to walk on. At the end of the sun-path surely there is a land without sorrow."

"Only in the Land of Promise," said Fionn, quoting the lines he had learned when he studied at Cethern's school.

"Without death or grief or sorrow,
Without health's thief, debility,
Of Emne fair that is the sign—
Uncommon such stability."

In Eriu the Sidhe might have their quarrels, but beyond the sea, as he had heard, things were otherwise. A white-winged gull wheeled gracefully above their heads, crying mournfully, and Fionn sighed.

Dusk was turning land and sea the same dim grey when they saw Caoinche coming back again. She was alone.

She stopped when she saw them waiting for her, her face working, and then, as if she could go no farther, went to her knees on the path.

"He would not come?" asked Caoilte, going to her.

"My grief, my grief! Ah, the dear, pig-headed, fool of a man!" she cried. "He is dying of hunger and thirst, there where he is, but he will not come out to you! I told him to take the flesh of the men he killed for food; I offered him the milk of my breasts to ease his thirst. But it is one of his *geasa* not to take advice from a woman, and him dying on his feet before me, so that you could count the bones of his body through his skin!"

Caoilte drew her in against his shoulder as she burst into weeping once more. But Fionn got to his feet.

"What are you doing?" said Oisin in alarm, as Fionn slung a waterskin over his shoulder and a pouchful of dried meat from his belt.

"I am taking Goll his dinner. I will pull my mantle over my head and in this light he will not be sure if it is Caoinche returning until I am across the neck of land."

"You brought me here to help you deceive him?" cried the woman. "I trusted you!"

"My dear," Fionn said heavily, "this is not a betrayal. I have feared all along that it would come to this in the end. He has his weapons and so do I, and it is his choice how to receive me." He had left Birga leaning against the rock, but he was wearing his father's sword.

"Father—" Oisin reached out to him, and for a moment Fionn clasped his hand. "I think that if you take that path, only one of you will return."

Fionn shrugged. "Would you rather we left him there to starve alone? I go to give Goll whatever gift he will take from me, and whatever mercy I can."

Oisin's hand fell and he turned away so that Fionn could not see his eyes. Fionn did not blame him. He had a rather unpleasant feeling in his own middle as well as he set out for this appointment with his ancient enemy.

THE PATH OUT TO THE POINT WAS TREACHEROUS EVEN in daylight. In the darkness it was a bone-breaker, made even more deceptive by the shadows cast by the rising moon. Vision was untrustworthy. The crags were populous with shapes drawn in moonlight and shadow; had they not been so still, he could have thought an army waiting there. And the night was full of voices that whispered from the wind and the sea. Fionn let his feet, trained by a lifetime of running over broken ground, find the way.

He was nearing the narrow ridge that connected the point to the promontory when one of the outcroppings moved. For a moment he thought his eyes had tricked him; then a fighting man's instinct reacted, and he drew his sword. The figure that faced him was swathed in a dark mantle drawn over its head so that all he could see of the face was the pale curve of the jaw and a gleam of eyes.

Not Goll, then. . . . Fionn felt his neck hairs prickling at the uncanny grace with which the figure was coming towards him.

"Save your sword for mortal prey, son of Cumhal—do you think to threaten Me?" It was a woman's voice, honey and harshness all blended together. He had heard it before.

"I did once," he said steadily. "Are you threatening *me*?"

"You were young then, though worn with madness. Now you are old, and I have a gift for you." The edges of the Morrigan's cloak settled like dark wings as she halted before him.

"Do you mean to offer me your love, as you did Cuchulain?" Fionn laughed. "As you have said, I am an old man, and I would be of little use to you."

"You are not so old as you think," she said sweetly. "But the gift I have for you is not love, but revenge. Fear not to fare boldly onward, for on yonder point your enemy lies sleeping. You can take his head easily. Strike him, Fionn, as once he struck at Cumhal, and let his blood feed the ground!"

At her words, Fionn felt his blood heating with an almost forgotten madness. It was true—he had killed all of his father's other enemies—why should Goll be spared? The dark figure of the goddess swayed nearer. He could smell her scent, a fragrance sweet to the point of corruption. She was very close now. Heart pounding, Fionn reached out to her.

Draperies swirled away like smoke at the touch of his hands. But the face beneath the hood was a skull. With an oath he recoiled.

"These are the holy and eternal bones," the wind sighed in his ear. "*Why are you afraid?"*

"Get out of my path—" he said in a strangled voice.

With a last whisper of laughter, the apparition disappeared.

My mind is failing, Fionn told himself. But his heart was still racing, and a hint of cloying sweetness hung in the air. Swiftly he hurried past the spot where the Morrigan had stood and started across the neck of stone.

"Goll! Goll mac Morna, are you there, man?" he cried as the path widened once more. At least he would not take him sleeping.

"I am here, and so is my spear—" came Goll's reply, but it was like a ghost speaking, like the wind.

Softly Fionn stepped past the outcrop of rock that leaned over the path and saw him, on his feet with his back to a boulder and his war spear braced on the ground. He was painted in silver against the dark stone, and behind him was a silver shimmer of sea. *Like Cuchulain against his pillar,* thought Fionn. *Well, I have met the Raven, and Goll is as great a hero as the Hound of the Ulaidh.* But any thoughts of vengeance the Morrigan had left in him fled as he saw how frail the old man had become.

"I have brought food for you," he said softly. "See, I will set it down here." He put the waterskin and pouch down and backed away, out of range of the spear.

"Ah Fionn, lad—" Goll sighed, and moving with great care, knelt down to take the food. He looked at the meat, then set it regretfully aside, but he tore the stopper from the waterskin and gulped the tepid liquid down. "That is better—" he said, sitting back. "But my belly is shrunken like an old wife's dugs and I cannot eat. I thank you—I did not expect to see you again."

"I made you an offer at the fords of the Sinnan. It still holds. Come home with me."

Goll shook his head with a hint of his old rumbling laughter. "I refused you with an army at my back. Do ye think, now that my back is to the wall, that I would choose different?"

Fionn hunkered down on his haunches, his hands resting on his knees. "I don't know. I hoped—man, if you do not come, what will become of you?"

Goll sipped some more water, savoring it this time. "Cumhal died young . . . You do not look like him now—he never got that old!" He laughed creakily. "But you know, inside, I feel no older than the lad who speared him. I thought I was dead . . . when I fell down beside him on Cnucha field."

"I am not my father," Fionn said, wondering what Goll was getting at now.

"You are Cumhal's son." Goll looked at him directly. "You are bound to avenge him."

For a moment Fionn wondered if the other man's mind was wandering. Then his belly clenched as it came to him, finally, what this old and beloved enemy was trying to do.

Goll picked up his spear and using it as a lever, got himself upright once more. Braced against the rock, he jabbed the air.

"Come and fight me, son of Cumhal, or are you afraid?" He laughed in self-mockery, but his eyes were burning. Very slowly, Fionn got to his feet as well. *I knew it might come to this, why am I surprised?*

He drew his sword, saluting Goll as a warrior honors his opponent in a formal duel. "This is Cumhal's sword, with which Fionnéices killed him after your spear had brought him down," he said grimly. "This is the sword with which I killed the *fili* when he tried to kill me. It still hungers for the blood of Cumhal's enemies. Are you satisfied?"

Goll's breathing rasped the silence, but his lips drew back in a feral smile. Fionn took a deep breath and stepped forward, bringing up his sword to guard against the flickering maneuvers of the spear. All of his being focused on what he was about to do.

The spear struck suddenly, grazing Fionn's chest, and Goll's eyes blazed with triumph. Fionn responded in a single smooth uncoiling of arm and sword, sweeping the spear aside, stabbing swiftly to pierce the old man's heart and bring the blade around to strike off Goll's head as his body began to fall.

The move had been performed perfectly. For a short time thereafter Goll's body twitched, pumping blood onto the thirsty ground. His head had landed a few paces away, its features still set in that snarling, triumphant smile. Fionn sank to his knees, breathing hard.

"Goll—" he whispered, but only silence answered him. He sat back, suddenly aware of the hiss of the ebb tide and the silver path the moon had laid across the sea. "Farewell, old friend, and fare swiftly," he said then. "It will be very lonely, now that you are gone."

Fionn did not know if he had served the Morrigan or defied her, but it was done. He kept watch beside the body while the moon set and the wheeling stars rolled across the sky. And when the heavens lightened enough for him to tell one stone from another, he put head and torso back together and piled rocks above them in a cairn, and set Goll's spear upright atop it in token that a hero lay buried there.

Chapter 16

THE *RÍGFÉNNID* OF ERIU STOOD IN HIS LADY'S GARDEN, examining the buds on the apple tree. The thin bark that covered the branch was hard and shiny, glowing with sap, and the tender nubbins that would become flowers already faintly green. There would be apple blossoms for the Feast of Brigid this year. So much changed and passed away with the turning seasons, but this remained constant—the yearly cycle of bloom and fading, growth and decay.

They had made the garden for Grainne in the first spring after she came to live at Almu, cradled in the hollow at the base of the hill with a stout palisade to shield it from the wind and protect it from marauding deer. In seven years, it had passed through the first anxious stages when one transplanted young plants and nursed seedlings and chanted spells over the new arrivals and hoped they would live. In the second year the garden had begun to flourish, and by the third the perennials needed thinning so that there would be room for all of them to grow.

It was not so different with the *fianna,* thought Fionn, as he turned away from the trees and surveyed the raised beds where Grainne grew herbs and flowers. Some men sprouted bravely, flourished for a season or two, then died, while others, perhaps slower of growth, clung to life and slowly increased in power until they threatened the others.

He and Goll had been both slow and enduring, Fionn thought wryly, but in the end there had not been room in Eriu for both of them. There were now no men of his age in the *fianna.* He stood like a hoary oak amid a crowd of saplings, and when the wind blew cold he felt the weight of every year. After Goll's death he had made peace with Cairbre, engaging to rule the *fianna* as he had before and continue to shield Eriu. But since the day of Cairbre's accession, he had not visited Temair.

Almu had become a pleasant place to him since Grainne had been here. Gradually the leadership of the *fianna* had shifted to Oisin, and now that the mac Mornas no longer threatened, Fionn was content to have it so. He would take the field for a major campaign, or go out to see the young men tested. But last summer there had been only minor skirmishes that Oisin could handle quite competently. Fionn was content to spend most of his time at Almu.

In the slow changes in Grainne's garden he found reassurance. It was possible to remember ancient wars and old friends and enemies as he remembered last season's blossoms. Now it was the turn of Oscar and Oisin. Fionn had lived his life, and though his health was still robust, he was content to exchange the forest for the garden. The life of a hero, however glorious, was not very restful, and there was peace here among the flowers.

A flicker of motion behind the lavender bush made him blink. Old eyes could be unreliable, to be sure, but it was also true that since the war in Faerie, many of the minor spirits, the *gruagachs* and *merrows* and *cluricauns*, had remained in the human lands. He saluted the spirit which had taken up residence in the garden and turned towards the gate, whistling to Sceolan, who had been dozing in the sun. Like Fionn himself, the dog was too pale in color to show much silvering around the muzzle, but he spent much of his time sleeping now.

"Come on lad," he called, "we'd best get moving or we'll miss our dinner!" It took both of them longer to get up the hill than it used to, but that was only partly from age. These days Fionn found himself easily distracted. He would take time to examine a stone or a flower that he would have passed without a thought when he was in his prime. He smiled a little, remembering how he had feared to find himself aging when he first wanted to marry Grainne. By the time she had come to him, he really was old. The difference was that now he was enjoying it.

At each bend in the road a different vista distracted him. To the west was the Forest of Gaible, bare branches just beginning to haze over with green. To the north an undulation of heath and hill faded into blue distance towards the River Liffe, and to the south scattered woods merged into the rich farmlands of Laigin. Eastward—he found himself smiling once more as he looked up the hill at Almu, its great gate open in welcome and its walls mellowed to gold by the afternoon sun.

He hastened his steps up the slope, suddenly eager for the sound of human voices and Grainne's smile. Halfway there, between one step and another, a wave of dizziness passed over him. He staggered, blinking at a world that had gone grey around him. The road was the same, but above it he saw the shining ramparts fallen and the courts of Almu overgrown with grass. From atop the remaining house timber, a raven screamed.

Fionn struck out, rejecting the image, and in another moment strong hands were upholding him, a young voice calling his name. Blinking, Fionn forced himself to focus. Above him, as before, the walls of his fortress smiled in the sun. The only bird sound was the call of a hunting falcon on her regular circuit above the hill. He sighed and turned to the dark-haired young man who had caught him.

"Thank you, Diarmuid—for a moment there I missed my footing."

"Eochaid—I'm Eochaid—" said the warrior. Fionn looked at him. Of course he was Eochaid, wasn't that what he had called him? Diarmuid had died fifteen years ago.

Eochaid still looked dubious, but Fionn strode out strongly enough to reassure him as they completed their ascent of the hill. Almu was whole and strong; he had simply experienced a moment of disorientation. Then he was through the gate and the life of the fortress surged around him and he forgot what he had seen.

That evening, as they were sitting down to their meal, a messenger arrived from Temair.

"From the *Ard Ri* of Eriu to Fionn of Almu I bring greetings—" The runner spoke with eyes closed, relaying the words stored in his memory. "And with them an invitation to a high feast and celebration on the occasion of the wedding of his daughter to Conbhron mac Aonghus, who is now king over the Dési of Mumu. At the first full moon after the Feast of Brigid he will hold the feast and the bedding of the bride and the celebration. Be you welcome!"

There was a moment of stunned silence when he had finished. Then everyone burst into conversation at once.

"Is it Sgeimh Solais he's marrying off? After all this time he's finally letting her go?" asked mac Lugach.

"So far as I know she is his only daughter," said Fionn. "As I remember, she was growing into a beauty."

"But to give her to the Dési!" exclaimed Oisin. "Surely Cormac's ghost will haunt them!"

"No doubt he hopes to pacify the south with this alliance while he puts down unrest in the Ulaidh," said Fionn.

"She would not be the first royal daughter to be married off to sweeten an alliance," put in Grainne, coming in with a dish of stewed apples, the last of the winter's store.

"Well, it is all one to me whom she marries," said Fionn. "I see no reason to bless the occasion with my presence there."

"I do," said Oscar, holding out his horn to be refilled as the serving maid went by. "We cannot stop it, I suppose, but at least we could sit there and make him feel guilty."

"You could always demand the old tribute." mac

Lugach grinned at Oscar's confusion. "Didn't you know? The tradition used to be that the *fianna* had first choice of the marriageable maidens. When a king's daughter was wed, the head of the *fianna* could either claim her first night or take a payment in ransom. Seems an easy way to earn a little gold, to me!"

"That hasn't been done for years!" exclaimed Fionn.

"There hasn't been the occasion!" answered the other man. "But Cormac paid you off, didn't he, when Grainne—" He broke off, seeing that she had come back in with the bread and cheese, and blushed.

"It is true," said Fionn, trying to cover the awkward moment, "and I wish that I could pay it back to him, now that I have the woman herself, who is better to me than any gold . . ."

Grainne smiled bitterly. As time went by the *fianna* had accepted her as Fionn's wife and mistress of Almu, but there were still some who blamed her for having rejected Fionn in the first place, and others who blamed her for being unfaithful to Diarmuid's memory. The sorrow was suppressed, but not forgotten.

"Well, I still think we should be represented at the wedding." Stubborn as a hound, Oscar returned to the original topic. "There's no need for you to go, Grandfather, but I could take my band up to Temair and look imposing."

"Look handsome, you mean—you want to turn all the girls' heads with your manly beauty!" teased Eochaid. Oscar reddened, and the rest of his men began to laugh.

"I would advise against it," Grainne said softly. "My brother is never so dangerous as when he is fair-spoken. He can do without your presence at this feast as he has done before."

Fionn was inclined to agree, but by this time the warriors, Oscar's men especially, were shouting with enthusiasm. It had been a long winter, and they were as eager as children at the prospect of a journey, and in the end he agreed that they should go.

BY THE FEAST OF BRIGID, THE APPLE TREES IN Grainne's garden were radiant with starry bloom. As the new moon rose through the gathering dusk the cart that carried the goddess was drawn past it, preceded by torchbearers, with her straw-masked warriors cavorting about her.

"She is coming!" came the call from the ramparts. "Hey, lads, you see how those poor oxen are laboring! Go you down and help them bring the cart within!"

It was always the same. As the oxen began to toil up the slope, Oisin and Diarmuid—but no, now it was Oscar and Uladhach and Glas and their friends who would run down to them, unhook the oxen from their traces and take up the yoke themselves, pulling and pushing the heavy wagon the rest of the way to the *dun*. Fionn remembered vividly how the wagon seemed to grow heavier the more fully the goddess came down into the woman who sat within.

As the cart was drawn through the great gate, Fionn came forward.

"Beloved Brigid," he said in a strong voice, "to you we are calling! Fire of burning gold, well of sweet wisdom, healer of every ill, to this *dun* be welcome. Lady, come down to us now!"

The still figure on the carven chair stirred. Moving surely despite the draperies that swathed her, she stepped from the cart to the bench they had set beside it. Beneath the white veil her cloak was crimson, parting to show a white robe beneath as she moved. Perhaps Fionn was confusing this priestess with women who had served Brigid in the past, but she seemed much taller than any of those now at the Shrine. The straw boys spread out into a circle, drawing the crowd after them.

"Noble Woman, be welcome!" the people cried. Surrounded by torches, the priestess moved forward, hands uplifted in blessing.

"Oh ye who have shivered in the cold of winter, behold, I bring you the warmth of the strengthening sun!" Her voice filled the space around her, sweet as honey, bright as gold. "Oh ye who have walked in darkness, I bring you lengthening of days! Oh ye who have hungered and thirsted, taste the sweet waters that make the green things grow! All ye who are weary and afraid, now hear Me—receive the upwelling of the spirit, and all things made new!"

Brigid moved slowly around the circle, bestowing her blessings. When she came to Fionn he felt the fine hairs lift on his neck, for power was radiating from that slender figure like heat off a forge. There was always to some extent a feeling of Presence when the goddess made her rounds, but surely tonight She had come in full measure, and he could not help wondering what need had called her. She left a fragrance of apple blossom behind her, and Fionn saw on more than one face the silver glint of tears.

She completed her circuit, took her seat in the carven chair and put back her veil. Bread and honey-mead were set out for her, and singly or together, the folk began to bring her their offerings. There were the usual tributes of food and animals, always welcome at the Shrine, which in time of famine sometimes seemed to be feeding half Laigin. Some presented gifts of their own fashioning, a length of embroidered linen or a lovingly carved bowl.

Last of all, Fionn and Grainne came forward. Grainne knelt, offering a spray of flowers from her apple tree, and as Brigid received it, Fionn saw suddenly the silver branch of Faerie shimmering in her hand. His head was buzzing; he had thought the eyes of the priestess were blue, but as he drew closer he saw that they were dark and liquid, and that he was seeing the face of the goddess who had saved him from the Morrigan once more.

Those eyes seemed curiously unfocused, as if she were looking, not at his surface, but at what lay within.

"Lady," Fionn said softly as he sat down on the bench at her feet and shifted his harp onto his knee. "My fingers are not so agile as once they were, but there is still music in my heart, and I have made a song for you." He cleared his throat and began to sing.

"Fair apple flower, honey's bright gold,
Sovereign power, safe flock and fold,
Brigid now hear us, Brigid be near us today—"

As he finished the first verse, the goddess smiled, and he felt the golden pulse of her power. For a moment he was afraid, then her Presence enfolded him, and suddenly his stiff fingers were flickering as swiftly as they had when first he learned harping in Cethern's poetic school.

"Wisdom upwelling, waters of healing,

Blessings compelling, holiness dealing
Brigid now hear us—"

Fionn's voice rang out, sure and strong.

"Bard's inspiration, harps' sweet rejoicing,
Song of creation, Words of Power voicing,
Brigid—"

The harp notes rang beneath his swift fingers; and the harp strings, catching the light of the torches, shimmered as if newly drawn from the forge.

"Forgefire's glow, craft to mold;
Hammer's blow gives life to gold!
Brigid now hear us, Brigid be near us today!"

Fionn lifted his fingers from the strings, but the overtones continued to echo, until they sounded so faintly they might have been coming from the Otherworld. As the last hint of music faded, the goddess laughed.

"You call to me, and because for this night I walk in flesh, you believe that I have come. Oh you foolish man—when was I ever far away?"

Fionn bowed his head, sure that he was blushing. Donait had used to chide him in just that way. He felt cool fingers smooth his close-clipped beard and lift his chin so that he had no choice but to look into her eyes.

"Ah, Fionn, Fionn, you cannot escape me so easily. Have you forgotten how I saved you from the warriors of the Sidhe? Have you forgotten the oaths you swore when I helped you to win Almu?"

Fionn stared at her. When he was young, forever had

seemed an eternity away. While the vigor of his manhood still flamed within him, he had been willing to take on a thousand enemies. And indeed he had retained that vigor far longer than most men. But now he was old, his fires burned down to coals.

"I have served you, Lady, while there was still strength in my arm. Now I make songs. . . ."

"Are you so sure that there is nothing left for you to do?" There was steel beneath the sweetness now.

"Are you trying to frighten me, or is the danger to those I love?"

Brigid shook her head, an ancient sadness in her eyes. "I do not threaten, but I see where the paths men take will lead. You cannot choose for others, my dear, but there are still choices before you. You were not born to go to seed in a garden, however beautiful, and from such oaths as you have sworn there are no unbindings."

He sat back, shaking his head. It was not fair! "If you require me to fight for you, I will do so," he whispered, "but I am tired of war."

"I require you to awaken, Fionn mac Cumhal. But remember, not every battle is fought with the sword."

In the days that followed Fionn often found himself remembering Brigid's words. But as the moon swelled, the weather held clear and bright. On the Curragh, the new grass was pushing the old growth aside; farmers began their ploughing, and the rich smell of new-turned earth drifted on the breeze. It made no sense to speculate on sorrows when the world was so fair.

On a morning two days after the moon passed full,

Fionn was on the eastern rampart of Almu enjoying the sunshine when Oisin joined him.

"See how the grasses are rippling beneath the wind"—Fionn gestured towards the Curragh—"like the waves of a great green sea."

"That's like what she said—" murmured Oisin, staring outward. "But she had it the other way round. The sea is like a rolling plain. . . ."

"*Who* said?" Fionn turned to him. "What do you mean?"

"Last night, in my dream. I was riding on a white horse behind a woman of surpassing beauty, but we were passing across the sea. And I woke cold and alone, and wept because to have her in my arms had been like holding the sun."

"Who was she?" Fionn asked urgently. "Where was she taking you?"

"I don't know," Oisin sighed. "But it was somewhere wonderful, and I was happy, as I have not been since I was young."

It was true—Oisin had been such a joyous child, but he had lost all his lightness of spirit when Eibhir returned to Rome. Fionn told himself that Oisin's trouble was a natural melancholy. Hadn't he himself brooded over Sadb for years? But he felt suddenly cold, despite the brightness of the sun.

They heard Sceolan barking and looked down. A moon ago Fionn might have waited for someone to call him, but it was a measure of how much Brigid's message had disturbed him that he moved immediately to the ladder and began to clamber down.

A sweated horse was standing in the gateyard; it took Fionn a moment to realize that the man who was still clinging to its neck was Eochaid.

"I'm sorry . . ." the young man forced a grin. "My legs aren't quite ready to bear me . . . I've been in the saddle a night . . . and a day and . . . half the night before."

The time it would take a rider to get here from Temair, pushing hard. Fionn's belly clenched.

"What has Oscar done?" asked Oisin in a still voice.

"Sgeimh Solais—" Eochaid gulped down the water one of the maidservants brought him and tried again. "At the wedding feast. He invoked the old custom—a night with the girl or a ransom." By this time most of the men who were still in the *dun* had gathered round. Grainne stood in the entry to her dwelling, her face paled to the color of the apron she wore pinned to her gown.

"And Cairbre didn't like it?" someone suggested helpfully.

"His reaction was . . ." Eochaid thought for a moment, "extreme. He can't have expected it—I mean no one would think that even Oscar—" he shook his head. "Cairbre exploded. Every resentment he ever had against the *fianna* back to his childhood came boiling out as if he had just been waiting for the opportunity."

"And what about Oscar?" Oisin spoke, still in that same quiet tone. *He is too controlled,* thought Fionn. *He cares more about his boy than he ever lets on. He won't want to wait while I work out what to do.* Without conscious thought Fionn had realized he was going to have to take control.

"Well . . . he had been drinking, and every time he looked at the Dési king he would say something about Cormac, and what a damn shame it was that Sgeimh Solais should marry into the tribe of her grandfather's murderers, and you know, I think he always had a liking for the girl. . . ."

Remembering the stunned-ox stare with which Oscar had watched the princess when they were children, Fionn thought that quite possible, but he had certainly chosen a poor time to do something about it.

"So he refused," Fionn cut him short, "and Oscar—"

"Grabbed the girl and carried her off." Eochaid swayed, and Oisin got an arm around him and supported him into the hall.

"Go find my messengers," Fionn said to the man who was leading the horse away, "every man and woman who can run, and send them to me in the hall." It was appalling, really, how quickly his old responses came back to him. He was already thinking in terms of times and distances and supplies.

When he joined the others in the hall Eochaid was explaining how they had fought their way out of Temair. But he had stayed long enough to hear Cairbre declare Oscar outlaw and summon the Gaelic chieftains of Eriu to war.

"DOES IT HAVE TO BE WAR?" ASKED GRAINNE, LATE that evening when they lay together in her bower.

"That is your brother's choice, not mine," Fionn answered, turning to face her. "My only options are to take all the men I can gather to help Oscar, or let him fight alone. If I choose not to fight, and Oscar loses, the balance of power between the chieftains and the *fianna* will be broken. Cairbre will never stop until he has destroyed us, and even if he spares me, I will be without force and alone. Better a violent death for a cause than a peaceful ending that has no meaning."

"Like my father's—" she said bitterly.

"But not like Diarmuid's," Fionn whispered into the darkness. They had never spoken of Diarmuid's death, since that first time, but it had to be said now.

"I begged him not to go up on the mountain!" exclaimed Grainne. "I pleaded with him not to go after the boar!"

"So did I. But I have wondered about it a great deal since then. I think that only when Diarmuid turned to face the boar did he finally stop running from me."

There was a long silence. Then Grainne reached out to Fionn and he gathered her against him. "Is that what you are doing now? Turning at bay?"

"I do not know—" Fionn breathed in the sweet herbal scent of her hair and sighed. "I know only that I must go. My dear," he went on, "I may be an old fool, but when we have marched out of here I want you to prepare for a siege. Eochaid will command your guard and stay here."

"Is there something you have not told me? Some premonition?" She reached up and he felt her long fingers smoothing his brow and the line of his jaw as if to reassure herself of his reality.

So lass, he thought, *do you love me at all, then?* Grainne, having made up her mind to be a wife to him, had done her job honestly. But he had never asked her if she loved him. It would have seemed a betrayal of Diarmuid's memory.

"I do not need to bite my thumb to see the dangers. If we strike swiftly, I think we can win, perhaps face them down, or offer a token fight and then negotiate compensation. But if things go wrong . . . well, Almu would be a target for folk who know more about attacking fortresses than Goll did."

* * *

WHEN FIONN AND THE *FIANNA* MARCHED OUT OF ALMU the apple blossoms were beginning to fall. It had taken him several days to gather his forces. He figured that he could afford the time to make sure his men had weapons and supplies, for the Gaelic chieftains Cairbre would be calling would be busy with the spring ploughing. But most of the younger, unmarried men who wintered at Almu had gone with Oscar. The men who lived on their own lands were engaged in their own ploughing and took longer to respond than he had expected. And some were reluctant to fight the high king, and did not answer his call.

Grainne stood at the gate to watch them go. Sceolan, whose old bones were no longer up to such hard travelling, had to be tied up in the stables to keep him from trying to come after them. They could still hear his whining. Fionn wondered if his bones were up to it either, but at the same age his foster father, Fiacail, had ridden across Eriu. Fionn was only going up to Temair.

"Farewell, my husband." Grainne offered the drinking horn. Her voice was steady, but her hands were trembling. "May the blessing of holy Brigid be a shield before you."

Fionn drank. The mead was cool and aromatic with a hint of sweetness, like the woman who had brewed it. As he returned the horn, Grainne's fingers tightened briefly on his.

"Fionn—" she whispered, "come back to me."

THE *FIANNA* PRESSED NORTHWARD THROUGH THE RADIANT springtide of Eriu. Runners ranged ahead of them, seeking news. So it was that they learned that

Cairbre had gathered an army from Midhe and the north, composed mostly of chieftains' war bands and younger sons who agreed with the *Ard Ri* that the time had come to break the *fianna's* power. He had been right to come, thought Fionn, as the reports came in; the longer the foe was unopposed, the more advantage he would gain.

They learned that as soon as Cairbre marched out from Temair with his men, Oscar had sent Sgeimh Solais home again. Whether the girl had been willing or unwilling, no one seemed to care. Running off with forbidden women was an old family tradition, but his grandfather Trenmor was the only one to have gotten away with it. Fionn supposed that even Oscar now recognized how dangerous a monster he had awakened when he challenged the high king, and had gotten rid of the girl to avoid distraction. As they travelled, a few more men joined them, including Caoilte, who had been wintering on his lands near Temair.

And as they moved across the rolling green fields of Midhe, they learned that Cairbre was pushing Oscar's *fian* eastward, and that the two forces were likely to come to battle near a place called Gabhra.

EASTWARD THE RAVENS WERE GATHERING, BLACK blots against the early morning sky. Oisin touched his rein and pointed, but Fionn had already seen them. He squeezed the pony's sides to urge it forward.

"Caoilte—you are the best runner with us," said Oisin. "How would you like to nip ahead and find out what has got those birds so excited?"

Caoilte grinned like the youth he had been, it

seemed not long ago, and started off, his long limbs covering the ground astonishingly swiftly. Without pausing, men began to check their shield straps and get ready to jettison extraneous gear. They knew what the birds meant as well as Fionn did. Somewhere ahead men were carving each other up for the ravens' next meal.

Fionn's shield and spear knew it too. He could feel the shield grow lighter as it always did when fighting was imminent, and hear the first faint humming that meant Birga was wakening as well. *Be patient, my old comrades,* he thought grimly. *There will be work for you soon.*

With every step the breeze off the ocean blew more strongly, cooling flushed faces and, presently, bearing with it the clamor of fighting men. They were almost due west of Temair, moving onto a hilly eminence halfway between it and the sea. The rising ground before them was ridged and rolling, left untouched except by grazing cattle though there were farmsteads with orchards not far away. A good place for a battle, thought Fionn, forcing himself to detachment. But something within whispered, *or a good place to die. . . .*

Oisin trilled the call to halt as Caoilte came loping back to them.

"Up there—" he gasped, "Oscar's . . . making a good fight of it. . . . But they have him outnumbered. Split the *fian*, come at 'em from two sides . . . we might be in time!"

Before he had finished speaking, a gesture from Oisin was dividing their forces. "Caoilte, take the foremost around to the far side of the battlefield, since you know the way. We'll follow and hit them from behind."

As Caoilte started off again, Oisin looked doubtfully at Fionn. "Father, you have led us this far, but—"

"But you're not sure you want me in the battle?" Fionn turned a cough into a bark of laughter. "Do you think you can stop me?" Oisin flushed a dull red and Fionn turned to the others, who were watching like spectators at hurley. Suddenly he felt almost cheerful.

"I call you all to witness that he did warn me, but I have been wanting to tan Cairbre's hide for him since he was ten years old, and I'll be damned if I'll let my own son deprive me of the pleasure!" He slid down from the pony and gave the rein to one of the lads to take it to the rear.

The warriors laughed, and he could see the apprehension in their eyes becoming belief. He could still do that to men. Once he had feared that power, but he was glad of it now.

"I don't suppose you considered that worrying about you could put me in danger too—" Oisin said crossly as they started off again.

"Now, my lad, you know how I felt when I first took you to war!" Fionn strode out. "We must all take our chances, my dear—you, and I, and Oscar. . . ." He stopped. The shouting ahead was very loud now; above the other clamor he heard the war cries of the *fian*. Without further words, he and Oisin started to run.

As they burst through the line of trees onto the battlefield, Fionn's first thought was that Cairbre had been able to field a much larger force than he expected. Strong and well armed, the Gaels had inflicted heavy losses on Oscar's *fénnidi*, who had gone to Temair outfitted for a wedding, not a campaign. But the battle-broom standard with its silken banner still tossed above the conflict, and Oscar himself was still standing, although the group of followers around him was achingly small.

But as Fionn pounded down the slope behind Oisin, Caoilte and his crew burst out of the ravine on the other side of the field, screeching like the *bean-sidhe*. Only when he gasped for breath did Fionn realize that he was shouting too.

Dry—try—die! sang Birga, wakening as the first foe loomed up before him and its point pierced the man's breast. An ecstatic pulse leaped up the spear shaft and through Fionn's arm, burning his fatigue away. He took an attacker's blow on his shield, jabbed in response, and felt more power flowing through him as the spear sank in. Once Fionn would have tried to master Birga's madness, but now he needed it. Snarling, he let the battle-fury take him as he waded into the fray.

For Fionn, the rest of the battle was fought in fragments of awareness. He glimpsed his half brothers Faobhar and Fearghusa fighting back-to-back against a crowd of enemies. He saw young Uladhach fall to the blows of a burly Gaelic champion. He found himself facing a young man with Cairbre's sullen eyes and only after he had struck him through the belly realized that he had killed the high king's younger son. He remembered Caoilte, his right arm hanging limp and bloody, holding off two enemy warriors with his sword. In a moment of freedom he caught sight of his grandson mac Lugach beating his way towards the heart of the fighting and stumbled after him.

Oscar stood in the midst of a crowd of foes, holding his standard in one hand and swinging his sword with the other. Mac Lugach's son Glas, who should have carried it, had fallen, and Oscar was straddling his body. As mac Lugach saw it, he launched himself at the men Oscar was fighting. Two of them turned to beat him back, leaving the third to fight Oscar. Fionn started to go to mac Lugach's aid, but at that moment a Gaelic warrior staggered into his path and began hewing at him with a war axe.

By the time Fionn had finished him off, mac Lugach was down. But so were his foes. On this part of the field, Oscar and his opponent were the only ones still fighting. With a shock, Fionn realized that the man with whom Oscar was trading blows was the high king.

They were both bloody; impossible to tell how much of it was their own. And they were tiring—the time between blows was becoming longer, and the cuts themselves wilder, delivered with more conviction than skill. Fionn started to move towards them and discovered that his battle-madness had departed. His own fatigue washed over him and suddenly it was all he could do to keep upright himself, leaning on his spear.

He could only watch as Oscar and Cairbre hewed at each other, their faces set in identical snarls. *You are young and strong,* thought Fionn, *younger than he is, and* fian-*trained. You can take him, Oscar!* But how many warriors had the boy had to go through to get to the king? Cairbre would have been protected by his houseguard until the end.

"It is growing dark—" gasped Oscar. "Confess that you are beaten, and for the sake of your daughter I may let you live. . . ."

Fionn looked around him, and his exhaustion became sharpened by fear, for to his eyes, it was still bright afternoon, and the sea wind was plucking the blossoms from the trees.

"Never! You are the wretched spawn of an evil race, and until your blood feeds the ground my honor will not be clean!" Cairbre stumbled torwards his enemy.

Fionn staggered a few steps nearer. Far too much of Oscar's blood had flowed already; where his skin could be seen it was as pale as bone. But he shook his head as if trying to clear his vision, and laughed.

"Then die! You are a bull-prince, Cairbre, and your reign has come to its ending; like a rogue bull I will strike you down." Oscar let the battle-broom fall and gripped his sword two-handed. For a moment he stilled, reaching into his center to gather his forces. Then he swayed forward, raising the sword.

Fionn saw Cairbre's thrust go into Oscar's belly, saw the younger man's eyes widen in surprise. But the blow did not stop him. As Cairbre reeled back, Oscar's own blade came down in a perfect arc, biting into the angle where head met neck and continuing deep into the high king's chest. Cairbre fell to one knee, blood spurting from the dreadful wound, then rolled over onto his back and lay still.

Oscar was still on his feet, looking vaguely around him as if wondering what had become of his enemy. Fionn got his own rebellious muscles under control at last and stumbled forward. The remnants of the Gaelic forces were fleeing. The survivors of the *fianna* looked around them and started towards Oscar. But Fionn reached him first, gripping his arms and seeing his face twist with the first stark awareness of pain.

"Oscar, dear lad—" he said hoarsely, "it is all right. The fight is over and you have the victory."

"Grandfather . . ." The sword slipped from Oscar's

hand. He shivered suddenly, and turned his face against Fionn's shoulder. Fionn took his weight, wondering how long he could hold it, but by that time Oisin and Caoilte were beside him, and together they lowered Oscar's long body to the ground.

Dark blood was pulsing sluggishly from Oscar's belly where Cairbre had stuck him. Oisin took the corner of the banner and tried to wipe it away.

"It's not bleeding badly—" His voice trailed off.

"He's bleeding from everywhere else," said Caoilte thinly. "And maybe that's a good thing." Men who died quickly from wounds to the gut were the lucky ones. Otherwise, it was a choice between the mercy stroke and weeks of agony.

"Father?" Oscar opened his eyes, trying to see, and Oisin bent over him. "I am sorry I failed you. I meant to keep the peace, but she . . . didn't want to marry him."

"Lad, it is all right. You have won a great victory," Oisin managed to say. His cheeks were streaked with tears, but Oscar could not see.

"None of them would believe . . . I had a heart . . . in my breast. They used to . . . tease me. . . ."

"No one will taunt you now." Fionn forced his own voice to stay steady. "You will be hailed as the greatest of heroes when the *fianna's* deeds are sung."

"We . . . swept them . . . clean!" Oscar's lips twisted in a smile. He reached out, and Fionn winced to feel his hand so chill. This was not happening, he thought numbly. It should be he himself that lay dying, and this some deception of the Morrigan to bring him to despair. If there had been a spring here, he would have crawled to it to bring water in his hands. But the hill was dry. He pressed the cold fingers and was answered by a momentary tightening. Then they loosened. "So tired . . ." Oscar whispered as his eyes closed.

Oisin called his name, but his son did not reply. His breathing became more labored; there was a last quiver of resistance as his body fought the final round of a battle his spirit had already abandoned. Then he lay still.

They were all still, waiting hopelessly for Oscar to speak again. But the only sounds were the cawing of the crows and the sigh of the wind as it chilled their tears and scattered white petals from the apple trees across the body like the first flakes of some untimely snow.

Chapter 17

IT WAS MONSTROUS, THOUGHT FIONN, THAT THE DAY should still be so fair. The sky should have been weighted with storm clouds; a cold wind should have been stripping the leaves from the skeletons of the trees. But as the survivors of the *fianna* bore Oscar's body and those of mac Lugach and his son Glas up the hill, the breeze that cooled their brows was soft as a mother's kiss, the sky a pure and transparent blue. Oscar had died in his springtide. Perhaps this grief was like the ache one sometimes felt when contemplating the evanescent perfection of a spring day.

Radiant you stood in the red light of dawning. . . . The words of a lament struggled within Fionn's awareness—if he could channel it into poetry, he might be able to bear the pain.

The battle, for all its fury, had been over by noon. To lay out their own dead and pile their shields and weapons over them had taken what time the survivors could spare for such honors. Bands of Gaelic warriors still roamed the neighborhood; soon they would recover from their panic and return for the body of their king. If it was accurate to say that anyone had won the battle of Gabhra, the *fianna* must be counted the victors, but they were in no condition for another encounter.

But Oisin would not leave the body of his son to the ravens, and so they made a bier of spear shafts and laid Oscar upon it, covered with the silken banner of his *fian*. Weeping, they bore it to the highest point of the hill, from which one could glimpse the blue shimmer of the sea.

Swordblades you broke, bright spearheads you shattered. . . .

Spearheads could be used to dig with, and for certain there were plenty of shattered weapons to choose from. Some of the men carved out a grave while others searched the hillside for stones to heap over it. It was nearly sunset before they were finished, and at that it seemed too soon.

Cloaked like a king you shall sleep this night. . . .

Loegaire had collected, from their fallen foes, cloaks with which to line the grave. The topmost was Cairbre's, woven with many colors and embroidered and fringed with gold. A king's cloak for a king of the *fian* . . . Fionn remembered painfully how Cormac had given him his cloak to keep him warm when he went out to face the fireserpent Aillén.

I am glad, old friend, he thought, *that you did not live to see this day!* But if Cormac had still been *Ard Ri*, this day need not have come at all. Fionn shook his head despairingly. No doubt each generation had to make its own mistakes, but he wished that he, like

Cormac, had not lived to see the disintegration of all they had tried to build.

"Bring him here," said Oisin in the same quiet tone he had used all afternoon. "I would have him safe before the darkness falls." It made Fionn shiver. The rest of them, still stunned by the magnitude of their loss, had obeyed him willingly, but Fionn could not help but wonder what would happen when they had buried their dead and the purpose that had sustained Oisin was gone.

"Gently, lads—lay him down on the south side here and let mac Lugach and Glas rest beside him. Set the clean stone beneath their heads . . . "Oisin twitched violently and then stood shivering as men brought branches of apple blossom and laid them over the bodies.

Fionn struggled to his feet and made his way to the graveside, leaning on his spear. His chest was tight; perhaps the lament with which he had been struggling could ease Oisin's grief and his own.

"Dig ye the bed of Oscar the brave,
A grave for the greatest of the fianna*'s warriors,*
Sore we shall miss you, from sight now gone,
A stone at your head, your banner for
bedclothes."

He drew breath and heard men weeping. Caoilte came forward, his arm in a sling, and looking into the grave, spoke in his turn.

"Many a bold band of foes you brought low,
So fierce were the fénnidi *you led to the fray;*

I say now that never was leader more needed,
Indeed, death has robbed us by striking you down!"

Now Oisin, mastering himself, took his place beside them.

"Lad that I loved, bright Eriu I would leave you,
Truly the whole world I'd give you to rule;
Cruel that with cold stones your flesh
we must cover,
And over your head raise this howe for a hall."

Fionn knew the tears were running down his cheeks, but now the song was surging strongly, and he let it flow through him once more.

"Warm though the sun shines, in our souls it
is winter,
Finished our future, for Oscar lies slain.
Pain fills my heart for the fallen,
the fair one;
The air fills with flowers that fall like
spring snow."

Oisin sank to his knees, sobbing, and Fionn, realizing that he must take over the direction now, motioned to the men to fill in the graves. As they began to do so, Fionn heard whining. A pale shape was coming up the hill; he blinked away tears and saw that it was Sceolan.

A ragged fragment of rope fluttered from the hound's neck; worn though his teeth were, with persistence, Sceolan had gnawed through it. Fionn cursed his own stupidity for not telling Grainne the whole story of Sceolan's birth and warning her that the dog was as intelligent as any man. He must have broken free and trailed them northward. For old bones it was a terrible journey; the dog's pads were bloody and torn. Clearly he had not even stopped to hunt, for he was like a skeleton covered with fur.

"My poor lad—" Fionn bent to embrace him. Sceolan leaned against him, trembling. "You had not the strength for this, my dear," he murmured. "Why did you think I told them to keep you at home?" The hound whimpered and pressed his head against Fionn's thigh. "I know, perhaps I should have let you take your chances with the rest of us," Fionn said, understanding. "But at least you can mourn with us now—"

The men watched in awe as the hound raised his head, testing the wind, and from his throat came a groan of human pain. Sceolan's eyes were failing, but he recognized the smell of death, and that needed no explanation. He pulled away from Fionn and took a few steps forward, sniffing Oisin's hair and licking his tears. Oisin would have held him, but the dog moved on until he stood at the edge of the grave.

A shudder ran along the gaunt flanks and Sceolan howled. At the sound some last restraint was lifted, and the rest of them cried out with him. A wail of anguish and pain and dreadful desolation went up from the remnant of the *fianna* of *Eriu*, so terrible that for a few moments even the ravens were still.

Then, as if that last outcry had exhausted him, Sceolan sank down. He sighed deeply, a long shudder ran through his body, and he was still. Oisin reached out, but Fionn stopped him.

A second time the limp form rippled, but this time it was not life, but a more final transformation. Sceolan was fading, the pale dog-shape becoming more ghostly with every moment, to be replaced by the emaciated limbs and white hair of an old man. Some of the warriors made the sign against evil, but Faobhar and Fearghusa, who had been with Fionn when Bran died, were weeping, and the eyes of Caoilte, who had seen how the were-stag Donn disappeared, widened in wonder as he began to understand.

For a moment they looked upon the form Sceolan would have had if he had lived as a man. Then the pallid shape shimmered, a rainbow light played briefly about the body, and with a final flare of incandescence, it was gone. An ashy outline seared into the grass was all that remained to show where Sceolan had lain.

THE SURVIVORS OF THE *FIANNA* MOVED THROUGH THE forest like ghosts in the twilight. Perhaps that was what they were, thought Fionn, as they wandered westward. On the second day after the battle they had traded their remaining mounts for supplies to carry with them. He longed to return to Grainne in Almu, but the fortress was too obvious a target, and although he had been able to keep Eochaid out of the battle, her oldest son, Donnchadh, had died fighting at Cairbre's side. For the moment, it would be safer if they could become invisible, and horses left too clear a trail.

On both sides, the losses of Gabhra had been terrible. The battle had decimated the fighting strength of the Gaels, and the surviving chieftains were forming new alliances as they struggled to decide which of the king's young grandsons would be the next *Ard Ri*. But two-thirds of the *fianna* of Eriu lay buried upon the field. Oscar's *fian* had died with him. The younger warriors—their future—were gone. Cairbre was dead, but his revenge had been terrible. The work of Cnucha was almost finished; of the blood of Cumhal, only Oisin and Fionn himself remained.

Faobhar and Fearghusa had both survived the battle; Caoilte lived, though his right arm was shattered; Loegaire and Cedach Cithach had only a few gashes, but fewer than a hundred of the lesser warriors had survived. Some, like Oisin, bore their wounds in the soul, where no man could see. In the hours after the battle Oisin had been superb, but when they had piled the cairn above Oscar's body all the heart seemed to go out of him. He walked and talked, sometimes he even smiled, but nothing seemed to alter the mute sorrow in his eyes.

Fionn's own battle-fury and the Hazel Shield had to some extent protected him. He was still limping from a sword cut on his right thigh, but was otherwise unscathed. It was exhaustion more than any wound that still troubled him. But as Oisin grew more withdrawn, Fionn found the *fianna* turning to him for leadership. Weariness bowed his shoulders, and the responsibility weighed on him even more.

At night he found it hard to sleep. After Gabhra, the fair weather had broken, and on the days when it was not storming outright it was damp or drizzling. Even when the men cut rushes for Fionn to lie upon, he ached in every bone. When he lay still he could feel his chest quiver to every beat of his heart.

Perhaps my heart will burst from this grief, he thought as he drew in deep breaths, trying to calm it. To die of sorrow was not so glorious as to fall on the battlefield, but at this moment Fionn hardly cared. He lay wakeful for a long time despite his exhaustion, listening to the breathing of the other men, and presently passed into chaotic dreams.

One night, a ten-day after the battle, it seemed to him that he was back in Donait's fair hall, and she was showing him her tapestries. He saw the fight in which Cormac lost his eye, and the death of Goll, and most terribly, himself and Oisin lamenting over Oscar's body on Gabhra field.

"See—your story is nearly over," Donait was saying, and he could see that the wall was almost filled.

"I thought it *was* over," he said bitterly. "I was content to live out the rest of my days between the garden and the fire."

She shook her head. "There are always more choices. . . ."

"What choices? My line is ended and Eriu has rejected me. What in Brigid's name is there left for me to do?"

"Ah my dear," she said sadly, "do not you yet understand? The ending will depend on you."

FIONN LED THE *FIANNA* THROUGH COVER WHEREVER possible, but even in the wilder lands expanses of open heath must be crossed from time to time. It was as they were moving across one of these that a distant shout halted them. Fionn motioned to Cedach Cithach, the tallest man among them, with the best eyes.

"Mounted warriors—" said the *fénnid*. "Gaels, by their arms. Coming this way—" he added. Fionn nodded. Over a moon spent in the field had restored many senses he had thought lost forever, and the drumming of hoofbeats had come to him as part of the earth song.

"How far?"

"We might reach that belt of trees ahead of them, if we run—" the Alban answered him.

Before he had finished speaking, Fionn whistled, and the men sprang into motion, obedient as hounds. *Now I know how Diarmuid felt when I was chasing him,* he thought as he pushed his own limbs to greater speed. Through the earth he sensed the glee with which the horsemen were closing in. *Now I know what it is like for the hunted deer.*

But the woods were just ahead. "Bows!" he gasped as the hoofbeats thundered loud behind them. A lance sped past his ear and he crashed through a stand of sallow and went sprawling. But a yell from their foes told him that at least one of the *fénnidi* had been able to obey. Heart pounding, Fionn rolled to his feet, pulled his own hunting bow over his head and grabbed for an arrow.

"King-killers! Traitors! Sons of slaves! Come out and fight with us!" yelled the Gaels, brandishing their swords.

A man on a horse shot between two trees and Rionnolbh and Caoilte seemed to rise out of the ground before him. The horse reared, whinnying, as a dexterous thrust of Rionnolbh's lance brought the rider down. Through the screen of leaves Fionn saw others. He nocked and released, and saw the arrow pierce the neck of a fair man with the golden torque of a chieftain.

Others were falling as the *fianna's* bowmen got their range. They were men of the Ulaidh by their colors, far from home. It was one reason he was trying to get away. Fionn wondered which candidate this bunch were supporting in the bloody internecine war that had been Cairbre's legacy.

The Gaels cried out as their leader swayed in the saddle. That should cool their ardor, thought Fionn, as he whistled to his men. With a few more well-placed arrows to discourage pursuit, they melted into the forest.

IN THE WEEKS AFTER THE EQUINOX THEY MET OTHER such bands. Fionn's heart ached, seeing the careful network of alliances and loyalties he and Cormac had been at such pains to build among the Gaelic clans unraveling. Once they even came upon a battle, but Fionn kept the *fianna* out of it. Their purpose had always been to defend Eriu from invaders, whether from the Otherworld or other human lands, not take part in the internal political struggles of the ruling tribe.

Fionn did not know how to choose a side even had he wanted to. He had toughened enough in body to keep up with his men, but he flinched from dealing with the wreck of Cormac's dreams. Let them kill off each other. When a victor emerged, the *fianna*—if there still were *fénnidi* by then—could offer their services to an *Ard Ri* once more.

But a ten-day before Beltane, they had an encounter of a different kind.

A DOVE CALLED SOFTLY FROM THE TANGLE OF HAZELS ahead and Fionn stilled, holding up his hand. As the others in his hunting party came to a halt behind him, Rionnolbh, who had been on point, came drifting silently back through the trees.

"Warriors coming—" He pointed southward. "I do not think they are Gaels, though."

Fionn frowned. He did not want to lose the deer they were trailing—keeping even a reduced *fianna* fed was a constant struggle, and he had divided his men into several parties to quarter the forest for game. But if it could be done safely, it might be wise to exchange news.

"Caoilte, do you watch them while the rest of us go after this doe. Find out who they are, and if you can do it safely, speak with them."

He had no doubt that Caoilte would succeed in his mission. His arm had healed, though it would never be strong enough for swordwork again. Other than that he was fit and healthy. Indeed, all of them were much thinner, browner, and generally in better condition, at least in body, than they had been at Gabhra.

Except, perhaps, for Oisin. Fionn frowned for a different reason as he looked at his son. Beneath the light bronzing the sun had given his skin, Oisin's flesh had a pallor that reminded Fionn uncomfortably of Sceolan, as if Oisin were imperceptibly fading away. He ate, though not much; he slept, though Fionn, who himself was often wakeful, knew he did not sleep well. He did his share in camp or on the hunting trail, but his heart was not in it. Once, long ago, Oisin had railed at Fionn for his inaction. If to stop fighting one's fate was death, then Oisin was dying now.

Fionn had loved his grandson, and of their times together he had only good memories. But as often happened between fathers and sons, Oisin had not known how to show his love. Too often what he had demanded from Oscar were things the boy did not have to give. And now there would never be a time for understanding, and regret was eating Oisin's soul away.

A whistle told Fionn that someone had sighted the deer, and other thoughts were forgotten as they moved into position for the kill. They had just finished gutting the animal and were tying it to a spear shaft for transport when Caoilte rejoined them.

"It is Bressal Bélach, king of the Laigin, that Rionnolbh sighted," said Caoilte, grinning, "and he would like fine to feast you, Fionn, just over the hill by the river where they are camping. What we saw was only a scouting party. He has an army over there."

"Well, and aren't the *fianna* worth an army?" asked Rionnolbh.

"I suspect that Bressal thinks so," answered Fionn. But there were several reasons why it might be a good idea to accept the hospitality of Laigin.

Later that evening, draining a horn of mead, he was not so sure. The mead was good, and after so many weeks of living on meat and herbs it was good to eat bread and cheese again. But he had an uncomfortable feeling that the king was going to ask him to pay for it soon.

"It would appear that there are two major groups now contending," Bressal was saying, "those who support Echu's boys, the Colla princes, and those who would rather see Falchu's son Muiredach in Temair."

"And who are you supporting?" asked Caoilte.

"Oh, a plague on them all! Laigin held Temair once, and if the Children of Tuathal want to kill each other off, I will not mind. I have refused to pay the Cattle Tribute already. In the meantime, though, I'll be content with reminding a few of the chieftains north of the Liffe that they used to belong to Laigin. You've done me a great favor already, Fionn, in finishing off that pig Cairbre and his sons. Join with me, and no one will be able to stop us."

Beyond Bressal's shoulder a young man with eyes like Diarmuid's was watching him. After Fionn's marriage to Grainne, young Olann seemed to have forgiven him his father's death, but that steady gaze was disturbing.

Fionn frowned. "If I were to ally with any faction, it would be that of Laigin, my home. But it is hard to think of serving one part of Eriu only when I have given my life to preserving the whole." Since the time of Tuathal, the high kings of Temair had imposed harmony upon Eriu's many tribes. Without a strong hand to control them, the vassal peoples were making the most of the chance to pay off old grudges.

"We could go to Alba," suggested Cedach Cithach earnestly. "Not for always, but until things are settled here. My uncle the high king would treat you royally."

"Crimall's old *dun* would be almost as remote and easier to come to," said Fionn. "Over in Connachta. I took my training there when I was a boy." But in truth, he was not sure if he liked that idea either. He remembered how the men of his uncle's *fian* had dwindled in mind and body, with nothing to do but hash over old glories and terrorize the countryside. But at least the place was hidden. The *fianna* would be a constant target and temptation to warring factions if they returned to Almu.

"You may find you have no choice, Fionn," said King Bressal. "You broke the power of the mac Mornas, but they are not all dead, you know, and Clan Urgriu and the Luagni are still your enemies."

"It is in my mind that in the days to come we will be missing Oscar sorely," said Caoilte mournfully. He had been taking full advantage of the mead.

"Truly, that was a heavy loss," the king nodded soberly. "I remember him at the kingmaking. He was like a young oak tree."

"He would have put paid to the Luagni." Caoilte nodded owlishly. "D'ye remember, Fionn, how he saved you when the fairy woman gave you the poisoned drink?" Bressal Bélach looked enquiring, and Caoilte launched into his tale.

"She said she had lost her ring in the lake, and when Fionn was blue and shivering from the cold water after diving for it, she gave him a drink of mead to restore him that nearly put him under the earth instead. It was in revenge, do you see, because he had killed her lover when we fought for Midir."

Fionn remembered too well the weakness that had left him half-paralyzed and trembling like an ancient. *Better a swift death in battle than that,* he thought grimly, *old as I am.*

"And how did Oscar rescue him?" asked one of the Laigin men. They were listening, wide-eyed as children, as if Caoilte were telling some tale of wonder from the elder days.

"It was Sceolan who brought him, though he had to bite his nose to wake him from his sleep. Fionn could not speak, but Oscar picked up his thumb and set it to his lips, and then he got back the power of motion, though no strength, and he told him how to break the spell." He paused, savoring the tension.

"Oscar had to go to the fairy hill and plunge Fionn's spear into it. They could not abide that, you know—that spear is poison to them—it has tasted too much blood of the Otherworld. And so the woman came out and gave him a flask of water from the Well of Youth, and he brought it back and gave Fionn some to drink, and—well—poured the rest over his manhood to bring him back to life again."

Fionn stared in as much amazement as the men of

Laigin as Caoilte's glib tongue embroidered the tale. It had not been like that—Oscar had carried him back to camp and nursed him tenderly until his strength returned—but he had to admit it made a better story this way.

"It would certainly revive me!" exclaimed Bressal, glancing at Fionn with a curious blend of respect and amusement. "Well, perhaps you do not need my help after all. But remember my offer of alliance if you change your mind."

As Beltane neared, the *fianna* made a temporary camp on the wooded shores of Loch Lein. On the eve of the festival, Fionn went down to the shore of the lake to bathe. Banners of cloud glowed golden in the western sky, but in the east it was clearing. As the light faded, the blue of the heavens deepened to a purple gloaming that reminded him of the Otherworld.

On just such an evening, he remembered, Fionnéices had caught the Salmon of Wisdom, and Fionn's life had changed. He twitched as something leaped in the still waters. It was a trout almost certainly—this lake had no connection with the Boann. And yet the *fili* had told him that on Beltane gateways opened between the waters as well as the lands of the human world and Faerie. He wondered what would happen if he ate of the Salmon reborn?

Perhaps I would lose my wisdom, he thought wryly, *not that it has done me much good lately.* His thumb tingled at the memory. He stripped off his tunic and waded into the cool waters. Whether the Salmon swam there or not, tonight they pulsed with magic. Perhaps it had not been a fish at all, but one of the scaly-skinned water folk such as he thought he had seen disappearing into the mist a few mornings before. As Beltane approached, they too would become bolder. The Song that he heard sometimes in the earth resounded even louder in the lake as the liminal moment drew near.

Trailed by the shards of his reflection he felt his way into the dark waters until they were waist-high. He looked down, wondering if he would see the fish, but as the ripples stilled it was a man's face that looked back at him. He stared, the rag he used for washing forgotten in his hand. Who was this ancient who stared up at him from the depths, gnarled and weathered like an old tree, with a beard like hanging moss and a crown of wild hair? The image glowered back at him as he frowned, trying to see in that face any resemblance to the boy Demne whom Donait had loved, or that Fionn who had been the radiant *Rígfénnid* of Eriu.

"And yet both of them are still alive within me—" he whispered, and it seemed to him that a voice from the waters replied:

> *"Water of life from the sky to the river,*
> *flowing forever, and ever returning;*
> *seaward 'tis yearning, the cycle rewinding,*
> *in losing the finding, unbinding once*
> *more. . . ."*

The music faded as a sudden wind ruffled the waters, dislimning his image, but Fionn's nostrils flared at a breath of salt air and for a moment the wind brought him the deep boom and surge of the sea.

The wind fell, but a restless expectance had replaced the stillness. Hastily Fionn scrubbed the grime from his body and ducked to rinse the dust from his hair. Then he splashed shoreward. As he emerged from the water another gust stirred the treetops with a sound like distant bells. Fionn shivered, not entirely from the wind.

The music was in the earth as well; he bit down on his thumb and let his awareness deepen and trembled at the answering surge of song.

"From the depths of the deep to
the waves we are rising,
the seabirds surprising, their
cries cheer us forward;
the distant shore beckons, from
the plains of the sea
we fare free, to the trees and
the fields and the forest. . . ."

Before, it was as if the waters had spoken. Now Fionn's heart leaped to the sweet singing of the Sidhe. Long it had been since he had heard those fair voices rejoicing—at Sid BodbDerg they had sung a different kind of song. The wind strengthened, bearing with it the scent of the ocean no longer, but the smell of new grass and wildflowers. And the music grew ever louder. It pulsed in the earth, in the air, in his ears. Surely by now even the men back in their camp must be able to hear it. Still pulling on his clothing, he began to run.

Oisin looked up in amazement as Fionn trotted into the clearing. For a moment he held to a tree, catching his breath, but the trunk vibrated to the hoofbeats of Faerie horses, growing ever louder as they neared the mortal world.

"Visitors—" he stammered. He knew he must look like a wild man, his face alight with joy in that music. In the forest the shadows of dusk were already deepening. He rubbed his eyes, trying to see. Oisin stood up, listening, and began to frown. One by one the other men stilled. A great wind rushed through the forest, and in its wake a final burst of song.

"Beltane is here, and the green grass is growing,
In the wind of our going it flows like the river;
Delight in each quiver of leaf and of flower,
unbinding the power of the hour we draw near!"

To the west, light glimmered suddenly on leaf and branches as if the setting sun had found a way through the trees. But it was not the sun. Men blinked as the shimmer shaped itself into men and horses, and foremost among them a maiden on a white mare who shone like the sunlight on the sea. She bore a silver branch weighted by three golden apples in her hand.

"Fionn of the *fianna*, I greet you." Her voice carried an echo of the music.

Was she fairer than Donait? Fionn could not tell. She was taller, her curling hair a paler gold, her eyes the blue of the deep sea. But the difference was not in beauty. In Donait's eyes there had always been a hint of sadness, as if she had studied the human world too long. This maiden's gaze was as pure as the wind off the western sea. It did not occur to him to compare her to Sadb, who had been a part of his soul.

"Woman of the Sidhe, you rejoice our hearts," he answered her. His own heart was pounding heavily. Had she come to release him from his long exile?

"Indeed, it is for the sake of love that I have come here," she replied.

Her mantle was made of some silken stuff the same deep blue as her eyes, embroidered with gold and pearls, but its lining was the pale greeny blue color of the sea above the ivory sands near the shore, and her gown was as white as the foam. There were pearls on her mount's golden saddlecloth as well, but neither bit nor bridle did it bear. The folk in her escort were nearly as splendid, clad in mantles of sea green and purple and blue.

"By what name shall we hail you, Lady, and for whose sake have you come?" Fionn looked around him.

The other men of the *fianna* were gaping in amazement, but on Oisin's face was something different. He was not gazing at the woman with wonder at the unknown, but with a joyous recognition that kindled his pinched features into the laughing countenance of the boy he used to be. Fionn saw it, and felt the first prickle of fear.

"My name is Niamh, and it is from Tir n'an Og, the Land of Youth, that I have come. Oisin son of Sadb is the man whose love I seek here. . . ." A daughter of the western sea she was indeed. The child of Manannan mac Lir. The Faerie steed sidled closer, until she was looking down at Oisin. "Fairest of warriors, I am calling you. Will you come away with me?"

"You do not know him," said Fionn desperately. "How can you love him?"

Niamh laughed, and the sound was like the chuckling of the waves when they run up across the sand. Her escort had spread out behind her and sat their slim-legged mounts silently, watching from sea-colored eyes.

"I first saw his image in Donait's tapestries. Since

then I have watched over him, rejoicing in his joys and mourning for his sorrows. How should I not love him? He is the fairest and the bravest of the *fénnidi* of Eriu. . . ."

"Niamh . . ." Oisin reached out to her, then his hand dropped again. "In my dreams I have seen you. But in my dreams I was a boy again, proud and unstained. If you had come to me in my youth I would have gone gladly. But sorrow has scarred me, my beloved, and I am worn out with war."

The woman shook her head, but she was still smiling. "When you were a boy the world was still a cup of delights untasted—and Eriu needed you. You would not have left it had I asked you then. But you have drained it to the dregs. Your work is done, Oisin—come with me now."

Caoilte made a convulsive movement towards his friend, but Oisin's gaze was fixed on Niamh.

"Where? Where would you take me?" His voice wavered.

"Over the sea, Oisin, to the western Isles. . . . to the land where it is summer always, and fruit and blossom together on every tree. In that land is neither age nor sickness, but mirth and music and good company. The stag that is killed in the evening shall arise from his bones in the morning; the grain that is ground at noon shall sprout up from its chaff the next day. Fair women shall serve you, and goodly champions be your companions. Every sport and diversion will you find in that land, Oisin, and you and I together on one couch always, exchanging joy."

"Be still!" Fionn found his voice at last. "You shall not steal him. He is all that remains to me!"

For the first time since her arrival Niamh looked at

Fionn, and her eyes flashed. "Do you see this branch?" She lifted it, and the faint shimmer of sound that came as the apples touched made Fionn's senses swim. "I have only to shake it and you would sleep, all of you. I could have carried your son off long since if that was my will!" Smiling scornfully, she turned to Oisin once more.

"With songs I could bemuse you, with sorcery enchant you, but I will not lay upon you even so much as the *geas* that Grainne laid upon Diarmuid, that you counseled him could not be denied."

Oisin looked up at her, his face working. "Niamh . . . ah, Niamh. In my dreams I loved you. But my strength is used up, my dear. I would be no good to you. . . ." Fionn took a step towards him, for in Oisin's eyes was the bleak regret of a man who looks for the last time on beauty, knowing his death is near.

"Indeed you will soon fall to dust if you remain in Eriu. But there is a spring upon my island from which flows the water of life. You have only to bathe in it and your manhood will be renewed."

What man could refuse such an offer? Remembering how Donait's bath had healed him, Fionn knew her words were true. And yet Oisin stared at the ground, mute and trembling. When he looked up at last, it was at Fionn.

"Father—"

He is asking me to decide for him, thought Fionn. *But what can I say?* He had tried to run away from his own choices often enough when he was younger, and knew its futility. Should he cry out and tell Oisin how much he needed him? Plead with him to stay so that Fionn would not have to die alone? Tell him he must breed up a new son to perish in Fionn's wars? Niamh had disdained to use her magic to compel Oisin's decision. Did he have the right to bind his son with spells of duty and love?

Fionn looked at Oisin, allowing himself to see the translucence of his skin, the bruised shadows beneath his eyes, recognizing how thin his son had grown. *I have lost him already,* he thought grimly. *He will die if he stays with me.*

"My son—" His voice was tight, but he managed to keep it from shaking. "You are your own master. I set you free."

"But I don't!" exclaimed Caoilte "I've followed you too long, man. Do not leave me now!"

Niamh raised one eyebrow. "Would you come with him, then, even to the kingdom of Manannan, whose father you killed?"

"I would dare it, if you will give me leave!" Caoilte answered stoutly. Oisin looked from one to the other helplessly.

Take me too! The plea beat against Fionn's closed lips. But she had not asked him, and the Otherworld was closed to him by his own bond.

"Well, my love?" She smiled down at Oisin. "Would you have him?" At his nod, Niamh gestured, and a rider on a grey horse swung around her, holding out a hand to Caoilte to mount up behind him.

Oisin's eyes were shining, and Fionn's heart was wrenched, remembering how he had smiled just so as a child. He took a step towards him, and suddenly his son was gripping him tightly.

"I'm sorry . . . I love you . . . but I have to go—"

"I know, lad," Fionn murmured in return. "I know. Do you not think I would be off in a moment if your mother should come for me?"

The white mare knelt down on one knee. For a moment longer Fionn held his son. Then Oisin settled himself behind the fairy woman. With a bound the horse gained her feet once more, shaking her head impatiently. A sudden wind shook the leaves, or perhaps it was only the movement of the Faerie riders as they swirled away. The white mare reared, growing ever brighter, until the image of horse and riders was imprinted on Fionn's vision.

And then—Niamh's final mercy—he heard a shimmer of sweet music as she shook the silver branch. Sleep came upon him like a great wave and drowned him in a deep and dreamless sea.

Chapter 18

SUMMER CAME IN WITH DAYS OF MIST AND DRIZZLE alternating with periods of blinding sunshine, an unsettled kind of weather that matched the confusion in Fionn's soul. He was going the same way as Oisin, but where was the fairy woman who would carry him away? While the men foraged for food, he sat by the ashes of the campfire, hunting memories. They should have moved on long since, but where? No matter how far they wandered, they would find neither Oscar nor Oisin.

In that fashion the next moon passed, and it became clear that they must find another hunting ground or starve. If he had cared to make the effort, Fionn could have lived on roots and berries, but the men needed meat. As the days lengthened towards Midsummer, the remnants of the *fianna* moved slowly northward through the hills, hunting as they went along.

One evening, as the long summer dusk was darkening the forest, Fionn found himself alone. He had promised to meet the men back at the campsite, but as the mist rose from the damp ground he became unsure of the way. And what did it matter, after all? Once his grandfather had cursed him to wander alone and homeless, but only now was Tadg's curse striking home.

The woods had grown very quiet. The catch of damp air in his lungs reminded him suddenly of the cave in which he had been trapped by the daughters of Conaran. But it was a hut, not a cave, that he found beneath the oak trees, beside a little spring. Fionn smiled, for it was very like the ones that he had lived in when he was a child in the forest of Fidh Gaible. Before the door a cook fire was flickering merrily, heating a cauldron of riveted bronze. A thin steam spiraled from its surface and his nostrils flared.

Scent is the oldest of the senses, and this one brought back to him a vivid memory of Bodbmall's stews. Suddenly he was hungry as he had not been for many a day.

"Ho the house—is anyone at home here? I seek a drink of water from your spring."

For a long moment there was silence, but its quality had changed. He could tell that now someone, or something, was listening. He cocked his head, debating whether to call again.

"Is it a golden drinking horn you're waiting for?" Fionn jumped, for the voice came from behind him. "If you are thirsty, then drink—the spring will not run away."

Gods! She even sounded like Bodbmall! Fionn turned and saw an old woman, her face so creased and the rags that wrapped her so shapeless that she could have been anyone.

"Forgive me, mother. I meant only courtesy."

She snorted disbelievingly as he leaned his spear against a tree and knelt beside the spring. The water was cold and good, with the taste of stone.

"You have not been eating right, that is clear. You may as well have some stew," she said ungraciously, as he sat up again.

"I thank you—" Looking up at her, Fionn felt even more like a boy.

He eased down on a log and accepted the bowl she filled for him. There was rabbit in it and wild carrot, ground oats, a little garlic and wild onion and other herbs, so delicately blended he could not name them. For a moment it was enough simply to savor the flavorings.

Then he looked at the old woman sharply, for never in all his wanderings had he found anyone who had Bodbmall's hand with a stew. The fire flared and died, painting her worn features with stark highlights and shadows.

"Who are you?"

"I am called Cama," she answered him. "And who is it I have been entertaining at my fire?"

Fionn sighed. Of course, Bodbmall was dead. She had been old when he was a child, and he had seen her gasping out her life at Tailtiu.

"I am—" he broke off. Alone and aging, he could hardly recognize himself as the Fionn mac Cumhal who had been lord of Almu. But eating this stew he could pretend this woman was his old foster mother, and he was a boy once more. He grinned suddenly. "You can call me Demne."

"And what are you doing here—Demne—out in these woods where no man comes?"

Somewhere in the woods behind him an owl called mournfully. Grief tightened Fionn's throat. "I am waiting to die."

She snorted. "Everything dies. But you don't see me sitting around moaning, do you?"

"Soon or late, I bring death to everyone I love!" Fionn exclaimed. "I was more powerful than any king, a commander of armies, but only a remnant remain to me. I possessed lands and treasures too numerous to name, and now I am a ragged wanderer!"

"All those things you may be, but first and foremost, you are a fool! You followed the Red Path of the Warrior, and now you see where it ends."

"I tried to avoid it!" Fionn cried. "But I was needed to shield the land. Brigid Herself called me to be Her defender. And I have not done so badly—for more than fifty years Eriu has been protected."

"Then you have not lost everything," the woman said sternly. "You whimper like a child who has broken all his toys!" She spat into the fire and it flared suddenly, turning the hut and the tree trunks and the woman's garments to gold. "Those years, and those deeds, cannot be taken from you—the crops that were harvested, the children who grew up safe in their homes."

"It is true . . ." he sighed and rested his face in his hands. "And it is more than I ever expected, in the days when all I wanted was to know who I was. It is all very well to have won a name that will never die—my legend seems to have a life of its own! But the man behind the tales is all too mortal, Bodbmall—" He realized what he had called her and started to apologize.

"Call me what you wish," the old woman growled. "If that name means something to you, perhaps you will take my advice more readily."

It was Fionn's turn to smile. He had fought hard enough against Bodbmall's instruction when he was a boy; could he profit from it now?

"She wanted me to be a druid," he said softly, "but I was always too busy with other tasks to follow the Way of the Wise." He blinked; a full belly and the warmth of the fire were making him sleepy.

"A separate path— Is that what you think it is?" Now there was honey in the woman's low laughter and for a moment her hair seemed pure white, crowned with a wreath of green.

"Airmedb . . ." he whispered, thinking of the old priestess of Brigid who had counseled him how to win Almu. "Speak in that name and I will listen to you. . . ." If he could stay awake. He eased down upon the ground with his back against the log.

Suddenly the woman seemed taller. Fionn was a little afraid to look at her, and her voice was so soothing; it was easier to close his eyes.

"I want to do it the right way . . ." he mumbled. "So that you will love me . . ." It seemed to him she sighed, or perhaps it was only the whispering of the flames.

"The Way of the Wise is not where you walk, but how; it is the art of living every moment fully, of savoring what each day brings. It is yourself, not the world, that you must bend, responding to its tides and cycles as the salmon flexes with the currents of the stream. Wisdom lies in doing what you must, no less and no more. Then death is not an end, only a transformation. . . ."

A transformation . . . He rested his head against the log. Truly, he could feel the change even now, bearing him away on a dark tide, and whether it was death or sleep, he welcomed it. He heard her singing, soothing as the wind in the trees, constant as the sigh of the sea—

"In the warmth of my mantle my love
will enfold you,
Sleep now, sleep safely, oh child
of my heart;
Be at peace and remember, 'tis my arms
that hold you,
Sleep safely till the morning—"

He felt the blessing of her lips upon his brow; softness enveloped him and he knew no more.

WHEN FIONN WOKE, IT WAS MORNING. EARLY SUNlight glittered on the leaves and the birds were trying out their songs. He sat up and saw that he had been sleeping in the shelter of a fallen log beside a chuckling spring. There was no hut beneath the trees, no cauldron, and no fire. But a cloak of fine crimson wool had been tucked tenderly around him, and the scent of apple blossom still clung to its folds.

He drank from the spring, and the water tasted like honeymead.

"Ah, Brigid," he shook his head ruefully, "fool that I was to think myself alone!"

Wrapped in the cloak, he passed like a flame through the forest. He did not quite understand how he could have been lost, for the way seemed quite clear to him. But then, many things were clear now. A great peace was on him, and he rejoiced in the misty gold of the summer dawn.

He came upon his men soon after, and with an effort kept from laughing as fear and wonder, relief and exasperation, chased across their faces.

"My lord, we searched for you," exclaimed Loegaire. "Where—"

"I am sorry to have worried you," Fionn said simply. "But I slept safe and warm." He could see their eyes upon the new cloak, but there was now no man among them with the standing to question him.

"Well. All right." The man pulled his gaze away with an effort and smoothed down his brush of grey hair. "But we must be moving on—" He paused, obviously wondering if he dared to press for orders, and Fionn felt shame to have led them so badly.

"It is so." He had not thought about what to do next, but suddenly it was clear. "We are doing no good skulking around these woods, lads, and it is time we faced the world."

"Are we bound for Alba, then?" asked Cedach Cithach, his blue eyes kindling.

"Not there, nor to the western mountains either," answered Fionn. "Our way leads east and southward, back to Almu."

To Almu, he thought, where Grainne was waiting. He should send word to her of what had happened, he thought, to warn her he was coming. His two half brothers, Faobhar and Fearghusa, were in better condition than most of the men. He summoned them to take the message, and sent them on their way.

The rest of the men moved more slowly down from the hills of the Sliab Guaire and across the western edge of the plain of Brega towards the tributaries of the Boann. They went carefully, for these were the tribal lands of the Luagni, and there was no telling which side they were taking in the current conflict.

But in the open country they could not avoid being seen, and on the day before Midsummer a messenger came to them with greetings from Fer-tai son of Uaithne Irgalach and an invitation to feast with him that night in his hall.

"I do not like it," said ruddy Daolghus. "It was the Luagni who turned against your father, Fionn, and they are implacable enemies."

"But Fer-tai was with us for a time in the *fian*," answered Cedach Cithach. "He is a good man, and can be trusted."

Trust . . . thought Fionn. *That is what it comes down to now, and the courage that forbade old Goll to flee a foe.* He turned his gaze on the messenger.

"Take my thanks to your master for his hospitality."

FER-TAI OF THE LUAGNI WAS A WEALTHY MAN. HIS FAther had been *fian*-chief to their tribal king and had only the one son to inherit his treasure. His feasting hall was spacious, with comfortable couches covered with embroidered cloths. The house pillars were carved and painted, upon the floor were laid fresh rushes, and colored hangings covered the walls. Fer-tai himself had only one son by the daughter of Goll—Fer-li, who had been Fionn's fosterling.

Fionn watched him across the fire, wincing whenever the shifting flames highlighted the young man's features. He had been with Garad in the mac Morna war. After Garad died the survivors of his *fian* had fled back to Loch Dergdeire, and Oscar had scorned to pursue them. In manhood, Fer-li resembled his grandfather more than ever, from the strength in his big hands to the fox-pelt glint of his hair. But Goll's feelings had been all in the open, while Fer-li's smile never reached his eyes.

"Have some more of this pork," said Fer-tai. "We have given you the Champion's portion."

Certainly Fionn had no fault to find with the welcome. He and Loegaire and Daolghus had been bathed and clad in new tunics and given seats near the chieftain while Cedach Cithach presided over the feasting of the rest of the men in another hall.

"You are too thin, my lord—all of you need feeding. And your clothes! Tomorrow you must let me outfit you and your men."

Fionn smiled his thanks. After Gabhra, they had abandoned all but the necessities. But though their clothing might be in tatters, no one could find fault with the condition of their weapons.

"When darkness falls the farm folk will kindle the bonfires and dance around them," said Fer-tai, gesturing towards the open doorway, whose hide curtain had been drawn aside to let in the last of the light. "It is a fine sight. They drive barren cattle through the flames to cure them, and carry burning brands through the fields to make the corn grow."

Fionn nodded. "They do the same in Laigin. It is a magic of the elder races who were here before the Sons of Mil came into the land." And yet from this moment the power of the sun would begin to diminish despite men's magic. Fionn closed his eyes, feeling himself, like the sun, poised on a pinnacle in perilous equilibrium.

When he looked up, young Fer-li and his cousin Emer Glunglas were watching him. *Goll's grandson and Garad's . . .* thought Fionn. He had not quite wiped out the mac Mornas—these two remained, like the last green shoots in a cleared field. The young men with them were from the clan of Urgriu. He met their hostile gaze calmly, and after a moment they flushed and looked away.

But someone was still staring—he turned and saw a woman holding a pitcher who looked at him with naked hatred. Her gown was too finely embroidered around the neck and hem for a maidservant. She was black-haired and proud, and it came to him that he had seen her before. Then she turned, and in the curve of her cheek he saw Diarmuid, and knew whose daughter she was. Eachtach was her name.

Daolghus was right. There is danger here. He wondered why he did not feel afraid.

The long golden twilight gave way at last to darkness. From outside the *dun* came singing and the deep booming of drums. Even inside, Fionn could hear the earth song pulse in answer. Thus the people had danced before the Gaels ruled them, and before the Galéoin, and no doubt would continue to do so no matter what conquerors might come.

He heard the strains of one of the *fianna*'s drinking songs from somewhere nearer. Fer-tai was rolling out his vats of ale and his barrels of mead to entertain them, and the *fénnidi*, deprived of drink all spring, were making up for lost time.

> *"We hauled our booty homeward*
> *an' we had a lotta fun,*
> *for to fight is all our pleasure*
> *until the day is done."*

Fer-tai himself refilled Fionn's horn and he drank deeply.

"An' then we'll empty all their barrels,
an' then we'll drink up all their beer.
We'll trade them horn for horn, from sunset
till the morn,
an' come back an' do the same next year!"

The last chorus resounded through the air. Fionn smiled. If Daolghus had reason to warn him, Cedach had been right to trust. His host was an honorable man and would not stain his own hospitality.

In the next moment he became less sure. There was a clamor outside, and men thrust through the doorway, half-naked and bloody, crying out for aid.

Fer-tai leaped to his feet shouting for silence. "One at a time now! Who has attacked you?"

"It is the people of Fionn and the *fianna*!" cried the tallest. "They are slaughtering and attacking the cattle and the farmers. And you are our chieftain and our avenger—"

"Seize him!" Fer-li sprang from his couch and pointed at Fionn, looking more like Goll than ever. "It is an outrage that such sudden raids should destroy our people!"

Fionn remained perfectly still. He did not need to set his thumb to his teeth to see a trap here. If his own gut were anything to go by, his men would be bloated already by the feast that had been set before them, and in no state to be slaughtering anything.

"If you are being raided, it is not by my men," he said calmly. "But if it can be proved against us, we shall make good the damages—for two cows shall be given for each single cow slain, and two sheep for one."

"Traitor! Do not try to turn our minds with your lies!" yelled Fer-li. "It is not to feast you have come here, but to slay us as you slew our grandfathers!"

He does not believe that, thought Fionn, watching his eyes. But his rage against Fionn was real enough. Only reflexes newly honed by several moons in the field set Fionn rolling off his bench as Fer-li snatched a javelin from the wall and sent it speeding towards him. Fionn lifted the bench as Emer sent a second spear after the first and the weapon thunked into it. The Sons of Urgriu had weapons out as well.

"Hold!" screamed Fer-tai. "My son, all of you, stop this! You dishonor my hall!" He stepped in front of Fionn, arms spread wide, and Fer-li paused, the sword he had drawn poised in his hand.

The respite was all Fionn needed to free his own blade. He batted a stabbing spear aside and slashed its owner's arm. In another moment Daolghus and Loegaire were beside him, presenting an unbreachable defense in the old triple fighting formation of the Galeóin.

Grinning fiercely, Fer-li thrust his father aside and the older man, swearing, scrambled to get his own weapons from the wall. Fionn brought his sword up to guard and felt the shock of Fer-li's first blow. He was strong, but was he subtle? Steel hissed as blade beat against blade. He heard a cry behind him as another of Fer-li's companions went down.

Fer-tai had his shield before them now, and was trying to bring himself to attack his son, when a scream like the battle-keen of the Morrigan split the air.

For a moment shock held them still. Uncanny as

some apparition, a woman strode into the hall. Her breasts were bared and her fair hair flew wildly about her. Fury blazed from her eyes.

"My son, put down your sword! It is the ruin of honor and a disgrace to a warrior and the loss of all luck for you to betray the noble Fionn of the *fianna* in our hall!"

It was only when she spoke that Fionn recognized her as Fer-tai's wife Iuchna. She had seemed a noble and gracious lady when she welcomed them that afternoon; now she was entirely Goll's daughter, and worthy of her sire.

"Woman, cover yourself—" muttered Fer-li, his face flaming. From Fer-tai came a great sigh.

"I will cover myself when you put away that blade and take yourself and your companions out of here!"

With an insulting deliberation, the young man slid his sword into its sheath. But his eyes were on Fionn.

"I will go then," he said softly, "but before I depart, upon you, oh Fionn, I cry challenge to meet me in battle tomorrow morn."

"And so do I!" exclaimed Emer Glunglas, stepping up beside him, "for the sake of Garad mac Morna!"

"As do I!" came a lighter voice, "in my father's name!" And Diarmuid's warrior daughter came forward to stand with the two men.

Ah, Grainne, thought Fionn, *this girl of yours will be more dangerous to me than all the others.* But he kept his features stern.

"I answer your challenge with my own, though little justice or fair play have you shown to me. You two were my foster sons, and if I am brought down you will fall with me. Well do I remember the Battle of Cuinmoinn, when Garad cut down the warriors of the *fianna* in his wrath, but I remember also how he cried out when we overcame him in the end."

Iuchna pointed towards the door, and her son lifted his chin and strode out, followed by those of his friends who could walk. On the floor one man lay unconscious and several others were bleeding. With the same chill efficiency she gave directions for their care. Then, still wearing that disdainful smile, she herself left the hall.

"I am ashamed," said Fer-tai. "I knew he was angry, but I never dreamed—" He shook his head. "They have plotted this because you are so poorly attended and they think they can overwhelm you."

"Few though my men may be," Fionn answered, "they are worth a multitude. Do I not have Loegaire by my side, who is the son of the king of the men of Fannal? Do I not have Cedach Cithach of Alba, who came here to avenge his brothers and stayed to defend the land against his countrymen? Each man of them could hold off three hundred warriors from me." Cheerfully he began to enumerate the virtues of his other men.

Fer-tai shook his head pityingly and pressed more mead upon him, but as Fionn spoke, he realized that in truth he was not feeling the sorrow and apprehension that he might have expected, and wondered how long it would last.

Much later, when they were preparing to sleep, Iuchna came into the hall with bedding, and Fionn went to speak to her.

"I have to thank you for stopping the fighting. I would not willingly have broken the peace of your hall."

Iuchna shook her head. "It was our own honor I was

defending. My son worshiped his grandfather and took his death hard. As for me, I grieve for the old man, but I have spoken to Caoinche and I know he had the death he wished for. I am only sorry it had to be at your hands."

"I grieve for him as well," said Fionn. "But I must tell you this—if I have been a Shield, I am also a Sword and a sword has no choice but to slay. If your son comes against me, I may have to kill him as well."

"Be it so—" Iuchna said grimly. "I was bred to bear heroes. If he ends his life with honor, I will be satisfied. But look to yourself, old man. Do you not think it far more likely that if you and Fer-li meet, it is you who will fall?"

SURELY SHE SPOKE TRULY, AND THIS IS WITHOUT doubt my last night in the world, thought Fionn when he lay in the bed they had made for him and all was still. Despite his fatigue he could not sleep. There was a sickness in his gut and his heart was pounding and he knew that now, he was afraid. The first few times he had fought he had been too enraged for fear, and later he grew confident because, having survived so much already, it did not occur to him that he could die. When he had sought death, it eluded him. Now that he had chosen to live, it menaced him with teeth bared.

I must not allow my fear to matter, he told himself. *The warrior lives to the fullest as long as he can. Cormac and Goll and Oscar did not try to flee this moment; surely I can meet it as well as they.*

It was good advice, but hard to follow. He wished that just once more he could have lain in Grainne's arms. In the end, he could only draw Brigid's cloak around him and lie still, pretending to sleep.

But in the midst of his pretense the reality came upon him and he slid into a dream. It seemed to him that he was back in the Otherworld, and he was clasped in a woman's arms. Brigid's red cloak was wrapped around them, but when he looked up from her soft breast it was the face of the Morrigan that smiled down at him. He stared at her in wonder, for there was only compassion in her dark eyes. He sank into their depths until from dream he passed into a deeper slumber, in which the only thing he knew was the sweetness of her lullaby.

FIONN LOOKED OUT OVER THE BATTLEFIELD, A GREEN sweep of meadow that sloped down to the Boann. Fer-li had drawn up his forces on the other side of the river, just above the ford of Brea. He was having trouble making out their numbers, for the sun had barely risen, and the morning mist still lay heavy on the land, but there seemed to be a great many of them. Behind him his own men seemed in good heart. A night's rest and a feast had done wonders for their morale, and indignation over Fer-li's treachery had improved it even more.

When they arose in the hour before dawn Fer-tai had been painfully helpful, bringing out weapons from his own stores and giving Fionn a helmet and a battle dress sewn from layers of waxed linen and a stout fighting belt to wear. He still hoped to manage a reconciliation, and had taken Fionn's offer of compensation for the deaths of Goll and Garad with him when he left them to go join his son. That figure loping across the field must be their messenger returning now.

"Well, and what have they to say?" asked Loegaire.

The man seemed reluctant to meet Fionn's eyes. "No other substance or terms will be accepted from you except battle, that they may avenge their ancient wrongs. So say Emer Glunglas and the Sons of Urgriu and the chieftains of the Luagni that are with him. And Fer-li says that you are a worn-out, feeble-handed old man—" The messenger broke off, flushing, but Fionn, who knew that it had been said to sting him into giving battle, gave a bark of laughter.

"Does he so? Well, I pledge my word that I will fight them like a youngster!"

The sons of Urgriu and the Luagni and the heirs of the mac Mornas . . . thought Fionn, his laughter leaving him. All his father's old enemies. Would this battle lay the old feud to rest at last?

With some surprise he realized that beneath his sadness lay relief. He had lost everyone he loved already. There was no one to fear for, no one now whom he must shield. Pain and hard battle lay ahead of him, but they would not last. In a very long life of striving, Fionn had always had to meet each moment with something held in reserve. But he need hold back nothing now. Existence was narrowing to a terrible simplicity. He could spend what strength remained to him with lavish abandon, until one of those young men who were glaring at him over the rims of their shields finally struck him down.

Through the mist across the river came a rumble that resonated like muted thunder in the damp air—the sound of Luagni spear shafts beating against shields.

"Well lads, can we find no answer?" said Fionn, and Loegaire, grinning, opened his throat in a stag's belling challenge. From Cedach Cithach came the howl of the wild wolf of his homeland, and from Daolghus the coughing grunt of a wild boar. Each man of the *fianna* cried out in the voice of the creature that was his totem, and as the mass of the enemy began to advance through the ford and up the slope towards them, they leaped and shouted in challenge, shaking their spears.

Only Fionn, who had been all those creatures in his time, made no sound. The Hazel Shield was still slung across his back. As carefully as if he were competing in the games at Tailtiu, he set his five lances butt first into the ground, two on the left and three on the right, with Birga behind them, muttering its eagerness for the fray. The Luagni were coming fast, white blurs above armor becoming faces with glaring eyes and mouths twisted in rage.

I will do this right, he thought, *as if the Liath Luachra were still watching me. . . .*

A thrown lance arched towards him, fell short and rattled like a serpent across the grass. Fionn reached out with his right hand, grasped a spear and cast it, reached with his left and threw again before the first brought down its man. By the time the second struck, the third was in the air. The fourth spear pierced two warriors, for the enemy was very close now, and the fifth he lofted high so that it came down from above like a bolt from heaven and took out a man in the rear.

Then it was Birga in his hands, and the singing of the spear became one with Fionn's own roar as he plunged it into the breast of the nearest foe. The warrior fell back, knocking over the man behind him, and Fionn shrugged the Hazel Shield forward onto his arm.

"So, old friend, will you aid me one last time?" he murmured, and the Shield sang out in reply:

"I am the help that holds back harm,
Companion of the hero's arm;
Though men betray, I shall not fly,
For faithful unto death am I!
I am Hazel, hallowed Tree,
Between the worlds I ward the way!"

The lie of the land had turned the enemy's charge at an angle, so that the "pillars" of their army, their leaders, were fighting on Fionn's flank. There was a great clamor of breaking spears and clanging swords and the death cries of men from that direction. Fionn was attempting to fight his way towards them when a voice like the Morrigan's shrieked his name.

He turned, and for a moment thought that the goddess herself had come for him, seeing the tossing black hair and a woman's fair face above the corselet, distorted by rage.

"Now you shall pay for Diarmuid's blood!" she screamed, and he knew her, and wrenched the shield up barely in time to receive her first blow.

"Find another opponent," he gasped. "I have promised . . . your mother . . . to spare her children."

"Fight or bare your neck to my blow!" Eachtach snarled. "It makes no difference to me!"

She had a good sword, with a bright, keen-edged blade. *The Moralltach—Diarmuid's sword . . .* thought Fionn, then staggered as her next blow came down. He felt something give way and heard a groan from the shield. Birga struggled in his hand, and he fought to control its hunger. *Not this one—not this girl!*

She struck again, and the shield shook, whimpering.

The third stroke broke the metal rim, sliced through the outer skin, and shattered the plaited wood behind it, and the Shield screamed in pain.

The blow had loosened the fastenings of the arm-strap as well. As Fionn tried to dodge, the pieces banging against his side, Daolghus leaped in between them. Eachtach's next blow took him on the crown and drove downward so that he fell in two pieces on the grass.

Fionn was still struggling to get the remains of the Hazel Shield off of his arm as she whirled, blood spraying from her crimson sword; he reeled as the sharp tip sliced through the stiff layers of his battle shirt and his flesh and bounced across his rib bones. A convulsive shake threw the broken shield against the sword, sweeping it away from him. Still gasping with pain, Fionn tried to guard with Birga's shaft.

Her face alight with exultation, Eachtach raised her sword once more, completely focused on her prey. And it was then that young Lodhorn, Daolghus's companion, leaped forward and plunged his spear beneath her lifted arm and into her heart.

Ah Grainne, he thought as he watched Eachtach fall, her mask of fury changing to surprise. *I tried to save her for you—I did try!*

"Are you all right, sir?" Lodhorn was at his side, steadying him.

Fionn touched his side and brought his hand away red, but the blow had touched nothing vital. Around him the battle had broken into knots and tangles of struggling warriors. Many were down, and the Boann was beginning to flow red where men had been fighting back and forth across the ford.

At the edge of the water the fighting had been especially furious. Now men were drawing back to make room for the combat between Loegaire and Fer-li. Fionn would have wagered on his own man, but Goll's grandson was younger, and he, too, had been trained to fight in the *fian*. As he watched, Loegaire's spear darted past Fer-li's shield and gashed his thigh, but in the next instant, Fer-li thrust his own shield forward, knocking Loegaire off balance long enough to stab him in the arm.

It was his spear arm. He danced away, casting his shield aside and catching his spear in his left hand as the grip of his right gave way. *Fénnid* warriors were trained to fight equally well with either hand, but Loegaire was losing blood from that arm. Still, Fer-li's leg wound seemed to be impeding him. He crouched behind his shield, swiveling to meet each new attack by his foe.

Fionn was not close enough to see what finally made the difference; perhaps it was simply loss of blood and fatigue. Suddenly Fer-li seemed to spring to life. Like a striking falcon his spear struck downward, dashed Loegaire's weapon aside and pierced his belly. The *fénnid* went down, mouth open in silent agony, clutching at the spear. But Fer-li yanked it out and drove the spearhead up under the jaw and into his enemy's brain, and Loegaire jerked and lay still.

Cedach Cithach roared with rage and, leaving his own battle, plunged down the hill. Emer Glunglas rose up to stop him, and the sound of their encounter was like two bulls meeting on the plain. Back and forth their combat raged, and neither could get the better of the other. In the end they were trading blows like drunkards, and together their final blows fell and they died.

Fionn looked around him and saw that of all the more notable warriors who had stayed with him in the *fianna*, he alone remained. *Goll told me I would regret his loss one day,* he remembered. *I would have no doubt of the outcome, even now, if he or Diarmuid were by my side. But Diarmuid's daughter is dead, and Goll's grandson waits to slay me.*

Suddenly that seemed funny. *The wise man does what he must,* he thought, *and what I must do is show these children how a warrior of the* fianna *dies!* It was not rage but a strange delight that upheld him as he sped down the slope, stabbing with the spear in his left hand, and using his right to slash with his sword, blinding in his swiftness, dazzling in his skill.

By the time Fionn reached the ford no one opposed him, but pain stabbed his lungs with each breath and spots swam before his eyes. Across the river foes remained, but at the water's edge only one man was standing, splattered with blood and grinning.

"You fought better than I expected, old man," said Fer-li, "but it is time now for me to take revenge for my grandfather Goll and all my kin."

"These feuds will be the death of you, Fer-li," Fionn answered breathlessly, and the other man laughed.

In the next moment his sword swung high and he came rushing in. Fionn blocked the first blow with his spear, and felt its force shock down Birga's shaft. Thought fled in the moments that followed; Fionn was fighting by instinct, and only when a head blow sent him staggering did he realize that Fer-li's sword had broken on his helm. With an oath, the younger man swerved away, bent to snatch up a spear, and threw.

Fionn saw it coming but, still off-balance, he could not even get a weapon up to guard. The impact spun him round, but he did not, quite, fall. He sucked in breath, and saw that the spear had pierced through the battle dress and all the way through his body between his ribs and the hip bone and out the other side. Quickly, before the shock wore off enough for pain to fell him, he wrenched it out and cast it away.

Fer-li's eyes widened. He saw his death coming towards him, but he was weaponless, and for just a moment too long, disbelief held him still. Fionn lifted his father's sword and in a single swift stroke struck from his body the head of Goll's last heir.

From somewhere beyond the mists a raven called as Fer-li's body fell. Fionn felt warmth coursing down his leg and looking down, saw blood pouring from the hole in his side. It would not be long now, he thought, but who would finish him?

"That was a great deed," said a quiet voice behind him.

"It was so," Fionn looked up and saw Fer-tai, his honest eyes hot with grief. "There have been many great deeds on this field. What took you so long?"

"I was hoping that you would be killed by Fer-li rather than by me," said the Luagni chieftain, looking at the head of his son, which had come to rest near Loegaire's body, its mouth still open in surprise.

"Have you come to attack me or to sympathize?" asked Fionn. With each breath his wound was beginning to send sharp jolts of pain through his body, and he felt rather ill.

"I must attack you," Fer-tai said sorrowfully. "There is no compensation that will pay for the death of a son."

Fionn, who knew that already, lifted his weapons to guard. Fer-tai came in like a madman, swinging wildly. Chips flew from Birga's shaft as he hacked at it. Fionn switched arms so that he could guard with the sword and stabbed at his opponent with the spear. *Feed me!* cried Birga as Fionn's arm came down. But the spear point caught on the boss of Fer-tai's fighting belt, the weakened wood of the shaft snapped suddenly, and the point, deflected, spun past him and away, wailing in almost human agony.

Fionn stared as the bright metal turned in the air. At first it seemed to fall very slowly, and then, with a splash and a hiss of steam, it plunged into the Boann.

His own moment of inattention was almost fatal. He turned as Fer-tai lunged and gasped as the sword pierced his chest. Reflex brought his own blade down across his enemy's back, and the sharp sword, with the last of his strength behind it, sliced through armor and backbone and guts and Fer-tai fell.

Fionn sucked in damp air and bit back a whimper of pain. A breath of wind swirled the mists over the river and kissed his brow. For a moment sunlight gleamed on the water, then cloud flowed back over it. *It will be a beautiful day,* thought Fionn, *but I will not see it. . . .*

A wave of dizziness passed over him. If he had been Cuchulain, now would be about time to look for a pillar to tie himself to. Or even a tree. He did not want to lie in the mud while his life ebbed away.

He looked around him. There were no trees near, and no friend left to give him the mercy stroke. He was alone with the dead. Above the Boann mist curdled and parted. A little way above the ford on the other side of the river, men were standing . . . five of them . . . the Sons of Urgriu. . . .

Even though it hurt his belly, Fionn began to laugh. "Come on—" he called. "Here I am, waiting! Or do you want me to come to you?"

His head started to sink on his breast, and he lifted it to keep from fainting. To cross the river would be better. They could not know how badly he was wounded, and perhaps they were afraid of him. He grinned again. How simple it had all become, in the end. Perhaps he would fall into the river and find a salmon. At least he would be going forward, towards the enemy, towards Grainne.

Painfully, Fionn hobbled forward. He had lost his helmet in the fight with Fer-tai; the breeze lifted his matted hair.

"*Run, brother,*" it whispered in his ear. He felt a small hand tug at his. "*The way is open—and Donait is calling you—*"

Fionn coughed and tasted blood, but the wind was growing stronger. He took a step and then another. He set his teeth and broke into a lurching run. Sight came and went, but the edge of the river was near. He could no longer see the enemy, but now his own momentum was carrying him forward.

Fionn leaped into the mist, and the world disappeared.

Epilogue

MIST . . .

Cold and choking, it swirled around him. In a moment he would feel the shock of the water, or else his enemies' spears. . . .

But Fionn did not fall, and strangely, he no longer felt pain. He was suspended, neither dead nor living, between the worlds.

"Sister—" The words formed, but he had no voice here. *"Where are you? Where am I?"* He sensed contact, as if a slim hand had closed on his. *"Tuireann? Is it you, then? I thought you hated me—"*

"I did . . ." the answer came, *"but it was I who doomed my sons by sending them to the world of men."*

"I am doomed as well . . ." thought Fionn.

"Not entirely," she answered him. *"That hero-leap of yours has carried you out of your world, but you are not yet in mine. I have been sent to offer you a choice,*

my dear. In the mortal world your flesh will fall to dust, and your spirit will go where our father and Goll and all the champions of Eriu have gone. That is the gift of men—to give up the world entirely and pass on."

"That is one choice. What are the others?"

"As you have served Brigid, she grants you this, to return to Faerie and dwell in Donait's hall."

"To go out of the world like Oisin and see Sadb again?" Emotion shook him. Of what else, all these lonely years, had he dreamed?

"But if you take this way, you will never again see Eriu."

"What other way can there be?"

"The third choice is the hardest, for if you make it, you will never entirely lay your burden down. It is to sleep, Fionn, while your body slowly heals and is renewed, and your spirit watches over Eriu . . ."

To Fionn it seemed that the voice had somehow changed, and in this place without breath there was nonetheless a hint of apple blossom on the air.

"Lady, I know you now." And indeed, as Brigid's love surrounded him, it came to him that it was always She whom he had been seeking, whether he loved Donait, or Sadb, or Grainne. *"Why do you ask this of me?"*

"One of the five masters of every art you have been, and men shall count you one of the three sons of comfort to Eriu. If you die, you shall not return with your own shape on you. If you live in Faerie and try to set foot in the mortal world, all the years that have passed shall come upon you and your flesh will fall to dust. But if you choose sleep, you may return, in spirit or in the body, in the hour of Eriu's need."

"To watch alone while all I love passes away? Why should I desire it?"

The sense of Her presence grew stronger, a mighty flame that burned the mist away until there was only Light.

"You will not be alone. . . ."

Fionn chose.

IN THE DAYS THAT FOLLOWED RUMORS FLEW THROUGH Eriu like ravens from the battlefield. Some said that the mac Mornas had taken Fionn's head, which prophesied to them from beside the fire. Others were sure that was a lie, and swore that Fionn had bled out his life beside the Boann. But his body was not found. It was true that there were a great many bodies, some of them mangled beyond recognition, but surely they could have identified him by his height and his sword. And some said that the Sidhe had borne his body to a secret cave.

But there was one man, whom they found lying by the riverside exhausted by wounds, who told another tale. He had seen Fionn mac Cumhal come running towards the river, but when he reached the edge he gave a great spring and leaped outward as if he would cast himself into the waters of the Boann. From across the river a flight of spears sped towards him, and a few moments later the Sons of Urgriu scrambled down the bank to see what they had hit, but they found no body, neither in the river nor on the other side.

And that man who was watching had heard no splash. All he could remember, as he saw Fionn disappear into the mists that covered the river, was the sound of silver bells.

* * *

DONAIT WATCHED OVER FIONN'S SLEEP.

His bed was woven of hazel boughs, but he did not lie fully upon it, for his form was sheathed in a haze of silver light that shimmered as he breathed. Through its radiance she could see him, and each time she looked his flesh had grown fairer, as the ravages of the years were dissolved away. She leaned over him, lovingly noting how the strong limbs had filled out with new muscle, the high-arched feet and long-fingered hands grown supple once more. And though his face still bore the marks of character that years and experience had sculpted into it, she could also see in it the beauty of the boy she had loved.

Fionn had seemed dead when he first appeared in her hall, almost empty of blood, his colorless skin torn by gaping wounds. Weeping, she and Tuireann and Sadb had cut away his bloody garments and washed him, but old and broken, his hurts were beyond the powers even of her healing bath. He did not open his eyes throughout their ministrations; only the faintest flutter of pulse told them that he still lived.

And then Brigid had come, and commanded the trees to shape a bed to cradle him. And they had laid him on it, and as the goddess sang, the silvery light had gathered about him, and the remaining tension in his body finally eased as his pain faded away.

Sometimes Sadb came to watch with her, and sometimes Tuireann. Once or twice it was even the Morrigan, looking down with an expression Donait could not interpret in her dark eyes. Brigid was always with him, in the whisper of the fire and the murmur of the spring and the wind that stirred the leaves.

Fionn slept, and Donait worked at her tapestries.

It seemed to her that their colors were already a little

less vibrant. They were fading, as the Sidhe themselves were fading, though the others might not realize what was happening. In the end, she thought, they might all become no more than myths and memories, their reality withdrawn entirely from mortal knowing except in dreams. One by one the great ones of Faerie would depart, until all that remained were the lesser spirits of hill and wood and stream.

All but one, perhaps, thought Donait as she considered the figure of Brigid emerging from the fire. *She*, at least, would remain to watch over her people, no more able to abandon them than a mother her children.

And so would Fionn. His images remained bright as well. So long as Brigid watched over the land of Eriu, Fionn's oath would bind him. And all that Brigid Herself had blessed would be defended so long as the spirit and story of Fionn mac Cumhal remained alive in the land.

Donait looked from the sleeping man to the tapestry before her. It showed a forest, with trees as noble and leaves as green as those that roofed her hall. And as she watched, something seemed to move through it—the shape of a man, or perhaps it was only a flicker of light or the wind in the leaves.

Afterword

AND SO IT IS TODAY, FOR BOTH HOLY BRIGID AND Fionn mac Cumhal have altered and adapted to fit the times, and though the country be torn by enemies from abroad and her own dissensions, so long as they are remembered, the green land of Eriu will endure.

How, indeed, could Fionn's story come to an end? Even in the most complete account of his last battle, told in a manuscript called the *Fianaigecht*, the final pages have been lost. The story breaks off just as the Sons of Urgriu begin to cast their spears, as if some medieval reader tore off the last page because he could not bear to see Fionn die. Perhaps it is this quality which has accounted for the peculiarly vigorous quality of Fionn's tradition.

In the history of Irish literature, the Fenian cycle holds a position similar to that of the Robin Hood ballads in English, being popular and episodic in comparison to the Ulster cycle, which, like that of King Arthur, was courtly in nature and given a final form at an early date. The stories about Fionn exist in many versions, inconsistent and contradictory in both chronology and details.

One of the interesting (and frustrating) things about writing these books has been the challenge of fitting as much as possible of the original material in, and arranging it in some kind of coherent order. However, we know from the *Book of Leinster* that "He is no *filidh* who does not harmonize and synchronize all the stories" (quoted by Eoin MacNeill in the Introduction to the *Duainaire Finn),* so the attempt would seem to be justified.

The tradition is particularly rich in episodes which appear to belong to the latter part of Fionn's career, when both Oisin and Oscar were grown. This three-generation Fenian "triple threat" dominates the traditional image of the *fianna.* The largest collection of stories about Fionn is found in the *Duainaire Finn*—the *Book of the Lays of Fionn*—edited and translated by Eoin MacNeill for the Irish Texts Society in 1908. A number of the tales, including the Pursuit of Grainne and Diarmuid and the wonderful battle at the end, are included in *Ancient Irish Tales,* edited by Tom Peete Cross and Clark Harris Slover, originally published by Henry Holt & Co. in 1936. However, almost any book of traditional Irish folktales will have something about Fionn. For a somewhat different view of Fionn, readers may want to explore the Ossianic cycle compiled by MacPherson. For the source of some of the details of our natural history, presented with a poetry of language almost too rich to assimilate, see *Where the Forest Murmurs,* by Fiona Macleod (Charles Scribner's Sons, 1906).

In addition to mining the traditional material for episodes, we have tried to convey some of the archaic flavor through the inclusion of poetry based on traditional sources or written (although Irish verse forms can be almost as complex as Irish grammar) in a form derived from their style.

The Summer spell with which Fionn disenchants Sadb in Volume II was inspired by a fourteenth-century Welsh description. The source of the song with which Fionn welcomed Beltane after eating the Salmon of Wisdom in Volume I, however, is an Irish poem written down in the ninth century and attributed to Fionn himself. Both, in much more literal versions, may be found in *A Celtic Miscellany,* ed. Kenneth Hurlstone Jackson, published by Penguin (1971). Grainne's sleep song for Diarmuid is adapted from her song as given in *Tóruigheacth Dhiarmada agus Ghráinne (The Pursuit of Diarmuid and Grainne).* The advice offered by the druid Cathal to the high king is adapted from the precepts as given in the seventh-century text, *Audacht Moraind* (*The Testament of Morand),* source also of the definition of the "bull-prince."

And as for the rest, may Brigid of the Blessings her own self guide you, as she led Fionn, to inspiration. . . .

March 17, 1994